Celebrations for the Woolworths Girls

Also by Elaine Everest

The Woolworths Girls series
The Woolworths Girls
Carols at Woolworths (ebook novella)
Christmas at Woolworths
Wartime at Woolworths
A Gift from Woolworths
Wedding Bells for Woolworths
A Mother Forever
The Woolworths Saturday Girls
The Woolworths Girl's Promise

The Teashop Girls series
The Teashop Girls
Christmas with the Teashop Girls

Standalone novels
Gracie's War
The Butlins Girls
The Patchwork Girls

Elaine Everest

~

Celebrations for the Woolworths Girls

MACMILLAN

First published 2023 by Macmillan
an imprint of Pan Macmillan
The Smithson, 6 Briset Street, London EC1M 5NR
EU representative: Macmillan Publishers Ireland Ltd, 1st Floor,
The Liffey Trust Centre, 117–126 Sheriff Street Upper,
Dublin 1, D01 YC43
Associated companies throughout the world
www.panmacmillan.com

ISBN 978-1-0350-2057-7

1 3 5 7 9 8 6 4 2

A CIP catalogue record for this book is available from the British Library.

Typeset by Palimpsest Book Production Ltd, Falkirk, Stirlingshire
Printed and bound by CPI Group (UK) Ltd, Croydon, CR0 4YY

Visit **www.panmacmillan.com** to read more about all our books
and to buy them. You will also find features, author interviews and
news of any author events, and you can sign up for e-newsletters
so that you're always first to hear about our new releases.

This book is dedicated to the memory of
our late Queen Elizabeth II in thanks
for her dedication and service.

Prologue

~

Ruby Jackson huddled beneath the bedcovers. As hard as she tried, she couldn't sleep.

Hushed voices from downstairs reminded her she wasn't alone in the house, even though Bob was not here.

Would her life ever be the same again?

1

~

6 February 1952

'For goodness' sake stand still, Nanny Ruby. If you're not careful I'll be pinning this hem to your stockings. Why you haven't asked Aunty Maisie to hem this frock, I'll never know.'

Ruby Jackson snorted with laughter. 'If I'd spoken to my great-grandmother like that, I'd have been shut in the coal hole for a fortnight without any food,' she said, admonishing the child. 'Anyone would think you were forty rather than eleven, the way you talk. For your information, I don't like to bother Maisie as she is so busy with her factory and dress shops. Besides, she'd have me standing on the table while she pinned up the hem, and I'm not sure I'd be able to get back down.'

Georgina, known to her family as Georgie, sat back on her haunches, removing a pin from between her lips. She looked at her great-grandmother with affection; she'd not really thought of her as old, as she was always up for a lark with the children who visited the house. There again, she did wear clothes for older ladies and her hair was more grey than brown. But she had a twinkle in her eye, unlike her friend, Mrs Munro from up the road.

'You could stand on the stool,' she suggested, giving Ruby a grin. 'Or perhaps wait until Mum comes back? I am supposed to be ill, you know.'

Ruby tutted, before leaning over to kiss Georgie on her forehead. 'You've had a cold and you seem to be as right as rain now. Perhaps you could return to school?' she said, before laughing at the shocked look on the child's face.

'I still feel poorly,' the girl replied, giving a deep sigh. 'Can we look at your photographs?'

'I suppose so. Get yourself off the floor and fetch me the photograph album from the sideboard. Not that one; find the one with the faded navy-blue cover,' Ruby said as Georgie pulled out the album from Ruby and Bob's wedding. 'It's time I gave you a history lesson. Come and sit beside me,' she added, patting the arm of the armchair where she'd settled, as Georgina pulled the album from beneath a pile of knitting patterns.

Georgie snuggled up beside Ruby and the wide chair arm, and slung her arm around her great-grandmother's shoulders. All the youngsters called her 'Nanny Ruby', although some were from different generations, whilst others weren't even blood relatives; Ruby was a nanny to everyone. Even though she was seventy-one, her mind was as active as it had been when she was a young woman and had moved into her home in Erith with her first husband, Eddie, and their first child.

Ruby flicked through the pages until she stopped and pointed to a faded sepia photograph of an upright man in an army uniform. 'This was my first husband, Eddie. He is your Granddad George's daddy and passed away before the last war was even thought about.'

Georgie nodded her head thoughtfully as she ran her finger over the photograph. 'I thought he'd been a sailor. That's what Mummy told me.'

'Yes, you are right, in a way. It was while your mum was still a small child. Eddie wasn't sure what to do with himself and he had the chance to go to sea on one of the ships that docked down on the river. I was against it because . . . well, let's say I'd miss him too much. However, it was a short occupation for him, as he suffered from terrible seasickness.'

Georgie chuckled. 'Mummy never told me that.'

'It's a secret,' Ruby replied, putting a finger to her lips. 'Don't you go telling a soul.'

'Cross my heart, Nanny Ruby,' the child said seriously, making the sign of the cross on her chest. 'Tell me about some of these other people,' she said as she turned the pages.

Ruby flicked over the pages, explaining about relatives and old neighbours, her mind travelling back to the past while patiently answering Georgie's questions, until she noticed the time. 'My goodness, we need to finish pinning my dress.'

Georgie's cheeks flushed bright red. 'Looking at these photographs is more interesting than pinning up your dress. I'm no good at these kinds of things. Can't you wait for Mummy to come back?'

Ruby sighed, but couldn't be angry with the child. 'Your mum could be a while over the road visiting your Aunty Freda; she's not feeling so good this morning, and young William is being fractious. It is best you help me or how else are you going to be able to make repairs on your own clothes, and those of your children, when you grow up?'

Georgie tossed one of her long plaits over her shoulder. 'I shall just have to pay someone to sew for me.'

Ruby fought hard not to smile. 'I take it you don't see your future as a seamstress?'

Georgie looked horrified. 'Oh no, I'm going to be a cook and run my own tea room, like the one Granddad George and Nanny Maureen took us to before Christmas. Nanny Maureen is teaching me how to bake cakes and has promised to take me to Woolworths to help her cook for the staff when she's on duty there.'

Ruby closed the photograph album. She wasn't so sure about a child working in the Woolworths staff canteen, as Georgie was far too young: what if she burnt herself? She'd have to have a word with her daughter-in-law. 'How about we finish pinning up the hem of this dress and then you can help me start lunch? It's only toad-in-the-hole with a few vegetables, but you can mix the batter.'

Georgie's eyes lit up. 'Can I wear one of your pinnies?'

'That goes without saying. I don't want your mum after me if you spoil your nice dress. I take it she bought it from Aunty Maisie?'

'Yes,' she said, jumping to her feet and giving a twirl, so that the full skirt flared out. 'It was free, as Aunty Maisie said it wasn't good enough to go into the shop. One of the panels in the skirt is upside down. Dad said it must have been made on a Friday afternoon. What does that mean?'

Ruby peered at the floral pattern on the dress. The error was hardly discernible. 'It means something that was spoilt, as the person making it had their mind on going home rather than working.'

'I'm glad they did, as I love this frock and I didn't have to shorten the hem, either,' Georgie added as she picked up Ruby's pincushion. 'Can I put the wireless on while we work?'

Ruby shook her head. This was what had come of the child's dad owning a wireless shop. They had one continually turned on in the shop in Erith High Street, and also in their small house around the corner from Ruby's home in Alexandra Road. 'Go on then, but don't be surprised if Bob switches it off when he comes in from the garden, as he likes to read his newspaper in peace.'

Georgie hurried to the large brown Bakelite box that sat in pride of place in the corner of the room. She twiddled with the knob before leaving it to warm up. 'I've just realized you've had two husbands. That's unusual, isn't it, Nanny Ruby?'

Does the child ever stop asking questions? Ruby thought to herself. 'It's not so unusual, when a woman loses a husband early in her life. Your Aunty Maisie is on her second marriage to David, and your Nanna Maureen and Granddad George have been married before. You can ask your mum to explain more, as it gives me a headache thinking about the past too much. Now, let's get this dress finished; I want to tack it, ready to hand-stitch the hem this evening after tea,' she said as she straightened her skirt and checked that the pins Georgie had inserted had not fallen out.

'Shall I put the kettle on before we start?'

'No, let's get this done and dusted first,' Ruby said as a

solemn voice started to make an announcement from the wireless set.

'*This is London. It is with the greatest sorrow that we make the following announcement . . .*'

'What does it mean?' Georgie asked as her bottom lip started to wobble.

Ruby wrapped her arms around her great-granddaughter. 'It means our beloved King George has gone to heaven,' she replied with a heavy heart. 'I want you to be a sweetheart and pop out to the back garden and tell Granddad Bob to get himself indoors, then run over the road and ask your mum and Aunty Freda to come over. It's at times like this our family needs to be together,' she said as she reached for a handkerchief tucked up the sleeve of her cardigan, quickly blowing her nose. It wouldn't do to cry in front of the child. 'I'll go upstairs and take this dress off; we can finish it another day.'

Georgie nodded her head and disappeared out of the back door, calling for Bob as she went.

Ruby hurried upstairs as fast as her legs would allow. She'd not confess to any of her family that she was finding the steep stairs hard to climb on cold days when her old joints ached. 'At least I'm still alive, unlike our poor King. Why, he's about the same age as my George; it would kill me to see him pass away at such a young age,' she murmured to herself as she struggled out of the navy-blue dress, being careful not to catch herself on the pins. She was already feeling sad after thinking of Eddie and, on top of that, the news about the King had made her quite maudlin. Thank goodness me and Bob found each other, she thought. Bob has been a comfort during the hard times, and he truly

8

loves me. She looked at a framed picture of them both, taken by George when they married on VE Day.

Out of respect for the late monarch, she pulled a black dress from the wardrobe before checking her hair in the dressing table and brushing a few stray hairs from her face. The short bob suited her. She wasn't sure when Sarah suggested having her hair cut short, to save having to pull the shoulder-length hair into a neat bun each morning, but her granddaughter was right, it suited her. She was soon ready to go downstairs and join her family in mourning their much-loved King. Taking a deep breath, Ruby decided there and then that, if she was able, she would go to London to pay her respects. The Royal Family had stood firm with the people during the war, and now was the time to say thank you.

'How are you feeling?' Sarah asked as she looked at Freda's pale face.

'Much better, thank you for sitting with me. You must think me a fool to act like this? I so wanted to enjoy this pregnancy and not have Tony worry about me while he's away.'

Sarah pursed her lips. She wasn't about to say what she thought of Freda's husband going off and leaving his wife alone while she was pregnant, even if she still had some months to go. 'I'm just relieved you are back with us, where we can care for you, and not stuck up in Birmingham on your own, caring for William while Tony is at work all day. I couldn't imagine not having friends or family nearby when I was expecting.'

Freda pushed herself up into a sitting position from

where she'd been resting on a burgundy velvet-covered sofa set in front of the bay window of the front room; it was her favourite piece of furniture and, although second-hand from Hedley Mitchell, she thought it made her home in Alexandra Road look different from others. 'He'd be here with me if he could,' she replied, her eyes shining at the thought of her husband.

'You should use Nan's telephone and let him know you are poorly. She told you it's there any time you want to use it.'

'That was nice of Ruby, but I don't want to bother Tony right now. Our Olympic cycling team needs him more than I do. He is arranging for us to have our own telephone installed; it should be here soon.'

Sarah wrinkled her nose. 'The Olympics aren't until the summer. I really think he should be home with you.'

'Please don't think for one moment that I don't want Tony here by my side, but the opportunity to coach our national team is such an honour, considering his age and him not winning a medal at the last Olympics.'

'That was unfortunate, but he did win something much better,' Sarah smiled.

Freda grinned. 'You mean my hand in marriage? It was so romantic when he proposed to me. That's why I want him to grasp this opportunity with both hands. Did I tell you head office is keen for him to write reports for the Woolworths staff magazine? I said I'd help with a window display, as I've collected posters and can use some of Tony's cycling equipment as well. I shall have to start making notes.'

'The baby will be here by then. I can help you, by caring

for him or her while you are busy, along with William,' she said, glancing to where Freda's firstborn was sleeping soundly in his pram in the hall. 'We can work it around my shifts at Woolies. My only experience of two-wheeled travel is Alan's motorbike, *Bessie.* I'm not sure greasy overalls and oily polishing rags will look good in a Woolworths store's window,' she chuckled.

'I don't think I'll ever be able to ride Alan's motorbike again; well, not in this state,' Freda added, gently stroking her tummy and thinking back to the days when she jumped at any chance to ride a motorbike. These days she was happier to care for her babies, thinking of how at one time Tony had been an orphan and now had his own little family, with another on the way.

The two women continued chatting about motorbikes and the time when Freda had ridden one whilst working for the local Fire Service during the war.

'It's hard to imagine you dashing everywhere on that motorbike,' Sarah grinned.

'I was glad to be able to do my bit for the war,' Freda replied as something caught her eye out of the bay window. The front room, like all the other three-bedroom terraced houses in Alexandra Road, had a large bay window in the front room, where Freda often sat watching the world go by. 'Here comes your Georgina; she looks as if she's upset about something,' she said as there was an urgent knock on the door.

'Oh dear, I hope she hasn't been naughty. At least she can't fight with our Buster, as I packed him off to Dad's this morning for a boxing lesson. He's almost over the cold the children went down with, and the pair of them keep bickering.' Sarah sighed as she let her daughter into the house.

'Boxing?'

'Don't ask,' she replied as Freda raised her eyebrows whilst trying to sit upright on the comfortable sofa.

'I have all those joys to look forward to, when William and the new baby are older,' she said as she greeted the red-faced child. 'You look puffed out, Georgina, whatever have you been up to?'

'Nanny Ruby said you are both to go over to number thirteen at once. He's died,' she announced dramatically, before throwing herself down into the armchair just vacated by Sarah and bursting into tears.

2

~

'It must be Bob.' Freda struggled to her feet and took the coat Sarah had thrust at her. 'Perhaps you should run on ahead, Sarah,' she said before grabbing Georgina's arm. 'You can help me with the pram; we can't leave William here alone.' She chuckled, trying to lighten the girl's mood, thinking that if Bob had died, it wasn't something for a child to see.

Georgina looked puzzled, but did as she was told.

Sarah entered her nan's house using the key tied to a string inside the letter box. Ruby had never removed the key in all the time Sarah could remember. 'Nan!' she called out, hurrying in the direction of the sound of Ruby crying. 'Oh, my goodness, you're not dead,' she said without thinking, as she came across Bob doing his best to comfort Ruby.

'Not the last time I checked,' he answered gruffly as he wiped his own tears away. He was a man who was not frightened to show his emotions, which was what had attracted Ruby to him in the first place. Now long retired from the police force, he still kept his grey hair short and his face clean-shaven and took a pride in his appearance when the occasion dictated. 'It's the King. Seems he passed away this morning. He's no age at all. It certainly makes you think, doesn't it?'

'Oh, it does,' Sarah said as she knelt by her nan's armchair to give her a cuddle. 'Come on, Nan. If I'm not mistaken, you will have a houseful before too long, as the family hear the news; you know how everyone comes to number thirteen to be together in times of trouble.'

'And to celebrate. Not that this is a celebration,' Bob added quickly, as Ruby gave him one of her stares.

Sarah gave him a sympathetic smile. 'Nan, shall we get out your best china, and toast the King's memory with a nice cup of tea?'

Ruby perked up. 'I'm a silly old woman. Yes, you're right. I'd hate anyone to think I wasn't up to offering a decent cuppa.'

'I'll help you,' Freda said as she parked the pram in the hallway and checked William was still sleeping. 'Georgina told me we got the wrong end of the stick,' she grinned. 'I almost went into labour with the shock. Thank goodness you are well, Bob,' she added quickly.

'I do have a few aches and pains.' He started to explain, before Ruby told him to go and put a clean shirt and tie on. 'No peace for the wicked,' he muttered, giving Freda a broad wink, which made her giggle.

'Close the upstairs curtains,' Ruby bellowed after him as he hurried upstairs. 'Georgina, be a love and close the curtains in the front room.'

'Why do I have to do that? It won't get dark for hours?'

'It's a mark of respect, love. Do you remember when old Mr Michaels, who lived up the road, passed away and

14

we closed our curtains on the day of the funeral?' Sarah said.

Georgina was thoughtful. 'But the King only died this morning.'

Ruby shook her head. The child had an answer for everything. 'It's the way we show how much he meant to us, now the country is in mourning. Now, why don't you help me lay out a tea tray? Thank goodness I made a jam sponge cake the other day.'

Georgina nodded and set about helping Ruby. 'I can help you make more cake if you wish?' she asked, but Ruby had her mind on other things as Bob came downstairs.

'Bob, take off your bicycle clips,' she bellowed as she spotted him peering at the cake she'd placed on her best cake stand. 'Whatever do you look like?'

'I thought I'd cycle over to George and Maureen's and tell them the news, in case they hadn't heard. I could knock on our Mike and Gwyneth's door on my way.'

Ruby bent to remove the clips from around his ankles. 'You don't need those to walk into the front room and use our telephone. George will be there, even if Maureen's out. He is looking after Buster; mind you, let it ring for a while as they could be in the garden. After that, you can walk over the road to number one to tell Mike and Gwyneth and the kids to come over. I'd best rustle up some sand-wiches as well,' she added thoughtfully.

'There's no need to put on a spread, Nan. People will come here because they are sad. It's not a party.'

'She's right. A cup of tea is good enough while we remember our King,' Bob agreed.

'Then keep that bottle of whisky in the sideboard,' Ruby

called after him as he left the room; she knew all too well what Bob was like. He'd be topping up the men's teacups with the whisky if she didn't keep an eye on him; it was the same at every funeral and family get-together. 'What is it with you men?' she muttered, before paying attention to Georgina, who had pulled on an apron and had her head in a cupboard, reaching for a large mixing bowl. 'What are you up to?'

'Making another cake; there won't be enough for everyone, and they will all want feeding,' she said in a grown-up voice.

Ruby roared with laughter. 'Don't you go worrying your young head about such things. I reckon people won't arrive empty-handed. Leave it to the adults, eh?'

Georgina scowled and pulled off the apron. 'But I'm going to be a cook, like Nanny Maureen. I need to practise.'

'Another time, love,' Sarah said as she straightened the child's hair and gave her a kiss.

'Nobody listens to me,' she huffed.

Georgina was such a handful these days. Sarah thought with longing to the time when the children were younger; even with the war raging around them, she had loved that time with her babies. She sighed out loud as a smile crossed her face.

'A penny for them, even though I have a good idea what's on your mind,' Freda said.

'Oh, was it that obvious? You will feel just as I do when your baby grows up. Enjoy the early days, as they pass so quickly.'

'You're not too old to have another,' Freda suggested.

'Perhaps . . .' Sarah replied. 'I'd have to convince that

16

husband of mine first. His head is more into his business these days than it is babies. Now, if I was to suggest having a bigger wireless in the house, or perhaps a television, I'd soon get his attention.'

Freda chortled with laughter as the front door opened and their friend, Maisie Carlisle, appeared.

'I heard the news and felt so sad I thought I'd come straight down and be miserable with you. I thought this was supposed to be a sombre affair, and here you are laughing like a drain,' Maisie said with a twinkle in her eye. 'What have I missed?' she asked, throwing off her bright-red coat and joining her friends in Ruby's front room. 'It's blooming perishing out there.'

Sarah looked guilty. 'It's bad of us to be light-hearted when our Royal Family must be so terribly sad. I suppose that means Princess Elizabeth is our Queen now?'

'And there she is, a young mother with two kiddies,' Maisie said, looking thoughtful. 'She's just like us really, as we women have to carry on regardless whenever there is a problem.'

Sarah nudged Freda's arm. 'Don't forget her husband should be a great support to her in these times, exactly as ours are . . . or should be.'

'I take it Tony's not home yet?' Maisie asked, catching on quickly to Sarah's knowing look. Freda started to look upset, causing Maisie to cut in quickly, 'I'm just saying I'd love to have fewer people under my roof right now. I swear I'll need a shoehorn to even get through the front door before too long, what with my youngsters growing so quickly.'

'I don't suppose when you and David purchased your house you expected to be a grandmother so soon.'

Maisie snorted. 'Don't forget that makes David a

grandfather. I do like to pull his leg about that,' she grinned before looking serious. 'But you're right. I didn't expect it, and now we must do the best for our Bessie and the baby, regardless of what people say about one of my kids being an unmarried mother.'

Freda looked annoyed. 'I take it Vera from up the road's been adding her two penn'orth again? She's such an irritating woman; I don't understand how Ruby's been her friend for so many years?'

'I suppose it's because they go back a long way, and Nan likes to get on with most people. If you think about it, we three have been friends now for over . . .' Sarah stopped to count on her fingers. 'Why, it's over thirteen years.'

'But we don't go around running each other down to other people, do we?'

'Forgive and forget; that's the sign of a good friend, and perhaps that's why our Ruby gets on well with Vera. She forgives the old bat's outspoken ways,' Maisie said.

'It's more that Nan stops Vera in her tracks and takes no nonsense from her,' Sarah said. 'What are you going to do about the sleeping situation in your house?'

Maisie lived at the top of Alexandra Road in one of the two double-fronted houses. It looked larger at the front, but was a similar size to the bay-fronted homes, and all had three large bedrooms.

'David approached our next-door neighbour to ask if we could buy their house. They said no and dug their heels in, even when he offered a decent price. It would have saved us moving.'

Freda gave her a confused look. 'Why would moving next door have given you more room?'

'Did you mean you would keep both houses and knock a wall down, to make it one house? That would have been rather grand,' Sarah said, thinking how much she longed to move out of her two-up, two-down in nearby Crayford Road.

'I thought so too, and told David as much. That would have given Vera enough gossip fodder to keep her going for many a year. No, I reckon we are going to have to move, and soon, before the younger kids get much bigger. Young Ruby and the twins are squeezed into the back bedroom, while the baby is in with her mum and our Claudette. As for queuing up to use the loo . . . well, let's just say it is murder, even though David had the outside toilet reversed so that we don't have to stand in the cold garden any more. The other day I was tempted to use the little ones' potty.'

'Now, that is luxury,' Sarah giggled. 'I'm sure you will find somewhere to suit you all and, being selfish, I'm glad it will have to be local because of your businesses. And don't you move miles away. I'd miss you,' she added.

'Bless you,' Maisie said, patting her friend's shoulder. 'David did mention selling up and moving away, but I soon put a stop to that.'

'I would've liked to have been a fly on the wall when you put him straight,' Freda chuckled. 'If it would be any help, I could have Bessie and the baby move in with me for a while,' she offered. 'We get on so well these days, now that we can chat about babies. Little Jenny is such a dear sweet thing. And only a few months older than my William.'

Maisie was thoughtful. 'I'll have to talk with David and Bessie. It would certainly help while we make plans, but I don't want to impose, what with you and Tony having another baby arriving in a few months.'

Freda gave a harsh laugh, causing her two friends to raise their eyebrows in consternation. 'Tony's hardly home these days. I'm wondering if he will even be here to meet his child when it is born.'

'Aw, don't talk like that,' Sarah said as she leant over to give her a hug. 'Tony adores you and is only doing his best to learn his job and give you and your children a comfortable future.'

'Yeah, and it's not his fault he's such a good cyclist that they want him to train our Olympic team,' Maisie chipped in, shrugging her shoulders at Sarah, who gave her a questioning glance as she continued to hug Freda.

'What's going on here?' Ruby asked as she came into the front room.

Freda pulled away from Sarah, taking a handkerchief from the cuff of her cardigan and blowing her nose. 'Oh, it's just me being silly,' she said, giving a weak smile.

Ruby looked between the girls. Something was going on here, if she wasn't mistaken. 'There's nothing silly about having a few tears. There'll be a fair few shed across the nation today. It's like we've lost a member of our family. The King was there for us all through the war. It doesn't bear thinking how Queen Elizabeth and the two princesses are feeling at this moment.'

'We have a new Queen Elizabeth now, and she's only twenty-five,' Maisie said. 'Fancy being that age and being the head of a country; I couldn't do that.'

'She will be head of the Commonwealth,' Sarah corrected her, thinking how adept Maisie was not only at caring for a large family, but also a successful clothing company, with a small factory and several shops. She knew no other woman who could juggle such a busy life. Maisie put them all to shame. Looking around at the downcast faces, she went on, 'We ought to be thankful we have such a loyal Royal Family. Our new Queen will do a marvellous job, I'm sure. Things could be a lot worse. Why, we could still be at war and have our menfolk away from home, defending our country . . .'

'Or organizing a team of cyclists.' Freda burst out laughing, seeing the look of horror cross Sarah's face as she realized what she had said. 'Come on, let's go out to the kitchen and sort out the washing up. I take it there is rather a lot?' she asked Ruby.

'That's what I'd come in here to see you about. The children are complaining they are hungry, and Bob's mentioned once or twice that his stomach thinks its throat's been cut.'

'Blimey, look at the time,' Maisie said, looking towards the black marble clock on the mantelpiece over the fireplace. 'I'd best get down home and get some housework done. I know I closed the factory early as a mark of respect, but it's a shame not to put the extra time to good use.'

'Stay and have a bite of food here. We can all muck in together. The kiddies are playing Snakes and Ladders with Bob in the other room, and it would be a shame to disturb them. Bob and Maureen will be here soon, to bring Buster back, and Maureen said she'll bring a loaf with her as she's been baking; we can make toast and have a fresh pot of tea.'

'Make that cheese on toast.' Freda struggled to her feet.

'I've a large lump of Cheddar in my pantry that I can donate. It tends to give me indigestion these days.'

'In that case, I've got a bowl of fresh eggs down home,' Maisie said. 'I'll come with you, Freda, and then we can walk down to my house as well. Anyone who doesn't want cheese on toast can have a fried egg instead,' she said, taking Freda's arm as they left number thirteen.

'I'll keep an eye on William,' Sarah called after them as she followed Ruby into the kitchen.

'What was that all about?' Ruby asked her granddaughter as they started to wash up the cups and saucers and prepare for making a meal. There wasn't much room in the small kitchen as they worked around each other. A stone pantry in the corner took up much of a side wall, next to the white stone sink and wooden draining board, while on the opposite wall a stove and cupboards filled the space. Thankfully the large living room had room for a table and chairs and a large sideboard, as well as Ruby's beloved wireless. A couple of armchairs set each side of an open fire made the room very cosy, leaving the front room with its bay window for more formal occasions. Ruby was often to be heard pointing out that the road was once called Piano Street, as many people kept a piano in the front room, which was a sign that the houses were a little further up the social scale than the surrounding streets.

Sarah smiled to herself. Her nan didn't miss a thing. 'Freda's upset about Tony not being home much at the moment; one minute she's defending him, and the next she wants him home. I can't say I blame her. What with him being sent all over the place by Woolworths, and then he's been given leave because of the Olympics. It's time he realized he's got a wife and a toddler at home, let alone another on the way,' she huffed.

'He went with Freda's blessing – and ours as well. If you remember, we promised to care for Freda, and that's the only reason Tony agreed to go to the training camp.'

'Yes, but then there's his work . . .'

'Don't see problems where there aren't any, Sarah,' Ruby admonished her. 'Tony will in time hold an important job with F. W. Woolworth, and at the moment if they say jump, he must do so. He's done well working in the Erith store; you've said yourself you got along with him when you worked with him?'

'If more women ran the stores, there would be more understanding about women needing their men at home at times like this.'

'It's the way of the world, and we can't go changing things. We're here for Freda, and Tony will be back in a flash when the baby decides to arrive. There's time for that yet.' Ruby stopped and thought for a couple of moments. 'Perhaps I'll have her move in here with me and Bob. I can keep an eye on her and lend a hand with William.'

'We've solved that problem. With Maisie's house fit to burst, we thought it would be a good idea for Bessie and her baby to lodge with Freda for a while until Maisie has sorted out her housing problem; if Bessie agrees.'

'That is a good idea, but if it doesn't work out, I have two bedrooms here going begging. I enjoyed having you, Maisie and Freda living here when you first came to Erith.'

'And I loved living here with you, Nan. Those were the days.' She chuckled as they both turned their minds to a time before the war started and the babies came along.

Georgina wheedled her way into the kitchen and gave a big sigh as she leant against the door frame.

'Whatever is wrong with you?' Sarah asked, stroking her daughter's cheek.

'I want to do some cooking.'

'Now's not the right time, love. Nanny Ruby has guests and doesn't have time to watch you bake. Why not put your coat on and go out into the garden for a breath of fresh air, or perhaps join Granddad Bob and play Snakes and Ladders with the others?'

Georgina gave another exaggerated sigh. 'All right, I'll go out into the garden . . .'

'She's got a bit of a bee in her bonnet, going on about baking cakes. I had to put her off earlier.'

'Oh, Nan, she's been a complete pest. Maureen allowed her to help make some buns. Now she wants to be a cook and work in Woolworths, just like her Nanny Maureen. I'm all for girls learning to cook, but she won't let go of the idea. Last night Georgie started to tell me how Nanny Maureen makes her steamed syrup puddings differently to me. I could have screamed.'

Ruby chuckled. 'She will learn the hard way; no cook likes to be criticized in their own kitchen. I'm sure it's a fad and will soon pass. Next week she'll want to do something else when she leaves school.'

'I pray it is something that won't have her in my tiny kitchen every five minutes. She won't do her own chores, and thinks she can simply cook all the time. As for her leaving school, well, that's three or four years away. I doubt I can cope that long.'

Ruby thought for a moment. 'I do have an idea that may help,' she said, before checking the child wasn't loitering outside the door, then speaking to Sarah in a hushed tone.

'What a day,' Bob said as he walked into the front room, carrying a tea tray. 'I thought you could do with a cuppa, now the hordes have gone home.'

'You've read my mind,' Ruby said from where she'd made herself comfortable in her favourite armchair by the fireside. It had seen better days and the cushions were lumpy, but it was the place where she liked to sit and relax. 'It's been a sad day, but all the same lovely to have some of the family together. It reminded me of the days when I was needed more.'

'What are you talking about, woman?' Bob asked, settling down on the settee and stretching his legs. 'Friends and family are here all the time. You're never short of visitors.'

Ruby tutted. 'You don't understand. They now come to see if I want a bit of shopping done, or to check up on us. They don't want my help or advice, like the old days. It makes me feel old.'

Bob laughed out loud, ignoring Ruby's scowl. 'I hate to remind you that we are both old. And as far as I'm concerned, I like people popping in to give me a hand in the garden or up the allotment. Did I tell you our Mike's going to help me distemper the toilet next week? He's a good lad.'

Ruby shook her head; trust a man not to understand, but she had to admit that Bob's only son, Mike, was an affable man. If he wasn't helping his wife, Gwyneth, bring up their two youngsters, he was doing more than his fair share of tending their family allotment. All that and being a local bobby. 'We'd be lost without him,' she said with a smile.

'As we would without yours; you did a good job caring for them, and now they are reciprocating.'

'That's a long word, coming from you,' she said warmly. 'I don't begrudge their help and today was a good example of that. It's just . . .'

'It's just that you want to be telling them how to live their lives,' he said warily, knowing that his wife could take offence if she thought he meant she was being bossy.

'I'd never interfere, and well you know it. I simply want to be here for them, and to be able to play my part. I never did tell you how hurt I felt when Maureen went part-time at Woolworths so she could help our Sarah look after the kids while she was working. I'm Sarah's grandmother and should have been the one to carry on helping.'

'Now you're being silly,' Bob said. 'Maureen's as much family as you are to those kiddies, and she's younger than you. Let her take on the daily care, and then you can enjoy them even more when they come to visit. Didn't I hear you advising Sarah this afternoon?'

Ruby smiled. 'Yes, I was able to help her with our Georgina. The child's got a bee in her bonnet about being a cook, and Sarah's that busy with her job at Woolworths that she can't show Georgina how to bake cakes and such, much as she wants to. I said Georgie can come here on Saturday morning and she can cook to her heart's content while I guide her.'

'See, you are helping the family,' Bob said as he picked up his cup and gulped his tea.

Ruby gave up trying to explain how she felt. Yes, she would enjoy her time with Georgina at the weekend, but she felt it wasn't the same as her life had been in years gone by. She shuddered inwardly as the thought how she was reaching her twilight years and things would never be as they used to be.

They both jumped as someone hammered on the door. 'Who the hell is that, at this time of night?' Bob asked as he got to his feet.

'You'll never know unless you take a look,' Ruby replied as she glanced at the clock on the mantelpiece. Her heart skipped a beat; it was gone eleven o'clock. Only trouble came knocking at this time of night.

3

~

Ruby looked up as a handsome dark-skinned man entered the front room. 'Why, James, you look frozen. Sit yourself down by the fire, it's freezing out there,' she said, wondering why he'd arrived at this time of night. 'Bob, stick the kettle on,' she commanded, noticing that James was still standing. 'Is there something wrong, lad?'

James shuffled from foot to foot, twisting the cap in his hands that he'd removed on entering the house. 'I don't like to bother you at this time of night, Mrs Jackson,' he said politely. 'It's just that Sadie's so worried about her grandmother.'

Ruby frowned. 'Is Vera no better? I'd have thought she'd have been over the worst of her bad chest by now.'

'She's certainly no better. I didn't like to worry Sadie, by saying I thought she was fading fast. Mrs Munro's been sleeping, then woke, calling out such things it frightened us both. She shouted out for you, before falling asleep again. I don't know what to make of it.'

Ruby got to her feet, wincing as her knees objected. 'I'll go to her now. Bob, perhaps you'd make a telephone call to Dr Baxter. Tell him Vera has taken a turn for the worse.

Don't let him fob you off by saying he will see her in the morning. You remind him that we belong to the National Health Service, who pay his wages, and Vera needs his help now, not when he's had a good night's sleep and filled his stomach with eggs and bacon.' She shook her head. 'He's a saint and so much better than his father ever was.'

Bob helped Ruby on with her coat, tucking a woollen scarf around her neck and reminding her that she still wore her slippers, before James escorted her out of the house, offering her his arm to hold onto as they started out on the short walk up Alexandra Road, past identical bay-fronted houses, to where Vera Munro (or, as her family called her, *Vera from up the road*) lived.

'I've made some changes to the house to make Mrs Munro more comfortable,' James explained as he opened the gate for Ruby. 'The front room is now her bedroom, so she needn't use the stairs. She still has her wireless and armchair and seems quite settled. We take it in turns to sit with her when we can, and when she is up to it, she joins us in the living room for her meals.'

So this is what it has come to, Ruby thought to herself. How long would it be before she too had to sleep down-stairs? The thought filled her with dread, as she imagined Bob taking care of her in her final days.

'You've been very good to Vera, considering that she can be an awkward woman at times,' Ruby said.

'It is she who has been kind to me. I know it was hard for her to accept me into her family, due to . . .' He stumbled over his words, unsure what to say next.

Ruby finished what he was trying to say. 'Due to the colour of your skin, perhaps?'

29

James signed. 'Yes, it can be difficult, and she is a stubborn woman. The thought I keep foremost in my mind is that she is Sadie's grandmother. I love Sadie, and for me that means I must love Mrs Munro as well. I would have my mother to answer to, if I did not.'

'You have a good soul,' Ruby said as they walked the few steps to the front door. Before James had fished his door key from his pocket, the door swung open, with a distraught Sadie ushering them inside.

'How is she?' Ruby asked as she removed her coat, handing it to James to hang on one of the hooks on the wall.

'It's as if she is delirious and she keeps calling out such strange things. Do you think she is going to die?'

James put an arm around his wife and whispered words of consolation. 'If it is the Lord saying her time is close, we must be brave.'

Ruby bristled. She didn't take with such talk and would have told James so, if it hadn't upset Sadie. 'Vera has years left in her, so we won't speak of such things,' she said kindly. 'A bad chest infection can drag us older people down. James, why don't you pop back down to my house and see if Bob's had any joy contacting the doctor? It won't hurt for him to come out and check Vera over. That's if he hasn't had one too many, to toast the passing of our beloved King.'

'Oh no,' Sadie said. 'Caring for Nan, I'd not listened to the news. She will be upset, as she loves the Royal Family.'

'As does my mother,' James added.

'It is a sad time, but he hadn't enjoyed good health of late,' Ruby said as they all fell silent, thinking of their monarch. 'However, let's get cracking. I'll go in and sit with

Vera while you, James, get hold of the doctor. Tell Bob he may as well retire for the night, as I could be here for a while. Now, Sadie, how about a hot drink?' she added, thinking how the young woman would feel less distraught if she had something to do.

Gently tapping on the door to the front room and not waiting for an answer, Ruby stepped in with a smile on her face. 'What's all this I hear about you being poorly?' she asked, going over to the single bed set against a wall opposite an open fire. Quickly looking around her, Ruby could see that Sadie and James had worked hard to make the room welcoming and bright for Vera. It fleetingly crossed her mind that the same could be done for her own bay-fronted room, if necessity demanded.

'This is a fine time of the day to be visiting?' Vera wheezed. She'd lost none of the waspishness she'd been known for all her life.

'I felt like coming to see you. What's wrong with that? I welcome people into my home night or day, as well you know,' she answered back, knowing that if she spoke sweetly, Vera would be aware there was something wrong. Vera was never slow in coming forward when visiting number thirteen, using the key tied to a piece of string and calling out, 'It's only me' as she stepped over the threshold, regardless of whether she was invited in or not.

'Can you put the wireless on for me? I did ask James, but he seemed reluctant. I miss a bit of sound to break the silence. For some reason he wanted to read to me and keep me quiet,' she said, trying to laugh and instead breaking into a bout of harsh coughing.

Ruby rubbed Vera's back until the cough subsided. She

plumped up her pillows before taking a seat close to the bed. 'It's gone off for the night, love,' she said preparing to impart the sad news of the King's demise. Sick or healthy, Vera would not wish to miss a juicy piece of news or gossip. James didn't know Vera like she did; the woman wanted normality rather than to be handled with kid gloves. She'd want to know what was happening until her dying breath.

Vera looked up at the clock. 'Something's happened, hasn't it?'

Ruby took her hand, just in case she was shocked by the news. 'The King's died. It was peaceful and in his sleep.'

Vera frowned, causing more frown lines to appear in her lined face. As Ruby watched her, she thought how Vera had never had a young face in all the years she'd known her. 'So we've got a Queen, have we? She's no more than a slip of a girl. I'm not sure she'll be up to the job of running our country.'

Ruby shook her head. Trust Vera to see the dark side of something. 'Time will tell, and she is sure to have advisers to help her. My heart goes out to King George's consort; she is only in her early fifties. That's no age to be a widow.'

'You married again, and in your old age, so she may do the same.'

'I'm not the Queen of England,' Ruby admonished her, at the same time thinking how lucky she had been to meet Bob. But then Vera had set her cap at the poor man, causing a sticky situation and making the friends fall out for a while, until Bob made his intentions clear.

'Neither is she any more, as she's just the mother of a queen,' Vera snapped back before starting to cough once again.

Blimey, you may be poorly, but you can still come up with a waspish comment, Ruby thought to herself, before becoming ashamed of her thoughts. This was the way Vera had always been. If Vera had only a little time left in this world, then she could put up with her harsh words. 'It is very sad all the same. I quite liked our King.'

'They didn't need to shut off the wireless early, though,' Vera huffed, before becoming convulsed in another bout of coughing. 'Some of us like to listen to it.' She forced out the words as she gasped for breath.

'Not to worry,' Ruby said, biting back a pithy retort. She had to remind herself Vera was very ill. 'Now, James told me you wanted to speak to me about something?'

Vera flapped her hand for Ruby to pass her a cup of water, which she held to her lips for her to sip. After taking a deep breath, she looked Ruby squarely in the face. 'I've been a wicked woman and want you to help me make amends before I pass away.'

'In what way have you been a wicked woman?' Ruby asked; she could think of a few instances from the past.

'I had a child out of wedlock and gave him away.'

'Bugger me, you kept that quiet,' she said as Sadie walked into the room with a tray.

'Nan, I thought you'd like a cup of cocoa, along with me and Mrs Jackson.'

'Have you put a tot of brandy in it?' Vera croaked. 'It is medicinal,' she added, seeing a smile cross Ruby's face.

'I have, here you are,' the young woman said, placing the cup and saucer where it could be reached. 'I'll leave you alone,' she said, hurrying from the room.

The poor child's petrified at the thought of losing her

grandmother, Ruby thought. Vera might appear harsh to some people, but she brought that girl up after her good-for-nothing mother abandoned her. If Vera was about to meet her maker, the young woman would be inconsolable. She gave Sadie a knowing smile as the girl left the room, before checking Vera was comfortable. 'Now, what's this you're going on about?' she asked, trying to lighten the atmosphere.

Vera sighed. 'I'm dying,' she wheezed, 'I want to put a few things right before I go.'

'Stop talking like that or I'll take myself off home. There's plenty of years left in you yet, Vera Munro. You are just feeling sorry for yourself. Why, I'm older than you, and I've no intention of popping my clogs any time soon.'

Vera glared at her, before taking a deep breath in clearing her throat. 'I may be old, Ruby, but I'm not daft. I've seen many a person taken off by what's wrong with me. Please understand that, for once in my life, I want to do the right thing, and that means finding my son and apologizing to him for abandoning him as I did, when he was a baby. I won't lie by saying I've thought about him often, because . . .' Her body shook as another bout of harsh coughing halted her words.

Ruby put down her cup and saucer and leant over to rub and thump Vera's back until she started to breathe easier. Vera took the proffered handkerchief and scrubbed at her streaming eyes before spitting into the piece of cloth.

'There's no need to keep talking,' Ruby scolded her. 'It can wait.'

'It can't wait. I don't have much time. Please, at least humour me.'

'Drink this,' she said, holding the cup to Vera's lips. As her friend slowly sipped the warm drink, Ruby's mind was ticking over. Vera had had bouts of illness in the past and could really make a meal out of it, having Sadie and everyone else running around, waiting on her hand and foot. However, Ruby had witnessed times when Vera had really hit rock bottom and then she would speak from the heart, knowing that what she said would go no further. Ruby's gut was telling her this was one of those times, but rather than humour her friend, she would do her best to help her. 'I won't humour you, because it's not in my nature to do so. However, I will listen to what you have to say, as long as you promise me one thing.'

Vera nodded her head, trying to clear her throat. 'Thank you,' she whispered as Ruby took the cup.

'Now is not the time. Once the doctor has been, I will help Sadie to settle you for the night, and in the morning I'll come back and sit with you for a couple of hours and you can tell me everything. What do you say to that?'

Vera reached out and took Ruby's hand; there was no need for words as the two friends sat in companionable silence until the doctor announced his arrival with a sharp knock on the door.

'Can I have a quick word, Doctor?' Ruby called out as she hurried up the road. She'd slipped away from Vera's house, not wishing to intrude, and had loitered by her own gate, waiting to see the man go to his car. Even though Bob had nagged her to come indoors, he'd understood when she explained that she'd not be able to sleep until she knew the doctor's conclusions.

'Now, Mrs Jackson, if you wish to speak to me you need to make an appointment. I can't examine you in the street, especially at this time of night,' he scolded as he tucked his scarf into his overcoat and started to pull on his leather driving gloves. Though only a young man in his early forties, there were flecks of grey in his dark hair and shadows around his eyes. She thought being a doctor must be a tiring business.

Ruby leant against the wall to catch her breath. 'No, I'm fine,' she gasped. 'I wanted to know about Vera . . . Mrs Munro? Is she going to die?'

'We are all going to die at some point,' he answered, not unkindly. 'And if you go rushing about in this night air, you will be taking to your own bed and who knows what will happen.'

Ruby brushed away his comments. 'I can take care of myself. I've hardly visited your surgery, and well you know it,' she answered back. 'I've been sitting with Vera and know how poorly she is. In fact she's been saying some strange things, and I wondered if it was part of her illness?'

'Mrs Munro is a very ill woman, but I'd not say she is rambling or hallucinating. You know her better than me, so you will have to judge her words. Now, if you'll excuse me . . .'

Ruby gave him her thanks and watched as he drove away; she could sleep easier now, but she would go up to see Vera when she was on the mend and find out what she'd been going on about. Hopefully by then she'd have forgotten imagining that she had a long-lost son.

4

~

'Alan, I'm trying to tidy the kitchen before I go to work,' Sarah Gilbert huffed at her husband. 'Why ever have you covered the table with all this paperwork when we both need to leave shortly, and your mum will be here to walk the children to school?'

Alan looked up at her and grinned. 'I had an idea about stocking more televisions in the shop. There's talk that the King's funeral will be televised and our business could be quids in, with everyone wanting to watch it in their homes.'

Sarah couldn't be annoyed with her sandy-haired husband for long. He only had to give her a warm smile and her heart would flutter, just as it did the first time she met him on the day she attended the Erith branch of Woolworths for her interview as a counter assistant. 'I'm not sure it's the right thing to do. He's only been dead for two days. It seems rather mercenary to be profiting from his passing.'

Alan raised his eyes to the ceiling and tutted. 'For goodness sake, Sarah, the man died. He did not "pass" or anything else, for that matter. You are starting to sound like Vera from up the road.'

Sarah snorted with laughter. 'And you are starting to sound like Freda and Maisie. We all gave Vera that name when we lived with Nan at number thirteen.'

He groaned in jest. 'Then there's no hope for me. I'm a lost cause. Maisie will be teaching me to make rag rugs next.'

Sarah leant over and gently kissed his lips. Alan responded, wrapping his arms around her and pulling her closer.

'Why are you a lost cause?' a voice enquired from the doorway.

Sarah jumped with shock, forgetting for a moment that their two children were in the house, as Alan chuckled, noticing her embarrassment and holding onto her hand so she couldn't move away. 'It's nothing for you to worry your head about,' he told Georgina.

'In that case, can I do some cooking after school?'

'Oh, darling, not today. I'm working a full day at Woolies, and your daddy won't be here to help you, either,' she replied, hinting to Alan that this was his problem as much as hers.

'You know I'm not good in the kitchen and leave all that to your mum,' he replied, giving Sarah a sideways grin.

'Oh, you two. I don't know why you had children,' Georgina huffed, before stomping off, her two long plaits swinging behind her.

'I blame your mother for this,' Sarah scowled. 'She's put the idea in the child's head about being a cook when she leaves school, and you know what Georgie is like. She won't let go of it now.'

The smile left Alan's face. 'I had no idea you blamed

my mum for this. She's done a lot to help us out so that you can continue to work at Woolies, now you've been promoted.'

Sarah bristled. 'Don't forget my dad is also helping us out, so your shop can prosper,' she spat back, not realizing how much she looked like her daughter, when riled.

Alan stood up and kissed her forehead. 'I don't have time to discuss this now,' he said as he pulled together the brochures and paperwork from the table. 'But let's both agree that our parents are marvellous and we couldn't cope without them. Georgie will get over this fancy of hers, and life will continue as usual.'

'I suppose you are right,' she said, giving him a quick hug. 'We are lucky that our parents fell in love and married so late in life, and then spare us so much time . . .'

Alan gave a belly laugh. 'Now you are sounding like one of those romantic magazines you and Freda like to read.'

Sarah slapped his arm; he was always joshing her over her choice of reading material. 'Gosh, thank goodness you mentioned Freda. She's popping into the store during my dinner break, and I have a knitting pattern I want to give her. She wants to select the wool while she's there. Sadie was joining us, but she has her hands full, with her nan being poorly.'

'It's a shame Vera is unwell, as James doesn't have his full mind on things at the shop.'

'Why not give him a special task, like choosing those television sets you've decided to stock?' She smiled, looking towards the brochures tucked securely under Alan's arm.

His face dropped. 'I was thinking of giving him more responsibility while I purchased the new stock . . .'

Sarah chuckled as she pushed him towards the door. 'Oh, Alan, you are as bad as our Georgie, once you have a bee in your bonnet. Off with you, so I can tidy up and get myself ready for work.'

'You look ready, from what I can see,' he said admiringly as he opened the front door. 'Is that your new suit?'

'Yes, I thought I should wear black today as our King has died. I have to interview new staff and it sets a good example, especially now that I don't have to wear that ghastly overall any more.'

'I quite liked you in your Woolies uniform,' he smiled, raising his eyebrows suggestively.

'Oh, be off with you.' She chuckled as she closed the door after him and smiled to herself. She was a lucky woman to have such a loving husband, beautiful children and a good life.

'Are you sure we are alone?' Vera asked as Ruby settled herself in an armchair close to her friend's bed. Two days on from her health scare, she had more colour in her cheeks and was even more demanding than usual.

'Don't you worry about that. I convinced Sadie you would be all right with me and sent her packing, to do some shopping. James was more of a problem, as he felt he should be here in case you needed the doctor again. I told him Bob's down home, so if we need anything I'd give him a shout. It would be good if you had a telephone installed. Have you thought about it?'

Vera shifted herself against the pillows and snorted. 'I don't need one. I've heard they are expensive. You'd think it would be cheaper, with an exchange at the end of the road. I keep on using yours and leave a few coppers in the pot,' she added, as if she was doing Ruby a favour.

'What if it's the middle of the night and pouring with rain? You don't want to catch your death, do you?'

Vera shrugged her shoulders before giving a chesty cough. 'I can send James to use your telephone. He's young, so a bit of rain won't hurt him.'

Ruby tried not to laugh. Sick or perfectly fit, Vera was always the same. 'Well, you are always welcome if there is an emergency. Just remember to knock loudly or we won't hear you if we are in bed.'

'I'll tell him to use the key that's tied to the inside of your letter box . . .'

Ruby shook her head. Honestly, Vera had no shame. 'Now, why don't we have a chat about what you told me the other night? I'm hoping it was your illness and that you were rambling. If not, you've got some explaining to do.'

Vera eyed Ruby with her dark, beady eyes. 'There's nothing wrong with my memory; it's my chest that's the problem, and now I'm taking that jollop the doctor prescribed I'm on the mend. Everything I told you the other night is true.'

'Perhaps remind me what it was you said, to refresh my memory,' Ruby said tactfully, as all she could remember was Vera mumbling about having a son.

'I can do better than that. If you go upstairs to my bedroom and look in the back of my wardrobe, you'll find a small leather attaché case. Bring it down here and I'll tell you everything.'

Ruby swore to under her breath as she climbed the steep staircase to the bedrooms. She loved her home at number thirteen, except for the stairs, and was starting to avoid using them as much as possible during the daytime. She felt uncomfortable rummaging about amongst Vera's personal property. There was a strong smell of mothballs as she pushed aside old coats and Vera's best finds from the jumble sales. Spying the small leather case, she grabbed the handle and stood up straight, stretching her stiff back. 'There'd better be something interesting in this case,' she muttered as she carefully went back downstairs.

'You took your time,' Vera said as Ruby placed the case on the bed.

'I was being careful on the stairs; I didn't want to fall and break my neck,' she replied, sitting back down by the bed. 'Did you know you've got a couple of loose stair rods? I'd get James to fix them, if I was you, before someone hurts themselves.'

Vera ignored Ruby's words as she carefully snapped open the brass catches and started to pull out various documents. 'I know they are here somewhere,' she muttered to herself, before pouncing on a roll of newspaper clippings tied up with string. She handed them to Ruby. 'Be careful, that's all I've got of him.'

Ruby picked at the knotted string until the clippings unrolled onto the bed. 'They look old,' she said, not liking to pick them up to read them. 'Can you tell me why you've kept these?'

Vera had started to sort through the yellowing paper, but stopped to hand a snippet cut roughly from the *Erith Observer*. 'This is when he won Bonniest Baby at the Erith show,' she said proudly. 'I was there, but stayed well back, in case they thought I was up to no good . . .'

Ruby frowned as she read the words: '*Daniel Carrington was chosen by the mayor of Erith as the Bonniest Baby at this year's show. Young Master Carrington is ten months old and lives with his proud parents in Avenue Road.* He's certainly a bonny baby,' she smiled.

'That's my Gerald,' Vera said proudly as she started to sort through the clippings again. 'Mrs Carrington changed his name, goodness knows why as I like the name Gerald and will continue to call him that. Here he is when he won a prize at Sunday school, and this one is with his classmates before they left to go to grammar school. He's a clever lad, is Gerald,' she smiled as she gazed into the distance, deep in thought.

'I'll make us a cup of tea,' Ruby said, wishing to escape from the room while she collected her thoughts. As she set out the cups and warmed the teapot in the small kitchen so like her own, she still wasn't sure what Vera was going on about, because until her recent outburst there had never been any mention of her having a son. Was she going a bit doolally in her old age? Adding a few malted-milk biscuits to the tray she'd prepared, Ruby walked carefully back to the front room to face whatever Vera had to tell her.

'Now, can you explain to me what this is all about? As far as I know, you had just the one daughter, Sadie's mum . . .' She froze as Vera lurched forward from where she was relaxing against her pillows.

'Don't you even mention her name. She's no daughter of mine, after what she got up to. Besides, she left this earth a long time ago. As far as I'm concerned, Sadie is my only family, and of course Gerald.'

'Now, calm yourself and drink your tea,' Ruby scolded

her, wishing she had someone else with her at that moment, as Vera was looking distraught. 'What's done is done and I won't say anything to upset you. Your Sadie is a credit to you; she's a wonderful mother to her two kiddies, considering what she has been through in her young life.'

Vera slurped her tea nosily whilst nodding in agreement. 'She's a good girl.'

Ruby winced, thinking back to when Sadie went through a bad patch and found herself expecting her boss's baby, Vera had thrown her out on her ear, and the girl ended up in a maternity home for unmarried mothers run by the Church. Sadie would have had the baby taken away from her at birth, were it not for friends who had stepped in to help. Then later to lose her husband in a tragic accident just after she was married. Many women would have lost their mind. Now she was settled with James, the brother of her late husband, and was bringing up two beautiful children. Yes, Sadie was lucky, but not because of anything Vera had done back then. 'She is. Now can you explain to me about the lad in these newspaper clippings, before she comes home from doing her shopping?'

'He's my son,' Vera said, looking at the pile of yellowing papers as if they were set in a gold frame. 'I've already told you that . . .'

Ruby put down her cup and looked Vera straight in the eye. 'Vera, love, you have never given birth to a son. Don't you think all this is a bit fanciful and perhaps brought on by your illness? Why, this lad doesn't even have your name.'

Vera grabbed at the clippings and hugged them to her breast, giving Ruby a malevolent glare. 'I've kept my secret until now and, when I ask for your help, you say that? Do you think I'm making it all up?'

Ruby thought exactly that, but stayed quiet for a few moments until Vera sagged back into the pillows, still holding onto what she thought were her memories. 'Perhaps you could start at the beginning?'

Vera sighed and started to straighten the papers on the blanket that covered her knees. 'No, my old man was still away at the end of the First War. I had my head turned by a chap who used to deliver the groceries to the house where I put in a few hours a day as a cleaner. I know I was a fool, but I was lonely, and I missed my husband so much, and it was a mistake.'

'I'm not one to judge and, as far as I'm concerned, what happened in the past is best forgotten. All I'll say is that I've been no saint myself,' she replied, handing Vera back her drink. 'Best get that down you before it gets cold.'

Vera's paleness had disappeared, with her now-pink cheeks burning brightly, although she had an aura of peace about her. 'I'm glad I got that off my chest. You won't tell anyone, will you? I don't want our Sadie finding out. I had another man's child while her grandad was away serving his country. The last thing I want is her thinking badly of me.'

Ruby put the back of her hand to Vera's forehead; she was a little warm. 'Sadie won't hear anything from me about this,' she promised, although it was a little late now for anyone to think of Vera as a good person. 'I want you to settle down and have a short nap. I'll stay here,' she promised, seeing a look of alarm cross her friend's face. 'May I read the cuttings while you sleep? If Sadie returns, I'll hide them away.'

Vera nodded and was very soon asleep, after Ruby had settled her down and straightened the bedcovers. Collecting the newspaper clippings, she did her best to put them into date order and slowly read each one. They mainly charted the life of a little lad who lived a comfortable life in this very town. Ruby prayed Vera wasn't going to do anything to disrupt another family's life. After all, if she had decided to tell her about this, what was to stop her speaking to the boy's parents? She frowned and checked the dates on a few of the cuttings. The lad was now a grown man and would, more than likely, have a family of his own. He could have a distinguished career and might not be happy to find out that Vera Munro from Alexandra Road was his mother – if, in fact, she was.

Ruby's eyes strayed to the leather attaché case leaning against the bed. Being careful not to make a sound, she opened it and flicked through the contents. There she found Vera's marriage certificate, her husband's death certificate along with the notice from the *Erith Observer* of his passing, and two birth certificates for Sadie and her mother. There was nothing for a Gerald Munro.

'I never registered him,' Vera whispered.

Ruby was embarrassed to be caught going through her property. 'I'm sorry for being nosy. I was just wondering . . .'

Vera gave a gentle smile. 'Let me close my eyes for a little longer, then I'll tell you more, and what I want you to do for me.'

5

As Sarah approached the Erith branch of Woolworths in Pier Road, she felt tears prick her eyes. The windows had been edged in black ribbon, and on a pedestal sat a portrait of the late King. She made a mental note to speak to their temporary manager to check there was enough black fabric and elastic for people to make armbands as they mourned their monarch.

Holding open the door for two elderly shoppers, she greeted them with a smile and a polite hello.

'Hello, ducks, how's your nan? I've not seen her for a while, so I hope she is well,' one of them said.

'She's keeping well, Mrs Froggatt, thank you for asking.'

'Well, give her my best, won't you?'

'And that Betty Billington. I miss seeing her working in Woolies. That latest manager isn't a patch on our Betty,' her friend said.

'I'll pass on both your best wishes,' Sarah replied, watching as they headed towards the haberdashery counter.

She grimaced, even thinking of the new manager, and wished they could go back to the days when Betty Billington managed the store. Freda's husband, Tony, would be ideally suited and got on well with all the staff and customers. However, at the moment he was of course away, helping train cyclists for the Olympics. Hopefully upon his return the powers-that-be at head office would offer him the store's management full-time, and there'd be no more roaming around the country standing in for absentee general managers. Until recently Tony had been overseeing one of the larger Birmingham stores, but with Freda's pregnancy, and her wanting to return to her home in Alexandra Road, his career path within Woolworths had changed. 'It couldn't happen soon enough,' she murmured as she walked towards the staff door.

'Talking to yourself, Mrs Gilbert? I don't know, you young women want management jobs, then turn up late muttering to yourselves . . .' a male voice said just behind her.

Startled, Sarah spun round to find herself face-to-face with one of the two floorwalkers employed by F.W. Woolworth, standing there with a smirk on his face, a little too close. She attempted not to shiver and instead gave him a look of contempt. 'Mr Argent, I can assure you I am not late for my shift. In fact I'm a little early,' she replied, looking up at the large clock that dominated the shop floor.

He frowned, as the clock showed three minutes past the hour. 'I beg to differ.'

'You can beg all you want, but anyone who has worked here for a while knows that by ten o'clock each day the clock has gained three minutes. You can blame the war for that,' she said, giving him a superior smile.

'Then I suggest you ask head office to change this clock

for something more reliable, and then at least the female staff could tell the time.'

'Head office is aware, and agree with the old staff that it should remain as a reminder of what this store went through during the war. Of course you wouldn't know that, would you, not having worked for the company for very long?' Sarah continued to stare back at him, willing him to be the first to walk away.

'You had better get to your office before you are later than you are now,' he sneered, turning and walking purposely away from her with his nose stuck in the air.

Sarah shrugged her shoulders, deciding not to let the man get under her skin. He'd only worked in the store for a few weeks, arriving just after the temporary manager, Mr Harrison, had been moved to Erith from another area. Rumour had it that the two men were related in some way, but Sarah didn't listen to rumours.

'Mrs Gilbert, can you spare me a minute?'

Sarah looked at the young woman's flushed face and puffy red eyes. 'Of course I can, Barbara. Come along in,' she said, ushering her into the small office that just had room for a small desk, two wooden chairs and a row of shelves and a filing cabinet, where she kept personnel records and employee details. There had been a time when she shared an office with the manager, but since the arrival of Philip Harrison she had been moved to work in what was no more than a small storeroom. 'Now, you sit yourself down there and tell me your problem. I take it you do have a problem?' she asked as she removed her black woollen coat and hung it on a hook behind the door.

'Yes.' The girl sniffed into a damp handkerchief. 'I'm not quite sure how to explain what has happened.'

'Then start at the beginning. Are you unhappy in your work?'

'Oh no, I love working here. In fact I was worried about speaking to you, but my mum said if I didn't, she'd come and speak to Mr Harrison.' The look of horror as she spoke was echoed in Sarah's own eyes.

'I'm sure whatever it is, I can help you sort it out,' she said, sitting down opposite Barbara on the other side of the desk and taking a notepad and pencil from the top drawer. 'Do you mind if I take a few notes? I promise they will not be seen by anyone else and will not be shown on your work record.'

'I trust you, Mrs Gilbert,' Barbara said, giving a glimmer of a smile. 'You've been good to me since I came for my interview, and showed enough trust in me to put me on the household-goods counter.'

'You are a good worker, Barbara. I hate to see you looking so upset. Now tell me everything, before the bell goes for the end of your break.'

'Well, it's Mr Argent . . .'

Sarah sat deep in thought, long after Barbara had returned to her duties. She had never liked the over-confident man from the day he'd been introduced to her by the new manager, but she had kept her thoughts to herself. After all, it would be a strange world if she liked everyone. She treated him the same way as every other colleague, even though she wasn't enamoured of his slicked-back hair and thin black moustache or the way he stopped to check his appearance when he walked by the mirrors displayed on one wall in the shop. However, what Barbara had told her was most disconcerting. Sarah decided to get on with her work and push the problem to the back of her mind for a while. It wouldn't help if she went in like a bull in a china shop and caused problems when there weren't any.

Taking several ledgers down from a shelf, she started to enter figures onto a page that listed staff working hours. After half an hour she stopped and rubbed her eyes as a thought came to her. Taking a key from the top drawer of her desk, she unlocked the filing cabinet tucked away in a corner and pulled open a metal drawer, then started to flick through the sections until she reached the employment records for the store's male workers and frowned as she ran her fingers over each staff member's notes: Brown, Benfield, Davis, Henson, Jones, Palmer, Stevens, Tomkins . . .

'I must have missed him,' she muttered as she started again, checking to see if Alfred Argent's file had been put in the wrong place. No, she couldn't see it. After pulling out the folders and checking at the bottom and back of the drawer, she knew for certain that Alfred Argent's personnel folder was not there. With a deep sigh, she started to check the other three drawers, going through the female folders as well as other paperwork. Mr Harrison had specifically told her that he would file the folder when he had a moment, as it was somewhere on his desk. Brushing down her skirt – black did show up every speck and was not a good colour for working in Woolworths – she left her office and walked along the corridor to knock on Mr Harrison's door.

'Enter!'

She felt as though she was back at school and was about to be told off by the headmaster. Straightening her back and taking a deep breath, she entered the room. 'Excuse me, Mr Harrison, I wondered if you'd finished with Alfred Argent's employment record? I'd like to file it away in the proper place.'

Philip Harrison looked up at her from where he'd been reading a newspaper. A thin weasel-faced man, there wasn't an ounce of spare flesh on the whole of his body. She could imagine her nan saying how he would need both belt and braces to keep his trousers from falling. 'Whatever are you talking about?'

'Mr Argent's personnel file; you told me you were going to give it to me once you had finished with it?'

The man frowned at Sarah. 'I returned it to your office weeks ago. Don't tell me you have misplaced a document containing personal information? Head office will hear of this.'

Sarah's stomach churned as she started to doubt herself. Perhaps she had missed it while she was searching? 'Would you mind telling me where you put it, as it is not in the section where we keep the male employee documents?'

A look of incredulity crossed his face. 'Are you stupid, woman? I placed it on your desk. Surely you've seen it, or are you too busy chattering to the female staff all the time that you have not done your job competently?'

Sarah clenched her fists behind her back and tried to stay calm. Perhaps he was right and she had overlooked the file, but there was no need for him to talk to her like that. 'I'm sorry, I'll check again. But, sir, I don't like the way you just spoke to me.'

His mouth dropped open at her words. 'You don't like the way I spoke to you?'

'No, sir.'

'I'm afraid you will have to put up with me, from now on. The days are gone when Betty Billington ran the store, because no other men were available. You won't find me organizing tea parties for old folk and being a shoulder for staff to cry on.'

'But, sir, Mrs Billington was a very good manager. Everybody liked her.'

He started to mimic Sarah. 'Everybody liked her . . . For goodness' sake, woman, we do not manage Woolworths stores to be liked. Managers are here to run the bloody place.'

'May I remind you that I am also a manager – a personnel manager,' Sarah replied, struggling to hold on to her composure.

Harrison scowled. 'Merely words; you are not, and never will be, a proper manager,' he snapped, waving his hand to dismiss her. 'Now I suggest you go back to your office and find that file or you will receive a letter of dismissal come Friday – unless you wish to resign before then? I can easily promote one of the male staff to take your place; they never cause a fuss.'

Sarah backed towards the door; the fight had left her and she didn't wish to let herself down by crying, even though tears of anger were threatening. 'Thank you,' she mumbled before fleeing the room. Sitting at her desk, she tried to calm herself by taking deep breaths as her heart beat nineteen to the dozen. 'That wretched man is a night-mare,' she said out loud, thumping both fists on the wooden-topped desk as the door opened.

'Is that your husband or another man, and is it safe to come in?' Freda asked as she put her head around the door.

Sarah brightened immediately. 'Come along in, Freda. I'm just venting my anger because of Mr Harrison; he is an odious creature with a nasty nature. I swear he doesn't like women.'

'Perhaps his mother dropped him on his head as a baby?' Freda chuckled as she eased her growing frame into a chair. 'Ooh, that's better. Those stairs damn near done me in; next time I'll ask one of the storeroom lads to bring me up in the goods lifts. I may look ungainly, but it would be heaven; thank goodness I left William with Ruby, as I'd never have got the pram upstairs.'

Sarah couldn't help but smile, and thought back to when she was expecting her children. The uncertainty of what lay ahead and getting used to her changing body was an experience she would never forget. 'You have a while to go yet, so you need to start pacing yourself. I found I was thinking ahead all the time and trying to avoid steep staircases and anything that made me puff. I'm sure you will be fine, as you are a fit young woman. Imagine how Betty felt, having her two later in life?'

'I can't even begin to imagine having two children,' Freda said as she peered at Sarah's face. 'Have you been crying?'

'Not so much crying, just getting very angry. To be honest, I could easily give up working at Woolworths; it's not the same any more without you, Maisie and Betty. I miss the old days when we all worked together; even Maureen only works a few mornings a week in the staff canteen, so I can't wander in there for a shoulder to cry on. It doesn't seem like the old Woolies we knew and loved.'

'Oh, please don't feel like that. I was only saying to Betty the other day, when she popped in to see me, that we rely on you to be our contact with this store until such time as we are back working with you. Betty is ready to return in any capacity, now her little ones are older, and she feels she can leave them with her housekeeper.' She noticed a small grin cross Sarah's face. 'Don't smile like that. I too had to keep a straight face when she told me. Imagine being able to have someone live in and do your housework, let alone take over caring for the children – not that I want anyone else looking after this little person,' she said, patting her stomach lovingly. 'To begin with, I want to take care of him or her all on my own, as I have with William.'

'That's as it should be, but our Betty is an older mum and things are different for her. I do admire her,' Sarah sighed.

'Did I tell you Sadie has told me she would willingly care for the children if I wished to return to work part-time? She is a godsend. I told her what I've just told you, but to have a friend living close by who cares for children will be so handy. Tony knows I've always wanted to return to work, and he agrees there is no reason I can't, but it is up to me. I know some women have no choice, but in this day and age there's no reason we can't be a mother, run a home and work part-time as well.'

'As long as it all runs to plan, and we have a nice boss . . .'

'You are really down, aren't you?' Freda said, looking concerned. 'And I am holding you up. I shall go away and let you get on with your work. Will you be ready to meet for lunch at one o'clock? I was going to pop into the canteen to beg a cup of tea from Maureen, but as she's not in work today, I'll take myself off to Maisie's Modes and see if there's anything to fit my growing girth. I'll see you later,' she said, struggling to her feet and reaching over to kiss Sarah's cheek. As she walked to the door she started to giggle.

'I'm so pleased you are in good spirits,' Sarah said, fighting hard to smile.

'It suddenly came to me that the first time we met here for our interviews, I was a skinny little thing who wouldn't say boo to a goose. Now look at me!'

Sarah couldn't help but join in with her laughter. 'That was quite a few years ago,' she said as she started to count on her fingers. 'Crikey, I make it over thirteen years. How time flies!'

Freda, still laughing, started to open the door as it was pushed hard from the other side. She stepped back as the door hit her. 'Oof, mind out there!' she snapped.

Mr Harrison stepped into the room. 'For heaven's sake, woman, why are you blocking the door?' he asked, giving Freda a questioning look. 'Do I know you?'

Freda, who was unhurt by the experience, raised a hand to stop Sarah, who was about to leap to her protection. 'I am Mrs Tony Forsythe, the wife of one of your colleagues. I was also a supervisor here at one time. I popped in with a message for Mrs Gilbert,' she retorted, giving him a haughty look. 'I'll see you at one o'clock,' she said to Sarah, before pushing past the store manager and giving him a shove as she did so.

'Did you require me for something?' Sarah asked the man as she watched Freda depart the office, wishing she could leave with her. Mr Harrison made her feel so tired and useless.

'Yes, I wondered if you had found that file yet?'

'I only left your office some fifteen minutes ago,' Sarah said, trying her hardest not to snap back at him. 'I'll let you know if I come across it, but as I don't recall you returning the file, I'm at a loss to know where it could be.' In a way she was glad Freda had interrupted her thoughts, as otherwise she would by now either be shouting at the man or telling him she would be leaving the employ of F. W. Woolworth as she could not stand working with him. 'I am rather busy at the moment, but will try to find time later today to search for it.'

Philip Harrison raised his eyebrows. 'You seem to have time to entertain ex-members of staff in your office. I just hope you don't make a habit of allowing your social life to affect your duties.'

Sarah shook her head as the odious man left the room. She knew for certain he had not returned that file and was trying to cause problems – but why?

'I'm so sorry for getting you into trouble,' Freda said as Sarah joined her in Mitchell's tea room across the road from the Woolworths store. 'I've ordered for the four of us, as I know you won't have much time, now that tyrant is watching your every move.'

'Four?' Sarah asked, wondering what Freda was up to. Before she could receive an answer, there was a flurry of noise at the door to the tea room and in burst Maisie Carlisle followed by a pink-cheeked Betty Billington.

'I thought you needed cheering up, so I summoned the gang,' Freda said as she stood up to hug them both.

Betty hurried to Sarah's side. 'I feel responsible for your

ELAINE EVEREST

situation in the store,' she apologized, enveloping her in a delicate waft of face powder and Je Reviens perfume. Sarah took a deep breath and couldn't help thinking how she would recognize Betty anywhere, as this was her distinctive perfume. 'I'm so pleased to see you all,' she beamed as the girls took their seats around the table, while Freda beckoned the hovering waitress to bring their order.

'Why do you blame yourself?' Sarah asked as she watched Betty remove her gloves.

'I should not have left; I know that now. As much as I love my family, I should have requested to have my job held open until I was ready to return. You all know I'm better suited as a store manager than as a mother.'

'Don't put yourself down,' Maisie scolded her as she peered at her image in a pretty gold compact, before dabbing on more powder to her perfect nose. 'If you want to look at a bad mother, look no further than me. What other mother pushes her stepdaughters into working for her in a factory and leaves her younger kiddies for hours on end?'

'For goodness' sake, Maisie, you are a very good mother, and your girls adore you. As for leaving the babies, you know very well that Sadie is an excellent person to care for them – and she is on your payroll,' Sarah admonished her. 'I'm just so pleased to see you all. It's been an age,' she smiled, looking around the table. 'However did you manage this?' she asked Freda, who was looking rather proud of herself.

'Maisie was in her shop, and I told her how annoyed you were with Mr Harrison. She picked up the telephone and contacted Betty. They both decided to drop everything and join us for lunch.'

'Thank you all,' Sarah said, feeling quite emotional to see her friends. 'You really shouldn't have put yourself out, just because I'm not happy in my work. I've near enough decided to hand in my notice. Alan is always reminding me I don't need to work, now he is doing well. Besides which, I should spend more time with my children.' Howls of disagreement were aimed at Sarah, who looked surprised. 'Well, I must say, I'm shocked by the way you've taken this.'

'Are you surprised?' Maisie said, wagging a finger at her. 'You'll be bored to death inside a fortnight. What will you do with yourself, once you've scrubbed the floors and cleaned your oven?'

'You could do more knitting,' Freda offered, trying not to laugh as she knew how much Sarah detested it.

'I could have you come to my factory, and I'd teach you how to cut patterns and sew garments . . . ?' Maisie contributed as Sarah wrinkled her nose.

'Much as I admire the way you have built up your own business, I'm afraid sewing is not for me. Thank you for the offer.'

Maisie frowned. 'What about running my office?'

Freda beamed. 'That would suit you down to the ground, Sarah. Go on, say yes.'

'Have Maisie as my boss?' Sarah laughed. 'We'd be at each other's throats by the end of the first day. I'd want to stamp my own mark in the office, and Maisie would over-rule me. Besides, it is only fair that one of your daughters takes up the reins.'

'I have the perfect idea,' Betty grinned. 'You could take up the reins from Freda and run the Brownie pack; that takes up a lot of free time, from what I've seen.'

Sarah slapped her hand to her mouth in horror. 'I can just about cope with my two children. As much as I love them, I could not imagine overseeing twenty or so girls younger than my Georgie, even for one hour. No, there must be something else I can do?'

The girls continued to offer suggestions as their food was served, with Sarah putting up objections at every turn.

'Oh, gosh, I really ought to get back to work,' she said, checking her wristwatch. 'As tempting as it is to while away the time with you lovely ladies, I have a job to do.'

Maisie snorted with laughter. 'Here we are, trying to give you ideas as to what to do with your time, and all you want to do is return to work.'

'She has a point,' Betty observed. 'I wonder, if things were different, if you'd want to stay working for Woolworths?'

Sarah pulled on her coat while considering Betty's words. 'If only we could turn back the clock and I was working with you all again. As it is, I have to interview a young woman this afternoon, so I must pin a smile on my face – as you would say, Betty – and get on with the job. You may recall the woman, Freda, although she was a girl the last time you met her.'

A frown crossed Freda's forehead. 'You can't leave without telling me who it is.'

'I tell you what: why not pop over to the store at half past two and meet her yourself? Mr Harrison will still be down the pub at that time, so the coast will be clear. But keep away from the floorwalker as, from what I was told this morning, his hands are all over the place, although you will probably be safe in your condition.'

'What?' the three girls said in unison.

'I'll accompany you, Freda,' Betty said. 'It's about time I met these new people.'

'I must get back to the shop. I'm putting together a display of maternity wear, but I want to know all about it. Make sure you let me know,' Maisie said, giving them a stern look. 'If this chap is giving you trouble, let me know and I'll pay a visit,' she huffed while a dreamy expression crossed Freda's face.

'Oh, maternity wear. I'll be your first customer. Nothing fits me properly any more; I seem to be carrying a giant baby this time . . .'

6

~

Freda pulled her scarf closer around her head as she headed down the road from Mitchell's into the High Street to where Maisie's Modes was situated. Although she was walking beside Maisie, she was deep in thought about her friend's business. To think Maisie had been a sales assistant and had started at Woolies at the same time as her in December 1938, and now had two shops and a clothing factory to her name. It made her wonder if she too should have done something with her life rather than remain at Woolies, working her way up to supervisor before marrying Tony and moving to the Midlands when he was promoted to temporary manager. Now she was back in Erith and expecting their second child.

'A penny for them?' Maisie said as she tucked her arm through Freda's. 'You are miles away.'

'I was thinking how our lives have changed since we first knew each other. You've done so well for yourself.'

'You've not done so badly. When I think of that timid waif and stray that I first met and then look at you now.'

Freda laughed. 'I've turned into a baby elephant.'

'An adorable baby elephant who is a wonderful mother.

Now get yourself inside the shop. That wind is fair whipping off the river and freezing my bones.'

Freda chuckled, before pulling away to investigate the window of the clothing shop. 'You've made this look wonderful. I've never seen it so crammed with clothes.'

'And all made in my factory. I've put the second-hand stuff in a room at the back of the shop for now,' she said, pulling her friend inside the shop and closing the door on the biting wind. 'You'll catch your death out there.'

Freda sat down gratefully on the chair a sales lady offered to her, then unbuttoned her coat. 'Thank you, I don't think we've met before,' she said, giving the elderly woman a smile.

'This is Yvonne; she usually works down the factory, but I asked her to give me a hand with the stock I brought over. Thanks for clearing up all our mess; the shop looks spick and span now.'

'I enjoy doing it,' she replied. 'It's nice to see the clothes we make being sold. Those maternity clothes look good on the mannequin. I sold two maternity tops and a skirt just now.'

'Show me, show me,' Freda begged. 'The waistband on my skirt is cutting into me and I can't let it out any more.'

'Shall I show the stock to your friend, Mrs Carlisle?'

'No, I'll do that. You get yourself off home. There'll be a little something extra in your pay packet on Friday as my way of saying thank you,' Maisie replied as the grateful woman put on her coat and left the shop.

'You are good to your staff.'

'I've found that if I look after them, they look after me by working that little bit harder. Besides, I like the people

I've hired and want them to stay. Now, look at this,' she said, wheeling the mannequin closer to where Freda was sitting.

'Oh, I adore the colour of this maternity smock,' she said, running her fingers over the blue gingham fabric. 'The white collar and bow set it off so nicely.'

'I have other colours with full-length sleeves, and some don't have such wide collars,' Maisie said, going to a rack and flicking through the hangers, stopping to pull out an array of pretty outfits. 'I have dresses and formal wear in production, and by the summer we will have a full range, including sun dresses.'

Freda screwed up her nose. 'I'd almost want to remain pregnant longer, just to wear the super clothes you make. May I try this one on?'

Maisie took a deep-red smock with large white buttons down the front from the hanger and handed it to Freda. 'Hang on a minute and I'll give you a hand,' she said, going to the door and turning the sign to 'Closed'.

Freda hurriedly pulled off her outer clothes. 'I can slip it on over my blouse,' she said, holding out her arms for Maisie to help her into the voluminous garment. 'Oh, it's too long for me,' she sighed. 'I wish I was taller, like you.'

'That's not a problem,' Maisie said, reaching for a pincushion and holding several pins between her teeth. 'Stand in front of the full-length mirror while I pin up the bottom to the length you prefer. Then you can make us a cup of tea while I stitch the hem.'

Freda stood still and watched in the mirror as Maisie knelt down and deftly raised the hem several inches, commanding her to turn round slightly every so often.

'There, what do you think?' she asked, standing up and stepping back to get a better view.

'God, I love it; I reckon it will see me right through my pregnancy,' she added, holding out the front as if she was further gone than she already was.

'While you are trying things on, slip on the skirt to see if it fits.'

Freda frowned. 'I'm already having problems with my skirts, like I told you. When I had William, I got away with a larger-size skirt, but this time it's not so easy. Ruby told me to open the buttons and stitch a length of elastic between the top button and buttonhole. I reckon it will be a tad draughty, though,' she chuckled. 'Sarah offered to lend me a skirt as she is a size larger than me, but it swamped me.'

'Never fear,' Maisie winked. 'I designed this to have openings on each side with extra buttons, so that women can move them as they grow. There's also elastic in the waistband, for extra give.'

Freda's eyes sparkled. 'You've thought of everything.'

'I just thought what I'd have liked to wear, when I was expecting.'

'But no siren suits,' Freda laughed, thinking of the comfortable garments Maisie had made for friends and their families during the war, often out of men's clothing that they found at jumble sales.

'Hmm, leave that with me,' Maisie said with a glint in her eye.

As Sarah expected, the coast was clear when she returned to the store. Mr Harrison had gone to the pub, along with the floorwalker, for a liquid lunch. She sighed; there seemed to be one rule for the men in this store and another for the women. She said as much when she bumped into the cashier, Doreen, as the woman returned upstairs with the takings from the tills, accompanied by one of the lads from the store.

'Give me a shout if you decide to copy the manager, and I'll join you,' the woman laughed. 'I could do with a break. I'm only glad I retire next week.'

'I'm sorry to hear you are leaving,' Sarah said, wondering if Mr Harrison had found a suitable replacement.

'It's just not the same here any more, without Mrs Billington in charge. Even Freda's husband was a good temporary manager.' She shrugged her shoulders. 'My old man's been nagging me to resign for a while, now he's retired.'

'I will miss you; this place is changing so much. I'm not sure I'll be here much longer. My heart isn't in the job any more, as so much has altered,' she replied, thinking of the awful floorwalker and the complaint from the young assistant, which she still needed to speak to Mr Harrison about.

Doreen patted Sarah's arm. 'Fight for the store, love, or there will be others leaving, you mark my words. They're not a happy lot down on the shop floor.'

Sarah thought of how there was a time when she knew everything that was going on in the store, when Betty was manager and Freda worked as a supervisor. Her mother-in-law, Maureen, was also cooking full-time in the staff canteen and was there as a shoulder to cry on, or just to share news. Now she felt so alone. 'I'll do my best,' she promised.

Doreen unlocked the door to a room that was even

smaller than Sarah's office. It contained a desk and a large safe. She beckoned to the lad who stood patiently nearby, holding a heavy hessian sack containing the takings from each till. He placed the bag on the desk and left them alone. 'You will join me in the staff room for my leaving do? There's an open invitation stuck on the noticeboard. Please invite the old girls; I know you still see some of them, and don't forget your nan. Maureen is laying on a buffet and there will be a bottle or two of sherry. It's after the store closes, so we won't have to worry about being inebriated in front of the customers,' she laughed.

'I'll look forward to it, but it won't be the same without you,' Sarah said as Doreen went into the room and locked the door behind her.

Checking her watch, she could see that she had ten minutes before the interviews for counter assistants started. She expected two young women, as there had been a telephone enquiry early that day. Sarah preferred written enquiries, as she could gauge more from someone's handwriting and the way they presented themselves, but she would have time to talk with the woman, and there was an arithmetic test and an application form to complete. She quickly tidied her desk and found another chair, so the two women could sit together for the first part of the interview. Taking a comb from her bag, she ran it through her shiny chestnut-coloured hair and checked herself in the mirror hanging on the wall. It used to belong to Betty and, when she left the store, Sarah had put it in her own small office. Thinking she should apply a little lipstick, she did exactly that and straightened her jacket, thankful she was wearing her smartest suit. If she'd learnt nothing else from Betty

Billington, she knew that a smart suit spoke volumes when working in management.

Sitting down at her desk, she checked that she had application forms and sharpened her pencils, then took a deep breath as there was a knock on the door. Taking a deep breath, she called out, 'Enter' and two young women came through the door, looking nervous.

'Please take a seat.' Sarah smiled, recalling how nervous she was when she attended her interview. 'I'm very pleased to meet you both. It is a little cramped in here, but I'll take you through to the staff canteen while you complete the paperwork,' she said as she looked down at the sheet of paper in front of her. Although she recognized one of the women, she felt it was right not to say so. 'Now, who is Christine and who is Jessie?'

'I'm Christine Jenkins,' the younger woman said. 'I rang this morning on the off-chance there was a vacancy. I've just moved here from Gravesend. I do have references, but I've not worked as a sales lady before,' she said, handing over an envelope.

Sarah was impressed that the woman was honest about her work history. 'I'll look at these while you're both in the staff room. So you must be Jessie?'

'Yes, I used to work in Hedley Mitchell and served you once. We chatted about your father, Councillor Caselton.'

'Of course, I thought you looked familiar,' she said, recalling that wasn't the first time they'd met. 'We can talk more when I speak to you individually.'

Jessie nodded her head. She looked nervous as she passed a couple of folded letters across the table. 'I'm not sure if these are any good; I've not worked for a little while. I have young children,' she said, averting her eyes from Sarah.

'Children can be a blessing,' Sarah replied, wondering why Jessie looked so furtive. 'Why don't I take you both through to the staff canteen and you can complete the application form and do the arithmetic test. I'll arrange a cup of tea for you both and leave you for three-quarters of an hour. That should be enough time,' she said as a look of alarm crossed Christine's face.

As she showed the two women into the canteen, she spotted Freda at the top of the staircase. Mouthing, 'I'll be a few minutes' to her, she ushered Christine and Jessie to a table at the back of the canteen and ordered two cups of tea and a plate of biscuits. 'I trust you both not to cheat,' she smiled. 'I'll come back at a quarter to three.'

'Wow, you look very smart,' Sarah said as she entered her office to see Freda giving a twirl in her new clothes.

'I feel wonderful. Maisie has done a marvellous job with this new range of clothing.'

'I wonder if her Bessie had a say in this idea?'

'I thought the same. With her baby, Jenny, now a year old, she knows what women like to wear. Maisie told me she is sketching design ideas for the factory. The maternity smocks are so youthful; I don't feel like an old granny this time round.'

Sarah giggled. 'I doubt a granny would need to wear maternity clothes.'

'Oh, you know what I mean. She's going to extend the range for the summer.'

'Even though it's too late for you. Come the summer,

you'll be pushing young Master or Miss Forsythe in a pram and showing it off to the world, while William will be toddling alongside.'

'I can't wait, but in the meantime I'll enjoy wearing these new clothes.'

Sarah smiled. It was good to see Freda so happy. 'Can you do something for me?'

'Of course, if it doesn't include going up and down stairs or lugging sacks of potatoes to the veg counter.'

'Nothing like that. I want you to go into the staff canteen and take a peep at the two women who are here for their interviews. I want you to tell me if you recognize one of them.'

'That sounds rather furtive. What am I supposed to be looking for – a shoplifter or something?'

'No, nothing like that. Let's just say it is someone from the past . . .'

Sarah smiled to herself as an intrigued Freda scurried off to the staff canteen. Sitting down at her desk, she opened Christine's references and read them carefully. She could see no reason to contact the two employers. Granted, one job had been factory work towards the end of the war, and a second, more recent one in the office of a local builder, but both companies praised her diligence and pleasant nature; and that's what Sarah expected from someone working on the shop floor. Jessie's reference letters caused her a little concern, as one was over five years old, written in a rough hand by a farmer who simply stated that she had worked in his fields picking vegetables one summer, whilst the other showed that Jessie had been a cleaner at the Burndept works in Erith. Sarah knew the woman had worked in Hedley Mitchell; had she not mentioned this less than an hour ago? She was still deep in thought as Freda returned with a grin on her face.

'Oh my, that's Jessie, who was hiding here one Christmas during the war when we had that unexploded bomb to contend with. She was no more than a kid then. I wonder what she's been up to these past years?'

'I met her around the time of your wedding. She was a waitress at Hedley Mitchell at the time. I do recall her saying that Dad had helped her, in his position as a local councillor, as she had a problem with her housing. I suggested that she applied here for a job as she said she was unhappy in her current position.'

'How strange it took her this long to apply . . .'

'I did wonder about that, but hopefully it will come to light when I interview her, once she has completed the paperwork.' Sarah looked up at the clock. 'Another ten minutes, then I can collect what they've written. There may be something on her application form that explains what has been happening.'

'I hope she has had a good life, as she was in such a fix when I discovered her. I feel bad for not keeping in touch.'

Sarah agreed. 'It was a difficult period for us all, at times.'

'It was, and look how life has moved on for us all.'

'Now tell me more about Maisie's new range of clothing. I wish I'd had lovely clothing like that when I was carrying my two.'

'As long as Mr Harrison doesn't catch us chatting. I'd hate you to get into trouble.'

'Don't worry about him, as I doubt he and Mr Argent will be back from the pub for at least another hour. He's on good terms with the landlord of the Crossed Keys, so he will be in there after hours,' she tutted.

Freda shook her head. 'Oh, to be a man and make up your own rules. I wonder what head office would say about it?'

'I'll not say anything, as he talks as if he has friends in high places.'

'Have a word with Betty; she might be able to advise you about that. She knows lots of people. She did say she might pop in and see you when she has finished her errands. She came into town to do them, as she was keen to meet Mr Harrison. Shall I collect the application forms and get the women another drink while you read them through, once their time is up?'

7

~

Bob came in from the back garden, stamping his feet on the doormat to remove any lingering mud before he was told off for making the linoleum dirty. He spotted Ruby at the table, deep in thought. 'What's up, love? You've been so quiet, you're worrying me. Do you feel ill?'

Ruby's head jerked up with a start. 'Sorry, I didn't hear you come in. I was sitting here thinking.'

He looked at the washing up sitting in the sink and at a pile of newspaper cuttings on the table. It wasn't like Ruby not to keep on top of her housework, even though she'd looked after young William for a couple of hours. Rolling up his sleeves, he lifted the large kettle sitting on the gas stove and poured warm water into a white enamel washing-up bowl, adding a generous handful of soap flakes. 'Why don't you put your feet up in the front room? I'll bring our afternoon tea and biscuits through when I've finished here.'

'Oh, Bob, I'd have done that in a minute. I just got caught up in my thoughts.'

'These thoughts . . . they've been on your mind for a couple of days now. How about you share them with me?'

'I promised Vera I'd not tell anyone her secret,' she said, going through the open door that separated the small kitchen from their living room and sitting at the table.

'Come on, love, I'm not anyone, I'm your husband. Surely you can confide in me? You know whatever you tell me will not go elsewhere. What is it they say about a trouble shared is a trouble halved?'

'You're right. I'm being a silly old woman. Sit your bum down there and I'll tell you everything I know. With luck, you'll be able to come up with something because I know, as sure as eggs is eggs, I am truly stumped.'

Bob abandoned the washing up and, wiping his hands on a towel hanging on the back of the kitchen door, walked into the living room and sat down next to his wife. 'I've been thinking I might take off that kitchen door, as we never close it and, that way, everyone can move about freely.'

Ruby looked up from sorting through the newspaper cuttings. 'You'll do no such thing. What if someone turned up out of the blue and the kitchen was in a state? I'd die of shame. At least, as it is, I can close the door on any mess.'

Bob laughed. Ruby might be down in the dumps, but scratch the surface and the woman he loved was still there. 'Now, what's all this about?'

'I don't need to tell you Vera's been very poorly; I thought at one point we were going to lose her. Well, when I was sitting with her, she shared a secret that she's kept to herself for many years. It seems she had another child, a boy. She wants me to find him, so that she can see him before she passes away.'

'Bloody hell, that's a bit of a tall order. Why didn't she

ask her Sadie to do it for her? Come to that, why didn't she look for him while she was fit and well, rather than leave it to you to be at her beck and call. Tell her you can't do it. In fact, I insist we put all this stuff in a box and take it back to her, and let that be the end of it.'

'Now, now, Bob, don't go getting on your high horse or I won't tell you any more about it,' Ruby snapped. 'I thought you would at least have been interested enough to want to know more. I'll ask my George instead.'

'Ask George what?' a voice called from the hallway, causing Ruby to almost jump out of her seat.

'You gave me the fright of my life, creeping about like that,' she said, clasping her hand to her chest.

'I do come bearing gifts,' George Caselton said, placing an enamel baking tin covered in a tea towel on the table in front of the pair. 'I did tap on the door before I let myself in.'

'That's all right,' Bob said, lifting the edge of the tea towel and sniffing appreciatively. 'I do believe that's a steak-and-kidney pie, if I'm not much mistaken?'

'It is,' George said. 'Maureen got carried away while she was cooking this afternoon and thought you'd help her out by taking this off our hands.'

Ruby shook her head and chuckled. 'You mean my son and his wife are making sure we are eating properly? I'm not quite in my dotage that I can't cook a square meal for us. Besides, Bob would nag me to death if I forgot to feed him.'

'I'm quite capable of looking after myself,' Bob was quick to answer. 'All the same, we are very grateful. While you are here, I've got a box of vegetables for you to take back with you. I was up the allotment this morning and got carried away with the picking. Do you have the car with you?'

It was George's turn to laugh. 'I'd not have walked across Erith carrying a meat pie now, would I? I'd have had half the strays in the area following me. I could kill a cup of tea, though, if you've got one on the go. I'd only just stepped inside our front door and Maureen had me making deliveries.'

'How many pies did she make?' Ruby asked as she indicated to Bob to put the pie in their stone pantry and check the kettle was full.

'Only the three, but as I was driving the children back to Sarah and Alan's, it was easy to leave one with them and bring yours round at the same time. That reminds me. Georgina told me to let you know she helped Maureen with the pastry.'

'Bless her, she's really into her cooking at the moment,' Ruby beamed.

'To be honest, Mum, she's a pest. Maureen needs eyes in the back of her head with that child in the kitchen. We've told her not to touch the knives, but will she listen? I've moved everything and put a lock on the drawer, we are that worried she will cut herself.'

'Someone needs to give her a good talking to,' Bob said, returning to the room. 'The kettle's on, and it won't take long to boil.'

'I'll speak to Sarah and tell her the girl needs a hobby, so that she forgets about wanting to cook every five minutes. There's time enough for that when she gets up to the big school and has lessons.'

'Thanks, Mum,' George said. 'I know Maureen will be

grateful. Now, what's all this?' he asked, peering at the newspaper cuttings strewn on the tabletop.

Bob nodded to Ruby. 'Tell him, as he may be able to help you.'

Ruby looked between the two men; was she doing the right thing in sharing Vera's secret? There again, she wasn't getting anywhere on her own. Granted, she had all the newspaper cuttings and had scribbled down a note of what Vera had told her of the baby's birth, but she was at a loss to know what to do next. Making a quick decision, she looked at her son. 'Please don't say a word about this, not even to Maureen.'

'I promise to keep what you tell me to myself,' he said, looking serious. 'I want to help you all I can to stop you looking so worried.'

'I'll help, love, but you know what I'm like with paper-work. Having given that all up when I retired as a policeman, I've got out of the habit of thinking about things.'

'Anything the two of you can do would be a big help; even making a cup of tea, when it's needed.'

'I think that's a hint,' George said, nodding to Bob.

'I'll get that done while you tell George. I can listen from the kitchen,' Bob said, thinking that he could finish the washing up and tidy the kitchen. Ruby would be morti-fied if George spotted how messy it had been left.

Ruby picked up her page of notes. 'Vera had a baby that none of us knew about. It was not long after her husband went off to war, and she had a toddler at home – you know, the daughter she won't talk about.'

George shook his head. 'You mean Sadie's mother?'

'Yes, that's the one. Well, she had her head turned by a

man who visited the house making deliveries for the local grocer. When she realized she was expecting, she got herself into a right state and her work suffered. That's when the lady of the house sat her down and gave her a talking-to. I got the impression Vera was about to be given the sack, until she explained her predicament.'

'Could it have been Vera's husband's?' Bob called from the kitchen.

'No, he'd been gone for eight months by then.'

'Hmm, that was a problem, I remember her husband and although he was a decent chap, that's a lot to accept, and he was a good deal older than Vera, much more set in his ways,' George said thoughtfully. 'Wasn't that part of the problem when Sadie's mother was shown the door after finding herself pregnant?'

'It was, but that was before they came here. Moving to Alexandra Road was supposed to be a fresh start for the family, with Vera bringing up Sadie.'

'Then history nigh on repeated itself when Sadie got herself in trouble,' Bob said.

'It takes two to tango,' Ruby reprimanded him. 'But getting back to her bombshell. Vera couldn't face losing the baby and couldn't face losing her job, either. Women had it just as hard as the menfolk you know,' she said, trying hard not to think of when she was a young mother.

'So what did happen, Mum?'

'It's the age-old story of a young girl being sweet-talked by a man, but Vera landed on her feet, as the lady who employed her offered to adopt the baby. It seems she'd never been able to have children and, as far as she was concerned, Vera's dilemma was the answer to her dreams.'

Bob walked into the room with a tea tray. 'What about Vera's old man? Surely he came back while she was carrying the kid?'

'Ah, that's where her employer was crafty. Vera told me she rented a cottage in the West Country and they all went down there, and when they came back some months later, the woman had a baby and Vera didn't.'

'Blow me down,' George said, scratching his head. 'I'd heard of women going away to have a child, then having it adopted, but this takes the biscuit. Did Vera stay in her employ?'

'Until the baby was weaned, and by then her husband was back and none the wiser. Her employer was grateful and very generous. The agreement was that Vera left her job and severed all contact. Vera told me it was for the best, but I couldn't have done that in a million years. How she lived with herself, I don't know.'

'Needs must,' Bob said as he sat back down at the table. 'She's a hard woman.'

'It seems to me that life has made her the way she is,' Ruby said.

George agreed. 'I take it Vera being ill has made her think about this child?'

Ruby placed her hands on the newspaper cuttings. 'I do wonder if she ever forgot about him. Look at what she's collected over the years,' she said, pushing them towards him and watching as George started to read.

'He seems to have accomplished quite a bit in his early years: prizes at school, music lessons, school sports days. But then it all stops when he was ten.'

'It was about then that the family moved away. Vera got

wind of the move and enquired where they were moving to, but they wouldn't say.'

'I wondered if our Vera was being a bit of a pest. If I was the woman who adopted him, I might have thought she'd spill the beans to the lad.'

Ruby stirred her tea thoughtfully. 'That did cross my mind. I couldn't say that to her though, as she's so poorly.'

Bob reached for the cuttings and flicked through them. 'The way I see it, we could find the lad and then Vera opens a hornets' nest and causes all kinds of trouble. Could you pretend you are looking for him and hang it out until she passes away?'

Ruby was horrified. 'Oh no, I'd never forgive myself. She so wants to see him and know he is well. Knowing how bloody-minded Vera is, she could well hang on until she sees her son . . .'

George spluttered into his tea. 'Mother, for goodness' sake, I know Vera can be annoying, but show some compassion.'

'I am, and that is why I'm asking you both for help. I just wish I knew what to do. Do you have any answers?'

George thought for a moment before taking a deep breath. 'What I'm about to say must never go beyond this room or I could get into a lot of trouble. If we think the son is still in the area, I may be able to look at council records and find out where he lives. Some information is available for anyone to find, but if you or Bob go asking the wrong questions, it could reach this man, and then goodness knows what could happen. It could scare him off and Vera will never see him.'

Ruby beamed. 'Thank you, I knew you would be able to help me; that's a weight off my mind.'

'Let me take some notes from these cuttings and then you can return them to Vera. It would help if you could ask her if she remembers anything else, since she first told you. For instance, does she recall if the family had any relatives? Things like that may help the search.'

'I'll do that,' Ruby said. 'Now, have another biscuit; they're your favourites.'

8

'There's no need to look so worried,' Sarah said when Jessie returned to the office. 'I'm extremely impressed by the results of your arithmetic test; you only got two slightly wrong,' she said as the young woman sat down.

'I'm sorry,' Jessie stammered. 'I was so nervous and couldn't add up to save my life. I lost count of the times I checked my answers, and each time I made them different.'

Sarah chuckled. 'I'm the same, and it never hurts to double-check. I do have one question, though, and it has nothing to do with your adding up. Your references seem a little out of date. I wondered what you'd been doing since, as there is nothing on your application form?'

Jessie looked down into her lap, avoiding eye contact with Sarah. 'I thought this would be my downfall. I'm sorry for wasting your time,' she said as she got up to leave.

'For goodness' sake, sit down. I have no intention of turning you down for the vacancy. I just want you to be honest with me. After all, there may be a time when you want my advice over something and, as the store's personnel manager, I need to know all about you. You do understand, don't you?'

She beamed. 'Oh, thank you so much. I thought I'd messed up.'

Sarah looked at the young woman; she'd not changed much over the years, and the mop of dark, unruly curls and her slight frame did little to show that she was a mother in her mid-twenties. 'Never think that, as we all make mistakes at times. No one is perfect. Now tell me why there is not a reference from Hedley Mitchell, as the last time I bumped into you, you served me tea in their tea room and told me how my father had helped you out with a housing problem.'

'That's right, and you said that if I ever wanted to work for Woolworths to ask for an interview.'

'That's correct. After all, you know the store very well, from the time you hid away here during the war.'

The girl went bright red. 'I did explain at the time . . . I was running away from someone. It was cold and there was a window open. Everyone was very kind to me.'

Sarah was thoughtful, as it all came back to her. 'Are you now happy with your life? I see you have young children.'

'My life isn't perfect, but I want to be able to earn enough money to pay the rent and feed my kids. I promise I won't bring my problems to work with me.'

'Tell me about your time as a waitress at Hedley Mitchell and why you don't have a reference?'

'I'm ashamed to say I was sacked for causing a rumpus in front of customers.'

'Oh dear, that doesn't sound good. Was it an unpleasant customer?'

Tears started to fall onto Jessie's cheeks as she fumbled in her coat pocket for a handkerchief.

'Here, take this. It is freshly laundered,' Sarah said, taking a white cotton handkerchief from a small pile in her desk drawer, thinking how often Betty Billington had done the same when she looked after the staff. Betty had been a good teacher.

'Thank you,' Jessie sniffed.

'Take your time,' Sarah said gently.

'When I ran away and hid in this store just before Christmas, I was afraid of being caught. My family have a travelling funfair, and an uncle wasn't very kind to me and some of my cousins. I can't even think about it,' she trembled.

'Then we won't discuss it,' Sarah said, trying not to imagine what Jessie meant.

'Please, I need to explain. I want to be honest with you. I thought my life was back on track, but while I was working at Mitchell's this uncle spotted me and tried to cause trouble. You see, I'd spoken to the police at the time, and he'd been given a six-year prison sentence and he blamed me. He'd been brooding about it, and then when he heard where I was working . . .'

Sarah thought it didn't seem enough time in prison, but didn't like to say so. 'I take it you fought with him and for that you got the sack?'

'Yes, he could always charm the birds off the trees, and he made me look like the one in the wrong. My supervisor thought I'd been rude to a customer and wouldn't listen to my explanation. Since then, I've done a bit of this and that to get by. There's always work to be found on the farms, and I went hop-picking with the children just to keep my head above water. But deep down I knew I needed a proper job that I could be proud of. It was then that I remembered meeting you.'

'I'm glad you did, as I can't begin to imagine what life has been like for you. I am a little concerned about your uncle. Is he likely to turn up?'

'I doubt it, as the fair will be off on its travels again. They do have a yard in Belvedere, but mainly they are on the road.'

'Well, Jessie, I am more than happy to take you on as a sales assistant. I don't want you talking about this to any of the staff. What has been spoken about here will go no further. However, if at any time you want to speak to me, please do so.'

'I'm ever so grateful,' Jessie said, looking as though she was about to fling herself across the desk and hug Sarah.

As Sarah started to explain more about the duties of a counter assistant, there was a knock at the door and Betty and Freda walked in. Freda hurried over to hug Jessie.

'I'm so happy to see you,' she said. 'I've often wondered about you.'

'I too recall you from that Christmas,' Betty said as she shook Jessie's hand.

'Will you be my boss?' she asked.

'No, I took early retirement as I have a young family at home, but you will often see me about the place. A Mr Harrison is the current manager. I was hoping to see him, to introduce myself.' She looked at Sarah with an enquiring glint in her eye.

'He is not yet back from lunch,' Sarah said.

'Then I will have a cup of tea in the staff room and say

hello to a few of my old staff. I suppose I'm allowed to do that?'

'Of course,' Sarah grinned. 'It seems like old days to have you here.'

'There was another lady,' Jessie said. 'She was rather poorly that Christmas. Does she still work here?'

Freda looked sad as she explained. 'That's Maisie, and she lost her baby; it was a difficult time for her. However, she has a lovely family now and owns Maisie's Modes in the High Street.'

'Oh my, I often look in the window at the beautiful frocks, and my kids have a few outfits from her make do and mend section. Who'd have guessed!'

'You will meet her once you start work, as she can't keep away from the place,' Freda laughed. 'As for me, I'm a lady of leisure,' she said, pointing to her bump. 'I also have a young son.'

'Make the most of it,' Jessie said as she congratulated her. Turning to Sarah, she enquired, 'May I ask if the other lady was successful in her interview?'

'Yes, she was, so we have two new Woolworths girls!'
The women cheered.

'Well, well, well, what's all this then? Are you all having a ladies' tea party while the hard-working boss is having his lunch break?' Mr Harrison said from the doorway.

'Mr Harrison, I am Betty Billington, one of the previous store managers,' Betty said holding out her hand, which he ignored.

'Time to be on your way, ladies. You should be at home

preparing your husbands' dinners, and Mrs Gilbert should be trying to earn her wage.'

Sarah was seething. How dare he speak to them in such a way! 'This is one of our new counter assistants,' she said as Jessie smiled politely.

'I'm looking forward to working here,' she said.

Ignoring the women present, Mr Harrison turned to leave, calling over his shoulder, 'Gilbert, a word in my office right now.'

Sarah went to follow him, her face like thunder.

'No,' Betty said, placing her arm on Sarah's. 'You may say something you regret. Let me deal with this,' she said, leaving the room and closing the door behind her.

'Oh dear, he seems rather grumpy,' Jessie said, looking worried. 'Does he often speak to the staff like that?'

'You will see very little of him on the shop floor, so please don't worry. I'm looking forward to you working here. I'll see you bright and early on Monday morning. Please come to my office first, and I'll have your uniform ready for you and will talk you through your duties.'

Jessie made her thanks and hurried away.

'Crikey, I thought for a moment there I'd lost a new staff member. What an odious man he is,' Sarah said, falling into her seat and indicating for Freda to sit down.

'I could smell drink on his breath and he was slurring his words,' Freda replied. 'Why ever was the man hired?'

'I have no idea, but wait until you meet our new floor-walker; he will give you the creeps. I've had a complaint from one of the counter staff about his wandering hands. I did mean to speak to Mr Harrison about it, but I'll not do so today, as the drink will be affecting his judgement and he won't be open to a sensible discussion.'

'Hmm, it makes me wonder how Betty is getting on?' Freda said. The two girls looked at each other, before creeping along the hall towards the raised voices coming from Mr Harrison's office.

'I have no idea why you are even in my store,' Philip Harrison growled, 'but while you are here, you can fetch me a cheese sandwich and a cup of strong coffee from the canteen.'

Betty frowned. 'I came into the store to speak to Mrs Gilbert, as she has a problem that I might have been able to help with,' she said, giving him a hard look and hoping he didn't ask what the problem was. He'd not be too pleased to learn it was his bad management that had had Sarah considering handing in her notice.

Harrison ran a hand though his thinning hair and groaned. 'Did you notice the name on the door?'

'Yes, it is your name . . .'

'Correct, and above it the word *Manager?*'

'Well, yes,' Betty replied, wondering what he was getting at.

'I am the manager of this store and, as such, I – and not you – advise the staff. You, Mrs Billington, were a temporary stand-in while we men were off fighting for our country. Do you understand?'

Betty sighed. It wasn't the first time a man in management had made jibes about female staff only being good enough to stand in during times of war until the men returned to take up the reins. 'That is your opinion, Mr Harrison. From where I sit, the women who worked for F.

W. Woolworth did a jolly fine job, on a lower wage than what you were receiving. However, I am not here to argue with you, as I am a busy woman and I can see you have a lot to be getting on with,' she said, looking aghast at the heap of papers on his desk. 'I came here to introduce myself and to ask if you needed any advice about the Erith store. If you do, then I'm more than happy to offer it. However, I suggest that before you start work, you collect your own food and drink and don't expect a woman to do it for you.'

She wanted to say more, but knew she was on a sticky wicket as she was no longer on Woolworths' payroll, something she was starting to regret. Checking her watch, she went on, 'I must leave you, as I must be at my husband's office to discuss business matters. He does value a woman's input.'

Harrison snorted. 'I'd heard your husband was some big shot in this town. No doubt we will meet before too long.'

Betty kept a straight face. 'I hope you meet soon in a professional capacity.'

Harrison nodded his head approvingly.

'You do know my husband is a funeral director?' she said, before holding her head high and leaving.

'Whoops-a-daisy,' a tall man said as he gripped Betty around the waist as she hurried into the hall, intent on seeing Sarah to discuss her boss.

'Remove your hand from me,' she spat at him, before wrinkling her nose. 'You, sir, have been drinking.'

'A little of what you fancy does you good,' he smirked as she slapped his hands away before hurrying down the passage.

What had become of her beloved store? She was still

fuming as she approached the Erith branch of the funeral directors that her husband, Douglas, owned along with Maisie's husband, David. It wouldn't do for their recently bereaved clients to see her in such a state. She stopped to gaze into the florist's shop next door and took a few deep breaths to compose herself before entering the office at the front of the undertakers' business. Apart from several flower arrangements, an oak desk and various armchairs, there was little to show it was a place to arrange funerals. They had decided not to have posters and brochures on show; discretion, sincerity and sympathy were always observed. Betty was visiting today to help her husband for a couple of hours as their receptionist was unwell.

'Hello, my love.' Douglas appeared through a door that led to the back of the building. 'Are you sure you are feeling well? You look a little flushed.'

'Oh, Douglas, I've made a terrible mistake; I should never have left F. W. Woolworth,' Betty said as she pulled off her coat and gloves and placed her handbag in the top drawer of the desk.

Douglas Billington looked concerned. It wasn't the first time Betty had left the company to care for their family. 'We agreed you would devote yourself to our family, my love. If you wish to return to the workplace, David and I would gladly find a place for you in this business. Having four premises, as well as the florist's next door, we are in dire need of reliable staff.'

Betty took her husband's hand and held it to her cheek. 'As much as I would like to be by your side every waking hour, I don't see the funeral business as being right for me. My heart is in retail. I miss working for F. W.

Woolworth. I wonder . . .' She stopped talking and looked away from Douglas, as she took a deep breath to gather her confidence and voice her feelings. 'I wonder, would you approve if I contacted head office and asked for my old job back? I'm not needed so much at home, now Clemmie and Dorothy are older, and the little ones are just as happy with our staff. Gosh, that makes me sound like a bad mother.'

'You have never been a bad mother,' Douglas was quick to interject. 'You are simply one of those women who is not complete being a wife and mother. I've often thought there were three in our marriage: you, me and Woolworths. You've worked for Woolworths a lot longer than you've known me, and I'd be the first to say you are nothing if not loyal to the store.'

'Oh, Douglas,' Betty said, holding tightly to his hand. If they had been anywhere else, she'd have thrown herself into his arms, but it would not be seemly, here in the funeral establishment. With his silver hair and strong stature, he reminded her more of a matinee idol than an undertaker. 'I don't deserve you. I promise I'll make it up to you and the children.'

'There's no need, my love. You come alive when you are busy running the Erith store, and I'd rather have a wife full of life than one stuck at home turning into . . .'

'A wilting lily?' Betty asked, looking towards the flower arrangement on the desk. 'Besides, they may not want me back.'

Douglas didn't want to agree, although the thought had crossed his mind. 'What has made you come to this decision so suddenly? I can see something has happened to upset you. We have ten minutes before our next client, so tell all.'

Betty quickly outlined her brush with Mr Harrison, along with how low morale seemed to be among some of the staff. 'I'm not saying I'm perfect, but that man is a terrible manager. There's something about him I'm not sure of.'

'Why not speak to Tony Forsythe? Freda is sure to have a telephone number she can give you.'

'That's the other problem. As far as I know, when Tony finishes helping to train our Olympic cycling team, he will want to return to management, and he was shortlisted for the Erith branch. With Freda expecting their second child and them having a home in the town, although nothing was decided before he left.'

'My advice would be to take things slowly. After all, there is no point in rushing in and causing problems.'

Betty agreed, but shook her head, looking glum. 'My goodness, life can be such a conundrum at times.'

9

~

'That child is making a hell of a mess,' Bob grumbled as he squeezed past Ruby and Georgie to reach the pantry. 'Is there anything to eat in this house?'

'Nanny Ruby told me practice makes perfect,' Georgie said, shaking flour from a large packet onto a board where she was kneading suet pastry, closely supervised by Ruby.

'What's it supposed to be?' Bob asked as he peered over her shoulder.

Ruby frowned at Bob. 'We are making steak and kidney puddings, as well you can see, from the pan of meat cooling on the hob.'

'The smaller one will be for Mrs Munro, as she is still poorly. I'm making that one,' Georgie said proudly.

'Thank goodness for that,' Bob murmured as he reached for a loaf. 'I really don't want my meals to be something a child has practised on,' he muttered to Ruby.

Ruby's glare was enough to have Bob backing into the living room. 'I'll go up the allotment for an hour or so,' he said, thinking he could pop into the New Light for a pint on the way.

'It would help if you could bring some veg back with

you. The big pudding will be for our dinner tonight. We have visitors.'

Bob nodded his head, thinking of what there was up at the allotment. February wasn't much of an interesting month for vegetables, but he was sure there was a cabbage. He started to whistle cheerfully as he left the house, contemplating a steaming plateful of Kate and Sidney pudding.

'Why doesn't Granddad Bob like my cooking?' Georgie asked after hearing the front door close behind Bob.

Why indeed? Ruby wondered as she looked at the mess in her kitchen. 'Let's just say he's a bit set in his ways, being on the older side of life, and likes me to cook his meals.'

'He is rather old, and he can be grumpy sometimes, but then so can my daddy,' Georgie said thoughtfully, picking up a rolling pin to tackle the suet pastry on the board in front of her. 'Perhaps I should make them a cake. Cakes are so much more interesting than pastry, don't you think?'

'I do, lovey, but you should never forget that making nutritious meals for our family is much more important, even though we all enjoy a slice of cake.' She grinned, seeing her great-granddaughter's glum expression. 'I know, let's get these puddings on to steam and then we can clear up and eat the cake Granddad Bob failed to find in the pantry.'

'Perhaps I'll make a cake when I'm at home,' Georgie said as she passed the pastry to Ruby. 'I know where everything is in the kitchen there.'

'You do that, lovey,' Ruby replied distractedly as she carefully lined the pudding bowl with the pastry, before adding the meat mix. 'You do that.'

*

Ruby looked around the room and at the satisfied faces of her extended family. 'If you have room, there's steamed pudding for afters. Do I have any takers?'

George groaned and rubbed his stomach. 'Mum, I couldn't eat another morsel.'

'I don't know how you managed,' his wife Maureen said, giving Ruby a crafty wink.

'Many hands make light work, and your contribution to our meal was gratefully received,' Ruby said. She was pleased when Maureen took half the ingredients, so that she could concentrate on her great-granddaughter's cooking lesson. Ruby was thoughtful; perhaps they were wrong to dissuade the child from her dream of being a cook? Georgie was growing up fast and although she could be a pain in the neck, Ruby knew it was time the girl learnt about keeping house, and that included cooking nutritional meals for her own family one day. It wouldn't be that many years before she left school, and perhaps cooking would be her path in life. Granted, the girl had a bee in her bonnet about baking cakes, but that would pass and one day her great-granddaughter would be a competent cook. That was, if she could learn to clear up after herself. No amount of telling Georgie about rationing, and how they went without during the war, could hammer home to her that she should be prudent with her ingredients.

'There is a reason for me to invite you all for a meal this evening. There's no need to look at me like that, either, George. I'm not about to announce I have some terrible illness and to tell you about my last will and testament.'

'Oh, Nan, hurry up and tell us what it is you have to say. I feel quite flustered,' Sarah said, holding one hand to her chest while flapping the other in front of her face to cool herself. 'Whatever is the problem?'

Bob patted his wife's hand, while Maureen looked towards George to see if he knew what his mother was about to say. George simply shook his head at his wife to indicate that he was in the dark.

'There's no need for you all to look so worried. It came to me that no one has mentioned going to pay their respects to our late King. This family has always prided themselves on travelling up to London to mark royal events, whether they be happy or sad. What do you have to say?'

Freda was the first to speak. 'I would very much like to go, as long as one of you would come with me. I'm sure I could take William in his pram; he won't remember anything about it, but one day I can tell him he was there.'

'I don't think that's advisable, not in your condition,' Maureen was quick to say.

'I have a while to go yet, so as long as I take it steady and have a sit-down when I'm puffed, and we know where the public toilets are, I don't see it would be a problem at all,' she said, looking towards Sarah, whom she thought would be an ally.

'I'll accompany you. Our King stood by us during the war and set an example to us all; it is only right we say thank you. I reckon Maisie will want to be with us. What about you, Gwyneth?'

'Most certainly,' Bob's daughter-in-law chipped in. 'My family back home in the Valleys have already written pointing out that, as I live so close to London, it is important for me to do my duty. I take it you are keen to be part of our trip, Ruby?' the soft-spoken Welsh woman asked.

Bob and George both objected at the same time.

'Mum, you'd be daft to undertake the journey,' George spluttered.

Bob was more to the point. 'You're too old to be galli-vanting off up to town.'

'I'll decide whether I'm daft or whether I'm too old,' Ruby said to her husband and her son. 'However, any doubts I had have been swept away by your objections.'

'Thank goodness for that,' Bob said, looking relieved.

'I mean I'm going, and I don't want anyone arguing about it,' she went on, giving Bob a steely look.

'I'll stay behind and look after the children. My gammy leg wouldn't be up to standing in a queue for such a long time, although I'll be sad not to be able to pay my respects,' Maureen said, giving the children around the table a bright smile. 'I'm sure we can find something interesting to do.'

'We could do some baking,' Georgie was quick to chip in, causing many of the adults to groan.

Sarah's youngest child, Buster, looked up from where he'd been trying to hide cabbage underneath a pile of suet pastry. 'Why do ladies always want to know where the toilets are?'

'Don't worry your little head about that,' Ruby replied. 'It's just a case of being prepared, in case we . . . well, in case someone with us wants to go.'

'Then you'd better make sure you have a purse full of pennies, as Dad is always asking if we want to spend a penny when we go to the seaside,' Buster said, looking serious.

As the laughter subsided, Gwyneth thanked Maureen for offering to look after the children. 'Mike reckons he will be on duty in the days leading up to the funeral, so I can't rely on him being off duty to have the kiddies. He wanted to be here tonight, as he loves your steak and kidney pudding. Thank you so much for saving some,' she said to Ruby. 'I take it your Alan is very busy as well, Sarah?'

'Gosh, yes, he's working all hours at the shop; that's why he's not here this evening. Since it has been announced that the funeral service is to be shown on television, he's had no end of enquiries about purchasing television sets. Dad, you know more about this than I do.'

'I don't mean to say this in a disrespectful way, but the King's passing has been a great help to the business. Not only that, but we have also seen an increase in wireless sales as well as repairs. Some people will be disappointed because, even if we doubled our staff, we won't be able to keep up with the demand. I've managed to secure some stock of televisions that will be delivered in the next couple of days.'

'Fancy watching a funeral on the television. I'm not quite sure I approve,' Ruby said. 'Something should be private, and for the family alone.'

'I suppose it's no different from people standing in the street, watching it go by,' Bob replied, still annoyed with Ruby for saying that she intended to travel to London.

'I disagree with you,' Gwyneth said, looking embarrassed to be speaking against her father-in-law's opinion. 'When there is a funeral of someone we know in the town, don't we stand still as the cortège passes by and silently pay our respects? In a way that is no different to standing on a pavement in London as our monarch goes to his final resting place.'

'You're right, lass. I didn't think of it that way,' Bob replied, giving her a sheepish grin.

'You'd best not forget to close all our curtains,' Ruby told him. 'I don't know what people would think if they were left open during such a sad day.'

Bob groaned. 'How will I see anything, with the curtains pulled? You know my eyes aren't as good as they used to be. I can't really turn the lights on in the daytime, as that would be silly.'

'Why not come to our place?' George asked. 'I want your advice on our garden, and we can watch the funeral on our television set.'

The children cheered at the mention of George and Maureen's television set.

'Can I watch the funeral too?' Myfi asked her mum, Gwyneth.

Gwyneth stroked the young girl's hair. It was as dark as her own, with people often commenting on how the apple hadn't fallen far from the tree, even though Myfi was her late sister's child. She was growing up so fast, and in a few years she would be a beauty. Gwyneth was thankful that Myfi was shy and not one to take the lead, unlike Maisie's eldest two, who seemed so worldly-wise. 'I'm thinking you could come with us to London, cariad,' she smiled, looking to Freda and Sarah for their approval.

Both women agreed, with Freda giving Myfi a broad smile. 'Perhaps you could keep me company on the trip? We could look out for a shop where we could purchase more knitting patterns.'

'Aren't there enough in Woolworths?' Myfi asked innocently.

Sarah hooted with laughter. 'Freda has every single one already; that baby is going to be the best turned out child in Erith by the time it comes along.'

'And will be royally spoilt by all his or her aunties and cousins, just as William is. I know none of you will be blood relatives, but as far as I'm concerned, each and every one of you are my family.'

Ruby wiped her eyes while Bob blew his nose noisily. 'I've always thought of you as a granddaughter, Freda, but to hear you say how we are all part of your family has touched me deeply. Now, who has room for spotted dick and custard?'

'I told you to go and sit down and rest, Mum, you've been on the go all day,' George said as Ruby joined him in the kitchen, where he had his sleeves rolled up and was tackling the washing up, assisted by Bob.

'I'll do that in a moment, but first I wanted to catch you on your own and ask if you'd found out anything about Vera's son?'

'Give him a chance; it's only been a couple of days since he offered to help,' Bob scolded his wife.

Ruby turned to leave the kitchen as George called after her. 'Actually there is something, but best not say anything to Vera at this early stage, as it may get somebody in trouble.'

'Then keep it to yourself, lad,' Bob said with a grin. 'Loose lips and all that.'

'Stop it, or you can go and sit with the girls in the front room. They are talking about problems in childbirth,' she replied, seeing how his face turned pale. 'Now, what have you found out? Be quick, as no doubt one of the kiddies will be out here in a minute.'

'I thought there would be a possibility that Vera's son still lived in the area. I was in the town hall yesterday and stopped to speak to a couple of women in the housing department about something else. I've known both for quite a while and they're helpful ladies, so I asked if they'd come across the man, as I needed to speak with him and had misplaced his address.'

'Be careful, George. I don't want you getting in trouble because of Vera's foolhardiness years ago.'

'It's all right, Mum. I wasn't asking anything untoward. With me being a local councillor, I'm always in there asking for help with a housing problem for the constituents. I was told to pop back in tomorrow and they would have had time to go through their index system. I did mention the address where he lived as a child, before the family moved away. I've not done anything wrong or rung any alarm bells. It is more than my political career is worth to do that.'

'Thank you, love. I'll not say a dicky bird to Vera. I'd hate to get her hopes up. I'm taking a small steak and kidney pudding up to her tomorrow and will see if she has had any other thoughts that could help the search. By the way, I've not told her you are helping me. She knows I told Bob, and her response to that is unrepeatable.'

'Tell her I think fondly of her too,' George said with a grin. 'She may be a strange woman at times, but I'm keen to help Vera. I can't imagine what it must be like to lose contact with a child, let alone give one up, as she did.'

Ruby kissed his cheek. She'd never felt so proud of her son as she did at that moment.

*

Freda made herself comfortable in an armchair close to the fire and held her hands out towards the flames. 'I could sit here forever,' she sighed.

'It's all right for some. I have a basket of ironing waiting for me at home, and these two will need a bath before they go to bed,' Sarah said as she knelt on the hearth rug beside her young friend.

'Make the most of this time,' Gwyneth said as she bounced her young son, Robert, on her knee. 'You will be run ragged once the little one arrives. I'm in awe of anyone who has two babies close together.'

Freda smiled at her friends. 'I'm looking forward to it so much. Tony adores the thought of his own little family; being an orphan, he never had a normal childhood. There is still a fair time to go and, to be honest, I'm a little bored with the waiting, even though I have William to care for.' She smiled at the fair-haired baby in her arms. 'By the time baby number two comes along, this little lad will be toddling. The small back bedroom is as ready as it can be. I've even chosen a new pram that will hold the two of them.'

Sarah and Gwyneth both gasped. 'Whatever you do, don't bring it home until after the birth,' Gwyneth said, her words rushing out before Sarah could say anything.

'It is customary to put a deposit down, and then your Tony can collect it when you are ready to come home.'

Freda kept quiet, rather than mention that she'd had William's pram at their rented home in Birmingham two months before he'd arrived. She wasn't one for superstition.

'I wish I'd hung on to our Buster's pram, as you'd have been welcome to it. As it was, I donated it to the WVS, and no doubt by now it is doing a good turn for another mother,' Sarah apologized.

Gwyneth's cheeks turned pink as she spoke quietly, making sure her daughter Myfi could not hear. 'You would have been welcome to our pram, but . . .'

'Is there another baby Jackson on the way? I'm so pleased for you,' Sarah said.

'I may be wrong, and I've not even said anything to Mike.'

Freda sighed. 'How glorious, our babies will be growing up together. I won't feel so alone, being the last of the friends to give birth.'

'You will never be alone, Freda, that is as long as Tony doesn't go taking you off to another part of the country again,' Gwyneth said. 'I'm grateful Mike is happy to work at the local police station and has no desire to move to another police force. He may work strange duties at times, but he's always ready to care for the children.'

'I'm really hoping Tony will be given the Erith store to manage, once his Olympic duties are over,' Freda replied. 'I want my children to grow up here in Alexandra Road, as it's a place I've come to love so much.

Gwyneth agreed, before clapping a hand to her mouth. 'I meant to tell you, Sarah, one of the young girls on the biscuit counter had a run-in with that awful floorwalker.'

Sarah groaned. 'Oh no, not another. I'm going to have a word with Mr Harrison about the chap. Tell me what you know; it will go no further, I promise.'

'He cornered her at the bottom of the staff staircase and made certain suggestions to her. The poor child was petrified, but fortunately another colleague came along, and Mr

Argent scarpered. I do wonder whether you could have a word with the female staff before some of them decide to leave. After all, you are the senior female member of staff in the Erith store.'

'Yes, I'll do just that, as we can't have women being treated like this. Thank you for bringing the problem to my attention, Gwyneth. I'll make sure something is done, and as soon as possible.'

'Why the glum faces?' Ruby asked as she joined the women in the front room. 'Stay where you are, Freda, I'll sit here with Gwyneth,' she added as Freda started to stand up.

The girls explained about the problem they had with the floorwalker. Ruby tutted in annoyance. 'In my day we carried a hat pin to defend ourselves in such circumstances, but I doubt you girls require hat pins to secure your work caps.'

'It's a pretty good idea, though,' Freda said.

Maureen had been sitting knitting quietly in an armchair set in the bay window. 'I know I only work a few hours a day, but please make it known to your colleagues that I'm always there as a shoulder to cry on, if Sarah isn't on duty. This does need to be brought to the attention of Mr Harrison, as Mr Argent's actions are unacceptable. I can see a few husbands hearing about this and paying him a visit.'

'I'll ask Mike if there is anything we can be doing,' Gwyneth said, looking shocked at Maureen's words. Violence in the store would not look good for F. W. Woolworth.

'I shall speak to Mr Harrison first thing in the morning

and then we will know what course to take,' Sarah said. 'I promise I will put a stop to all of this.'

Ruby looked thoughtful. 'There is something else you could consider. Why not take a leaf out of Maisie's book? She'd not stand for being propositioned. She'd be bellowing at the top of her voice, so that other staff members knew what was going on and came to her aid.'

Sarah chuckled as she imagined the scene. 'Gosh, that'd soon stop his wandering hands. But, seriously, I don't have confidence in our manager. My feelings are that he will side with the floorwalker, as Mr Harrison and Mr Argent are drinking buddies.'

'I've heard that as well,' Gwyneth said. 'Whatever can be done?'

The women fell silent until Sarah spoke. 'We were safe when Betty was in command, and the store was such a happy place to work in. I'm going to ask her if she would apply to return to work. That will make us all happy.'

Freda's quiet voice piped up. 'As much as I love Betty, I'd not be happy to see her installed as the new manager, if Mr Harrison were moved on. If my Tony doesn't get offered the Erith store, we could end up living and working in another part of the country.'

10

'Aunty Sarah, may I speak to you privately?' a worried-looking Dorothy Billington asked as Sarah entered the staff canteen for her morning break. Although Betty's youngest stepdaughter was not a blood relative to Sarah, the young girl was part of the extended Caselton family and respectfully called Sarah and her friends 'Aunty'.

Sarah glanced around the canteen. It was her mother-in-law's day to work behind the counter and, apart from a few storeroom lads sitting in one corner playing cards, they were alone. 'Why don't we collect our lunch and sit over by the window, where we won't be disturbed,' she suggested.

They both went to the counter and collected cheese and tomato sandwiches with a cup of tea, refusing Maureen's suggestion that they tried her rabbit stew.

'I've made a shepherd's pie for dinner this evening, so I dare not have another heavy meal at lunchtime. It does look delicious, though,' Sarah sighed. 'How about you, Dorothy?'

The young girl wrinkled her nose before saying no, thank you.

Carrying their food to the Formica-topped table, they

ate in companionable silence for several minutes until Sarah spoke. 'It is always lovely to spend time with you, Dorothy. However, I have the impression there is something on your mind.'

The girl finished chewing and swallowed. 'There is, and I'm rather embarrassed to have to talk to you about it. Please promise me you won't tell my mother,' she said beseechingly.

'I'm not sure I can promise such a thing; it all depends on what you are going to tell me. If it is something of a personal nature, then Betty really ought to know. In fact I wonder why you are not speaking to her, when you girls get on with her so well these days,' she said, thinking back to a time when Dorothy and her older sister Clementine did not accept Betty as their mother, after Betty married their father, Douglas.

'I really like Betty, and I can't believe Clemmie and I were so beastly to her when we were younger. Normally I would speak to Clemmie when I have a problem, but she is so bound up in her young man these days that I don't want to burden her. Also, I know how much Mother wishes she was still a manager here, so I don't feel it right to bother her.'

'I see, then tell me your problem and I'll do my best to help you.'

Dorothy fiddled with her teaspoon until Sarah gave a small cough. 'Sorry, I'm not sure how to start . . .'

'Then dive straight in,' Sarah suggested, noticing how the time was passing and she had a heap of work to get through.

'It's that floorwalker, Mr Argent. He keeps making

embarrassing remarks to us girls while we are working. We have tried to laugh it off, but some of what he says is so personal I can't even repeat it to you,' she replied, looking down into her lap.

Sarah groaned inwardly. The wretched man was becoming a problem. As Dorothy continued to talk about what the man had been up to, and mentioned other colleagues who were thinking of leaving, her mind roamed to an incident that very morning when she had shown the new employee, Jessie, to her counter and the damned man had gone up to her and put his hand on her arm, welcoming her in an over-friendly way, and suggesting they shared a tea break sometime so that he could get to know her better. Jessie had shaken Mr Argent's hand away and had glared, before saying, 'No, thank you, I know your kind.' She then apologized to Sarah, and said she hoped Sarah did not think badly of her by reacting in such a way. It had been Sarah's turn to apologize and say that no male employee of F. W. Woolworth should act in such a way, and she promised it would be dealt with. With complaints piling up, she knew she had to act swiftly to nip this in the bud before her female staff started to hand in their notice.

'What do you think, Aunty Sarah? Are we being silly by reacting in such a way to his comments?'

'You are not being silly at all. In fact there have been several other complaints, and I am doing something about it. Your mother is aware of what is happening at Woolworths, but perhaps it's best not to say that you have become involved as one of his . . . his victims. Let's keep it between ourselves for the moment, shall we? I promise you I will sort it out.'

'Thank you, Aunty Sarah. I told the other girls you are a good egg and will look out for us.'

Sarah couldn't help but giggle. Dorothy was the product of a private school for young ladies and, as such, could come out with some funny phrases at times. Sarah had become used to them, but to be called a 'good egg' was something new. 'Tell me what you've been up to in your spare time. I've heard mention of amateur dramatics?'

In between eating her sandwich, Dorothy explained how along with Maisie's daughter, Claudette, she had joined a group of enthusiastic amateurs at Erith Playhouse down by the riverside. 'I can't sing and I can barely dance, but Claudette is just wonderful. They are already talking about auditioning for parts in the Christmas pantomime, and it is still only February. I reckon she will have a starring part, as her singing voice is so beautiful, while no doubt I will be the back end of the pantomime cow,' she chuckled.

'Make sure you keep me informed when tickets become available, as I would love to take the children to see you both perform. I've tried to get my Georgie into ballet lessons, but she's not interested and wants to take up tap dancing. I fear for the floorboards in my kitchen if that should happen.'

'What about your Buster? We do have several young boys in our group.'

'Buster thinks of nothing but his boxing club; some days I have trouble getting him to take off his boxing gloves to eat his dinner.'

'Now that I would like to see,' Dorothy laughed, standing up to brush the crumbs from the front of her overall. 'I do appreciate your help, Aunty Sarah. If you would like me to babysit any time, so you and Uncle Alan can go out, I'd be more than happy to do so,' she continued, before hurrying back to her work, as the bell for the end of the lunch break rang through the store.

Sarah thought of how her friends' children were so delightful; granted, there had been troubles along the way for a few of them, but all in all they were a decent bunch. As she returned the plates and cups to the counter and said goodbye to her mother-in-law, she became thoughtful. It was up to her now to step up to the plate and show that she could take care of her staff; she had told her friends she would talk to Mr Harrison, and now was the right time. Walking past her own office door, she continued along the long corridor until she reached the store manager's office and knocked confidently before walking in.

'It's only me,' Ruby couldn't help calling out as she knocked on Vera's front door. She'd lost count of the times her friend had said those same words, before letting herself into number thirteen. She was surprised when it was Vera herself who opened the door.

'Get yourself in quickly, before you let the cold in,' she huffed, pulling her dressing gown close around her throat. 'They've left me on my own today,' she moaned.

'You seem to be on the mend, so that's good news,' Ruby couldn't help saying. If Vera was moaning about the world, she was certainly getting better.

'I wouldn't say I'm any better, but if I didn't get up out of my sickbed I would starve to death.'

Ruby tried hard not to laugh as she placed her shopping basket on the floor and shrugged off her coat. Keeping on her headscarf, she picked up the basket. 'Should I take this straight through to the kitchen?'

Vera sniffed appreciatively. 'What is it?'

'It's a Kate-and-Sidney pudding, as my Bob would call it. There's also a bowl of vegetables to accompany it.'

'That's cockney, you know. He's not from the East End, is he?' Vera said, without a word of thanks.

'No, none of us are, but we all use a few phrases from time to time. Should I put this in the oven, as it won't take long to warm through? You get yourself back to your bed and I'll pop the kettle on at the same time.'

'I'm up now, so I'll sit here for a while.'

Vera and Ruby's homes were mirror images of each other. Some people in Alexandra Road had started to brick up the door to the outside toilets, so they could be accessed from inside the houses, creating a very small lavatory. Ruby was hoping one of the men in the family would volunteer to do this for her, as it was mighty chilly going out there in the cold weather, not to mention the spiders fleeing to safety when the light was switched on. It would be so much more preferable than having a china pot under the bed.

'I've got some news for you,' Ruby said, after she'd prepared a tray and joined Vera at the table while she waited for the kettle to boil.

Vera's eyes gleamed. 'About my boy, do you mean? Have you found him?'

'Not exactly, and I hope you aren't angry as I asked my George for help, what with him being a local councillor and having contacts.'

Vera glared and slammed her hand on the table. 'I said

111

not to tell anyone. I don't want all and sundry knowing my private business,' she spat.

Ruby got to her feet. 'Then I'll be getting back to my own house. I don't take kindly to my son being called "all and sundry". George went out of his way to see if he could find out anything about the child you gave away.'

Vera flinched at Ruby's words, and flapped her hand for her to sit back down. 'I'm sorry, you know I didn't mean what I said.'

'Then you shouldn't have said it. You can be very unkind at times, Vera Munro.'

To Ruby's surprise, Vera burst into tears. She passed her a tea towel to wipe her eyes.

'I know I can be a mean woman at times, and I hate myself when it happens. It's just my way, and I'm too old to change now. Being so ill and knowing it won't be long before I meet my maker, I wanted to put things right. I apologize for being rude about George; he's a good lad, and you must be very proud of him,' she said before bursting into a fit of coughing.

Right then the kettle started to whistle. Ruby hurried to the kitchen to warm the teapot, before adding three generous heaps of tea leaves and pouring the boiling water on top. Adding a faded tea cosy, she carried the teapot through and placed it on a cork mat in the middle of the table.

'Have you taken your medicine or should I get it from the front room?' she asked, too astounded by Vera's words to be able to comment on them. Never, in all the years she'd known Vera, had her friend been complimentary about her family.

'I took some just now, thank you,' Vera replied humbly. 'If you would like a biscuit, there are some in the tin on the sideboard. I'll have one, if you're having one,' she added.

'I'm fine, thank you, and your meal will be ready soon. Do you think we should save some for Sadie and James?'

'No, I'll manage it all; I've been told I've got to build up my strength. Now, what's this you found out about my child?'

Ruby pulled the scarf from around her head and kept it on her shoulders; she was starting to feel a little warm. George had dropped in to see her before she headed up the road to visit Vera; the note he'd left was folded up in her apron pocket. 'What George has found out could have got him into hot water in the council, you do realize that, Vera, don't you?'

'I do and I'm truly grateful. Please say thank you to him, won't you?'

Pleased that Vera had voiced her thanks, Ruby started to pour out the tea as she spoke. 'George often works with the ladies in the housing department; it is part of his work as a town councillor to check on housing and help constituents. With the name given to him, by the lady who took on your baby, he was able to see if he still lives in one of the town's council houses.'

Vera frowned. 'I don't think for one moment he lives in a council house, do you? The family who brought him up were well to do. I would have thought he'd have a good job and a lovely home,' she added, blowing on her tea and taking a slurp.

Being used to the way Vera spoke, Ruby was not offended, but felt she could not let the comment slip by without addressing it. 'It doesn't matter where somebody lives or how well they've done in life. Surely you know that by now?'

'You're right. I need to start thinking before I open my trap; we have no way of knowing what hand life has dealt my boy. He was off to a bad start as soon as I met his father. I should have known better,' she started to sob.

Ruby didn't wish to pander to Vera's emotions, as the woman could turn tears on and off like a tap. 'Do you want to know what George has found out or not?'

'Oh, I do, please tell me.'

'His name was not listed amongst the people on the housing list.'

'I'm pleased about that, but does it mean George hasn't found him?'

'You were lucky because, as George went through the index cards in the housing office, one of the office clerks spotted his notes. George had to make up some cock and bull story as an excuse for looking for the man. Fortunately the woman was too busy explaining that your son plays bowls with her husband.'

'Well, I never!' Vera exclaimed. 'They don't take just anyone in the bowls club,' she said approvingly. 'He must have done well for himself.'

Ruby shook her head. Already Vera was preening herself about a child she gave away at birth; the woman was going to be unbearable if it turned out the man had done well in life. Vera would never settle with knowing that he was happy and content with his lot.

'I've come to a decision,' Vera told Ruby, after she sat thinking about her friend's news. 'Once I'm back on my feet, I'm going to visit the bowls club and introduce myself to my son.'

Ruby had had a feeling in her waters that Vera would want to do something like this, as she would never be content simply knowing that her son was alive and well. No, she would want to be involved in his life and make sure people knew she had a successful son.

'I suggest you wait a while until we have more information about the man. You don't want to frighten him off, do you?'

'Why would I do that?' Vera snapped back. 'He's my son, and I want to get to know him. Don't you think he will want to acknowledge me after all these years?'

Ruby sucked in her breath. 'It all depends on . . .'

'On what?'

'What his situation is now, and how he feels about having been given away at birth.'

'My son will know it was for the best. I couldn't have given him that kind of education and a decent home.' Vera sniffed haughtily, starting to get on her high horse.

Ruby gave her time to consider what she'd said, before adding, 'He may not even know he's been adopted.'

Vera's face turned pale. 'Surely she'd have told the lad?'

'Who's to know, love . . . who's to know?'

'It's not what I expected to happen. Once I decided it was time to find my son, I thought he'd be happy to see me and want me to be part of his life. I may even have more grandchildren – possibly even great-grandchildren. Why, with him being well educated, he's probably done well in life, and I could move up in the world as well.'

'Why, Vera Munro, I never took you to be a snob,' Ruby

chuckled, trying to lift their spirits. 'You'll be saying next you can see yourself taking afternoon tea with the lah-di-dah folk in posh London hotels.'

Vera smiled. 'So would you, Ruby, and don't tell me otherwise. You know you like to dress up occasionally and go somewhere smart.'

'Talking of which, I'm off to London tomorrow. The girls are taking me to pay my respects to the King.'

Vera looked surprised. 'Blimey, aren't you a bit long in the tooth for gadding up to town – will your knees stand up to it?'

'Bloody cheek! I'm lighter on my feet than you are,' Ruby scoffed, although she had wondered if she was up to it; hopefully Sarah would take good care of her. 'My reason for telling you is because I shan't be able to come up and see you tomorrow and, as your Sadie is coming with us, you'd best make sure you are able to take care of yourself. I'm not even sure you should be out of bed just yet. You seem to be rushing things.'

'The doctor told me I could sit out of bed for a few hours, so that my legs don't seize up, although I'm feeling tired now.'

'Then let's get you back to your bed. I'll have a tidy round and bring you your meal on a tray when it's hot enough.'

'Don't worry yourself about that. Sadie can clear up once she's home.'

Ruby shook her head. 'That granddaughter of yours puts in long hours working at Maisie's house, caring for her children. She doesn't want to get home and have to start housework and preparing food for you. Besides, what if your long-lost son was to knock on the door, you'd not want him seeing a messy house,' she said with a glint in her eye. She knew Vera occasionally needed a nudge to stop her being selfish.

'In that case, I'll accept your help. Thank you, Ruby,' Vera said, giving her friend an unexpected hug as Ruby helped her to her feet. 'You are a good friend. I appreciate what you've done for me, even though I don't always say it. I wonder . . .'

Ruby had got Vera to her feet and, with one arm around her waist, was guiding her towards the front room and her bed. 'What are you wondering, love?'

'I wonder what you'd do if you were in my boat?'

'Well, I'd eat that meat pudding before it dries out, for one thing.'

'Don't be daft. What I meant was what would you do if you'd just found out where your long-lost son was?'

Ruby stopped to push the front room door open, before leading Vera to her bed. 'Hmm, now you've put me on the spot. What I'd do is let sleeping dogs lie. I'd not go rushing in and frighten the poor man. Possibly I would ask someone who visits the bowls club, and who I could trust, to seek him out and see how the land lies. Then, after a few months, I'd approach him and tell him I was his mother.'

Vera leant forward as Ruby plumped up her pillows. 'That makes sense. I just need someone to join the bowls club and get to know him.'

'What about Sadie's James?'

Vera scoffed at the idea. 'I'm not being funny, and you know I'm one to say, "Live and let live", but with James being a darkie, there are people in this town who wouldn't have anything to do with him. Some even cross the road rather than talk to Sadie when she's with him. No, James would not be the right person.'

Ruby bit her tongue from saying what had come into her head. Vera was always the first with her comments about people, and never thought she was hurting someone by mentioning the colour of their skin or the way they spoke. 'Then what's to be done?'

'Your Bob would be the perfect person to check him out. Or perhaps your George. There's no point in asking Mike, as he's a policeman and might scare people off if he were to ask questions.'

'I'll bide my time and ask Bob and George when I think the time is right, so don't you go expecting news straight away,' she replied as she noticed Vera's eyes start to close.

Ruby began to creep from the room, but pulled up short when Vera said, 'Don't forget I'd like some gravy on that pudding. And tell your Bob and George to be polite to my son when they meet him.'

Ruby chuckled to herself. Vera would never change.

'Can't you see I'm busy?' Philip Harrison snapped at Sarah as she entered his office. 'Come back later.'

'This can't wait,' she replied, standing in front of him and folding her arms across her chest. 'I've had some serious complaints made to me about Mr Argent, and they can't be ignored.'

Philip Harrison placed his pen on the desktop and leant back in his chair. 'Why are you listening to tittle-tattle from the shop floor? Those women have nothing better to do than gossip.'

Sarah could feel the anger rising inside her, but pushed it back. Now was not the time to be angry with the man. She had to use every piece of common sense she had, and be as professional as possible, as she argued her case and defended the staff that she was employed to care for. 'I wish to have somebody sit in on this meeting, so that my evidence is minuted.'

Harrison frowned. 'You walk in here, out of the blue, and demand to have a meeting with somebody else present?'

'If it isn't convenient, we can set a time for the meeting. However, Doreen is working in the cash office at the moment and would be the ideal person.'

'If you wish,' he huffed, 'although I would have preferred a male employee, preferably an assistant manager.'

'We only have one trainee assistant manager, Mr Harrison, and as you know, he is standing in at the Bexleyheath branch. This cannot wait a moment longer. However, if you prefer, I can write a report and send it to head office,' Sarah replied, turning towards the door.

'No, wait, we will deal with this right now. No doubt it's just one of your female fancies, and nothing to bother head office with.'

Sarah hurried along the corridor as fast as she could. On the way she passed several assistants who asked if they could speak to her, one of whom was Clemmie Billington. Quickly saying that she would catch them later, she knocked on the cashier's locked door. Almost immediately a shutter slid open and she was looking through a row of bars at Doreen's face.

'I'm sorry to bother you,' she said. 'I'm in a bit of a fix. Can you spare me ten minutes?'

The woman smiled. 'Of course I can. Do I need to bring anything with me?'

'A notebook and pen would be a good idea – oh, and have your wits about you. I'll wait in my office.'

Sarah paced the floor, trying hard to remember all that she had to say about the way the female staff had been treated. Grabbing a pencil and a sheet of paper, she jotted down the names of the staff who had made complaints, along with several other points that she wished to make. A few minutes later Doreen knocked on her door and entered.

'Thank you for sparing me the time.' Sarah smiled.

'I'm agog at what it is you need me for,' Doreen said, looking concerned. 'I only have two weeks left at work before I retire, so I'm assuming I'm not in for a telling-off?'

'No, nothing like that,' she said to the older woman, thinking how much she would be missed and wondering if Mr Harrison had given any thought as to who was going to replace Doreen when she retired. When she had brought up the subject before, when she was going to place an advertisement in the Situations Vacant section of the *Erith Observer*, the manager had told Sarah to leave it with him, as he wished to interview senior staff. She quickly made a note on the paper in front of her. 'I would like you to accompany me to Mr Harrison's office and take notes while I explain to him how our floorwalker, Mr Argent, has been propositioning some of our female workers. It is essential this is done formally, as I may have to take the problem to head office if he dismisses my allegations.'

'Let's get cracking,' Doreen said. 'I may be locked away

in the cash office for much of the time, but I do hear what is happening on the shop floor. You can rely on me.'

'Thank you. I know I did right in asking you,' Sarah replied as she opened the office door and they headed towards Mr Harrison's office.

11

~

'I hope this isn't going to take long,' Philip Harrison said as he looked over the rim of his spectacles at Sarah and Doreen. He indicated for them both to sit down, but was taken aback when Doreen opened her notebook and sat poised, ready to take notes.

'I will type up the notes and give you both a copy, so that neither of you forgets what has been said,' Doreen said politely.

'Then you'd better tell me what this is all about,' Mr Harrison said, leaning back in his seat and lacing his fingers together.

Sarah took a deep breath and glanced at her notes, feeling glad she'd written them down as she was starting to believe she'd even forget her own name under Mr Harrison's gaze. Get this right and take care of your staff, she urged herself. 'I've received some complaints about our floorwalker, Mr Argent, and as you hired him, I felt it was not something I should have to deal with myself.'

Mr Harrison looked thoughtful as a thin smile appeared on his lips. 'Don't tell me he's been caught helping himself to the Pick'n'Mix?' he said, giving a small yawn. 'I thought you were capable of doing your job and sorting this out, Mrs Gilbert?'

'If only it was that simple, Mr Harrison. I fear this is much more serious.'

He frowned. 'Please explain.'

'Mr Argent has a penchant for making unpleasant comments to our younger female staff.'

'Oh, come along now, Mrs Gilbert. When women work on the shop floor, they must get used to customers being rude at some point in their working lives. In fact on most occasions they are to blame, being slow to serve and speaking quietly, so customers cannot hear them. I suggest you have a staff meeting and explain this to them. Now, is there anything else?' he asked, ignoring the open mouths of both women as he stood up. 'I'll be out of the office for a couple of hours.'

'Hold on one moment,' Sarah said as she found her voice. 'I have not yet explained what Mr Argent has got up to,' she said, glancing down at her notes as Doreen gave her a look of encouragement. 'This man has been catching my girls at inopportune moments and . . . and touching them, uninvited. His insinuations about their virtues are not what they should expect from senior staff, let alone older men.'

'What?' Mr Harrison said, sitting back down quickly. 'You should not be making allegations like this about my staff. Why would he do such things? That's if he has,' he muttered, starting to turn red in the face.

'I can assure you he has done these things,' Sarah replied as she started to list the complaints given to her by the female staff. 'And those are only the ones who have been brave enough to come forward. Most fear for their jobs, by

123

speaking out; I have assured them we will look at each complaint and deal with it sympathetically.'

'You had no right to interfere like this. I should have been the one handling this.'

'I am the staff personnel manager,' Sarah said calmly, holding his gaze. 'As such, it is my duty to protect my staff, especially the younger girls who have not experienced the ways of the world – not that they should have to,' she added through gritted teeth, thinking back to when there was only innocent banter amongst male and female staff when she first joined the company. In fact her Alan had been a trainee manager at that time and would stop by her counter to crack harmless jokes. 'Perhaps we should also have a meeting of the male staff members and educate them in the ways they should treat female staff?'

Mr Harrison scoffed at the idea. 'Don't be so ridiculous, woman. How would they feel, being told they cannot even speak to female staff in case they are pulled up over some innocent remark?'

Sarah knew she was losing the battle; if only Betty was here, she would know what to do. As she looked at her notes, she spotted Jessie's complaint about the floorwalker and recalled how, when much younger, Jessie had run away from home due to being abused and had hidden away in this very store, such was her fear. 'Perhaps I should point out that one female member has already faced abuse from a man in her young life. Why should she have to put up with it in her employment for a respectable company?'

'Name her.'

'I refuse to, as I took her statement in confidence, but you have my word it is very true, as I knew her at that time.'

'And you still employed her? That is rather careless of you,' he started to shout as he thumped the top of his desk.

Sarah was confused. Why should he say she was careless for employing a woman who was turning out, in the short time she'd worked there, to be a valued member of staff? 'I don't understand what you mean. Why was I careless in employing her?'

'Because, Mrs Gilbert, if the woman had blamed a man once for abusing her, she could do it again. That puts me and every male staff member at risk.'

Sarah couldn't believe her ears. She heard a sharp intake of breath from Doreen and hoped she was taking down every word that this odious man had said. 'I think perhaps this meeting has gone as far as it can. I will have that meeting with female staff members, and as soon as possible,' she continued, trying hard to keep her temper. She gave him a curt nod and left the office, with Doreen close on her heels. They both headed to Sarah's office.

'No wonder you wanted a witness and note-taker,' Doreen said as she sat down and started to flick through her notebook. 'I got everything down and will not leave my office until I have typed it up.'

'I can't begin to say how grateful I am for your help. I'll assign someone to help you count the takings, so you aren't under too much pressure.'

The cashier looked grateful. 'Thank you. It's rather a busy day and I'd like to get off on time, as my husband's been to our allotment and he'll be expecting a hot meal on the table.'

'Give me ten minutes,' Sarah said, already starting to think who was on duty and would be able to help Doreen, counting the takings from each till as well as entering figures into the ledgers.

Doreen returned to her office and Sarah started to check the staff rota. As she was doing so, there was a knock on the door. 'Come in,' she called out.

'I'm sorry to bother you, Aunty Sarah,' Clemmie Billington said as she entered the room. 'I wondered if I could check the staff rota, as I want to go with you to pay my respects to the King tomorrow. Mum said it was best to see if you could juggle my work times. I'm sorry to be a pest. I can make up any lost time,' she went on, with a pleading look.

'You couldn't have walked in at a better time,' Sarah said, sitting back down at her desk. 'I'm in need of someone with a sharp mind who can add up correctly.'

'You've lost me,' Clemmie said as she joined her. 'But if you think I can help, then I'll do my best.'

'Before I explain my predicament, I can see by my schedule that you are due to work tomorrow. However, you are on duty in the office with me and as I won't be here, it makes sense to swap your days, and leave Mr Harrison to hold the fort. I've told him I'm not available tomorrow.'

'Then I'll accompany you,' Clemmie beamed. 'Jimmy was going to take me, but he must work, and there are only a couple of days when we can pay our respects before they start to prepare for the funeral. He did suggest we go up to London to watch the funeral procession, but I wasn't so keen, as the weather is so miserable and it will be crowded.'

'I did wonder about doing the same and taking the children. Alan was keen too, but then he's become so busy, with so many people wanting to purchase televisions to watch the funeral. It seems so strange to want to do that. I really don't see the attraction,' she said. 'Besides, our Buster would no doubt escape my clutches and I'd spend the time searching for him amongst the crowds,' she continued, shaking her head ruefully.

Clemmie chuckled. 'I take it little girls are much easier to care for?'

'Goodness, no! Our Georgie runs me ragged at times with her demands. She has no concept of how we coped during the war, although she has been told often enough. Even now, with so much still rationed, all she talks about is making cakes. Now if she was keen on housekeeping or dressmaking, I would be a happy mother,' she sighed.

'They are both a credit to you,' Clemmie said. 'If I could be half the mother you are, I'd be happy.'

Sarah gave a startled look. 'You're not . . . ?'

'Goodness, no. Mother would have a fit. Could you imagine?' she laughed. 'No, Daddy won't be arranging a shotgun wedding any time soon. My Jimmy has two young children, as you know, so I'm keen to be able to help guide them as they grow up, and who knows what will happen in the future? May I ask: would you like to have more children?'

'I hadn't really thought about it,' Sarah said. 'My two pregnancies were both complicated; Buster's was long and arduous, while Georgina's was memorable for her quick arrival during an air raid, while we were in my nan's air-raid shelter in the garden.' She was thoughtful for a moment. 'It would be lovely to have another baby, now the country is at peace and Alan is settled in his business. I suppose my answer is that if another one came along, it would be very welcome.' She smiled. 'I'm not sure we have room in our house; there again, we would make room. Perhaps for now I'll just fuss over Freda's babies.'

'It is still hard to imagine Aunty Freda with babies,' Clemmie sighed.

'I agree. I still see her as the shy sixteen-year-old who first came to work here before the war. Another few months and she will have added to her own little family, and of course she lends a hand with Bessie's child.'

'Of course I heard Freda had invited Bessie to move in with her until Aunty Maisie finds a house with more rooms. I wonder if she will move very far away?'

'I hope not, as I've got used to seeing her most days, with her living at the top of Alexandra Road. Does that sound very selfish of me?'

'Not at all, as I like to meet up with Claudette and Bessie and if they moved to another town, it would put a strain on our friendship if we had to catch buses to go to the cinema or meet for a chat. It's bad enough my Jimmy being moved to the Bexleyheath branch, although it is a larger store with more prospects for a trainee manager.'

'It is something you will have to get used to; look how Freda's Tony has moved around the country, and even though he has been so successful with his career so far, Freda wants nothing more than to have him living at home and working in a store nearby.'

'I had heard that,' Clemmie said, biting her lip and looking worried. 'You do know that Mother is hoping to return to work? I overheard her talking to Daddy and saying how she regrets giving up her job. Perhaps I shouldn't have said anything . . .'

'Perhaps not, but I am aware Betty misses the store. What will be will be,' Sarah replied, knowing that there would be a conflict if both Betty and Tony expected to work in the Erith store and were vying for the same position. She hoped it would be settled amicably. Whichever of the pair became manager, it would be heaps better than the awful Mr Harrison, who was after all a temporary manager. 'I'm hoping Mr Harrison will not be with us much longer as, between you and me, he is not the best of managers. He does tend to think of himself as a permanent fixture.'

Clemmie was sympathetic. 'I know I am still part-time here, but I was considering asking for a full-time position, now my college course has finished. I know I had dreams of working in London, but my life is linked so closely to Woolworths, now that I'm walking out with Jimmy, that I feel travelling to and fro each day would put pressure on our relationship.'

'I can see how you feel, but would just like to say that you are young, and you have many years in front of you. There may come a time when you regret experiencing the thrill of working in London and meeting other girls your own age. Mind you, for now your experience and education could help very well with a problem that I have.'

'I will heed what you say, Aunty Sarah, as Mother has very much said the same to me. She adores my boyfriend and knows we are serious about each other, but she would like me to stretch my wings before settling down. I am rather intrigued as to this small problem that you have . . .'

'We will have an opening for a cashier before too long. Doreen is retiring soon and Mr Harrison, who took it upon himself to find a replacement, has done nothing whatsoever.

I wonder: would the position be something you would be interested in?'

Clemmie's eyes lit up. 'I would adore to be considered for the position, but don't you feel I am rather young? The women I've known in that job have been quite a lot older than I am now.'

'I don't feel age comes into it. You've been taking a course in office machines at Erith college and now have a clutch of diplomas and exam passes. You are still the only person in this store who knows how to work our compto-meter and, apart from all of that, you have a sensible head on your shoulders. Would you like to give the job a try?'

'I certainly would. When can I start?'

'Would this afternoon be too soon? I promised Doreen I'd find somebody to help her for a few hours, so that she doesn't fall behind. I'll explain why later.'

Clemmie stood up and removed her coat. 'I'm ready,' she said, pulling off her knitted beret and shaking her hair free. 'Now is as good a time as any to put my future plans into action.'

12

~

15 February 1952

Ruby surveyed the friends and family sitting in George's living room. 'I don't know if it is right to be eating while the King's funeral is in progress,' she said as she bit into a ham sandwich. 'You've put on a lovely spread, Maureen. I don't know how you found the time, what with having Georgie and Buster all day yesterday. I'd have helped more if I'd known you were doing all this.'

Maureen looked slightly harassed. 'The problem was not knowing how many people would turn up to watch the service and procession on our television. I asked George to stop handing out invitations willy-nilly, but you know what he's like.'

'Generous to a fault,' Ruby beamed proudly. 'That's my son all over.'

Maureen grimaced. 'But when he offered to help me, and then disappeared because Alan needed his assistance delivering televisions to their new customers, I didn't see him until midnight. Then he wanted to tell me all about the customers, and how he helped people unpack the televisions and stand them in the optimum viewing place, when all I wanted to do was go to bed, I was that exhausted.'

'He's a good lad,' Ruby said, 'but you should have picked up your telephone and called me. Bob and I would have been round like a shot. Bob's a fair hand at buttering bread.'

'You've already done enough to help. How you managed to make so many sausage rolls, I don't know.'

Ruby gave her a wink. 'It was a lesson I learnt during the war. I padded out the sausage meat with breadcrumbs and added a pinch of mustard for flavour.'

'No one seems to have noticed, as the plate is almost empty. I thought I would hold back on the fairy cakes, and people can have them with a cup of tea once the proceedings are over.'

Both women fell silent as the funeral cortège appeared on the small screen. George had managed to fit almost every seat they owned into the large front room, while Maureen had scattered cushions on the floor for the youngsters to sit on. Already Buster had been packed off into the garden because he wouldn't stop fighting with his sister, who was now fidgeting and looking bored.

'Why don't you put your coat on and join Buster in the garden?' Maureen suggested. 'Don't forget to wipe your feet, so you don't tread in mud on my carpets.'

'I won't,' Georgie said glumly, before joining her brother in the back garden.

Maureen settled next to Ruby on the settee in front of the television. 'Have I missed anything?'

'They've just been showing the coffin being pulled by the sailors; the lads look so young and so solemn.'

'It's something that will stay with them forever,' Maureen

said, pulling her handkerchief from the sleeve of her cardigan and sniffing into it. 'Somehow it doesn't seem quite respectable to be watching a funeral on a television set. Do you agree, David?'

David Carlisle moved closer to where Maureen was sitting, leaning on the arm of the settee. 'Speaking as someone in the funeral industry, I don't feel the likes of us will ever see our final journey and interment filmed and kept for posterity. However, I do envisage state occasions becoming popular. Think how the generations to come will be able to watch historical events. Why, it could be quite educational for our children.'

'If anyone should consider broadcasting my funeral, I'm telling you now, David, I'll have something to say about it,' Ruby huffed.

Bob, who was sitting close to the table where Maureen had laid out the food, stopped loading his plate and turned to grin at the people in the room. 'I don't think you'd have much say in it, my love.' To which the room erupted with laughter, before quickly falling into silence as Ruby scolded them.

'For all intents and purposes, we are attending this funeral. Show some respect, all of you.'

They all kept quiet, although Maisie, who was sitting with Freda and Sarah, nudged her friends, who then had to fight hard not to giggle at Ruby's comment. 'Blimey, it's like being back at school,' she whispered as Ruby looked over at them and shook her head in warning.

'You look all in,' Bob said to Alan, who seemed to be dropping off to sleep while trying to prop his head up, with one elbow on the edge of the dining table. 'I take it the shop has done well out of this?'

Alan blinked and ran a hand through his fair hair. 'Sorry, I was about to drop off. Yes, you are right. I don't know the final figures yet, as George is still working on them, but we've done well, although I hate to think we've had to lose our monarch for the shop to turn a profit.'

'It's a rum world,' Bob said, 'but I'm pleased your business is doing well. Don't feel bad about profiting because somebody died, as it's no different from all the businesses that not only survived but expanded, due to supplying essential equipment for the war effort.'

'I suppose you're right, but all the same it does make me feel uncomfortable.'

'Don't feel like that,' George echoed, as he joined the two men. 'If you didn't sell somebody a television or wireless set, someone else would jump in. At least you are providing for your family and, with all the plans we have, I can see that in a year or two you will be competing with David and Douglas, with business premises in most of our local high streets.'

'Now that would be something to be proud of,' Bob said, patting his son-in-law on the back, 'and at least you wouldn't be treading on each other's toes, as both businesses couldn't be more different from each other.'

'Not unless Alan started filming funerals,' George said in a hushed voice, in case his mother overheard.

Bob stifled a laugh. George could be a bit of a wag and had a way to him that was rather like his mum; in fact he had Ruby's facial features, although his nose was larger and his jaw squarer.

'God forbid!' Alan chuckled. 'That's something we don't plan to do. However, George has a good idea.'

Bob was agog as the men explained how they were planning to hire out television sets, as well as washing machines, to people who couldn't afford to purchase an item outright. 'That does sound like a good idea, although I can see you having a few problems. What would happen if, say, a television set broke down? From what I've heard down the Prince of Wales, sometimes they can be temperamental.'

'That thought had crossed my mind too,' David Carlisle joined in. 'I'm already wondering if the television set at home will still be working when we get back. I've told the girls not to twiddle the knobs, but I'm not sure they were listening. We should have stayed at home with them, but Maisie was adamant she wanted to spend the day with you lot, so when Bessie and Clemmie offered to babysit, we jumped at the chance.'

'They are good girls; you won't have any problems there,' Bob said. 'However, you've not answered my question about what will happen if a television set you've rented out goes wrong. I've been told there are all kinds of things inside these sets that can break down. Does it mean you'll have to stock spare parts, and will you be able to fit them?'

Alan chuckled quietly. 'You aren't saying anything that we've not discussed. Although I've been on several training courses with manufacturers, I'm not qualified or confident enough to repair the television sets. We've already set up a small workshop at the back of the premises, where we can fix things.'

Bob thought for a moment. 'From what I remember, that room isn't very large; you'll be falling over those television sets, if many turn up for repair,' he said, nudging the others as Ruby gave him a glare for talking.

Alan lowered his voice. And kept an eye on Ruby. 'I've also rented an outbuilding of the shop next door that we can use as storage. It may mean hiring an engineer specifically to deal with televisions and wirelesses, if I don't learn enough.'

'It is certainly a growing industry,' David said thoughtfully. 'Do you envisage creating apprenticeships for your engineers?'

'Now that is a thought,' Alan said, as George agreed.

George was thoughtful. 'It's certainly worth thinking about. I'll start making enquiries.'

'Don't go making any plans for tomorrow, George, or you, Bob, as I want you to go up the bowls club for me, on that little matter we chatted about,' Ruby butted in.

'That woman has eyes and ears in the back of her head,' Bob muttered quietly. 'I reckon she heard every word we've said. Yes, dear,' he called over to where Ruby was still watching the television, while the other men grinned good-naturedly. 'The bowls season doesn't start until April, so I'm not sure how Ruby expects us to find this chap, simply because someone said he has played there.'

George rubbed his chin thoughtfully. 'I know a few of the members drink at the Wheatley Hotel. I reckon we could walk up to the bowls club and enquire, in case someone is there, and then move on to the Wheatley. What do you say?'

'That's sounds like a plan, but let's keep it to ourselves for now, shall we?'

Freda wriggled uncomfortably on the sofa. 'I'm glad we decided not to go up to London to watch the funeral procession. My legs still ache from standing so long, waiting to pay our respects the other day. If only we'd taken William, I could have leant on his pram.'

'I told you we should have asked somebody for a seat for you,' Maisie hissed, aware that Bob had been told off by Ruby for talking.

'I couldn't do that, when there were so many older folk queuing with us. Why, Ruby was a real trooper: she hardly complained at all.'

'Nan was telling me how she'd been up to London in her younger days to pay her respects when monarchs passed away. The only time she missed one was when my dad, George, was very young.'

'It makes you proud to be British,' Freda said, with a hint of a tear in her eye.

'Here she goes again,' Maisie said, passing a clean handkerchief to Freda. 'I think our Freda cries more than you do these days,' she said to Sarah.

'At least I have an excuse, with this baby,' Freda replied, gently stroking her stomach. 'The baby is not only making me tearful, but giving me strange eating habits. I found myself nibbling on a piece of coal this morning as I made up the fire. People will think I'm bonkers! I did nothing like that with William.'

'It's completely natural,' Maisie said. 'It'll go away, once the baby comes along. Just check your face in the mirror before you go out, in case you have coal dust on your lips. I craved pickled onions all the time and often carried a jarful with me in case I fancied one.'

Freda giggled. 'I do remember you and your pickles. How about you?' she asked Sarah.

'Raw pig's liver. Alan said he would divorce me for having such a strange craving. I would drool when we passed a butcher's shop. Although offal wasn't rationed, I did try to fight it, as my fancies could have been denying someone their dinner. Mind you, I would kill for a plate of liver, bacon and onions right now.'

'You're not . . . ?' Maisie asked.

'I'm not expecting, if that is what you are inferring. However, it would be lovely,' she added, gazing at Freda's happy face. 'Talking of children, I'd best check what mine are up to.'

'I'll come with you, as I could do with stretching my legs,' Maisie said. 'I'm not used to sitting on my bum for so long.'

'And I'll check on my boy. It was good of Maureen to let me park the pram in her kitchen; I was worried he'd be in the way.'

The three women left the room, glad to be in the natural light once more.

'My Alan's got all these big plans about the television business,' Sarah went on. 'I told him to sort something out, so we don't have to close the curtains to be able to see the screen. The kids can get up to all sorts outside while he's got his eyes glued to the television. Why, the other day the pair had escaped and were halfway to the park before we caught up with them. I was so angry I packed them off to bed without their supper. Anything could have happened to them,' she said as she started to look up and down the garden, calling their names.

George and Maureen's house, set just off Avenue Road, was on a new estate and as it had once been farmland, the builders had made provision for large gardens, which George had made good use of. Close to the house there was an area for sitting and enjoying the flower borders, while a wooden fence with a gate separated off a small vegetable plot. Sarah adored the house, with its light rooms and large windows, and was a little jealous of the three bedrooms, something she dreamt of, as her house in Crayford Road was so small.

'If they are digging about amongst the vegetable patch, I'll kill them,' she huffed. 'They're in their Sunday best, what with it being an important occasion. It is not really the kind of day for them to be playing outside.' She ran to the gate and flung it open, still calling their names. There was no indication they'd even been there, although she did check the shed, in case they were playing inside. 'There's no sign of them,' she said as Maisie joined her.

'Perhaps they've walked up to my house to join the other kids, or even gone to Mike and Gwyneth's. You know how much Georgie looks up to Myfi.'

'Let's walk up and down the streets,' Freda suggested. 'How long do you think they've been missing?'

'It can't be more than half an hour,' Maisie said, checking her wristwatch. 'But I don't think you should be marching about the streets. Why not go inside and use the telephone? Check with my house first and then try Mike and Gwyneth's. Thank goodness Mike has a telephone, what with him needing to be on call with the police.'

'Whatever the news, get my Alan to come out and find us, as the last thing I want is you overexerting yourself.'

Freda saluted them. 'Mission understood,' she said, before hurrying back into the house.

Maisie gave Sarah a concerned look. 'I didn't want to worry the kid,' she said, using Freda's nickname. 'But I did wonder if they'd gone back to your house. I take it they know where the key is to get in?'

'Yes, they are still too young to have their own front-door key, but I do have one hidden near the back door under a plant pot. Only Georgie is allowed to use it, if she gets home before me or Alan. You don't think she's messing about cooking, do you? She's got such a bee in her bonnet these days . . .'

'Probably not, but let's check, to be on the safe side,' Maisie replied as they both started to hurry. It took them no more than ten minutes to head down Avenue Road, over the railway bridge and past the Prince of Wales pub. Alan and Sarah's house was just around the corner and as they turned into Crayford Road, they heard a fire engine approaching, with its bells ringing.

'Oh my God, no,' Sarah gasped, thinking straight away of the time somebody had set Alan's workshop on fire and he almost didn't escape with his life.

'Don't start to panic,' Maisie said, grasping Sarah's arm. 'It may not even be going to your road,' she said, although she had her doubts.

As she spoke, the fire engine pulled up in front of them, blocking their view. They hurried round the vehicle as firemen jumped down and headed up the short path towards the house.

'It's all right, Officer, I have both the children,' Sarah's neighbour called from her doorstep, while a sheepish-looking Georgie and Buster peered out from behind the

140

woman's skirt. 'My husband put out the fire,' she said as she spotted Sarah.

Sarah couldn't speak as she ran towards her children and hugged them close, all three of them bursting into tears. After several minutes she looked up at her neighbour. 'Whatever happened? We were at my dad's house, watching the funeral on his television set, and the children were playing in the garden – they were told to stay there,' she explained as Buster started to cry once more.

'She made me eat her cake, Mum, even though I said I didn't like it as it wasn't cooked properly. I didn't mean to catch the tea towel on fire,' Buster explained, putting the blame on his sister.

Georgie reached out and pinched him. 'Don't tell lies,' she spat at him, diverting her eyes from her mum, who shook her arm to silence her.

They watched quietly, waiting for news of the damage, as more neighbours appeared, looking on from across the road.

'That'll give 'em all something to gossip about,' Maisie said as she glared back at them.

'I don't recognize any of them,' Sarah said, looking away. 'I feel so guilty.'

'Don't be daft; it's not your fault, and I'll tell them so if they as much as whisper a word about you.'

Sarah was relieved that Maisie was with her, as Alan would have been shouting the odds and causing her so much stress.

One of the firemen came out of the front door. 'You did a good job, sir,' he said to the neighbour's husband as he walked over to join Sarah and Maisie. 'It could have been much worse. Children should never be left alone in the house, let alone the kitchen,' he said sternly, looking towards Sarah.

'It's not what it seems, Officer. Sarah is a very good mother; it's her children who are naughty,' Maisie said, making it clear that she was talking about Georgina, who backed away and hid behind her mum.

'She's got this bee in her bonnet about wanting to cook all the time, and she must have grabbed the opportunity to sneak away while we were watching the King's funeral.'

'So you like working in the kitchen, do you?' he asked, bending down so that he was face-to-face with the girl.

Georgina nodded her head enthusiastically, seeing that the fireman was sympathetic. 'I do, but she won't let me do it very often, and neither will my Nanny Ruby.'

'I see,' he nodded thoughtfully. 'Perhaps you need some lessons. I can help you there.'

'Oh yes, please,' Georgina beamed. 'I can make cakes.'

The firemen stood up. 'If someone would like to walk her down to the fire station tomorrow afternoon, we can give the young lady a lesson in how to work in a kitchen. If she likes it, perhaps she could come back another time.'

Sarah could see, from the sparkle in his eye, that he had a plan of some kind. 'Thank you very much. I can certainly bring her tomorrow afternoon. Is there much damage in my kitchen?'

'Nothing a bowl of hot, soapy water and a scrubbing brush won't cure for now, although you will need to think about a new cooker and decorating the room. The upstairs rooms smell of smoke, but you shouldn't need to redecorate. Oh, and you will need a new tea towel. Thankfully your neighbours were home, otherwise it could have been so different. I suggest that perhaps you don't allow the children access to a door key.'

'I never thought . . .' she started to say as he patted her on the shoulder.

'Madam, it has been my experience that children can be like burglars; if they want to get inside the house, they will. I'll leave you now to start your clearing up.'

13

'Oh, Alan, look at the mess; it is going to take an age to get the kitchen straight. And as for the smell of smoke . . .'

Alan slung his arm round Sarah's shoulders and gave her a squeeze. 'I'm just thankful the kids didn't harm themselves. When I think of what could have happened. Two weeks from now, you won't be able to tell there's been a fire.'

'Two weeks? Surely it won't take that long to finish scrubbing the walls and give them a lick of paint? The cooker doesn't look too bad, now that your mum has helped me scrape the lumps of baked-on cake mix and burnt tea towel off the top. How will we manage until then?'

Alan tried to interrupt, but Sarah had far too many thoughts buzzing around in her head to be quiet.

'As it is, I should have been at work ten minutes ago. Mr Harrison will be fuming; it's payday and I should be there to hand out the pay packets once we've made them up. I can't expect young Clemmie to cope on her own.'

Alan ran a hand through his sandy-coloured hair. 'Look, Sarah, with all the goodwill in the world, I can't drop everything to finish sorting out this mess. Let's both get to work and we can continue this evening. Mum's collecting the children after they finish school, so we know they are safe. Even now, five days since the fire, I doubt they will ever contemplate doing anything without permission again; they've had such a scare.'

'But what about our dinner? We can't keep expecting our parents to step in and feed us. I thought by now we'd be back to normal, even if the walls haven't been decorated.'

Alan held up his hands to ward off her questions. 'We can have fish and chips; it will be a treat.'

'So now we are having a treat because of the fire? I don't feel we are setting a good example to the children.'

'Then let them have bread and dripping,' Alan snapped as he grabbed his jacket from the back of a chair and stormed from the house.

'There's not much chance of that, as the dripping bowl was in the oven . . .' she called after him.

She looked around the house, knowing that she had begun to hate living there long before the children caused the fire in the kitchen. With just the two bedrooms, it was time for Georgina and Buster to have rooms of their own. The cellar, with its whitewashed walls, had been kept clean and tidy since the war, when they used it as their own private air-raid shelter. She had pondered turning it into a bedroom for one of the children, until Alan had pointed out damp patches that would be costly to repair – if he had the time.

'It's time to move on,' she said out loud, knowing it would be a difficult conversation with her husband. Alan had been born in this house and had lived here quite happily with his mum and dad. Even after his dad died,

Alan had lived here right up till the time they married. Not many years after that, Alan's mum had married Sarah's dad, George; they'd been childhood sweethearts, but then separated until both of them were bereaved and rekindled their romance in later life. Maureen had been very generous and gave this little house to Alan and his family, now that she lived with George; this was a problem, because if Sarah suggested they sell up and move to a larger property, she could offend Maureen, and Alan would be so disappointed. 'Thank goodness we never had a third child,' she said aloud, because the only other dry place where a child could sleep was in the coal hole at the back of the house.

Deciding not to bring up the subject again with Alan, she pulled on her coat and hurried off to work.

'It's so good of you to collect me and drive me to work,' Clemmie said, as Jimmy stopped his car dead in front of the Erith store and switched off the engine. 'I hope I haven't made you late?' she asked, turning to look at him.

Even after a year of courting her handsome boyfriend, his features could still cause her heart to skip a beat. Not every girl favoured a man with copper-coloured hair, but Jimmy's hair seemed so different, sometimes looking darker, depending on the light. With his deep-green eyes and a scattering of freckles, he was, as far as she was concerned, perfect. Clemmie hoped that when the day came when they had babies together, they would look just like their dad. His two young children, both under the age of six, had taken after their late mother, with dark-brown hair and blue eyes. She felt sad for a moment thinking of how Amelia had died in a car crash while the youngest child was only months old.

'You look so serious,' he said, stroking the side of her face with one finger.

Clemmie shrugged her shoulders. 'It was nothing really; I was thinking how sad it was that Amelia wouldn't see her children grow up, and what a good father you've been.'

He looked away from her as a shadow fleetingly crossed his face. 'I'm lucky, in that my parents were able to take the three of us on. I wasn't able to function for a while, let alone look after a baby and a toddler.'

'They are good people and I'm as lucky as you, with them accepting me into the fold as they did. I appreciate now how hard it can be for a man's potential wife not to be accepted.'

'You speak from experience.' He smiled at her serious face.

'I've never told you this, but I was a beastly brat of a child when Dad brought Betty home to meet us. I'm pleased she stood her ground until we grew to love her; everything could have been so different.'

'She's an admirable woman, and I can see her in you; it's as if she is truly your mother.'

'For all intents and purposes, she is. I have few recollections of my own mother. You know, Dad has a very large oil painting of my proper mother and, when Betty married him, I kicked up such a stink when he took it down. I insisted that we had it hanging in our bedroom until it gave Dorothy nightmares. It's in his attic now.'

'Perhaps, when we marry, he would allow you to hang it in our home, so you have something to remember her by; after all, she will one day be the grandmother of our own children,' he said, rather liking the way Clemmie blushed.

'Gosh, look at us talking about children,' she chuckled, leaning over to kiss his cheek. If we don't crack on and get into work, neither of us will have a job in order to run our own household, let alone put food on the table for the children. Will I see you tomorrow evening?' she asked as she started to open the car door.

'Only if you are happy to come to my parents' house. Mum has a bridge match to attend, and I can't expect Dad to look after the kids. It's a shame we can't meet this evening, but with me working late it's impossible.'

'I'd love to. I'll catch a bus over there after work, so she can get ready and not have to rush.'

'I don't deserve you,' he called after her as Clemmie closed the door, bending to give him a last wave through the window before he drove off.

With a happy sigh, she almost skipped through the front doors of the building as they opened.

'Gosh, you look glum,' Clemmie said as she met Sarah on the stairs that led up to their offices. 'How is your kitchen coming along?'

'Let's just say I'm glad I'm here and not at home right now. I doubt I'll ever get the smell of smoke out of everything; it even crept upstairs and inside the wardrobes. Everything will need washing. As for using the kitchen, Alan can't cope with that as well as the business; it couldn't have happened at a worse time. Honestly, Clemmie, I'm that annoyed I feel like putting the kids up for adoption,' she added, before laughing at the notion of being free of her adored children.

'Oh dear, I had no idea it was as bad as that.'

Sarah pulled off her coat and scarf, hanging them on a hook behind her office door. 'I shouldn't complain, as our parents have been marvellous at giving us a hand. We slept at their house for the first night. As for the firemen, they went above and beyond their duties. Did you hear how they invited Georgie to visit the kitchen at the fire station?'

'I heard about the invitation, but nothing more. Did she have a good time?' Clemmie asked as she sat down on a spare seat.

Sarah chuckled. 'Let's just say that helping someone prepare a meal for twenty hungry firemen, and then being left to do all the washing up, didn't go down too well. Georgie was very quiet when she came home, and yesterday she announced she'd changed her mind about being a cook.'

'Oh, bless her,' Clemmie giggled. 'Has she told you what she would like to do instead?'

Sarah's eyes twinkled. 'She has decided to work here, but she doesn't want to work on the shop floor, as she prefers to be a manager . . .'

'Oh, my goodness,' Clemmie said as she wiped her eyes. 'This gets better and better. Can you imagine her being our manager? We already have too many people vying for that job.'

Sarah became serious. 'I've never wanted to see the back of a manager so much as I do Mr Harrison. However, it will mean that two people I love very much will be at loggerheads; Freda so much wants Tony to return to Erith and be a permanent manager, and your mum wishes to return to a job that suits her so well. I just pray head office make the right decision and it doesn't cause a fracture in the close friendships we hold so dear.'

'If it is any help, I do know Mother is aware of Tony's imminent return and feels torn between wanting to return to work herself and upsetting Freda, if she should be offered the Erith store.'

Sarah groaned. 'This does put us in an awful situation. Freda desperately needs to remain in her own home, especially once the baby is born, as she doesn't want to go traipsing around the country, living wherever Woolworths decide to place Tony as a temporary manager; it was bad enough when she had William while away from Erith. And God forbid if Tony is given a permanent contract in another part of the country, and Freda should have to pack up and move away from everyone she loves.'

Clemmie followed Sarah into her office and helped her off with her coat, before picking up the payroll sheet left on Sarah's desk. 'It was good that you and Aunty Maisie went to visit her and help out, but it is such a pickle, as someone is going to be disappointed. Mother said almost the same to me, and she really feels bad for wanting to return to work. It doesn't help that several people in high-up positions at head office, who she has kept in touch with, have tried to lure her back. I'm not sure how we can get through this without someone becoming upset,' she replied as a sad look crossed her face.

Sarah unlocked a drawer in her desk and took out a set of keys. 'Let's get the payroll money from Mr Harrison and make up the pay packets, before he realizes I'm late getting into work,' she suggested as they headed up the corridor to the manager's office. 'I've decided not to discuss the subject when we are in the company of either Freda or your mum, just so we all keep the peace.'

Clemmie nodded. 'That's a good idea. I'm certain Mother wouldn't mention it within Freda's hearing, but I will tell her what we have decided, although I feel it will become the elephant in the room.'

'Thank you for doing that; perhaps we should say the same to Maisie, in case she puts her foot in it, which, as you know, she can do sometimes.'

Clemmie chuckled. 'I do, I like Aunty Maisie, but I know what you mean.'

Sarah sighed. 'Hopefully it will all blow over. Now tell me, are you enjoying the position in the cashier's office? Have you come across any problems?'

'I'm thoroughly enjoying the work and wondered if you would consider me to be the full-time replacement?'

'Have you spoken to your mother about this?'

'Yes, I sat down with her and Daddy and explained how much I'm enjoying the work, and how my skills learnt at college have stood me in good stead for the position. It was Daddy who asked my reasons for changing my mind about working in London. He was worried I was throwing away my career dreams because ... well, because I'd fallen in love with my Jimmy.'

'Is he not happy about your romance?' Sarah asked as she entered Mr Harrison's empty office. 'Let's be quick and get out of here before he returns.'

Clemmie held the sturdy safe door open while Sarah collected a heavy leather bag containing the staff wages. 'Daddy really likes Jimmy; it's more that he thinks I'm still quite young to be serious about somebody. If he had his way, I would still be living with him when I was fifty and single,' she chuckled.

'That's a father for you,' Sarah said as she ushered Clemmie from the manager's office and closed the door behind them. 'I married Alan on my twenty-first birthday; it was the day war broke out, and I recall spending some of the time sheltering in Nanny Ruby's cupboard under the stairs – and that was before the wedding. My mother was alive then and was quite shocked, as I'd been there alone with Alan, and in my wedding dress. Apart from my frock being a little wrinkled, nothing really happened. Dad had jokingly said that if we hadn't planned to marry that day, he'd have been marching Alan up the aisle with a shotgun pressed to his back. I've often wondered if he was joking or not,' she grinned.

'Twenty-one is a good age to get married. I'm going to promise Mummy and Daddy I'll keep all my options open about my career, regardless of when I marry. It will give me time to add to my bottom drawer. Besides, you are a good example of a mother having a career.

Clemmie unlocked her office door and locked it again, once they were both inside. There was a protocol to follow where cash was concerned. 'Gosh, look at the time. We'd best get cracking,' she said as Sarah tipped all the money onto the desk and they started to count the cash, putting it into neat piles. 'That's correct,' she announced, checking the payroll sheet. 'So do you want to put the money into each pay packet while I check them?'

Sarah agreed, thinking how sensible Clemmie was. 'Perhaps when you speak to your parents, you could suggest that you have an engagement party. Of course your Jimmy will have to agree as well.'

'He's quite easy-going,' Clemmie smiled. 'He does worry that I'm not enjoying a traditional romance, what with him having two children and needing to be with them.'

'Does it worry you, being unable to go out alone as much as a young courting couple normally would?'

Clemmie shook her head. 'Honestly, I don't care if sometimes we have the children with us. I adore them as much as I adore Jimmy. He asked me that when he dropped me off this morning.'

Sarah was thoughtful. 'My advice would be to keep an open mind about everything. Don't hold off getting married for the sake of being a certain age. There were women who have regretted such things, having lost their fiancés during the last war or, come to that, the Great War. Just keep your parents informed of what is happening, so that they aren't surprised or even shocked by your actions.'

'I'll do that. We intend to enjoy our courtship, and Jimmy's two children make no difference to our plans. When Mummy was talking to me the other evening, she told me about her first love. His name was Charlie and, if the war hadn't taken him, they'd have married. It is so romantic: Daddy was a friend of Charlie's and that's how he and Mummy met.'

Sarah knew the story of Betty's early life and it wasn't quite as romantic as Clemmie was led to believe. Betty had known heartache and hardship before she came to Erith to work. 'Betty has lived an interesting life; you should ask her more about it when you are both alone,' she advised, not wishing to tell someone else's story. 'Now, let's get this job finished, as staff will be expecting to collect their pay packets after lunch.'

Clemmie looked up at the clock. 'I have a collection to make from the tills at eleven o'clock and I want to double-check something. Once I am sure I'm right in my assumptions, may I run it by you before I go to the manager? I don't wish to incur the wrath of Mr Harrison if I can avoid it.'

'That sounds sinister. Are you sure I can't help you now?'

Clemmie thought for a moment. 'Give me two hours to balance the takings, then I'll explain. It's probably me over-thinking something.'

Sarah watched Clemmie leave the office. The girl wasn't someone to worry unduly. With her mathematical training, if she thought there was a problem, then there probably was. She would do all she could to assist the young girl, as the last thing she wanted was for Mr Harrison to be nasty to Clemmie or she could lose one of her best younger staff members. As it was, she still had the matter of her meeting with Mr Harrison to deal with, as the man seemed to have brushed it under the carpet. She wasn't looking forward to insisting that he removed the floorwalker from the store.

Bob leant against the bar in the Wheatley Hotel, draining his pint of best bitter. 'Well, that was a waste of time,' he huffed. 'Who'd have thought the chap would abscond like that? This isn't my pub of choice,' he added, looking around at the unfamiliar bar. 'It's all polished brass, and too posh for my liking.'

'They don't do a bad pint, though,' George said as he

waved at the barmaid to refill their glasses. 'As for Vera's son, I blame myself for not sticking to the plans we made on the day of the King's funeral and coming here sooner; we might have caught up with him before he disappeared.'

'It's not your fault young Georgie set fire to Alan and Sarah's kitchen,' Bob tutted. 'She's getting out of hand. Her parents need to come down on her like a ton of bricks.'

George had said as much to Maureen, but didn't like to agree too much with Bob as he was proud of his little namesake. 'She'll grow out of it in time.'

'Let's hope it's before she causes a serious problem,' Bob replied.

George laughed out loud. 'I reckon helping the Fire Service the other afternoon made Georgie see that being a cook isn't just about making fancy food. I slipped them a few pounds for a round of drinks, to thank them.'

'They're a good lot of blokes; I couldn't do their job. God knows what they've seen.'

George was surprised at Bob's comment. 'You must have seen some sights in your time, what with being a police officer all your working life, even during the Great War?'

Bob thought for a moment. 'There were times I could have given up the job, but with my dad before me being a copper, I'd have been in hot water with him,' he said ruefully. 'I have some happy memories as well. Did you know I met Ruby during that war? She reminded me of it not long ago; it was during a Zeppelin raid. I was a very young copper at the time, and she was only a slip of a thing; I was on duty with my father. Strange how things work out. You'd have knocked me down with a feather if someone had said we'd meet and marry so many years later.'

'You've made Mum very happy,' George said with feeling. 'I'm grateful for that.'

'It works both ways. However long we've got left, I know I'll die a happy man for having known her – and her family.'

George coughed before changing the subject; he felt quite emotional. 'Getting back to why we are here, what shall we tell Mum?'

'Whatever we say, it's got to be enough for her to pacify Vera or all hell will be let loose. I don't want to say the chap hopped it to Spain before he had his collar felt.'

George thought for a moment. 'I'm not going to lie to Mum, as she will know. I've never been good at keeping a secret from her.'

Bob roared with laughter. 'And you a politician? I know what you mean, though. I can see through my Mike when he's not told me the whole story. He likes to keep police matters to himself, as he knows I'd worry if he was working on a dangerous case. Getting back to what to say to Mum. I suggest we tell her we found out the man has gone to work in Spain, and we've asked to be informed if he returns at some point.'

'That'll do it,' Bob said, finishing his drink, then wiping his mouth with the back of his hand. 'Fancy another?'

The men had finished their third pint when Sergeant Mike Jackson appeared from the private quarters of the hotel owner. 'I didn't expect to see you both here at this time of the day; you're not usually lunchtime drinkers,' he said, checking the large clock on the wall behind the bar before joining them at their table.

'I could say the same about you,' his dad said. 'Have you got time for a pint?'

'Not while I'm on duty, thanks. I've just had a cuppa with the landlord.'

Bob gave a quizzical look. 'Is there something happening?'

'Now, Dad, you know I can't tell you things like that,' he said, looking over his shoulder to make sure he wasn't being overheard, before leaning forward towards the two men. 'It's merely a general enquiry: a few public houses and hotels have found stock going missing over the past month or so, and I've been making our local publicans aware.'

'Is nothing sacred?' George muttered.

'How have you managed to escape at this time of the day?' Mike asked, noticing the two men giving a quick look at each other. 'Are you up to something?'

Bob tried not to meet his son's eyes. 'Well . . .'

'Come on, Dad, cough it up.' Mike knew his dad all too well.

George gave Bob a nudge. 'We might as well tell Mike. After all, he will hear about it eventually.'

'Don't tell me you've been selling bent crates of beer?' Mike laughed.

'Nothing like that, son. Ruby's had us looking for Vera's long-lost son. It seems he was a member of the bowls club, but it's out of season, so we were asking about, as he used to drink here. Vera's not seen him since he was a nipper and, now she's not in the best of health, Ruby has been charged with finding him.'

'Crikey, that is news. Who'd have thought it . . . Poor Ruby's pulled the short straw,' Mike laughed, before seeing the two men's glum faces. 'What have you found out about him?'

'It seems he was a regular at the bowls club and drank here, and in the New Light, before disappearing to Spain a few weeks back,' George informed him, thinking how alike father and son were, even though Mike stood a good head taller than Bob.

Mike pulled out a notebook and started to write. 'Don't worry, it's not official, and this is my own notebook,' he said, seeing his dad's worried look. 'The police force isn't at the beck and call of Vera Munro. However, I may hear something about the chap while I'm out and about. Unofficially, of course.'

'That's decent of you, Mike, but don't go getting yourself into trouble,' George said as he delved into the inside pocket of his jacket and pulled out an envelope. 'This is all the information I have on him, and that includes what Vera told Mum, which could be completely fictional. There are some newspaper cuttings of him as a youngster, after Vera gave him away, but Mum has them; I'm sure she won't mind you looking, although it's best we don't inform Vera, as she was grumpy enough when told that we knew her secret, even though we are helping track the bloke down.'

Mike gave a sigh of relief. Just the thought of interacting with Vera Munro gave him the jitters.

14

Sarah picked up the black Bakelite telephone on her desk as it started to ring. She prayed it wasn't Mr Harrison summoning her to his office. Since she had stood up to him, he seemed hell-bent on finding fault with every aspect of her work. He even had the temerity to suggest she wore the same uniform as the counter staff when, as office staff, she was allowed to wear her own smart suits. Even Clemmie, whilst working part-time in the office, was wearing a suit, often hand-me-downs from Betty. Sarah had pointed out to Mr Harrison that she did have an overall in her office, ready to wear if she should need to take over duties on a counter if an emergency arose. So far it had happened once, when a wave of sickness meant half the staff were off work at the same time. The three days she'd helped, moving from counter to counter, had been some of the most carefree days she'd experienced in the store for several years.

'Mrs Gilbert,' she said politely into the receiver, before holding her breath, waiting for the manager's bark.

'Aunt Sarah, it's me, Clemmie,' a hushed voice whispered.

'Clemmie, I told you not to call me "Aunt" when we

were at work,' Sarah said, relieved it wasn't Mr Harrison. 'Can you speak up a little?'

'I dare not, in case someone is outside my office door. Can you possibly join me? I have something to show you. Don't let Mr Harrison see you, as I'd hate him to make a fuss until we've decided what to do.'

'Give me two minutes,' Sarah replied, surprised that two hours had passed so quickly. She slipped her feet back into her brown leather shoes; her feet had been aching all after-noon and, after just half an hour of her bare feet on the cold linoleum floor, she felt revived. Picking up a notebook and pen, she hurried from her room, almost bumping into someone who was about to knock on her door.

'Good gracious, Sarah, why are you in such a hurry?'

'Oh, Betty, I didn't see you,' Sarah gasped, reeling from the shock. 'I'm on my way to Clemmie's office. Come along with me,' she said, grabbing Betty's elbow and hurrying her friend along the corridor before they were spotted by the store manager, or his friend, the floorwalker. 'It's good to see you,' she whispered, after looking over her shoulder. 'To what do we owe the honour?'

'I came to see if I could be of help, after your house fire. First, to invite you all to dinner on Sunday, and then to see what long-term help I could offer.'

'That's frightfully decent of you,' Sarah said as she tapped on Clemmie's door, and they were both hurried inside, before Clemmie locked the door and closed the small hatch window, fastening it so that no one could look in from outside.

'Hello, Mother,' she said, giving Betty a quick kiss on her powdered cheek. 'Two for the price of one,' she went on, looking nervously between Sarah and Betty, before offering them a seat each. 'I know I'm new at this job, but I'm pretty certain I've discovered something.'

Betty frowned. Forgetting that she was no longer employed by F. W. Woolworths, she moved close to the desk to look at the open ledger. 'What appears to be the problem?' she asked, before looking back at Sarah. 'You don't mind me looking?'

'Be my guest,' Sarah replied, knowing that Betty knew her way around the cash books far better than she did. 'I can see from here.'

'It's till number six, which is situated on the cosmetics counter. For the past five days the takings have been down. Here, look at my figures,' Clemmie said, flicking through the pages covered with columns of neat handwriting until she reached the current week's figures. Running her finger down the column, she pointed to the total. 'This is fifty per cent lower than what the till usually takes.'

'Hmm, I see what you mean,' Betty said as she looked between the current week and the preceding weeks. 'Can you see this, Sarah? Would there be any reason that the till wasn't in use?'

'Not at all,' Sarah replied, looking puzzled as she moved closer to the desk. 'That till is situated at the end of the counter, close to the main doors of the store . . .'

'You don't think there's been a theft, do you?' Clemmie asked.

'I doubt it, as one of the counter staff would have noticed. We should check the till, in case it is faulty and money has slipped down the back of the drawer.'

'I agree that it should be checked over, but that is far too much money to have disappeared down a crack or slid under the drawer of the till. Fine, if it was notes, but there are odd sums, so coins would have been involved,' Betty said. 'Do you have an idea of how much down you are on takings for this till?'

'Are there any other tills you are concerned about?' Sarah asked at the same time.

Clemmie reached for her notepad and turned it to face the two women. 'I calculate takings on that till alone are down by approximately one hundred and fifty pounds; and yes, there are two other tills that I'm concerned about, although they haven't lost quite as much money.'

'Oh dear,' Sarah said as she sat back in her chair. She felt at a loss to know what to do next, although she had one thought. 'We shouldn't tell Mr Harrison at this point; let's find out a little more. The last thing we want is to have him pointing the finger of blame at the wrong person. I have too many friends and family working in this store and don't want him accusing them out of hand.'

'I agree with you. I know I don't work here, but feel I can help, as I know the workings of the store inside and out,' Betty said, looking to Sarah for her approval.

'Oh, Betty, would you really?' Sarah said, feeling as though a heavy weight had fallen from her shoulders.

Clemmie's eyes shone brightly with unshed tears. 'Thank you, Mother. I've been worried that the finger of blame would fall on me. I can't help feeling that the manager would like to see me fail, because I am related to you and my boyfriend is an assistant manager at another store.'

'Never fear, my love, never fear,' Betty said as she hugged her stepdaughter tightly. 'I'll never let that happen.'

*

'Open up in there!'

Freda woke and stretched her limbs; napping on her sofa during the day never felt right, but if William was sleeping she took the opportunity anyway. 'Give me a minute,' she called back, recognizing Maisie's voice. Slipping her feet into her comfortable slippers, she hobbled towards the front, holding her back. 'Don't you realize there's a pregnant woman in here,' she called out good-naturedly.

'Excuses, excuses,' Maisie laughed as she entered the house, enveloping her friend in a bear hug that smelt of the February chill. 'I come bearing gifts.'

'In that case, get yourself inside while I close the door. Make yourself useful and get the kettle on while I put more coal on the fire. I've never seen a more miserable day,' she said, peering out at the fog that was still hanging in the air, although it was almost midday.

Maisie pushed a large brown paper carrier bag into her arms. 'As my official guinea pig, I want you to try these,' she ordered before disappearing into the kitchen.

'Crikey, you've been busy,' Freda replied as she struggled into the front room, putting the bag on the sofa that she'd just vacated and delving inside.

'It's part of my new range. It was chilly in the factory, and it made me wonder about pregnant women keeping warm in the cold weather,' Maisie said, appearing with a tea towel in her hand as she dried a teacup.

'From the magazines I've read, I thought clothing manufacturers worked a season ahead,' Freda replied, as she pulled out a soft woollen coat in a voluminous style. 'This is gorgeous and would see a woman carrying triplets all the way through her pregnancy,' she said, hugging the coat close.

'I manufacture in a small way, mainly to fill my three shops, so I can please myself. My Claudette is sketching designs all the time for later in the year, and I've had the girls run up a few samples, so who knows what the future will bring.'

'Hang on a minute. Did you say three shops? Have I missed something?' Freda asked, forgetting for a moment that she had one arm inside the coat, as Maisie grinned back at her.

'That's why I'm not at the factory. I met David and we went to sign all the legal stuff; he won't let me do it on my own, as I don't read the small print,' she laughed. 'This new shop's in Dartford, in the High Street close to Woolworths. I reckon we can be in there by the end of March.'

'As quick as that? I'll come and help, if you like; that's if you can make use of me and have a toilet that you don't have to share with the undertaker next door?' Freda grimaced, recalling how the first Maisie's Modes shared facilities with the premises next door, belonging to Maisie's husband, David. 'Of course I'd need to be able to park William's pram somewhere.'

'Your help would be fantastic, and I promise you I can give you a job sitting down close to the kitchen, and near the door to the staff loo. You can also be a model for the maternity collection. If customers spot you in our clothing, they may be tempted to spend more. I reckon they'd come in the shop just to drool over your adorable son,' she said, peering to where William was tucked up in a blanket, snoozing on the settee.

Freda smiled. 'I'm not sure I'll be much of a model, but I'll shout from the rooftops that you are a wonderful dressmaker and designer,' she smiled. 'Thank you, all the same. I was beginning to feel as though I was worthless.'

Maisie was about to give her a tongue-lashing when she remembered the time when she was carrying baby Ruby and felt alone and so scared. 'I was the same; I felt as though I didn't fit in anywhere. Do you remember how David packed me off to his parents' house and I thought I didn't fit in, what with them being toffs? So much so that I ran away and just made it back here before giving birth.'

'Almost on the doorstep of Woolies,' Freda giggled. 'Rather you than me.'

'It frightened the hell out of me at the time, but you were all so lovely and helped me; it put my mind at ease. I only wish my Bessie didn't have to find that out when she was so young – and unmarried.'

'Speaking of which, when is she moving in with me? I'm looking forward to helping care for young Jenny,' Freda asked, not wishing to mention Bessie's lack of a husband, or even a boyfriend, to stick by her. 'I've made room for Jenny's small bed in the back bedroom next to Bessie's room, and I thought I'd move William in there as well. He sleeps through the night now.'

'Are you sure Tony is fine with having a lodger with a baby? I was talking to my David about it, and he thought perhaps when Tony was home on his fleeting visits you'd both like to be alone. In fact we've had an idea about that . . .'

'You haven't changed your mind, have you?'

'No, we thought that when Tony was home, Bessie could come back to visit us, so to speak, and give you some time alone. You won't get much of that, once the second baby arrives.'

'Oh, honestly, Maisie. You only live at the top of the road. You talk as though you are going to miss her.'

'Believe me, I would miss her even if she moved next door. I love her and Claudette as much as the kiddies I gave birth to. I only work as hard as I do to provide them with a good start in life, even if I can't find a home large enough to keep them all under one roof.'

'Give it time. And for now Bessie and Jenny are welcome here for as long as it takes. In fact move her in today, as I could do with the company. Now, do you have time for tea and a few biscuits?' Freda asked, heaving herself out of her chair just as the telephone rang. 'Stick the kettle on the hob while I answer this. It may be my husband,' she said hopefully.

'Crikey, I thought you'd still be chatting to Tony,' Maisie said as she nudged the door open with her elbow when she struggled in with the tea tray ten minutes later. 'I was going to vanish again, if you were whispering sweet nothings,' she grinned.

Freda's face was troubled. 'That was Betty on the phone; she wants us all to meet this evening, as there is a problem at the store. I suggested they all come here after work and have a bite to eat at the same time.'

'Hmm, that doesn't sound good.'

'I thought the same. Whatever has happened?'

They both fell silent, thinking the worst, until Maisie piped up, 'Don't worry about feeding us. I'll pick up fish and chips, then none of us will have to be in the kitchen, if Betty is bringing sad news.'

*

'Any news?' Vera asked before Ruby had even sat down.

Ruby hadn't been looking forward to telling Vera they'd not yet tracked down her long-lost son. She feared what she had to say would have Vera relapsing, as lately the thought of meeting her son was what Vera had been living for. 'For goodness' sake, give me time to sit down,' Ruby said as she passed her coat to Sadie.

'Nan's talked of nothing else,' Sadie called out. 'I admit to wanting to hear more myself,' she replied as she hung Ruby's coat on the hall stand and joined them in the front room. 'I'm looking forward to having an uncle.'

Ruby felt sad for Sadie having to put up with Vera, who could blow hot and cold at the best of times. 'I'll get straight to the point.'

'Would you like a hot drink?' Sadie asked as she hovered by the door.

'Sit yourself down and listen,' Ruby said kindly. 'It's best you know what we've found out.'

'I thought you'd have found him by now,' Vera huffed, before starting to cough. 'Don't tell me you've had no luck?' she added once she'd caught her breath.

'We have and we haven't,' Ruby said, watching Vera to see how the news affected her.

'What do you mean by that, and who are the "we" that you mention?'

'Now, now, Vera, you know I'd told Bob and my George, as I needed help and George has contacts.'

'That's very good of him to help,' Sadie said. 'Mr Caselton will be sympathetic, Nan.'

'That's all well and good, but who will he tell, and who

will they gossip with? Before you know it, the whole of Erith will know that I have a son I gave away . . .'

Ruby flinched, knowing Vera wouldn't like what she had to say next. 'Bob and George spoke to Mike—'

'Mike Jackson? Well, now the coppers are in on my secret.'

Ruby grew red in the face as she tried to control her temper. No one could say anything nasty about her family. 'Mike happens to be my stepson and, as a member of my family, I trust his judgement. Just because he happens to be a policeman, and a very good one at that, it doesn't mean he snitches to his bosses. It's not as if your son is wanted by the law, is it?'

Vera fell silent for a while as she digested Ruby's words. Even she knew better than to answer back when Ruby defended her family. 'I don't want too many people knowing,' she added belligerently.

'In that case, perhaps I shouldn't share what Mike found out?'

Vera's eyes opened wide and her cough stopped abruptly. 'Tell me, where is my son?' she demanded.

'He has moved to Spain and isn't expected back until next year at the earliest,' Ruby explained, without adding that Mike had misgivings about why the man had left the country.

'It'll be business. He's a successful businessman and doing well.' Vera nodded sagely.

Ruby sighed. Already Vera was forming a story in her head that bore no resemblance to the truth.

15

~

'There's nothing to beat a meal I've not had to prepare myself.' Maisie sighed as she pushed away her empty plate and looked around the dining table at her friends, Freda, Sarah and Betty. Clemmie had joined them as well, but had hardly eaten one chip, and the battered fish had been left untouched.

'Perhaps we should have had our chat first,' Sarah said, noticing how quiet the young girl was. 'Clemmie, none of this is your fault, you know.'

'I'll put your food in the oven to keep warm,' Freda said as she took the untouched meal, placing a clean plate on top to stop it drying out. 'Shall we take our tea into the front room and get this over and done with? I'm aching to know what you've discovered. You may have said that it's trouble at Woolies to put our minds at rest, but I'm all agog to know the details.'

Betty led the way into the cosy front room and closed the curtains that hung in the bay window. 'Sit yourself down, Clemmie, and stop looking so worried. This is where your college training will come in handy.'

'Now I'm intrigued,' Maisie said as she handed Freda her tea and urged her to sit down. 'Spill the beans, Sarah!'

Sarah stared into the warm glow of the coal fire, trying to think where to start. Once she'd decided, she looked around the room and blurted out, 'Someone is stealing the takings from Woolworths.'

'Bloody hell, I didn't expect that,' Maisie choked, before wiping tea that had spilt down the front of her cardigan. 'You've obviously got proof of this, so why have you not gone to management about it?'

'Because we feel management is involved,' Clemmie said, no longer able to hold back the tears. 'I discovered this, and as I am the one counting the money from each of the tills, I'm worried I will get the blame.' She sniffed as Maisie put down her cup, enveloping the girl in her arms and soothing her until she calmed down.

'Don't think for one moment we will allow anyone ter blame yer. Why, yer Betty Billington's daughter, and no one in their right mind would accuse yer of doing anything wrong,' she said indignantly, her anger causing her to lose the way she spoke, now that she was a business owner, and resorting to her East End voice.

'Let's not get overexcited until we know all the facts,' Freda suggested. 'However, I do feel that if it is members of management that we believe are involved, they may resent a member of Betty's family working here in a responsible position, and may try to place the blame on her.'

Sarah was shocked by Freda's words and the colour drained from her face. 'I should not have given you such a responsible position,' she apologized. 'I'll have you moved from your office duties at once; better still, perhaps you should reconsider finding an office job in London?'

'No!' both Clemmie and Betty said at the same time.

'If I'm moved and these shortages are noticed, people may think I am guilty and that is why I've been moved,' Clemmie said, looking alarmed.

'It will also alert the guilty party to realize that we are on to them,' Betty added. 'We shall have to put our thinking caps on and come up with a plan.'

The room fell silent as the girls sipped their tea, thinking of a way ahead, with Maisie being unable to keep quiet for long before asking which tills were involved.

'There are six tills spread around the store,' Clemmie started to explain, 'although some days the takings are comparable to what they were before all this started.'

Maisie frowned. 'Bloody hell, how did you even notice that? You must be a whizz with figures!'

Clemmie blushed. 'I enjoyed learning such things at college.'

'And she is so quick at adding up on the comptometer that head office sent down to us, and which we shied away from,' Sarah said, looking proudly at the young girl. 'I'd never doubt you, Clemmie. However, just so the rest of you can see for yourself, I've brought home some pages from the cash book where the till takings are listed,' she went on, reaching down to the side of her armchair, where she'd placed a large shopping bag when she arrived. 'I'll have them back in the ledgers first thing tomorrow, before Mr Harrison notices they are missing; not that he ever looks at them,' she added, passing round the pages as Clemmie explained them.

Betty was thoughtful. 'Have you compared the staff on duty with the days the tills are low on takings, Sarah?'

'Gosh, I never gave that a thought. I can check that tomorrow morning.'

'I'll make a list of dates and counters this evening, and that way you won't be seen to be making notes at work,' Clemmie said.

'Are you saying Mr Harrison is involved in some way?' Freda asked.

'We can't prove anything at this time, but I do know he won't take any notice of what we say, as he is always so dismissive of the female staff and likes to point the finger at us when things go wrong. Look at how that floorwalker's personnel file went missing, and he had the audacity to blame me.'

Freda shook her head. 'How was that resolved?'

Sarah grimaced, recalling how she had spotted it under the blotter on her desk. She knew she'd not put it there. And how Mr Harrison had crowed when she informed him it had been found. 'I didn't like to say that much of the contents of the file were missing.'

Maisie looked disgusted. 'The blighter must have removed the paperwork, but why? Do you think he and Mr Argent knew each other before they came to the Erith store, and Harrison is covering up for him? Perhaps he has a dodgy past?' Maisie said as she started to build her version of events.

'Hold on, I don't think we should get overexcited about this,' Betty said. 'Let's stick to the facts and figures in front of us.'

Maisie fell silent for a few seconds as she thought of

Betty's words. 'All the same, it must be hell working there. It's time you were back in charge, Betty, as you always ran a tight ship.'

The girls all agreed, although Freda was thoughtful as she looked down into her lap. She would keep her counsel for today, while they worked together to sort out the problem at the store, but she so wanted to remind them that she'd prayed Tony would return to work at the Erith store, once his Olympic duties were over. It had been intimated more than once that he would make a good manager. 'When I next speak to Tony, I'll ask him what he knows about our Mr Harrison, but I'll not mention the problems you have with him,' she said, seeing a look of alarm cross Sarah's face. 'I'll ask him in passing, as I don't want word to get back and Harrison being alerted to our suspicions.'

'I'll do the same when I visit some of my former colleagues who now work at head office,' Betty said. She'd been peering at the pages from the ledgers, as Clemmie pointed out irregularities, so she hadn't noticed Freda's disquiet.

The girls were engrossed in making notes and discussing the situation until there was a knock on the door. 'My goodness, is that the time?' Betty exclaimed, looking up at the clock. 'That will be Douglas here to collect us,' she said, getting to her feet from where she'd been kneeling on the floor, looking at the rows of ledger pages lined up in date order. 'We will have to leave it there for tonight,' she said, straightening her skirt. 'Shall we set a date to meet again? I'd best not pop into the store as often, as Harrison may wonder why I'm there.'

'That's a good point,' Sarah said as she helped Clemmie

to fetch the coats and scarves. 'How about next Monday, if that's all right with you, Freda?'

'Most certainly, and this time I'll cook. I've been promised a rabbit by Bob, so we can have a stew.'

Betty licked her lips. 'That sound delicious. I've not had rabbit in years,' she replied as Clemmie wrinkled her nose. 'I'll bring cake, to have with one of our copious rounds of tea. Are you sure you won't be meeting Jimmy?' she asked her daughter.

Clemmie shook her head. 'No, I'll make sure to keep that evening free. I'll be seeing him on the Sunday, so he can't complain,' she said shyly, as the older women pulled her leg about courting her Jimmy.

'It makes me feel so old,' Maisie laughed as they closed the front door after bidding their friends goodbye. 'Shall we have another half-hour on this before we call it a night?'

Sarah rubbed her eyes. 'Yes, let's do that. If I go home now, I'll only have to clear up after Alan. I left him to prepare the children's meal,' she sighed. 'I just hope he hasn't bought fish and chips again. If he doesn't finish sorting out the kitchen, I swear the kids will turn into a chip before too long.'

'At least you were able to enjoy your fish and chips in peace with us,' Freda sympathized.

'Let's have pease pudding and faggots when we next meet, to save you cooking,' Maisie suggested.

Freda wrinkled her nose. 'No, thank you. That is something I've never taken to since moving down here that and rock salmon – oh, and jellied eels,' she said with a grimace. 'I said I'll cook, and I will. In fact I'll make extra, so you can take some back for the children, Sarah.'

'That's very good of you,' Sarah replied. 'It may shame Alan into pulling his finger out and sorting out the mess. I've done all I can.'

'Can't your dad help? I know he's handy around the house?' Maisie suggested.

Sarah sighed. 'I don't like to ask him; he has his own job to do, along with his councillor's work. He also steps in to help with the children, along with Maureen. I'm lucky to have their help, as I'd not be able to work otherwise. No, I'm just going to have to hire a builder to put things right. Alan won't like it, as he has a bee in his bonnet about doing it himself, but we can't live like this much longer,' she added with a tremble to her voice. 'It's bad enough that we have outgrown the house and the children are having to share a room; what we will do in a year or so when they get a little older, I don't know.'

'I feel rather guilty, when I'm here on my own with three bedrooms,' Freda replied, looking glum.

'Oh no, please don't talk like that,' Sarah pleaded. 'I wish I'd not said anything now; ignore me. Besides, you have William, and Tony will soon be home and then the baby will be here, and of course young Bessie is moving in with Jenny.'

Maisie looked between her friends. 'I don't know what we'd do without Freda and Tony's help. Our house is bursting at the seams, and I've threatened more than once to put the twins in the coal shed to make more room,' she chuckled. 'We shouldn't complain, as one day we will be sitting here bemoaning the fact that our children have all left home and we are rattling around, with only our husbands to talk to, and knitting for our grandchildren.'

'God forbid!' Sarah said in mock horror. 'Let's forget all about it for now and sort this mess out,' she said, waving one of the ledger pages in the air. 'When I'm in my office and Mr Harrison isn't likely to walk in, I'm going to make notes against the dates about who was working on those counters. Thank goodness Betty taught me how to keep detailed staff-duty records.'

'But can you prove anything? It's not as if you can point a finger at the counter assistants?' Freda said.

Sarah gave a cunning smile. 'Not really, but I've noticed all these tills are tucked away from the main aisles, so if we have staff on the fiddle, then I can control who works on those counters and move the ones who currently work there. After a couple of weeks we can compare Clemmie's figures to see if there are any changes. What do you think?'

'I think you're a bloody marvel!' Maisie declared, as Freda slapped Sarah on the back and congratulated her on her plan.

'I'd love to be a fly on the wall when you are able to point a finger at the culprits,' she grinned.

Sarah gulped. 'I'd not thought that far ahead.'

The next day Sarah found it hard to keep to her schedule. The morning had started off on the wrong foot when Alan, up before everyone else, sat at the table drinking tea, with his nose in a trade magazine while the children ran about, still in their nightclothes.

'Come along now, let's get you ready for school,' she called out, clapping her hands for attention. 'Alan, can you put the porridge on, so your children don't go to school on empty stomachs? At least we don't have to worry about that dreadful fog any more,' she said as she chased the children upstairs. 'Did I tell you about the time it was so foggy Nanny Ruby tied us all together, so we didn't get lost?' she asked, causing the children to shriek with laughter.

'I'm off, love,' Alan called up the stairs. 'I shouldn't be late home tonight.'

Sarah cursed to herself as she hurried back downstairs. 'Alan . . .' She was too late, as she heard the gate close behind him. 'Oh, for heaven's sake,' she muttered to herself. 'I feel as though I'm the only one who cares about this family.'

'Mummy, there's a funny smell in the kitchen,' Buster complained, sidling up to her and taking her hand.

Sarah ran into the next room and her worst fears were confirmed. Alan had put the porridge on the stove before leaving the house. 'Toast for breakfast,' she smiled, through gritted teeth, throwing the burnt pan into the sink.

'Mrs Gilbert?'

Sarah brought herself back to the present as Jessie approached her. 'I'm sorry, I was miles away. Can I help you?'

'I wondered if I could have a word about our stock?'

Sarah frowned. 'Surely you should be speaking to Mr Harrison or one of the stockroom workers?'

Jessie blushed. 'It's rather difficult . . .'

'Oh, I see. In that case, can you give me an idea of your problem, while your counter is quiet?' she asked, stepping behind the counter.

'I know I've not worked here long, but I'm confused about the way our stock is brought down to us. As you can see, we are quite low on sweets, but the lad who carried down our supplies this morning told me we were up to date with the list that I'd sent to replenish the counter.'

Sarah looked along the counter and Jessie was right. Instead of brimming with an array of different sweets for customers to select, the 'Pick-'n'-Mix' section looked depleted, although the shelves containing boxes of chocolates and other packaged delights were full. 'Show me the stock sheets,' she said, holding out her hand.

'That's the strange thing. The lists have gone missing. I usually keep copies on the shelf under the till, and they are mostly to remind me what I've asked the lads to bring from the stockroom, in case I forget and submit them again. It can be manic here at weekends and when the children are out of school.'

'Hmm,' Sarah said as she helped to check under the counters for the missing lists. 'You are right, they must have been taken away by the cleaners.' But in her heart of hearts, she knew that wasn't true. 'Leave this with me and I'll see if I can come up with something. For now, let's keep this between ourselves, eh?'

'Thank you, Mrs Gilbert. I knew I was right to speak to you,' Jessie said with a look of relief.

'Any time. I'd hate to think the staff were unhappy in their work.'

'I love working here. I wish I'd been brave enough to apply years ago.'

'I'm glad you have,' Sarah said as she moved on through the store, identifying the counters with tills that had dropped their takings, while wondering about the cause.

'Mrs Gilbert, I'll be leaving early as I have an appointment before lunch,' Mr Harrison said, as she bumped into him upon her return upstairs to her office. 'I assume you will be able to cope while I'm away?' he enquired pompously.

'I'm sure I can manage,' she replied, giving him a sweet smile. Any other time she'd have been seething at his condescending words. However, it suited her to be able to have some uninterrupted time to work on the problem of the missing takings and the lack of stock on the confectionery counter. Walking into her office, she rubbed her hands together, raring to get stuck in.

16

'Erith four-five-five, Mrs Jackson speaking,' Ruby said warily, wishing Bob was about to answer the telephone. What if it was bad news?

'Ruby? It's me, Maisie.'

'What's wrong?' Ruby asked, clutching the telephone receiver tightly.

Maisie guffawed, causing Ruby to hold the telephone away from her ear before realizing she needed to hold it close. 'There's nothing wrong,'

'Then why couldn't you walk down the road to tell me whatever it is you want to say?'

'Because I'm in Dartford, working in my new shop,' Maisie chuckled.

Ruby frowned. It astounded her how someone could talk to her all the way from Dartford. She would never understand how a telephone worked and, much as George and Bob explained it to her, became ever more befuddled. 'What is it you want to tell me?' she asked, taking her handkerchief out of the pocket of the floral crossover pinny she was wearing and dabbing at invisible marks on the telephone.

'Are you doing anything this evening?'

'Cooking Bob's dinner, but I can do it earlier, if you want me to come and sit with the kiddies?'

Bless her, Maisie thought. 'No, I don't need your help; I want you to come out with me and the girls. There's an *Old Mother Riley* film on at the Odeon, and I know you enjoy them.'

'Oh, I do; she is such a funny actress.'

Maisie smiled to herself. As much as they kept telling Ruby the character was played by an actor called Arthur Lucan, she would insist it was a woman playing the part. 'I'll knock on your door at six o'clock, then we can collect Freda from across the road before banging on Sarah's door. By the way, keep it to yourself, as I'm making it a surprise for her; she's been so down lately, what with the fire and her unpleasant boss.'

'That's a good idea. You know I told her to hand in her notice. No one should work where they aren't happy. It's not as if they need the money these days, what with Alan's shop doing so well.'

'She loves it there and would be miserable if she ever left. To be honest, I'd be back working at Woolies like a shot, if this business folded.'

'And it will, if you sit chatting to me all day long. Be off with you, so I can sort out Bob and put his dinner in the oven. Corned-beef hash won't cook itself.'

Maisie was chuckling as she put down the receiver and turned to Freda, who was busy putting price labels onto a pile of jumpers. 'I adore that woman.'

'And I adore these cardigans; wherever did you get them?'

'I have a team of women who live in Slade Green who knit them for me; it's another of my new ideas. I've had another idea . . .'

'Whatever next? I can't keep up with you.'

'You will like this one. When I drive you home, why not stay for your tea at my place. Bessie will be there too and will care for William for the evening; it seems daft for you to cook for yourself. Besides, I need you to remind me to take the tin of paint and the rolls of paper with me. Claudette's going to help me carry them to Sarah's house. I just hope Alan won't be annoyed.'

'We will soon find out.' Freda grimaced, wondering if Maisie's plan would cause an upset between the friends.

'It will be fine,' Maisie grinned. 'You sound like my David; he was unsure of my plan when I asked him to collect the decorating materials from the ironmonger's yesterday.'

Freda gave a nervous smile, still unsure of the outcome.

'You look very smart,' Bob said as Ruby came downstairs in her best coat and hat. 'Blue has always suited you.'

'I thought I'd make the effort, as Maisie is treating me,' she said, giving a little twirl before grabbing the edge of his armchair to right herself.

'Steady there,' Bob said, reaching out and taking hold of her arm. 'People will think you've been on the gin.'

'At this time of the day?' she chuckled. 'Not that I'm keen on the stuff at any time; a nice glass of port and lemon is more to my liking.'

'Will you be stopping off after, at the Prince of Wales? If you are, I'll walk round and join you.'

'I doubt it, as the girls all have to be in work tomorrow, apart from Freda. She'll be wanting to collect young William, apart from wanting her bed, in her condition. If you like, I'll stop off and pick up saveloy and chips for your supper?'

Bob licked his lips. 'They'd go down a treat. I'll make

sure to put the hot-water bottles in our bed and have the fire stoked up. It's nippy out there.'

There was a knock at the door, with Maisie calling through the letter box, 'It's only me!'

'Don't come out or you'll catch your death,' Ruby said, pulling on her best gloves and kissing Bob on the cheek. 'I'll see you later.'

'Hello, Claudette, are you joining us?' Ruby asked as she spotted one of Maisie's girls standing by her mum, with arms full of rolls of wallpaper. 'Why are you holding those?'

'It's a surprise for Uncle Alan. I'm helping carry these for Mum, then I'm back home to keep an eye on the kids.'

Maisie's mouth twitched. 'You could say Sarah needs a helping hand to get that kitchen of hers finished, before she lynches Alan.'

Ruby linked her arm into Freda's and they set off on the short walk to Sarah's house. 'I'm pleased someone is doing something. You know I offered to put them all up, but Sarah wouldn't hear of it?'

'She can be obstinate at times, but I hope she isn't offended by the gift,' Freda replied. 'You do look smart, Ruby,' she added, trying to change the subject.

'So do you. Is this a new coat?'

'Maisie treated me; it's from the stock in her new shop.'

'I did not treat you.' Maisie huffed as she moved the can of emulsion paint she was carrying from one hand to the other. 'I paid you in kind, as you wouldn't take money for working at my shop. She's been a big help, Ruby.'

'Then you deserve the coat, Freda,' Ruby said, admiring the garment as they walked past a street lamp that lit up the pavement. 'I may come and work for you myself,' she laughed. 'I could do with replacing my unmentionables.'

'Oh, Nanny Ruby, you are a one!' Claudette reprimanded Ruby for sounding like an old lady.

When Ruby stopped laughing, she patted the girl's head. 'You should be on the stage, my girl.'

'She's going to be,' Maisie said as the turned into Crayford Road. 'Our Claudette has joined the local amateur dramatics group. She will be on the stage at Christmas in their pantomime.'

'That's if we can get some more male performers; we need some men who can sing,' Claudette sighed.

'Ask Alan, he has a wonderful singing voice,' Freda suggested.

'But not until he's finished Sarah's kitchen,' Maisie said as they reached the gate to the Gilberts' house. 'Bang on the door, Freda, I've got my hands full.'

'No need,' Alan said as he opened the door and ushered the women inside. 'I heard you chattering as you came through the gate.'

Freda looked sideways at Maisie, as they both wondered if he had heard what they were talking about.

'Whatever have you got there?' Sarah asked as she greeted her friends. 'Is this a delegation or something?'

'We are here to whisk you off to the pictures with us. And these are for you, Alan,' Maisie said as they placed the decorating materials on the dining table. 'Call them a gift from my family, as we've not been around to help you much since the fire.'

Sarah beamed as she peered at the wallpaper. 'That's so kind of you. Look, Alan, that's the paper I told you about. How did you know I liked this, Maisie?'

'Don't you remember I was with you when you stopped to admire it in the window display?'

'Oh, of course, silly me.'

Alan stood there looking glum, before forcing a smile on his face. 'I'll see if I can start this at the weekend.'

Ruby, who had been watching his reaction to the gift, piped up. 'I'll have Bob come round and give you a hand on Sunday, and you can all have Sunday dinner with me, so the job gets finished.'

'My David said he'd help as well,' Maisie chipped in. 'Many hands make light work, as they say.'

'They also say too many cooks spoil the broth,' Alan replied, before breaking into a smile. 'Thank you all. I've been wondering how I could find time to get this done. Sorry for not getting things sorted sooner, love,' he said, kissing Sarah. 'Now go and get your coat on or you'll miss the B film. I hear it's one of Johnny Johnson's old films,' he said, winking at Freda, who had a soft spot for the actor.

Freda sighed. 'I adore watching the Clive Danvers spy films. He can still make my heart flutter.'

'Then let's get cracking, before Freda comes over all peculiar,' Ruby said, ushering them towards the front door. 'Claudette, why don't you stay and tell Alan about the amateur dramatics? Now that the decorating will soon be completed, he might be interested in joining you.'

'Look, there's Nanny Ruby with my aunts,' Clemmie said, from where she sat arm in arm with her Jimmy in the stalls of Erith Odeon, as the older women walked closer to the large screen.

185

He smiled indulgently. 'I adore the names you use, even though they aren't blood relatives.'

'They all mean so much to me and feel more like relatives than the few I have. My mum feels the same too. Or would you rather I called Betty my stepmother?'

Jimmy raised his hands in surrender. 'I'll not argue with you. I'm going to find it daunting having Betty Billington as my mother-in-law one day, let along calling her by the wrong name.'

Clemmie snuggled as close as she could, with an armrest between them. 'I can't wait to be your wife,' she sighed.

'I promised your dad we'd wait a year or two. It's asking a lot of you to take on me and my children.'

'I know, but I've been thinking about that . . .'

Jimmy groaned. 'That sounds ominous. Are you suggesting we have the children adopted?'

'Don't even joke about such things,' she said, thumping his arm. 'Seriously, and I know this isn't the right place to discuss such things, but I don't want there to be too large an age gap between any children we have.'

Jimmy was quiet for a moment. 'For my part, I don't want you to feel as though you've missed out on having fun with your friends. Marrying and having children is a big step to take. I'm nearly ten years older than you, and I'm grateful your parents have accepted me. I don't want to upset them, when they've been so welcoming. We need to think about this and take advice from your extended family.'

She gave him a beguiling look. 'People do say I'm mature for my years and, with you looking so youthful, no one would notice our age difference. Besides, in a couple of months we will both be in our twenties.'

Jimmy laughed. 'Just because you are clever with figures doesn't mean you can make us any closer in age, as a month after you are twenty I will be thirty. Imagine us in our twilight years, when you will moan about pushing me around in my bath chair and wiping dribble from my chin. Let's be sensible and consider how our life would be if you were a young mother and missed out on fun with your friends.'

'You're right. I'll have a chat with Bessie Carlisle.'

Jimmy frowned as the lights started to go down. 'What, Bessie who got herself pregnant at the age of sixteen and whose boyfriend got his collar felt by the police . . . ?'

Clemmie thumped his arm a second time. 'Don't be so stuffy; she's a decent sort and has her head screwed on right these days,' she hissed as someone in the row behind them tapped her on the shoulder and told her to be quiet.

'Hello, Aunt Sarah, are you enjoying the film?' Clemmie asked as she hurried down the aisle to speak to her aunts during the intermission.

'Oh, hello, Clemmie. Nan thought she spotted you and Jimmy as we came in. I am enjoying myself; it's such a treat to be able to watch a film without keeping an eye on the children. Buster made an escape once, and I spent half a film searching for him with the help of an usherette. We found him hiding behind the sweet counter in the foyer,' she chuckled.

'You've got your hands full with him,' Clemmie smiled. 'I shall have to come to you for lessons when I have children.'

Sarah raised her eyebrows. Perhaps she'd misheard Betty

when she told her Clemmie had promised not to rush into getting married. 'There's plenty of time for that. I wonder, could you come to see me as soon as you get into work tomorrow? I may have come across something to do with the till shortages and I would like your input. I want Betty's advice as well, so we could meet her at lunchtime and have a chat.'

'I'm relieved you've found something, as I've been worried.'

Sarah laid her hand on the girl's arm. 'Don't be. Now go and enjoy the film,' she told her as the lights started to lower.

17

'Thank you for getting in so early,' Sarah said as Clemmie entered her office just after eight o'clock the next morning.

'I caught the earlier bus and one of the cleaners let me in,' Clemmie replied, unbuttoning her coat and removing a jaunty felt hat. 'I can't say I slept well, wondering what you'd uncovered. Is it enough for you to be able to bring someone to account?'

'It's still early days. I'm afraid my detective work is not as fast or slick as the spy Clive Danvers is in his films,' she smiled.

Clemmie sighed. 'It was a wonderful film; I preferred it to *Old Mother Riley*. I could watch Johnny Johnson all day long, although my Jimmy doesn't agree with me.'

'Neither does my Alan. Men aren't as enamoured of handsome actors as we tend to be. Now, let me pull out my notes and I'll show you what I've discovered. Would you lock the door, please? It will give me time to hide the papers if Mr Harrison should wish to come in. Tell me, how easy is it for you to cry?'

Clemmie frowned. 'Cry? Is what you've found that upsetting?'

Sarah chuckled. 'I always find that if a male member of staff comes across a female crying, he will soon leave the room. Mr Harrison is no exception.'

'Ah, I get what you mean. I'll have my handkerchief handy in case he comes in, and I will sob into it as much as I can. Boyfriend trouble perhaps?'

'That should do it. Now look at this list first . . .'

Sarah passed her a list of the tills that had shown lower takings of late and, next to it, one of the staff working on those counters. 'Can you see a pattern?'

Clemmie picked up her pencil and, after reading the list several times, started to put small crosses next to some of the counters and tills. 'There seem to be a couple of newer staff working on these counters on the days when the takings are lower. I'm not saying the staff are stealing money, but there's definitely some kind of pattern. I'd hate to point my finger at anyone before we've investigated more,' she said, looking worried. 'What are your thoughts?'

Sarah knew she was right to ask Clemmie for advice; the girl had a quick eye and hadn't missed anything on the list. 'There are two other things: one is that we have a floorwalker covering that area of the store on the same days that the tills are taking less money.'

'Mr Argent?'

'Yes, spot on! Also, I've found what I feel is some fiddling going on with stock ordered by staff on the confectionery counter that is not arriving from the stockroom. Jessie brought it to my attention, and I plan to set a trap to see what, or I should say who, is at the bottom of things.'

Clemmie looked worried. 'Perhaps we should hand this

over to Mr Harrison for him to investigate; he can't really ignore this, can he?'

Sarah sucked in her breath. 'What I've not said yet is that I feel he already knows about it.'

Clemmie was incredulous. 'You mean he has brushed it under the carpet?'

'Well, no . . . I'm beginning to feel he has turned a blind eye – or he is involved in some way. I don't have concrete proof; it is simply my gut feeling.'

Clemmie frowned. 'Then perhaps it is best we keep this from him for the time being. I can see why you have taken precautions in case he should walk in. I thought it was more because he liked to poke his nose into your work.'

'That as well,' Sarah smiled ruefully. 'It's something that happens with some male bosses; we get used to it.'

'What is your plan for the confectionery counter problem?'

'I'm about to shuffle the staff rota.'

'I don't understand. How will that help?'

Sarah reached for a buff-coloured folder and pulled out a sheet headed with staff duties for the next week. 'I plan to be a spy, like Clive Danvers, except I'll be operating in Woolies rather than Berlin,' she said, pursing her lips.

Clemmie took the proffered sheet of paper. 'How can you spy on an unknown foe?'

'It helps to have friends I can trust,' she explained, pointing to the names of staff who had been moved to the problematic counters.

'Do you not trust all your counter staff, as you hired them?'

'It was while I was puzzling over the problem that I

noticed the names of the few staff Mr Harrison had hired while I had a week off just after Christmas, then came back to find a new floorwalker and three new counter staff. I may be wrong, but . . .'

'I don't feel you are wrong. In fact, add me onto the list and I can cover while your spies are at their lunch breaks, so the counters are never left alone with the foes.' She looked at Sarah and grinned. 'Next we will have to use passwords and wear dark glasses. I wonder what Mother will say about all this?'

'Come to lunch with me and Betty and you will find out.'

'I will, thank you. And now I'd better get to my office and prepare for the first money collection of the day. I'm on my own today, so I need a little more time to count the takings.'

'You won't be alone, as I'll come in and help you. It has been some time since I worked in the cash office, so I want to be up to speed, in case questions are asked once the problem becomes common knowledge. Be sure to knock on my door before you take the cash into your office.'

'I'll do that,' Clemmie said, heading off to catch up with her work.

Betty was quiet as she checked the detailed pages that Sarah handed to her when they met for lunch. All three had agreed not to discuss the problem until they'd eaten their meal of fried egg with bubble and squeak, but even so, as they chatted about family and children, it hung over them like the elephant in the room.

Clemmie pushed her half-eaten plate of food away from her. 'It was a good idea to eat at the railway cafe rather than at Mitchell's, in case we'd been spotted, but I seem to have lost my appetite. I see you've not eaten much, Mum?'

'I just want to see what the pair of you have come up with. I must say, you've worked flat out since we met at Freda's.'

'It was easy, with all the information to hand, and I had a good teacher.' Sarah smiled. 'What do you think of our idea to move staff around, so that we have, let me say, "knowledgeable staff" observing those tills?'

'I prefer to call them spies,' Clemmie smiled. 'We need reliable staff who have eyes in the back of their heads.'

'I agree with you.' Betty was thoughtful. 'May I hold on to these and think about things? I can drop them in to you later this afternoon. In fact I'll walk down to Douglas's office and use his typewriter.'

A look of relief crossed Sarah's face. 'Thank you so much. I was hoping you would give us the benefit of your knowledge. You must have come across this before in your long career with Woolworths?'

'Not to this extent, but pilfering and fiddles do happen. You should both be commended for noticing, and preparing a plan on how to tackle the problem. In your position, I too would be wary of speaking to the manager. Now, as we didn't eat our meal, could you manage suet pudding and custard before you go back to work? I know I could.'

'As long as it is quick, as I have another round of collections to make,' Clemmie said.

'And I will be investigating the case of the missing sweets from the confectionery counter,' Sarah added.

'Curiouser and curiouser,' Betty said as she waved to the waitress to take their order.

*

It was a happier Sarah who returned to work after lunch. Having Betty's input and guidance meant that she knew she was on the right track. Before heading upstairs, she stopped at several counters and asked chosen staff members to come up to her office at set times. Her idea was not to let each staff member know who else was participating in her plan; that way, if Mr Harrison wished to cause trouble, the women would not be able to say who else was helping to track down the thief. Because now Sarah was convinced there was money being taken from the tills, rather than the departments having slow days.

She had an hour before the first counter assistant was due upstairs, so after leaving her coat in the office and straightening her hair and checking her lipstick, she picked up a clipboard and headed to the storeroom.

'Derek?' she called, entering the large storeroom on the first floor.

'Sorry, Mrs Gilbert, he's got a half-day today,' a skinny young lad in an oversized brown overall said. 'Can I help you? I'm Colin.'

A thought came to Sarah almost immediately as she looked at the mousy-haired lad. It suited her plan not to have the storeroom supervisor on duty. 'I was going to ask if he required another worker, now that Sam has retired, but it can wait until another day.' She smiled at the lad, who looked decidedly nervous. 'Are you enjoying working here, Colin?'

'Yes, Mrs Gilbert. I'm keen to learn as much as I can and move up the ladder, so to speak, just as my brother, Sid, has done. He's now a trainee manager in the Dartford store.'

'Do you have any other family members working for Woolworths?' she asked, trying to recall the lad's application form when she interviewed him. 'Isn't it your mother who works on our electrical goods counter?'

'Yes, and my nan is a cleaner,' he added proudly.

'Rather like my family, who have worked here over the years,' she smiled. 'Woolworths seems to attract members of the same family.'

'My sister, Jean, is hoping to work here in the summer when she leaves school.'

'Ask her to come in and see me when she is ready. I'd like to add another member of your family to the payroll. I wonder . . .'

'What's that, Mrs Gilbert?' the lad beamed.

'Would you be able to spare me ten minutes to talk me through how the system works when a counter assistant places an order – that's if you aren't too busy?'

'I can do that,' he said, looking keen to be of assistance. 'I've only been tidying up, then I'll be twiddling my thumbs until we get a delivery in. I can show you how we deal with that as well, if you like?'

'Excellent,' Sarah beamed. 'Lead on.'

Colin showed her how, when an assistant handed in a list of items required to top up the counter, it would be taken to the storeroom where the supervisor, Derek, would complete an official Woolworths docket and instruct Colin, or one of the other lads, to put the stock into boxes and wheel them out to the counters on one of the sack barrows.

'This may sound like a silly question, Colin, but does anyone ever check the list that the girls hand in against the docket, and is it signed for at the counter?'

195

Colin scratched his head. 'It's funny you should mention that, as I asked Derek the same question and he told me not to be impertinent. It may have been a one-off, but when I took a box of cutlery out to the shop floor, it felt light, so I checked. There were half a dozen sets missing from the original order. I did point it out to Derek, but got a clip round the ear for poking my nose in where it didn't belong and telling him how to do his job.'

'Oh dear, if that should happen again, will you inform me? I promise you won't get into trouble. I wonder what happens to the lists the counter assistants give you?'

Colin nodded towards a small stove glowing brightly in the corner of the room. 'Everything goes in there, Mrs Gilbert. Derek is very strict about us getting rid of the rubbish and running a tight ship. The only thing is . . .'

'Go on, Colin, I promise it will go no further.'

'I hung on to some of the lists from the shop floor,' he said, going to a filing cabinet and pulling out a wad of papers from behind the large unit. 'I've marked on each one what was sent back to the counters.'

Sarah flicked through the various pieces of paper. 'I don't quite understand. It looks as though what was ordered had gone out to the counters.' She frowned, thinking back to the confectionery counter and how low it was on stock.

'Then look at this,' he said, going back to the cabinet and pulling out a stock book. 'Derek will kill me,' he said, looking glum, 'but I don't want anyone to think I had a hand in this. My brother told me I had to tell someone, but I was worried I'd get into trouble, what with being the new boy and all.'

Sarah looked over his shoulder as he opened the book, pointing to where Derek had logged the stock that had gone out to the shop floor. 'Oh, my goodness, it has been made to look as though more stock has gone out than really did.'

'Yes, and there were also times when he didn't send out what was asked for, but still booked the full amount in the stock book. I've been that worried about all of this that I even thought about handing in my notice. I would have done so, if it weren't for making it look as though I was the thief.'

'There is no need to think like that, Colin,' Sarah said as she collected the paperwork together to take upstairs. 'If anyone asks, tell them it is an official audit; and why there hadn't been one before now, I don't know . . .'

Deep in thought, she hurried back to her office just as Clemmie appeared with the lunchtime takings.

'Can you spare time to help me count these?' Clemmie asked as Sarah stopped to draw breath and try to collect her thoughts.

'Of course I will. I only hope nothing else untoward crops up today or I swear I will scream.'

Betty was as good as her word and dropped into the store later that day, discreetly passing the paperwork to Sarah, who placed it into her bag. 'I'm not leaving it here for someone to find,' she said. 'What do you think?'

'I need a cup of tea and one of Maureen's sticky buns. That's the thing I miss most about no longer working here.'

'Then let's go to the staff room and catch her before she leaves for the day. You know she is working part-time these days and is an enormous help to me with the children. I couldn't do this job without her and Nan.'

'How are Ruby and Bob?' Betty asked as she followed Sarah out of the office and watched as she locked the door behind her, something she'd never had to do in the past.

'Nan says she is well, but it's noticeable that she has aches and pains and isn't as nippy on her feet as she used to be. As for Bob, well he's the same as he has always been, pottering about in the garden and up on the allotment. I did suggest that my Alan took on the allotment, but both acted as though I'd taken away their sweet ration. Bob huffed that he wasn't ready for a rocking chair and comfy slippers just yet.'

'And Alan?' Betty asked as she steered Sarah towards a free table at the back of the room.

'He reminded me that he was busy with the shop and, if I wanted my cottage with roses round the door, we would need a bigger income.'

Betty chuckled, as the cottage and roses had been Sarah's dream for as long as she could remember. 'It'll happen one day,' she consoled her, as she spotted Maureen wiping down a wooden table and covering it with a clean gingham table-cloth. Maureen hurried over to Betty and gave her a hug.

'Blow me down, we don't see hardly enough of you these days, Betty. Please tell me you've come back and that Harrison chap has been given the boot.'

'Maureen!' Sarah said in a shocked voice, looking round the room in case she'd been overheard, although the manager was universally disliked for his brusque manner and rudeness to the staff.

'Sadly not,' Betty said, 'but never say never.'

'I thought that would be the case. You and Woolies are

joined at the hip. Get yourself back here, woman, where you belong.'

'I'll think about it, but what I could do with right now is a strong cup of tea and a bun, if you have any left. But aren't you just about to finish for the day?'

'Anything for you,' Maureen winked and went back behind her counter, producing two buns from a cake tin, then peering inside a large enamel teapot. 'I'll make a fresh pot; I could do with one myself. Here, take these and I'll join you when the tea's ready.'

Sarah took the two tea plates to the table, trying not to sigh. As much as she loved her mother-in-law and was grateful for all she did, this was time when she needed to be alone with Betty to discuss their problem. 'Sorry about that,' she said quietly as she sat down.

'Not to worry. What I have to say won't take long,' Betty replied, before biting into her bun. 'This is delicious.'

'Are you serious about returning to work? I know you've mentioned it before, but can you fit it in around your family commitments?'

Betty put down the bun and brushed crumbs from her fingers. 'Sarah, I'm shocked by your question; it almost takes women back to before the Great War. Haven't women's rights progressed enough for us to be able to work and have a family life, if we should choose to do so? I know I've taken time off for my family, but I realize it was a mistake.'

Sarah blushed. 'I didn't mean it like that. I know I find it hard to fit everything into my day, and there are times when I wish I could put my feet up and read a book . . .'

'We all have days like that. I confess that motherhood doesn't come naturally to me, and I miss my job.'

'Don't put yourself down,' Sarah said. 'We all look up to you.'

Betty thanked her. 'Let me have a quick word about your problem; and yes, it is a problem. You have pinpointed the area of concern. I also like the plan you have concocted with Clemmie, and I suggest that you proceed with caution.'

'I will. I'm seeing the first of my trusted ladies shortly, and everything will be put in motion tomorrow.'

'May I ask who,' she whispered, looking to where Maureen was starting to pour out their tea.

'Of course. It is Gwyneth Jackson.'

'A good choice; the wife of a police officer is above reproach, just like Caesar's wife.'

Sarah had no idea what Betty was talking about. 'I reckon within a week we will have the figures in front of us and will know if takings are truly down or if we have thieves in the store. What to do after that, I do not know.'

'I have a reliable contact in head office and, if you don't mind, when the time is right, I'll have a word with her.'

Sarah looked worried. 'I'm not sure . . . What if word got back to Mr Harrison and he poked his nose into what we've discovered? He could make life hard for those of us involved, and perhaps even sack us. That's if he is involved.'

'My friend is most discreet. I've known her for a very long time, in fact her mother gave me encouragement, and promotion, a very long time ago when I needed to leave the Ramsgate store. I'd not speak to her unless I was sure of the facts and knew we needed help. She's a good woman.'

'In that case, please do speak with her when the time is right,' Sarah replied as Maureen joined them, carrying a tea tray.

'Room for another bun?' she grinned, trying to ignore the way the two women had been locked in conversation.

18
~

'You wanted to speak to me?' Gwyneth asked as she tentatively stepped through the open office door.

'No need to look worried. I'm not about to sack you,' Sarah grinned. 'Can you close the door?'

Gwyneth frowned, but did as requested before sitting down. 'What's the problem?' she asked in her gentle Welsh lilt. 'I've noticed you have a worried frown on your face when you're on the shop floor.'

'I do have a problem and wondered if you'd be able to help me?' she replied, before outlining what had been happening with the takings on certain counters.

'You can't speak to our illustrious manager?'

'Well, no . . .'

'He's part of the problem, I assume?'

'I don't know, although I have doubts about him, as well as others. It's such a mess,' she sighed.

'I'll help all I can, just say the word. Oh, and I'll not tell Mike.' She smiled. 'That is unless you plan to rob the store, as he would know I had a secret. It comes with him being a policeman for so many years.'

'There's enough of that going on without me joining in,'

Sarah chuckled, feeling a weight drop from her shoulders, knowing that Gwyneth was part of the team. 'I want you to be my eyes on the shop floor, especially at times when Clemmie is collecting the takings from the tills. It will mean moving counters, though.'

'A change is as good as a rest, as they say, but surely you don't suspect Clemmie. Betty would be mortified.'

'No, not for a moment. Clemmie has been a star in all this, and it was she who noticed that takings had dropped on a few of the tills at certain times.'

'And with certain staff on those counters?'

'Yes, I'm afraid so, but I plan to put a stop to it. This is a list of your duties, and on which counters. All I want you to do is keep your eyes open and inform me if you have any concerns.'

'I can do that. I assume I'm not the only counter assistant you'll be speaking to?'

'No, there will be two others: Claudette and Jessie. I dare not make too many changes or the person who is doing this will get wind of what is happening . . .' She stopped speaking as someone knocked on the door. 'Come in.'

Maureen popped her head around the door. 'Sorry to interrupt you,' she apologized, looking between the two women. 'I hope there's nothing wrong. I thought you looked worried when you were in the staff room?'

'Everything's fine,' Sarah assured her, forcing a smile onto her face. She hated keeping things from her mother-in-law, but felt it best to keep mum for the moment.

'That's good to hear. I'm off home shortly, and me and your dad were going to take the kids up the park with a ball for a kickaround – that is, your dad and the kids will kick a ball and I'll cheer from the sidelines,' she chuckled. 'We'll drop them off at yours later on, after they have had tea with us.'

'That's so good of you, Maureen, thank you,' Sarah said, feeling grateful for the woman's help. She waited until the door had closed and Maureen's footsteps had faded away down the long corridor.

'There is something else, which means me putting you on the confectionery counter while I try out some new procedures.'

Gwyneth's eyes lit up. 'My favourite counter!'

'It may not be, once I've explained a little more about the missing stock,' Sarah said with a grimace.

'Oh, well, I'll give it a go,' Gwyneth said. 'I reckon I'm going to be doing more detective work than my husband. When do I start?'

Sarah spent the rest of the day speaking with the other counter assistants that she'd decided could help with her plan. Maisie's daughter, Claudette, suggested that Dorothy Billington should be taken on board, even though she only worked Saturdays and the occasional few hours after school.

'After all, Aunty Betty and Clemmie are aware of what's going on, and it would be awful if they had to keep a secret – even worse if Dorothy found out they were keeping a secret from her.'

Sarah had agreed and managed to speak to the girl when she arrived after school. Dorothy was keen to help, albeit a little nervous. She was a younger version of her sister, Clemmie, although her hair was longer and was plaited for school. 'We won't have to accost anyone, will we?'

'No, I just want you to keep an eye open for anything that you don't feel is right. If you see anything, you can speak to Gwyneth, if she is on the shop floor, or make a note to tell me in your break. Can you do that?'

'I think so. Is Claudette in on the secret too?'

'She certainly is. Would you like to work with her, if it makes you feel more confident?'

'Oh yes, please, I do like working alongside Claudette; she's a lot of fun.'

'As long as you work and don't chatter,' Sarah told her, wondering if she'd done the right thing.

Back in her office, she managed to sort out a few pay queries before it was time to accompany Clemmie on her final visit to the shop floor to empty the tills. Each till had a numbered leather bag, and the money in each till went into its own bag and was tightly fastened until all the bags were safely back in the cash office, with the door locked and the money counted. Sarah always took time to have a few words with the staff while Clemmie filled the money bags, while keeping her eye open for any problems that might occur when the tills were wide open. She was also able to check the counters to make sure they looked presentable. She held the door to the staff area open for Clemmie to walk through while she carried the cash.

'You were busy when I did the mid-afternoon collection, so I had one of the stockroom men accompany me,' the girl started to say. 'I found the takings were down on the haberdashery counter again. It's strange, as they've been quite busy today, with the new stock of wool and buttons coming in; our regular ladies know, to the hour, when we have new stock arriving.'

'They do,' Sarah chuckled, before looking serious. 'Tell me, was that when Gwyneth was with me?'

'Yes, that woman, Jean, who was hired by Mr Harrison, was on the counter on her own. Her name is on your list . . .'

'Oh dear,' Sarah said. 'Let's get the details down on paper while they are fresh in our minds.'

'Problems, ladies?' Mr Harrison said from the top of the staircase, making them both jump.

'Not at all,' Sarah replied as she tried to walk around him.

'I beg to differ; you were talking about writing something down?'

'It's a knitting pattern. We are making a layette for Freda Forsythe and noticed a discrepancy in the pattern,' Clemmie explained.

'Then talk about it in your own time. We can't have female employees chattering away all the time. Now get on with your work while I help Mr Argent lock up the store.'

Sarah held back from answering him. The man had been away from the store all afternoon. Although it suited her, it was still galling that others had to cover for him. 'Mr Argent has not been in work this afternoon,' she said, as Mr Harrison stood back for her to pass, trying not to flinch from the smell of whisky on his breath.

'Mr Argent was with me. We had a business meeting with a local supplier.'

'I thought head office dealt with things like that?' Sarah asked, knowing all too well that occasionally managers did meet suppliers. Hadn't Betty done just that during the war, when she arranged to stock vegetables from her Aunt Pat's farm in Slade Green? However, it suited her to let the man think she didn't know what went on in the store. Whatever he said, she knew he'd been skiving.

'Get on with your work,' he hissed.

'Mum, can I have a word with you?' Clemmie said as she helped Betty clear the dinner table, carrying everything through to the kitchen, where the housekeeper was washing up.

'Of course, dear, let's go through to the sitting room. The fire's lit and we will be alone,' she said, ushering the nervous-looking girl into the room. With its deep-green velvet drapes closed against the night, it had a cosy atmosphere. Betty straightened a newspaper that Douglas had left on the side table, before joining the girl on the chintz-covered settee. 'Now, what would you like to talk about?'

Clemmie fiddled with a brooch pinned to her cardigan. 'It's a bit difficult . . .'

Betty stroked her arm. 'You know you can talk with me about anything and I'll understand.'

Taking a deep breath, Clemmie blurted out, 'Jimmy and I would like to get married.'

'Of course, dear, we've discussed this. In a few years from now, you will have a wonderful wedding. You will make a beautiful bride.'

'We want to get married sooner than that. We love each other and can't see any reason not to marry now.'

Betty sucked in her breath. As Clemmie's stepmother, she couldn't really insist on any rules; and, after all, she had wanted to marry when she was younger than Clemmie

207

was now, if only her fiancé hadn't perished in the Great War. 'Perhaps we should speak with your father,' she suggested, knowing that wasn't what Clemmie wanted to hear.

'I thought you'd support my wish?' Clemmie said, staring Betty in the eye. 'Please, can you tell me why I should wait until I'm older? Jimmy is settled in his career, and I have my job at the Erith branch. I also have my bottom drawer – in fact I have a whole chest of drawers full of linen. A bride can have too much linen, you know,' she said with a tremor in her voice. 'I love Jimmy, and I want to be his wife.'

'Oh, Clemmie, you will be his wife. You know how much we approve of Jimmy, and he will make a fine son-in-law; it's just that if you make a mistake now, you may regret it for the rest of your life and have to live with it.'

Clemmie rose to her feet, an indignant look on her face. 'Pray tell me what mistakes you expect me to make?'

Betty sighed; she knew she was handling this all wrong. 'Sit down, dear. I seem to be distressing you and that wasn't my intention. You need to remember that your father and I have not encountered this situation before. Hopefully by the time Dorothy catches the eye of a young man, we will get it right,' she said with a twinkle in her eye.

Clemmie sat down next to Betty, kissing her cheek. 'Please, will you at least consider our wish? If I can't marry Jimmy, I know I'll remain a spinster for the rest of my life.'

'Just as I would have been, if your father hadn't plucked up the courage and walked into Woolworths to seek me out. None of us knows what's around the corner.'

'What's around the corner?' Douglas asked as he entered the room and sat in his favourite armchair.

Clemmie looked beseechingly towards Betty.

'The future, dear. Who knows what will happen in later life?' Betty smiled benignly.

'I'm content to remain in the present; let the future take care of itself,' he said, reaching for his newspaper.

'In that case, you won't mind me taking care of my own future,' Clemmie said, looking between her parents.

'What did you have in mind?' Douglas asked, peering over the top of his newspaper. 'I thought you were happy in your job at Woolworths?'

'Oh, Daddy, I'm not talking about my work; I adore my job. I want to marry Jimmy,' she added in a rush, before Betty could stop her.

'You will, dear, in time, as we discussed before when the subject came up. There's plenty of time.'

'But . . .'

Betty shook her head, signalling to Clemmie not to push her father, but the girl looked away.

'I've already said that we want to marry sooner rather than later. Why, plenty of girls marry at my age.'

'Is there a reason you wish to marry sooner rather than later?' Douglas asked, as the penny dropped with Betty and she gasped, clasping a hand close to her heart.

'Please don't say such a thing,' she cried out, watching Clemmie's reaction to Douglas's outburst. 'Think how it would affect your life.'

'Would it be such a bad thing? Look at Bessie Carlisle; she had her baby out of wedlock, and no one has thought badly of her.'

Douglas was thoughtful. 'I can't believe what I am hearing,' he said in a steely voice. 'I am saddened by the thought that my eldest daughter has been so foolhardy. As for Jimmy, who I have always admired, being so disrespectful as to put our daughter in the position of not being able to enjoy a lavish white wedding.' His voice cracked with emotion.

'Oh, Daddy,' Clemmie sobbed, hurrying to his side and flinging her arms around his neck. 'It's not what you're imagining. I've not . . . I mean we haven't . . .' She looked towards Betty for help.

'Douglas dear, what Clemmie is trying to say is that you can still walk her down the aisle and she will still be able to wear a white gown.'

Douglas looked uncomfortable. He coughed to clear his throat, before removing Clemmie's arms from his neck. 'I apologize for thinking otherwise. Now sit down and calm yourself. We would both like to know why this sudden change of plans. Betty – your mother and I – were under the impression you planned to wait four or five years at least.'

Betty smiled to herself. Douglas was like many fathers who didn't wish to see their daughters grow up. 'I like Jimmy very much, and I'm surprised he has not come to your father to officially request your hand in marriage. Are you sure he is in agreement with this change of plan?'

Clemmie stared down into her lap, lacing her fingers together distractedly. 'He knows how much I want to marry him, if that's what you mean?'

'Then may I suggest he comes to dinner on Sunday, so that we can discuss this like sensible human beings? Have a word with him, and he must bring his children with him. It's about time we got to know our soon to be step-grandchildren a little better,' Betty said.

Clemmie beamed with delight. 'Does this mean you agree . . .'

'Steady on, Betty,' Douglas objected, before turning to his daughter. 'Don't get too excited, as we have yet to decide. Betty is right in that we need to discuss the situation with Jimmy, but apart from that, nothing has changed. Do you understand?'

'Oh, I do,' Clemmie exclaimed, kissing them. 'If you will excuse me, I have to prepare for work tomorrow,' she said, hurrying from the room.

'Step-grandchildren?' Douglas groaned. 'Betty, we are far too young for such things.'

'Time waits for no one, my dear. Look around you at our friends and associates. So many have married children and, dare I say it, grandchildren. We need to embrace this opportunity, because otherwise we could push Clemmie away. Would you want that?'

Douglas folded his newspaper and put it to one side. '"Father of the bride" does have an attractive ring to it.'

'As does "mother of the bride",' she agreed, knowing that Douglas was warming to the idea.

'As always, you are right, Betty, but all the same – grandchildren?'

Betty felt more nervous than she had when she first met Douglas's young daughters. Of course she knew Jimmy very well, from when he had trained at Erith for six months before she retired, but this was different. This was about the future, Clemmie's future, and she did not want anything she or Douglas said to spoil that.

Even though their housekeeper kept the home spotless, Betty checked the shelves and ornaments again and again until she was sure there was not a speck of dust. She found it hard to settle, checking the ornate clock above the mantelpiece, even though it had hardly moved since the previous time she'd checked. She wished Jimmy was bringing along his two young children, but Clemmie had informed her parents that they both felt it would be best to be able to talk without the distraction. In her heart of hearts, she knew Clemmie was right and they could do without young children under their feet while they had important decisions to make. Jimmy's children were five and three years of age, his wife having passed away suddenly when the youngest was only weeks old; she admired the way he'd coped and how he respected Clemmie.

She'd arranged for her housekeeper to take her two youngest children out to the park for some air before giving them tea in the nursery, so that the adults could talk in peace. Dorothy, upon hearing what was planned, had shown such horror at being home for an adult conversation that she had declared she was taking herself off to see Claudette Carlisle for the afternoon and would take in a matinee at the Odeon until it was safe to come home.

'He's here,' Clemmie exclaimed from where she'd been watching the road behind a lace curtain. 'I'll get the door,' she said, trying to step around Betty.

'Just one moment, Clemmie . . . Are you sure? You can change your mind; we will support you either way.'

Clemmie flung her arms around Betty. 'I've never been

surer. I want to be Jimmy's wife for the rest of my life, whether that be fifty years or fifty days,' she replied, giving her a final hug, and hurried to let her intended into the house.

Betty shuddered. Why did she feel so uneasy?

They all talked about everything, apart from why Jimmy was there: his work; Clemmie's job; the weather; the new Queen and the date for the coronation; how quickly children grew out of their clothing; and Douglas's thoughts on expanding his thriving funeral business. It wasn't until Betty brought in the coffee tray that Douglas spoke to Jimmy. 'Shall we take our coffee into my study?'

Once the door to the study was closed, Clemmie groaned and sank her head into her hands. 'Why does it have to be like this? Daddy knows Jimmy very well, and he knows we love each other. Why do we have to be put through this?'

'It is traditional, my love. The man must formally ask the father for his daughter's hand in marriage; your Jimmy will know this. Everything will be fine, and if it is any consolation, your father will be more nervous than Jimmy. Now, why don't we drink our coffee and clear the table, then we can go into the front room, ready for when the men return?'

'At least it will keep me from wondering what is being said. I did drill Jimmy in what points to put across.'

Betty chuckled. 'Just as I did with your father.'

The two women were still laughing when the men joined them.

Clemmie quickly went over to Jimmy and he took her hand. 'If it isn't too long for you to wait, your father has agreed for us to marry on your twentieth birthday.'

Clemmie looked between Jimmy and her father. 'Oh, that's marvellous: the end of February 1953. Thank you, Daddy, I can't wait for you to walk me down the aisle,' she replied, quickly giving him a hug.

'We've got so much to plan,' Betty said. 'Especially as it will be a winter wedding. We should have a drink to toast the happy couple, Douglas. I could do with a glass of sherry, as the waiting has been interminable.'

'At least we don't have to worry about finding a home,' Clemmie said. 'You must both visit Jimmy's house in Belvedere and see where I will be living with my ready-made family.'

'Of course I will give you a free hand in redecorating the house, Clemmie. I want you to feel as though it is your home, rather than moving in with me and the children. In fact I will move out of the house and stay with my mother, so it will be like moving into a new home together after the wedding.'

'What a delightful idea,' Betty said, getting caught up in the romantic notion.

'In that case, I will need your help, Betty. I wouldn't know where to start,' Clemmie said excitedly.

'I will be delighted to help you,' Betty smiled, although she couldn't ignore a small nagging doubt at the back of her mind; no doubt it was just tiredness, she thought, as she took the glass of sherry from Douglas and they raised their glasses to toast the future.

19

Late May 1952

'Is anyone home?' Tony called out as he closed the front door behind him. Placing his suitcase down, he removed his overcoat. 'Freda?'

'She's not home at the moment,' Bessie said as he entered the living room and spotted her soothing William. 'She did say she'd be home by midday. There's something going on at Woolworths and she's helping Sarah and Betty.'

Tony shook his head in confusion. 'You've lost me. Have Betty and Freda returned to work?'

'Here, hold your son while I put the kettle on and I'll explain,' she said, handing over the child.

Tony hugged William, before swinging him round above his head, much to the boy's delight. 'Oh, I've missed you, little man. I swear you've grown since I was last home.'

'You'd best take a seat, as this will take a while,' Bessie said, before explaining all that had happened with the takings, and the wandering hands of the floorwalker; how today was the day when Sarah, Clemmie, Betty and her old friend from head office were facing the manager with their accusations. 'Others are involved too, as I know Gwyneth and my sister have been watching the tills, along with a few other trusted counter assistants.'

Tony shook his head in amazement. 'Trust Freda not to tell me any of this when I telephoned her; there again, I wanted to know how she and William were, and she was asking about my work training the cyclists.'

'She'd not want to worry you while you were miles away,' the young girl observed sagely. 'Would you like a top up?' she asked, looking at the cold cup of tea in front of him.

'No, I'll walk round to the store to see what's going on,' he said, stroking the cheek of the sleeping William in his arms.

Tony thought now was the time when he should offer to return to work and, whoever Betty's friend from head office was, they might be the person to talk to about taking on the store, especially now that there were problems with the current manager. After all, he had been the temporary manager before his sabbatical and he was confident they'd hand him the job. It had been intimated in the past.

'I'll see you later,' he whispered to his son as he handed him over to Bessie.

'I'm at a loss to know what this is all about?' Mr Harrison said as he faced the women sitting in front of him in the staff canteen. 'And who the hell is this?' he asked, looking towards a woman sitting at the back of the room.

'This is Mrs Cathcart from head office and—' Betty was cut short by a glare from the man, as he raised his voice at Sarah and waved a sheet of paper in the air.

'Mrs Gilbert, perhaps you can explain about the

anomalies in these ledgers. You too, Miss Billington, as they only came to light since you took on the cashier position.'

Clemmie and Betty gasped, with Betty slipping her hand into her daughter's, giving it a squeeze. When the decision had been made to confront Mr Harrison, Sarah had arranged for the meeting to take place in the staff canteen, so that there was room for all involved to be heard. It was half-day and the store had just closed. Betty's friend, Mrs Cathcart from head office, sat at the back of the room quietly observing the situation, after opening the meeting and distributing details of Sarah's observations.

Sarah cleared her throat and fought off the nausea that threatened to overcome her. 'Mr Harrison, I have outlined the problem we have here, so it is a little late to start pointing the finger of blame elsewhere. I would first like Mrs Gwyneth Jackson to explain what she saw and documented.' She nodded to Gwyneth to speak, giving her a kindly look.

'Mrs Gilbert explained to me that there was a problem with the takings on several tills and I was asked to move to the confectionery counter to watch for problems, both on my counter and also on the counter opposite,' she said with a nervous tremor in her voice.

'This was the household goods counter?'

'Yes. On several occasions I noticed that when one of the counter assistants went to lunch, the remaining assistant didn't always put the money into the till. Only minutes later, someone would come along and take the money from her . . .'

'I noticed the same thing happening on the haberdashery counter,' Claudette piped up.

Dorothy shyly held up her hand and spoke. 'It was the

same on the confectionery counter when Gwyneth – Mrs Jackson – went on her break.'

As the counter staff listed what they had seen, Mr Harrison's face became redder and redder. 'How do we know it wasn't these girls stealing from Woolworths? I am going to suspend you all until I have undertaken an investigation. Now get out of my office and back to your counters while you still have jobs. As for you, Miss Billington, you can leave the building now and I'll post your cards to you. Consider yourself dismissed, and be grateful I've not called the police,' he said, dismissing her with a wave of his hand.

'Hold on a minute,' Freda said bravely. 'I was one of the people who supervised Clemmie Billington as she collected the money and then counted it out in her office. Sarah – Mrs Billington – asked me to step in and help, as an impartial witness. Nothing untoward happened in her office, so you can't blame her.'

Sarah stood up, full of indignation. 'I was also with Clemmie Billington on numerous occasions, and the girl is above suspicion. In fact it was she who first noticed the anomalies and brought them to my attention.'

Betty had been seated close to the door. She opened it slightly and called for Doreen to join them.

Once Doreen had entered the room, Sarah turned to her. 'Mrs Nichols, can you tell us when you retired from Woolworths?'

'Why it must be over two months now,' she answered politely.

Sarah passed the cash book to the lady from head office and pointed out the change in handwriting, before looking up at Doreen. 'Are these your last entries?'

'Yes, you will see a few different entries when Clemmie was sitting with me to learn a little about the job, but I must say she hardly needed any teaching as she picked it up so quickly. I expected as much, what with her having been taught office practice in college, and she's a whizz on the comptometer. My opinion, for what it is worth, is that Clemmie has been made a scapegoat, but Mrs Gilbert and other staff were quick to find out what was happening.'

Clemmie, who had been close to tears, smiled her thanks and perked up. 'I'm as trustworthy as my mother, who has taught me well. My fiancé is also an under-manager currently at the Bexleyheath store. I would have too much to lose to pilfer from my employer,' she added, looking the man defiantly in the eye.

Sarah caught Betty's eye and mouthed, '*Fiancé?*'

Betty gave a small nod, causing Sarah to raise her eyebrows before returning to address Mr Harrison. 'We have other employees who have witnessed certain staff members taking money. I would say, without a shadow of doubt, there is a gang of thieves working within this store, and most are on the Woolworths payroll.'

'I would say you are to blame, as you hired our staff,' he spat back, looking as though he was about to spring over the desk and attack her.

'No, that is not the case,' Mrs Cathcart from head office said as she raised a finger towards him. 'You hired these new staff when Mrs Gilbert was on a week's leave. Do you want me to show you the paperwork? You had the opportunity to respond to my letter, sent two weeks ago, and you chose to ignore it, hence this meeting.'

Harrison blanched for a moment and stared into space

before pulling himself together. He held up his hands in frustration. 'You are all colluding against me. I would like you to show how I could have this money, when I'm hardly likely to be on the shop floor at these times?' He stabbed a finger on the cash book.

'It was your floorwalker, Mr Argent, who collected the money from these ladies and then passed it to you, no doubt during one of your long lunch breaks,' Betty said.

'Nonsense, nonsense, nonsense!' he roared. 'You have no proof!'

'Excuse me for one moment,' Sarah said as she left the room, followed by Doreen.

'Thank you so much for helping us out,' she said.

'My pleasure. He's made life here intolerable since he took over. Does this mean Betty will come back as manager? If she does, I may be interested in a part-time position. If the truth be known, I'm bored stiff at home since I retired.'

'I'll keep that in mind,' Sarah said as she made her goodbyes and hurried into her office, where more employees were waiting for her. She was unaware Tony was at the top of the staircase and had heard every word she said to Doreen. 'Nan, Mike, can you come with me now?'

Ruby followed Sarah into the staff canteen. Aware this was important, Ruby was wearing her best coat and was carrying the handbag Bob had given her at Christmas time. Clemmie vacated her seat, and Ruby sat down in front of the manager.

'What is all this?' Mr Harrison asked, as Mike stood in front of the door so that no one could leave.

Mike remained silent as Sarah addressed her nan. 'Can

you explain what you saw on the shop floor over the past week, please?'

Ruby settled her handbag on her lap and started to speak. 'As a long-time customer of Woolworths, I was worried when my granddaughter mentioned there were problems and staff were unhappy . . .'

Sarah coughed to stop Ruby speaking out of turn. 'Can you explain how you helped us out, Nan?'

'Of course. I purchased items from different counters using ten-shilling notes and they never went into the tills.'

'What she means is they never appeared in the takings; not a single one,' Clemmie said, looking Mr Harrison in the eye.

He shook his head, giving her a pitying look. 'It may have escaped your notice, Miss Billington, but we have many ten-shilling notes go through our tills, and nine times out of ten they will be handed back in a customer's change. Besides, how can you distinguish the notes this lady handed over from the ones other customers used to pay for their purchases?' he said, leaning back in his chair and crossing his arms over his chest with a self-satisfied smirk on his face.

'I used this,' Ruby said, reaching into her handbag and producing a fountain pen. 'It contains red ink, and I made a mark in the same place on all of the money, just like this one,' she added, producing a ten-shilling note and pointing to a small red mark in the top right-hand corner.

Mr Harrison swallowed hard as Sarah turned to Clemmie and asked, 'Were there any with the takings, Miss Billington?'

'Not a single one,' Clemmie replied calmly.

'Then I'm afraid, madam, your theory holds no water, so you may leave,' he said to Ruby.

'Stay where you are,' Mike Jackson said, laying a hand on Ruby's shoulder as she attempted to rise from her seat. Pulling an envelope from the inside pocket of his jacket, he held it out to Ruby. 'Are these the six ten-shilling notes you used to purchase goods in this store?'

Ruby took the money from him and peered closely, before holding them up for all to see. 'Yes, you can see where I made my mark in red ink; it is identical to this one,' she said, passing the original one to those seated nearby.'

'What the . . . Where did these come from?' Harrison demanded.

'The pocket of your floorwalker Mr Argent's overcoat; he is currently being held at the police station, helping us with our enquiries,' Sergeant Jackson answered.

'My goodness, I had no idea,' Ruby murmured, before being silenced by a stare from Sarah.

'What is this all about?' Harrison snarled. 'If members of my staff have been up to no good, then arrest them and let me get on with the job of running this store. I have management visiting this afternoon to discuss a promotion. I can't have them arrive and see a policeman asking questions, and my staff and their acquaintances cluttering up the staff canteen. It's not professional.'

'Just one more thing, Mr Harrison. Would you mind me checking the contents of your desk drawer – and your wallet?' Sergeant Jackson asked.

'Now look here, this is going too far,' he spluttered indignantly. 'You have no authority to search my office, especially in front of so many people.'

'Not even if one of those "people" happens to be from head office?' Mrs Cathcart asked, standing up to face him.

'Up till now you have chosen to ignore me, as well as my correspondence.'

Harrison turned to Mike Jackson. 'I'll ask again: what is this all about? If you are interviewing one of my floor-walkers, my first concern is that you should have come to me rather than embarrass me in front of my employees.'

Mrs Cathcart nodded thoughtfully. 'You do have a point. Ladies, would you all mind reconvening elsewhere? That is, apart from Mrs Gilbert and Mrs Billington, and of course you, Sergeant Jackson.'

'There are refreshments in my office,' Sarah called after them.

Mrs Cathcart watched as the women left the office, thanking Ruby, who had offered to stay. 'I'll have a word with you all once I'm finished here,' she said.

Once the door was closed behind the departing staff, she turned to the red-faced manager. 'I would be grateful if you would tell us what you know before Sergeant Jackson checks your office desk. It would help you very much if, at this stage of the proceedings, you cooperated by allowing us to see the contents of your wallet and pockets.'

He shook his head. 'I strongly object. You have no right to believe I have done anything untoward. For all we know, those marked notes were planted by a staff member.'

Mrs Cathcart sighed. 'Mr Harrison, you are doing your cause no good. We have information that makes you part of the conspiracy to defraud F. W. Woolworth.'

'I have no idea why the floorwalker should have the marked notes. Why am I being targeted like this?' he demanded of Mike Jackson, ignoring the woman.

Mike chose not to answer his question. Reaching for the man's overcoat on the seat beside him, he asked, 'Shall we start with your coat pockets?'

'This is all very strange,' Maureen Caselton said as she poured a second round of tea for the women waiting for news of what was happening. 'First I'm asked to stay on and set out tea in Sarah's office, then you say you played a part in catching the criminal, Ruby?'

Ruby nodded proudly. 'Only a small part, but don't tell Bob, as he will only fuss,' she said, accepting a slice of ginger cake from a plate Gwyneth was passing round.

'A big part, Nan, as we needed a customer to be able to approach the counters to pass over the marked ten shilling notes,' Sarah said as she joined them.

'You all did admirably well, as did the other counter assistants who helped us solve the puzzle of the takings dropping on certain counters,' Betty said as she entered the room.

'What's happening?' Freda asked, as Betty accepted a cup of tea and a slice of Maureen's cake.

'Sergeant Mike is escorting our Mr Harrison to the police station. Oh, and he asked me to let you know that he may be late home for his dinner,' she added to Gwyneth.

'It won't be the first time,' Gwyneth sighed.

'But what will happen to the store?' Freda asked.

'That's all in hand,' Mrs Cathcart announced. For the first time the staff looked properly at the woman from head office. She wore an understated navy-blue woollen suit and carried a black handbag that matched her shoes. Her brown hair had flecks of grey and she wore a pale-pink lipstick. Sarah thought she couldn't be much older than Betty.

'I'm pleased to say we will have a new store manager, starting tomorrow.' Mrs Cathcart spoke clearly.

'Tomorrow, isn't that rather soon?' Freda asked, wondering if Tony had been contacted and was already on the way back: perhaps he had tried to telephone her at home with the good news? Perhaps she'd best hurry back, in case he rang again. She got to her feet and reached for her coat. 'It's time I was heading home,' she said, not stopping to hear if there was an answer to her question. After all, she would soon find out for herself. It would be joyous to have Tony home again.

'I thought Freda would have wanted to hear the good news,' Ruby whispered to Sarah as they all congratulated Betty on her return to managing the Erith store. 'I'll pop over the road and see her later, just to check she's not under the weather.'

Sarah agreed. 'I wonder if she feels left out, now she's not working here. I'd love to have her back, once she feels ready to leave the baby and William with someone for a few hours a day.'

Gwyneth, who was sitting close by, leant in. 'I'm wondering if I could do the same, once I've had this little one,' she said, patting her stomach. 'I love my children, but for a few hours a week I can be Gwyneth rather than Mummy – does that make me sound like a bad mother?'

Ruby chuckled. 'I was the same when my two were young, and I was glad to be working; and yes, I did need the money.'

Sarah giggled. 'It does sound funny when you talk about

Dad that way; he didn't turn out too bad, did he? Gwyneth, I'd love to have you return to work when you are ready. Who will you leave the children with?'

'Can you all stop talking about children and explain to me what has happened? I know I get to hear lots of gossip, working here in the staff canteen, but this time I'm lost. I can see old Harrison has blotted his copy book, and that awful floorwalker has had his collar felt, but what has Ruby got to do with it and why are you all involved?' Maureen asked, looking bemused.

The women all started to talk at once until Betty clapped her hands together. 'Ladies, may I suggest we all head for home, as the store has been closed for some time. Perhaps Sarah and Ruby could explain to Maureen? There's no need to rush,' she added, before turning to Mrs Cathcart. 'I may as well get started this afternoon. I'd like to put the office back to the way it was before I left, if that's all right?'

'Be my guest. The sooner we get the store running smoothly again, the better. I want you to write up a full report on everything that has happened.'

Betty turned to smile at her friend and daughter. 'It is Sarah and Clemmie's story to tell, not mine. I simply added my support where it was needed. They make a good team.'

Freda hurried home as fast as her legs would allow. She got so out of breath these days and wondered if she would ever be able to ride a bike and walk miles with Tony, as she often did before she had William? Once Tony was back working in Erith, life would get back to normal; a thrill ran through her as she thought of her husband as manager of the Erith store. After all, he did a good job as temporary manager. It was such a shame Mr Harrison turned out to be a bad lot; but it had all worked out for the best, as she'd soon have her husband home with her.

Placing her key in the door, she faced Bessie and Jenny, about to leave. 'There's a surprise for you in the front room,' Bessie grinned. 'I'm going out for a while, so you can talk in peace,' she added, looking back to where Tony could be heard speaking in a loud voice on the telephone. 'Good luck.'

Freda listened for a moment before bidding Bessie goodbye. From the tone of her husband's voice, it didn't sound like good news. Whatever could be wrong?

20

'Gosh, what a day,' Sarah said as she stood watching Betty lock up the main doors of the store. 'There was a time I never thought we'd get to the bottom of that business with Mr Harrison. I'm grateful you had a friend at head office who agreed with our plan to catch him red-handed; and Nan played a blinder. You know, it's going to be like old times, with you back in charge of the store.'

Betty checked her bag. 'I want to take this gift to Ruby straight away, to show how much I appreciate her help. It's a silk scarf.'

'That's very generous of you; Nan will love it. I'll walk round with you, as I must collect Buster, who's been helping Bob up at the allotment since he came out of school. Georgie's playing with one of her school friends and will make her own way home at six o'clock. Alan should be home by then. He's off out tonight at the amateur-dramatics group.'

'Tell me more. I had no idea Alan was outgoing enough to perform onstage.'

'We have Maisie's Claudette to blame for that. You know how keen she is to sing at any opportunity?'

'She does have a lovely voice.'

'She joined the group a few months back, and it seems they have a shortage of male performers. She talked Alan into going along – he thought it was to help behind the scenes, but once there he was given a small part and he loves it.'

'Well, I never,' Betty exclaimed. 'I can't wait to see him perform.'

'Now, tell me all about Clemmie being engaged. I was so surprised when she mentioned it this afternoon.'

As they walked along Manor Road towards Ruby's house, being careful of the traffic as they crossed the busy road that led down to the Slade Green and Crayford marshes, Betty explained about the wedding and how Douglas had caved in, allowing Clemmie to marry, although he'd wanted her to wait a few more years.

'There's no reason to wait, when Jimmy already has a home, but I don't envy her taking on two children.'

Betty sighed. 'In so many ways it echoes my own life, as I too married a widower although, as you know, I was a lot older than Clemmie. Of course when I was a little younger than Clemmie is now, I could have been married, if it weren't for the Great War, but we waited, and then it was too late . . .'

They stopped at Ruby's gate in Alexandra Road as Sarah put her arm round Betty's shoulders. 'But look at you now. Surely it was meant to be?'

'Yes, but I can't help feeling that I need to support Clemmie as a young bride, as I see so much of myself in her, even though she is my stepdaughter and not a blood relative,' she said, giving a sudden shiver.

Sarah was concerned; she'd never seen Betty acting like this. 'Come on, let's get you inside. You must be freezing to shiver like that.'

'I'm not cold, I just can't help shake off this feeling I have that something will go wrong. You must think I'm silly?'

'Not at all. I've often had a sense of foreboding, and I'm not usually wrong,' Sarah replied as she pulled the string tied to the key of the door. As she ushered Betty in front of her into the house, she put a hand to the back of her neck, rubbing it thoughtfully; yes, she too wondered if all would be well with the young couple, although she wished Clemmie and Jimmy all the best.

'You shouldn't have done this,' Ruby scolded Betty as she ran her fingers through the silk scarf appreciatively. 'I'm only too happy to help you out. And to think you are now back at the store, and in charge, is such good news. And now to hear there is a wedding in the offing . . . What a day!'

'It certainly is. Clemmie is to be married at the end of February next year and there's so much to arrange before then. I have no idea about the church, let alone booking a place for the wedding breakfast,' Betty sighed. 'I may be able to run a branch of Woolworths, but arrange a wedding; well, I'm not so sure.'

Ruby was thoughtful. 'At least, being early in the year, it won't clash with our young Queen's coronation.'

'Oh, Nan, I doubt anyone going to Clemmie's wedding will also be attending the coronation,' Sarah chuckled.

Betty nodded. 'I agree with Ruby. People will either want to go to London to cheer on our new monarch or stay at home and watch it on the television. Alan will have a very busy year.'

'Of course. I'd not given that a thought. How sad it is that some people would prefer to watch the coronation on a television set in their front rooms rather than jump on a train and go to London. I know my family will benefit from the sale of all the televisions, but I fear for our children if they miss out on seeing real events. These days our Buster would rather visit his Granddad George and watch sport on television than attend his boxing club. I find it rather claustrophobic, sitting in a room with the curtains drawn so that we can see the picture,' Sarah said.

'I quite like it,' Ruby replied. 'I was at George and Maureen's the other day and watched a programme about walking through Wales. And there I was in my slippers, with a plate of biscuits by my side. Anyway, getting back to this wedding, why not ask Maisie to make the frocks? After all, she sells wedding gowns in her Bexleyheath shop. I bet she would run up a few outfits and give you a discount.'

'Oh, I don't mind paying the going rate. I don't expect any favours,' Betty said, thinking how embarrassed she would feel if Maisie was to offer to work cheaply for her. 'I'll have a word with Clemmie, and we can telephone Maisie to make an appointment. She's thinking of having two bridesmaids: Dorothy and Claudette. My two youngest are far too young to behave properly on the day.'

'Oh, bless them, I like nothing better than to see the little ones running amok in church in all their finery,' Ruby chuckled.

'Only because they aren't your children,' Sarah chortled. 'Do you remember Freda's wedding, when Buster played merry hell and hid under the skirts of her wedding dress? I could have died of embarrassment.'

Betty smiled. 'I've no doubt the children will get up to all sorts at Clemmie's wedding.' The smile dropped from her face for a moment. 'It is such a shame Clemmie's real mother isn't here to see her walk down the aisle on her father's arm; I'm sure she would have been so proud of the beautiful young woman she's become.'

Sarah kept quiet about the fact that Douglas's first wife came from the upper classes and would not have approved for one minute of her daughter marrying a man with two children, let alone of her working in Woolworths. 'It will be a wonderful wedding and I'm sure Maisie would do you proud. Do take into consideration that it will be pretty chilly in February, so perhaps a woollen suit for yourself and warm undergarments for the bride and bridesmaids.'

'That's a good point, thank you,' Betty said. 'I'm still unsure about the church. Clemmie isn't worried as long as she can marry her Jimmy, and he seems to be of the same opinion, not being a churchgoer.'

'But don't you have to attend a church, or be associated to it in some way, to marry there? I know, when Alan and I married, the vicar at St Paulinus was accommodating as he knew you, Nan.'

'He buried my first husband,' Ruby explained. 'I do have an idea. What about St Augustine's in Slade Green? The store did so much to help the British Restaurant based in the church hall during the war.'

Betty looked thoughtful. 'I do have a connection to the church and visit once a year with Douglas on Armistice Day.'

'You do?' Sarah looked confused. 'You've never mentioned this before.'

'It is something I have always kept to myself, but perhaps now is the time. You must recall my fiancé, Charlie, and his death at Ypres during the Great War?'

'I do,' Ruby said, reaching for a handkerchief. 'It was a sad time in your life.'

'And for many women. However, it is through Charlie that I met my Douglas, as they served together at that time.'

'I recall the palaver when he sought you out,' Sarah said through misty eyes. 'It was a very special time.'

'It was. We visit St Augustine's church each year to pay our respects and to think of Charlie, whilst looking at his name engraved on the war memorial.'

'I hope you don't mind me asking, but didn't Charlie come from Woolwich?' Sarah asked.

'His late mother's parents lived down the Green and it was they who requested that his name be added to the memorial, as he spent so much time there as a young boy. I was overjoyed when I found out, as it gives us somewhere to visit and think of Charlie. There was no grave in Ypres, although his name is engraved on the memorial at the Tyne Cot Cemetery in Belgium. Charlie and I plan to visit one day.'

'It wouldn't be my choice of place to visit,' Ruby shuddered, 'but I can see why you would want to pay your respects. I wonder what would have happened if he'd survived?'

'I'd never have known any of you, or worked at Woolworths. It is strange to think how our paths would have changed . . .'

The women fell silent as they thought of Betty's past life.

'I honestly feel the Reverend Donald Mills would be delighted to hold Clemmie and Jimmy's wedding in the church, but it would help to attend a few services, to be on the safe side,' Ruby winked.

'I will write to Reverend Mills and make myself known to him. Thank you for your advice, Ruby. To see Clemmie and Jimmy marry there would warm my heart.'

'You could ask about hiring the church hall for the wedding breakfast at the same time,' Sarah suggested. 'That's if you don't wish to hold it in a hotel somewhere?'

'That is certainly food for thought,' Betty said. 'I have a lot to think about, but for now I must bid you both goodbye and get home to my brood. Clemmie will be thrilled to know I'm making headway with the plans, as all she can think about is decorating Jimmy's bungalow in Belvedere to make it feel more like her own. The darling boy is going to move back in with his parents, so that Clemmie can do as she pleases and not disrupt the children.'

Vera nodded her approval. 'He sounds like a lovely lad.'

'Do you think you should let Freda know your good news, as she hurried off before it was announced?' Sarah suggested.

'I'll certainly do that at the earliest opportunity,' Betty replied.

'Clemmie is a lucky girl,' Ruby said as she showed Betty to the door.

'I'm the lucky one, being able to help Douglas's daughter arrange her wedding, and being accepted by Clemmie as a replacement mother. Being the new store manager, and with a family wedding in the offing, everything seems right in my world,' she sighed, before kissing Ruby and Sarah goodbye.

'Whatever has happened?' Freda asked as Tony slammed the telephone down. 'I've never seen you like this?'

'I've never felt like this before,' he replied as Freda hurried to him and flung her arms around his neck to give him a hug, before leading him into the front room, where she sat next to him on the settee. 'I fear I have let you down.'

'Don't ever say that, my love. Without you my life would be worthless,' Freda consoled him, still unsure why he was so upset.

'I went to meet you at the store and, as I was climbing the staff staircase, I overheard something. I could only think of getting home and contacting head office to ask what's happening.'

'But why are you angry, when the store manager's job is as good as yours? That's why I hurried home to telephone you. I didn't expect you to be here already, not that I'm not pleased to see you.'

Tony frowned. 'I'm not sure what you mean. I rushed back here to ring head office about my position, rather than wait for you.'

'Oh dear, this is all getting very confusing. Mr Harrison has been given the sack and that horrid floorwalker, Alfred Argent, has been taken to the police station. It seems they were in cahoots to swindle Woolworths. After it had all been sorted out, Mrs Cathcart started to announce there was to be a new store manager . . . It's you, my darling husband,' she beamed, trying to put her arms around Tony as he stepped back.

'Oh, Freda darling, you've got it all wrong. Betty Billington is to return as the new manager, effective immediately.'

Freda thought back quickly to what had been said at the store – she'd been so wrapped up in Tony returning as manager that she had misunderstood what had happened – before bursting into floods of tears.

'Don't upset yourself, my love. I can be angry for both of us. Think of the baby and our William asleep upstairs.'

Freda sniffed into the handkerchief he gave her. 'What makes me so angry is that while I sat in the office, watching the whole sorry story unfold, I started to feel a glimmer of hope that you would be recalled to take over the store. Not once did Betty, or Mrs Cathcart from head office, mention that Betty was to be manager. It got to the point when I had to leave. I wanted to speak to you, as the excitement was unbearable. I'm sorry you had to hear the news like you did.'

'And I'm sorry you had to get so upset,' he said, taking both her hands. 'What a pair we are!'

'Indeed we are. Do you think you've burnt your boats, shouting down the telephone as you did? I suppose we could always uproot and move to the coast and run a teashop . . .'

Tony gave a harsh laugh. 'We will soon find out, as I've been told to go round to the Wheatley Hotel this instant, because Mrs Cathcart is staying there overnight and wishes to speak with me.'

Freda was livid. 'No doubt throwing you a few crumbs,

or perhaps even giving you your cards. If she offers you something not worthy of your training, you are to refuse it, do you hear me? You are worth more than that. Besides, there will be other positions, perhaps at Sainsbury's or the Co-op.'

'I promise you I'll do just that,' he said, stroking her cheek while thinking that nowhere would be as good as working for F. W. Woolworth. 'Now I'll be off. Are you sure you'll be all right on your own or should I walk you and William over to Ruby's, so that you have company while I'm gone?'

'Oh, be off with you! I'll be fine,' she laughed, forcing herself to look positive, even though she wanted to howl her head off and throw a tantrum over the unfairness of the situation. She pushed him towards the front door. 'However, if your meeting takes a long time, I would love fish and chips for our tea; we will need something to cheer ourselves up.'

'The food of the gods,' he laughed. 'Put your feet up and rest until I return. William should be fine, as his nappy was changed before he was put down for his nap.'

Freda lay down on the settee and propped up her aching feet on a cushion. As much as she adored carrying Tony's baby and being spoilt rotten with new clothes from Maisie's shop, she'd be pleased when the child arrived and life got back to normal – if it ever would, with Tony's position at Woolworths being such a problem and two children to care for, with possibly no income. She wriggled and moved her position a few times, being unable to get comfortable. 'Oh, blow it, I'll go over and see Ruby,' she muttered, pulling herself up on her feet.

Writing a note for Tony, she pulled on a cardigan, then hurried upstairs to collect a complaining William, who did not want to be wakened from his slumbers. Opening the front door to go over to number thirteen, she spotted Betty walking away from Ruby's. Fury erupted inside her and she hurried as fast as her aching legs would carry her, whilst holding her son on her hip. 'Betty, I'd like a word with you,' she called out.

Betty turned towards Freda, about to smile, until she saw the angry look on the girl's face. 'Freda, is there a problem?' she asked, although she had a feeling she knew what it was.

'You may well ask,' Freda gasped, holding onto a garden wall with one hand while trying to catch her breath. 'Have you no idea that you've taken the position that was promised to my Tony?'

Betty reached out to touch Freda's arm. She looked as though she'd collapse at any minute. 'You need to calm down; it's not good for you or the baby. Here, let me take William while you compose yourself,' she said gently.

Freda wrenched her arm away. 'I'm fine. What have you done to my Tony's career prospects? They'd as good as promised him a permanent position as manager, and you've taken it from him.'

Betty sighed. 'Tony is not due back in work for some months; surely his work with the Olympic team will last until the Games in July?'

'No, he was due back for the last month before my confinement and at that point was taking up his management duties, but you've put paid to that now. I thought you'd retired?'

Betty felt as though she been cornered. Blinded by the thought of returning to the job she loved, she had forgotten about Tony. 'I'm sorry. Perhaps I could put in a word for him to be my under-manager?'

Freda was horrified. 'What? He has had more training and has been a replacement manager more times than you've had hot dinners. I thought you were a friend, Betty,' she cried out, before turning to walk back to her house.

Betty went to follow her. 'Please, Freda, I don't wish to fall out with you over this. Can we talk more?'

'I never want to speak with you again. You've destroyed my dream,' Freda spat back before hurrying across the road and slamming her front door.

21

~

September 1952

Betty was miles away as Maureen entered her office carrying a tea tray. 'Why, this is just like the old days, with you so busy you forgot your tea break,' she chuckled, trying hard not to comment on her manager's glum face.

Betty looked up at the clock – the same one that had been in the office since she was first promoted to manager during the war. 'My goodness, is that the time?' she declared, stretching her arms and yawning. 'I was up in the night with one of the children, and dawn was creeping over the horizon as I fell back into bed.'

'A woman's lot is never done,' Maureen said as she placed the steaming cup of tea on the desk, followed by a plate containing a sticky bun. 'Your favourite,' she nodded with a smile. 'That'll perk you up.'

'It certainly will, thank you, Maureen. Would you sit down for a few minutes for a chat? I wanted to ask a favour of you.'

'By all means,' she replied, stretching out her bad leg with a wince.

'Is your leg playing you up?'

'It's bearable; I like to think it's God's way of reminding me I'm lucky to be here, unlike others.'

'Very true. We are both lucky women to have survived the war,' Betty said, thinking of the way Sarah had dragged her from the burning Bexleyheath store.

'I know I'm lucky to have finally married the love of my life; not that I wasn't very fond of my first husband.'

'We are very similar in the respect of having a second chance of love. My Douglas is such a dear man; I'd not know what to do without him,' Betty said, stirring her tea thoughtfully. 'I pray Clemmie will have as happy a married life as I've had.'

'I'm sure she will. The wedding is coming round fast, isn't it?'

'Yes, and I have a million things to think about,' she replied, pointing to a large notebook on her desk with a cover labelled 'Wedding'. 'I wondered if you would help me with something?'

'I'd be more than happy to do so. I take it is to do with the wedding food?'

'It is, and I know I should have asked you ages ago. Clemmie and Jimmy could not decide on the wedding breakfast. Douglas wanted a formal sit down, with a top table and plated food served by waitresses. I'm sick to death of them not making up their minds, so I put my foot down. They must decide this week or I wash my hands of the whole thing and stop helping them.'

'Oh dear, I take it that didn't go down too well?'

'No, as both Clemmie and Douglas told me to decide, and Jimmy kept apologizing for being no help. The problem

241

is there are limited catering facilities in the church hall for a sit down meal, and being February . . .'

'It could be cold, even snowing, and your guests won't be happy to sit down to a ham salad.'

'Exactly! I knew you'd understand where I was coming from. Do you know the church hall at all?'

'Do I know it? Why, I've been to functions there more times than I care to think about and have helped out at a few. It stands to reason your guests will want to sit down, and I can assure you the hall has a heater, so they will be warm, whatever the weather. However, salads and cold food won't go down terribly well, although people would be too polite to say so and will forget, once the evening gets going and they are up dancing. If it was my child's wedding, I'd have pans of hot soup on the go, as well as some warm food and the usual sandwiches and cakes. It's not quite what the Co-op caterers would serve, but it would fill bellies and keep people warm – and is manageable in the church hall.'

Betty exclaimed her delight. 'That sounds wonderful,' she said, reaching for her notebook and making more notes.

'Of course I'd still like to make the wedding cake, as mine and George's gift, but if you like I can organize the food and arrange for a few women I know to serve and clear up afterwards? The soups could be made in advance, here in the Woolworths kitchen – if it would be allowed?'

'Gosh,' was all Betty could say. 'It goes without saying, you'd be paid for your time, but I couldn't be more grateful.'

Maureen was embarrassed. 'Well, you're like family, and family stick together, don't they?'

'They certainly do,' Betty agreed, looking to where a formal thank you card sat on a shelf, from Freda and Tony for the christening gifts she'd sent, even though there had not been an invitation. A wave of sadness flooded through her. When she heard Freda had given birth to twins, she wanted nothing more than to hurry to Alexandra Road and congratulate the parents, but it wasn't to be. Freda's anger knew no bounds over the way she felt her Tony had been treated, to the point where Ruby had suggested that Betty step back until tempers had cooled down.

Maureen could imagine what was on Betty's mind as she looked at the thank you card. 'It'll all blow over, so don't dwell on things,' she added, not liking to mention that there was a welcome back party for Tony on his return from the Olympics in Helsinki; with his help, the English team had secured twenty-sixth and twenty-seventh places, out of more than one hundred cyclists. They had also celebrated his promotion to store manager at the Dartford branch – a bigger store than the Erith one.

'Hello, what's this, a tea party?' Sarah asked as she entered the office, holding a file full of paperwork. 'I'm sorry to interrupt; these are the pay details to go to head office that you asked to see.'

'If I had time to throw a party, I certainly would,' Betty beamed, her sadness dissipating. 'Maureen has come up with the most wonderful suggestions for Clemmie's reception and wedding breakfast. Sit down and we will tell you all about it.'

'If you insist, but we should mind that we don't get in trouble with our manager,' Sarah grinned.

Maureen slapped her daughter-in-law's arm good-naturedly for being cheeky, as the women pored over the details.

'You have forgotten something,' Sarah said, once they'd discussed everything from sherry to extra food for the evening guests. 'The hall is looking rather shabby and could do with some decorations to brighten it up.'

'Hmm, you are right,' Maureen agreed. 'How about tablecloths for the trestle tables?'

'And vases of flowers,' Betty said.

'That many flowers could be a problem in February, even with Douglas being an undertaker and having contacts. Besides, they'd suffer in the warm hall. As for tablecloths, they'd need to be very long and all the same colour,' Sarah was quick to point out.

Maureen chuckled to herself. 'I was thinking of when Freda and her Brownies filled the store window with crepe-paper flowers one Easter; it certainly brightened up the store.'

'Oh, if only . . .' was all Betty could say.

'Leave it with me,' Sarah promised. 'Meanwhile, why not ask Maisie if she could get hold of a bolt of cotton fabric that can be chopped into tablecloth lengths?'

Betty looked between the two women. 'I don't deserve such good friends,' she smiled, while secretly feeling that Sarah would have no joy with Freda.

'You, young man, are a handsome fellow and your sister is a beautiful young lady, while your mother is an absolute fool,' Sarah said as she gazed in adoration at Freda and Tony's twins, which she held in the crook of each of her arms.

'Who are you calling a fool?' Freda asked as she joined Sarah in her front room. 'My husband says I am practically perfect, surprising him with twins in one fell swoop. No fool can do such a thing.' She smiled down at her babies before handing Sarah a bottle. 'Which one would you like to feed?'

'My goddaughter, if I may? Although I feel I should not choose between the two.'

'Then come back for the next feed and you can have Bertie; he is such a greedy child,' she said, kissing his downy hair before stroking his rosebud lips with the rubber teat. He eagerly opened his mouth.

'Margaret Rose is such a peach I could eat her up,' Sarah said as the two friends sat companionably side by side, listening to the babies suckle. 'Who'd have thought you were carrying twins.'

'I was as surprised as you, and as for Tony . . . But tell me why I am a fool, as if I couldn't guess?' Freda asked.

'It's about time you made up with Betty; the whole situation is ludicrous. Why, it's been six months since you fell out. No friendship is worth skirting around each other when you are at the same event; and looking the other way when you accidentally bump into each other is downright ridiculous. It's time you started to talk to each other again; even Tony chats to Douglas when they meet in the Prince of Wales.'

Freda frowned. 'I can't back down now. Betty took Tony's job without any thought for our future, and she has never apologized. Friends don't do that kind of thing.'

'Friends should be able to forgive each other,' Sarah added, watching the strained expression on Freda's face. 'You must miss Betty so much.'

'Betty is the one who needs to apologize. If it wasn't for her, my Tony would be running the Erith store.'

'Can you honestly say that? The job wasn't his, you know. Granted, his name was on the shortlist, due to him being temporary manager before he left to help the Olympic team, but what happened with Mr Harrison was unprecedented Besides, the Olympics was months away at the time. Head office required a manager at once, and it was keen to have Betty back on board. How could she refuse?'

Freda sighed as a single large tear dropped onto her son's head. 'I know you are right, and I've known it for a while now, ever since the christening, when Vera from up the road asked me why I'd not named my daughter Elizabeth, after our dear Queen's mother. She very pointedly told me that Albert and Elizabeth would have been more fitting, or indeed Philip and Elizabeth, but I was so bitter I refused to give my child the same name as Betty.'

'So that's why you looked so sad during the service?'

'Yes, I let people believe it was because I'd have loved my mum and dad to have been alive to see their grandchildren.'

'But your brother, Lenny, and his family were there.'

'It was lovely to see them, but even so . . .'

'You wish you'd invited Betty, especially as Tony has his own store to manage and it is larger than Erith Woolies?'

'I'm so proud of him. Dartford is not that far away, and now that we have our little car, he can drive himself to and fro without relying on buses or trains. Things have turned out well, apart from . . .'

'Apart from you being angry with Betty and removing her from your life?'

'Yes, it took the joy out of the christening, and the news of Tony's permanent position. If only . . .'

'If only you could turn the clock back?'

'Yes, but it's too late now. Betty must hate me for ignoring her and being so bitter.'

'Has she said anything – no, I shouldn't ask you; ignore my question,' Freda replied, lifting Bertie to her shoulder and rubbing his back until he gave a satisfying burp. 'See if you can do better than that,' she grinned.

Once the twins were settled in their cribs, Freda led Sarah through to the living room, where she showed her a box filled to the brim with baby clothes. 'Maisie dropped them down for Bessie and me to go through. She's been so generous.'

Sarah lifted some of the items from the box, exclaiming at the pretty garments. 'I'd completely forgotten that her two youngest are twins, as they are so different. At least they were the same size when they were babies, so you can make use of these. By the way, what is it like having three babies in the house?'

'Bessie's Jenny is a dream. Even when my two wake us up at night, she sleeps through, just like my William, who is out like a light as soon as his head hits the pillow. I'm thinking of swapping one of mine for Jenny,' she chuckled. 'Bessie is a love; I couldn't cope without her. Did you know she is going back to work for a few hours a week while I look after Jenny?'

Sarah pulled a face. 'I only wish she was coming back to work at Woolworths rather than working for her mum at the clothing factory. I could do with the extra staff. I don't suppose you . . .'

Freda's eyes widened in horror. 'As much as I love the store and all the people I've worked with, it just wouldn't be possible now, what with the situation between me and Betty; that makes me sad, as when I've been into Woolies a few times since the babies came along I've been watching over my shoulder all the time, in case I bumped into Betty. I confess to having shopped in Hedley Mitchell's store a few times.'

'Good grief, that is going too far; this has got to stop. Woolworths can't be losing money because you can't face Betty,' Sarah said in mock horror. 'But, seriously, you are missing out on everything that's going on. Why, only yesterday I sat with Maureen and Betty while they discussed Clemmie's wedding. Between you and me, I fear it is all getting on top of Betty. She hasn't experienced organizing as many parties and family celebrations as we have. I suppose that's what comes of being posher than we are.'

Freda giggled. 'We have had quite a few parties and weddings; even Maisie's upper-class in-laws enjoyed our get-togethers, although when you took doors off their hinges and propped them on bricks to create tables, even I was shocked. And you couldn't get more common than me.'

'Gosh, I remember that party. It was only because it was planned at the last minute and, try as we might, we couldn't borrow any tables. Nothing stops us enjoying ourselves.'

'I'd love to know more about the wedding plans, if you don't feel I'm being nosy? Is Maisie making the dresses?'

Sarah thought for a moment as an idea came into her head. 'Oh yes, that's all in hand and very secret. Clemmie doesn't want anyone to know what her gown will be like, or the colour of the bridesmaids' dresses. In fact you were mentioned yesterday,' she added, watching the expression on Freda's face.

'I hope it was something good?'

'Indeed,' Sarah said as she went on to explain how they'd recalled the crepe paper flowers that had adorned the front windows of Woolies one Easter, all made by Freda aided by her Brownies. 'It was agreed that the flowers would have looked lovely in the church hall for the reception and would brighten up what could be a dull February day.'

Freda fell silent and had a faraway look on her face.

'A penny for your thoughts?' Sarah said, wondering if the memory was a painful one now that Freda was estranged from Betty, and whether that included the store where she'd worked since she was sixteen.

'I was wondering if I should still offer to help. After all, it is Clemmie's wedding, not Betty's. I'll be back in a minute,' she said, hurrying upstairs.

Sarah busied herself putting the kettle on, while overhead she could hear Freda moving about in the main bedroom that she shared with Tony and the twins. She was just warming the teapot when Freda came back downstairs with an armful of brown paper bags. Sarah cleared items from the table as Freda laid the bags down, peering into each one as she did so.

'I thought I'd saved this crepe paper; it was on top of the wardrobe,' she said as she pulled out different-coloured paper from each bag. 'I also have some lengths of wire, as well as pipe cleaners that I used for stems. Betty and Clemmie are welcome to all of this. I have some more stored in the loft. Do you think they can make use of it?'

'That's awfully generous of you,' Sarah said as she touched the brightly coloured paper. 'There is one problem, and I hate to say it, but . . .'

'Come on, spit it out. I promise I won't sulk,' Freda laughed.

Sarah hated to voice what was on her mind because at that moment Freda seems so joyful. Creating crafts was something that her friend enjoyed, and being able to help others was right up her street. 'Not everyone is as good as you at creating flowers out of paper; I know I'm next to useless, and I fear Betty and Clemmie are the same. Look at Betty's attempts at knitting and sewing during their war efforts,' she said before escaping to the kitchen to pour their tea, rather than face what Freda had to say. By the time she appeared with the tea tray, Freda was busy at work, deftly twisting green paper around a length of wire.

'Look, it's easy enough to do, and I could write down the instructions. Here, have a go,' she said, passing a part-completed flower to Sarah. 'I'll pour the tea while you try your hand.'

Try as she might, Sarah couldn't get the hang of attaching petals to the green stem and each time she tried, most of the paper ended up on the table, limp and sad-looking. 'I'm just not any good at this,' she said for the umpteenth time. 'By the time I've made enough to decorate the church hall, Clemmie and Jimmy will be celebrating their golden-wedding anniversary.'

Freda chuckled. 'I'm sorry to laugh at you, but you must admit your skills do not stretch to creating a floral arrangement from scratch. There's nothing else for it, I'll have to make them myself and give them to you to pass to Betty. You can say you made them.'

Sarah was disappointed. She'd hoped it would be a way for Freda to resume her friendship with Betty. 'I'd rather

250

not get involved, if you don't mind? This is between you and Betty. I do have to work with her and, for the sake of tranquillity at work, I think it's for the best, don't you?'

'I'm sorry, I wasn't thinking,' Freda said. 'Let's not fall out over it or I'll not have any friends left.' She gave a weak smile.

Sarah felt relieved and, after helping Freda clear away the paper, they sat companionably chatting about this and that. 'Alan mentioned you are learning to drive; does that mean your days of borrowing his motorbike are over?'

'I did suggest to Tony that I have my own motorbike, but he put his foot down over me carting William and the twins about in a sidecar,' Freda laughed. 'He suggested that if I learnt to drive, we might be able to stretch to a car for me to use.'

'Rather you than me,' Sarah said, not in the least jealous of Freda and of Maisie, who bombed around town in a van emblazoned with *Maisie's Modes* on the side. 'I'll stick to using the bus if you don't mind!'

Freda gave a vague smile; her thoughts were elsewhere.

22

Betty walked around the shop floor, checking the counters and stopping to talk to her staff. Since the removal of Mr Harrison and the arrest of the floorwalker, life had settled down again and takings had risen once more. They were still short of counter staff, due to several of those employed by Mr Harrison leaving the company very quickly soon afterwards. She would have to ask Sarah when the advertisements for new staff would run in the *Erith Observer*, it would be good to have them trained and ready for the Christmas period. Already a large poster in one of the store windows had caught the attention of passers-by, with application forms being handed out.

She had reached the back of the store and was in conversation with two staff members about light fittings. Betty wanted to make more of a display by having lights hanging from the high ceiling, as she'd seen in a recent communication from head office, when there was a commotion at the front of the shop.

'I pray it isn't a shoplifter,' she murmured to herself as she hurried as fast as she could towards the large double doors, aware of shoppers and staff alike stopping to watch the commotion. She stopped in her tracks, watching the two doors being held open as what looked like a barrow containing flowers was pushed into the store. Completely confused, as she'd not been told of such a delivery, she rushed to ask the person wheeling them in to take them to the back door and was stopped in her tracks by a sight she never expected to see. 'Freda!' Customers and staff stepped aside, making a clear pathway for Betty to reach Freda. 'Whatever is this?' she asked, looking at colourful bunches of paper flowers piled high on what appeared to be a large pram.

A nervous-looking Freda scooped three bunches into her arms and handed them to Betty, uncovering the raised hood of a majestic twin pram. 'I thought you might like these for Clemmie's wedding?'

'Oh my,' was all Betty could say.

'I want to apologize for the way I've acted, but I do understand if you cannot accept my apology.'

Betty turned and handed the flowers to an assistant on the cosmetics counter, before pulling Freda to her and giving her the longest hug possible. 'I've missed you, and it is I who should be asking for your forgiveness. I was so het up about the problem with Mr Harrison, and Clemmie being involved, that I forgot about Tony; it was unforgivable of me.'

As the two women hugged, someone started to clap, and soon most of those watching them were cheering, even though they had no idea what had happened. It was obvious that a friendship was being renewed, and with the most beautiful flowers. 'My goodness, I'd forgotten we had an audience,' Betty said. 'Perhaps we should move to my office?'

Freda snapped back the hood on the pram and disclosed the sleeping twins, amid sighs from those looking on. 'I can't really leave these two on their own; as it was, I left William with Ruby, as there wasn't room for him and the flowers.'

'That is not a problem,' Betty said, reaching in and carefully lifting one of the babies. 'We will carry them upstairs and I'll have two stockroom lads carry the pram upstairs too. I have lots of cuddles to catch up on. Perhaps someone could bring up the flowers?' she asked and two counter assistants at once picked them up and opened the door to the staff area. 'Come along, Freda, we have a lot to talk about.'

Freda picked up the wide-eyed Margaret Rose, who couldn't take her eyes off the bright ceiling lights. 'Welcome to Woolworths, little one,' she smiled down at her daughter.

'I know our colleagues love to see a new baby, but I've never known so many staff members be so eager to meet your twins. Thank goodness there were tea breaks or I'd have lost everyone off the shop floor,' Betty laughed. 'Don't forget to drink your tea,' she added.

'At the moment finishing a cup of tea, or even a meal, seems to be nigh on impossible,' Freda replied as she checked the two sleeping babies. 'I'm so grateful to have Bessie living with me, as it means we can share baby duties.'

'It seems to suit you both. Is Maisie no further forward with her house-hunting?'

'No, work takes precedence in her household, but she's keen to find a larger home and then I'll lose Bessie, so I'm hoping it takes a little longer,' Freda said, draining the cold cup of tea. Don't look so horrified; cold tea is something we mothers get used to.'

Betty looked guilty. 'That's where we differ, as I had help with my little ones. I was so grateful, as I most definitely would not have coped.'

'You'd have coped if you had to; look at how you run this branch and solve problems instantly. Even my Tony can't do that.'

'How is Tony getting on at the Dartford branch?'

'He loves it and so far, touch wood, he's not had any major problems,' Freda said, touching the wooden desk for luck. 'You know, it is strange how, after all his disappointment, he was called in to see Mrs Cathcart from head office that day. They had a good chat, which put his mind at rest, even though it didn't stop me being angry over what had happened. The day he overheard you'd got this job he was ready to resign. That's why I was so upset when I spotted you and was so nasty.'

Betty gave a sigh of relief; she had no idea at the time that Tony was to be interviewed, but when head office was made aware that he was back in Erith that day, they quickly arranged an appointment, after his outburst on the telephone. Although Mrs Cathcart had waited a while, after meeting Tony, before offering him the Dartford store, she had at least stopped him resigning. 'Who knows what fate has in store for us all. I'm just pleased it all worked out for Tony, as Woolworths would have been the loser if he'd resigned. I only wish we could have remained friends, but I hope we are back on an even keel now?'

'I don't deserve you as a friend when I've been so rude and nasty, but I want to make amends by helping with the wedding. Sarah told me about decorating the church hall. I tried to teach her to make the flowers, but she was all fingers and thumbs. So in the few spare moments I've had this past week I made these bunches, and I can make more by February if that helps?'

'Oh, Freda, you have no idea how much it helps. The church hall is a little drab and although we really want to have the wedding there, I was beginning to think we should have the reception at a hotel instead, until Maureen and Sarah came up with a few ideas. That's when Sarah reminded us of the time you and the Brownies decorated our windows for Easter. She must have got it into her head to speak to you about it, bless her.'

'Bless her indeed, as I wouldn't have been brave enough to speak to you without an excuse,' Freda said, starting to get weepy as Betty took two clean handkerchiefs from her desk drawer, passing one to Freda and using the other to wipe her own eyes.

'What a pair we are,' Betty sniffed. 'Friends?'

'Forever,' Freda replied gratefully.

'There is one thing I'd like to ask of you.'

'Ask away. I'll help you if I can,' Freda said, once she had composed herself.

'Once you feel up to it, would you consider returning to work, even if it is only for one day a week? I desperately need a supervisor who knows her way around the store and remains unruffled when it is busy.'

Freda looked towards her two sleeping babies, tucked up under matching blankets at each end of the twin pram. 'I can't say yes, as I need to speak to Tony. He has told me about his part-time staff and how he values the women who can work around their families and who rely on others to help with childcare, so he wouldn't stop me wishing to work, as long as the children are cared for. I have missed working here . . .'

'Then speak to Tony and, if he is agreeable, you can choose your own hours; but only when you are ready, as I'd hate to be the cause of any discord between you and your husband.'

Before Freda could answer, there was a knock at the office door and Clemmie entered, apologizing for disturbing them. 'I wondered if I could steal the twins for a while? There are women on their tea break wanting to see your babies. If I don't do something, there could be a riot.'

Freda chuckled as Betty looked aghast. 'My goodness, just look at the time. I had no idea the third tea break had started. Would you like to take the twins to the staff room, Freda?'

'I could do it, if you wish to continue talking?' Clemmie said, looking eagerly towards the pram.

'Feel free,' Freda replied as she showed Clemmie how to release the brake on the pram.

'And thank you so much, Freda,' Clemmie blushed.

'What, for relieving me of my babies?'

'Well, yes, that as well, as I adore them, but mainly for the flowers for my wedding reception . . . and for making up with Mum. She's been so miserable, but wouldn't say so.'

'Oh my,' Betty said as her eyes filled with tears. 'I can't cope with people being so nice to me. Take those babies away right now, before I embarrass myself,' she told Clemmie, who left the room as quickly as she could, whilst manoeuvring the large twin pram around a bookcase, causing it to wobble.

'I'm sorry you've been so miserable. If it's any consolation, I too have been unhappy about the situation and I'm so pleased we have made up,' Freda said, giving Betty a watery smile.

'What a pair we are! Now, I was asking you about working a few hours a week, before my daughter interrupted us,' she smiled.

'That's very kind of you. Bessie is going back to work with Maisie from next week and I'll be caring for Jenny. She has promised to do the same for me, whether it is for me to return to work or just to have some time for myself with Tony.'

'She's a good girl. I remember her when she worked here as a Saturday girl, before she ran away to have Jenny.'

Freda nodded. 'She has grown up so much since those days and will be an asset to Maisie's business. I would think, all being well, that I can start back at work in December to help with the Christmas rush.'

Betty clapped her hands together. 'I'm delighted, but only if Tony is in full agreement. As for the paper flowers, do you think you could make me a few more for the wedding? I can supply all the materials and pay you for your time. Oh dear, do I sound pushy?'

Freda chuckled. 'I'd appreciate the materials, as I have trouble getting out to purchase them, but as for payment, no thank you. Consider it my wedding present to Clemmie and Jimmy, but I'll make more than a few bunches, I promise you. I want my contribution to the wedding to be spectacular.'

*

'Now you know me, I'm not one to complain,' Vera said, as she stood on Ruby's doorstep with her hands on her hips. 'But if Freda makes much more noise in that car of hers, I'm going to be having words.'

Ruby ushered Vera inside number thirteen, taking her through to the kitchen where she was preparing dinner. It was also the furthest room from the road out front, so it was much quieter. Ruby was aware that Freda was learning to drive and had been going up and down Alexandra Road for the past hour, revving the engine and jumping the car up and down like a kangaroo.

'How are you today?' she asked, knowing to enquire before Vera gave her a long list of ailments.

'I have good and bad days,' Vera moaned as she sat down. 'Today was a good day until that commotion started. That's why I thought I'd come down to ask you to tell Freda to stop.'

'She's just keen. It's not hurting anyone,' Ruby said with a smile. 'It's not like when Alan was teaching her to ride his motorbike, when she was a young slip of a girl, and she came a cropper out front. Alan was upset until he was shown that the bike wasn't damaged. I will say Freda has more courage than I would have, in charge of a machine like that.'

Vera groaned. 'Don't say that, as it might be an omen; she could crash into a house, and sod's law it'll be mine.'

'Don't take on so, I'll speak to her when I pop over there. I said I'll make her a shepherd's pie to save her cooking as she has a lot on her plate, with those babies and learning to drive.'

Vera sniffed the air. 'It smells good. How many are you making?'

Ruby knew that if she said the right thing, Vera would stop moaning about Freda, although she would suggest that the girl practised driving around the town rather than up and down their road. 'I can probably stretch to making another small dish for you. That's if your Sadie isn't cooking your dinner?'

'James is working late, as Alan is off to his drama rehearsal, and Sadie's going to the pictures with a friend once she's put her kiddies down for the night. I'll have it for my supper,' she said, with no word of thanks.

'Then I'll have Bob drop it down to you later on.'

'I did want a word with your Bob and George. Isn't it about time I heard from that son of mine?'

Ruby sighed. Vera often asked the same question. It was as if she never listened to what she was being told.

'There's nothing more than a few months ago, when they heard he was working overseas and wouldn't be returning until next year, so you will have to be patient.'

'He might have come back early. I would like to see him before I go to meet my maker.'

'George told me that if he returns early, then someone will let him know. We will be down to your house like a shot if that should happen.' She didn't add that it was their Mike who would know, as Gerald Munro was wanted for questioning because it had been discovered that money was missing from the bowls club bank account. How would Vera feel when she knew that her long-lost son wasn't the upstanding figure in society she'd built him up to be?

23

Midday, Saturday 31 January 1953

Sarah looked out of the large doors of the Erith store and shivered. 'I don't think we'll be seeing many customers today,' she said to Jessie. 'It's a day for staying home and sitting by the fireside.'

'I hope things pick up, as there's nothing worse than twiddling our thumbs and watching the clock for our tea breaks. I've already tidied under the counter and made a list of stock that I need. Shall I go and help the others?'

'Please do, as we only have one supervisor on duty today and she is upstairs with Mrs Billington at the moment. I suggest you go to the counter with the pots and pans and give the stock a thorough wipe over with rags, as those pots do attract the dust. Keep an eye on your counter, though.'

'I will, but I doubt many customers will be wanting to purchase sweets today,' she said, looking over Sarah's shoulder towards the front of the store as the rain lashed the glass.

'You looked worried. Are your family all right at home?'

'I'm not sure, as they caught the early bus to go to

Belvedere to visit my nan at the funfair site. She sent them a few shillings in a Christmas card and they begged me to let them visit, to say thank you. I kept putting them off, thinking they'd forget, but they have not stopped going on about it. For them, visiting a funfair is a dream come true. I know differently, but I can't tell them why, as they are still too young to know what happened to me.'

Sarah was thoughtful. Jessie had escaped from her brutal uncle when she was much younger and had taken refuge in the store, hiding away upstairs. Since then she had turned her life around and had returned to work for Woolworths last year. If she was honest, she'd not allow her own children to go within a mile of where they might be in danger, but Jessie must have been sure that her kids would come to no harm in a few hours; the eldest was nearly nine years of age, and the few times Sarah had met him she was astounded by how mature and responsible he appeared to be. 'I tell you what. If the weather doesn't improve, I'll give you permission to slip away early.'

'Would you really?' she beamed. 'I'll make up my time next week.'

'There's really no need for that. I'd rather your children were safe. And besides, you work non-stop when you are on duty.'

'I'll give those pots and pans a bit more spit and polish,' Jessie grinned, before hurrying away with an armful of dusters.

Sarah checked the other counters before heading upstairs to her office, only to be waylaid by Maureen.

'I've made a pot of stew and dumplings, and there are sandwiches for anyone who doesn't want the stew for their lunch. I'm going to get back home and relieve George from looking after Buster and Georgie, before this weather gets worse. I've never known anything like it.'

'Yes, you do that, and take my umbrella,' Sarah urged her mother-in-law. 'Dad's not going out in this, is he?'

Maureen harrumphed. 'Would you believe that he and Bob are going down to Belvedere to finish decorating Clemmie's front room. Why they can't wait, I don't know, as the girl doesn't get married for another four weeks.'

Sarah shook her head. 'That's Dad all over, and Bob's just as bad. Take care, won't you?' she said, kissing Maureen's cheek. 'I would think Alan will be closing his shop soon, so that he can collect the kids earlier.'

'There's no rush, as you know I love having them, and if George is off out, then they will be company for me,' she said, pulling on her coat and scarf and taking Sarah's umbrella. 'Won't you need this?'

'I doubt it, as Freda is here this afternoon and she will be driving, so I can get a lift home.'

'Why ever is she driving, when she only lives down the road?'

'She has some things for Clemmie for the wedding that were too heavy to carry.'

'It's going to be a lovely do,' Maureen said as she waved goodbye.

If the weather picks up, Sarah thought, as she tapped on Betty's office door and walked into the room.

'Just to let you know I've put the staff on dusting duties, as it's as dead as a doornail downstairs. Oh, and Maureen has knocked off for the day. There's hot food and sandwiches in the staff room, ready for the lunch breaks.'

'Who is going to serve the food?' Freda asked. 'I'd offer, but I'm due downstairs and as I'm the only supervisor on duty today, I can't really leave the floor.'

'That's no worry, as Maureen's assistant will cover the lunch break, but she may need a hand,' Betty said, looking towards Clemmie, who was writing in a ledger.

Clemmie looked up and chuckled. 'I'll volunteer. I'm almost done here, as it is. Besides, the staff room is nice and warm, and I can drink as much tea as I want.'

'But leave the sticky buns alone or you'll not fit into your wedding gown,' Betty scolded her. 'Maisie has had to let it out twice, as it is.'

Freda frowned and looked at Sarah, while Clemmie blushed.

'I was going to tell you, but now that you've mentioned letting out my gown . . . Please don't tell Daddy.'

'Tell Daddy what, dear?'

Sarah and Freda burst out laughing. 'Oh, Betty,' they said in unison.

'Oh, my! Couldn't you wait a few more weeks, dear?' Betty asked as the penny dropped. 'How will I find another cashier, if you go on maternity leave?'

That made the girls laugh even more. Trust Betty to think of the store rather than of being a grandmother, Sarah thought to herself.

'We love each other and, besides, we will soon be married. I'll help you train up a new cashier, I promise,' Clemmie said, still looking apprehensive. 'Please don't tell Daddy.'

'He's bound to notice before too long,' Betty pointed out.

'Men don't count the months like a woman does, so he'll be none the wiser,' Sarah said. 'When is your due date?'

'I have no idea. I've not even seen our doctor yet, in case he told you and Daddy.'

'Then before we start worrying unduly, I will make an appointment for us both to see him on Monday. Until then, we will keep things to ourselves, and that includes not telling your father. May I request that you and Jimmy are more . . . more circumspect until after the wedding?'

This made the three younger women start to giggle, with Betty wondering what she had said that was so funny.

'I don't think you should be going out,' Ruby said as she pulled the curtains across the bay window in her front room. 'It's getting worse out there and it'll be dark in three hours.'

'Don't worry yourself,' Bob said. 'I'll be in George's car, and it'll only take twenty minutes to drive down the Belvedere, then I'll be inside young Clemmie's house. I'll be as safe there as I am here.'

'What if the car crashes in all this wind?' Ruby said, turning away in case he saw the worry on her face. 'I want to know that you and George are safe.'

'There's a telephone at the house, so you can give me a call if anything should happen.'

'That's if the telephone lines don't come down,' she replied, going back to the window to peer between the curtains.

'You worry too much, old woman.'

'I have to, as you don't give enough thought to what could happen, old man,' she fired back at him in jest.

He shook his head at her. 'I'm grateful you care for me, Ruby, but sometimes . . .'

'I know, it goes in one ear and out the other. Make sure you write Clemmie's number in the little book by the telephone, then I'll not say another word.'

'I'd be grateful for a few sandwiches to take with me. I don't like to touch the food in their house, even though we've been told to help ourselves.'

'I've already packed up some food for the pair of you. There's some Corned Beef hash to warm up and a flask of soup. I reckon Maureen will have packed up some grub as well; I've never known her see anyone go short.'

Bob licked his lips. 'She's a good one, is Maureen.'

Ruby slapped his arm. 'You're only thinking of your stomach! Now go and change your trousers. You're not painting woodwork in your second-best pair.'

Bob did as he was told, while Ruby collected the food she'd put aside; she'd never let her menfolk go hungry.

'What time did George say he'd be here?'

'He was finishing up his council work early afternoon and was changing his clothes, then he'll be here; in fact, that sounds like his car now.'

'They all sound the same to me,' she replied, pulling a scarf around his neck and tucking it inside his coat. 'Wear your woolly hat as well, it'll keep your head warm.'

'I look daft in this,' he replied, about to pull it off.

'You'll wear it and be grateful; our Georgie knitted it for you for Christmas. She'd be mortified if she thought you didn't like it. Besides, she made one for George as well, so you'll both look alike. Now be off with you, and tell George to drive slowly.' Ruby kissed his cheek before opening the front door and ushering him out. 'I'll not hang about, as it's blooming cold,' she said, giving George a quick wave.

'Oh, blast!' Clemmie said as she spotted a large tin of paint and several brushes behind the door in her office.

'Whatever's wrong?' Freda asked from the corridor. 'Have you hurt yourself?'

'No, it's these decorating materials. I meant to take them home last night, so George and Bob had them today, ready to start work. They will be at my house now and won't be able to do any work. I hate to waste their time when they've been so good to us.'

'I'm sure Betty would let you go home early. She was talking of doing that before lunch. She and Sarah are making up a list of the staff who live furthest away and will need to catch buses before they stop running. By all accounts, a customer came in earlier and said there are trees down and the bus services are affected. It makes me glad I live only a short walk away.'

'The tins are too heavy for me to carry them on a bus, and perhaps I shouldn't at the moment . . . I meant to take them last night, as Jimmy was collecting me on his way home. It's just a nuisance,' she said.

'Hmm, I have an idea. Get your things together and I'll have a word with Betty and Sarah,' she went on, hurrying from the small office, then walking briskly along the corridor and entering the open door of the manager's office, where Sarah and Betty had their heads together over the desk, juggling the staff rota.

'Sorry to bother you. I can help with getting a few of the girls home safely.'

'That would be a great help. Who are you thinking of?' Betty asked. 'I've never known weather like this, and it is getting much worse. I don't want any of the staff getting stuck somewhere and not being able to reach their homes. Head office has given permission for us to close the store early. It seems this bad weather is coming down the east coast from The Netherlands.'

Freda and Sarah both shuddered and looked at each other as the store shook under a sudden gust of wind, before Freda spoke. 'Clemmie needs to get to her bungalow in Belvedere as she has the decorating materials that Bob and George will be waiting for; she forgot they were in her office. Jessie wants to go to Belvedere to collect her children. I could drive them both there and then bring Jessie back with her children, if you would allow me to do so? We've only got to walk round to Alexandra Road and get into my car. I'd rather like to pop indoors and tell Bessie to take the children over to Ruby's house to keep her company until we are all home, or the storm is over.'

'Then go now,' Betty said. 'Sarah and I can finish up here. Would you like me to contact Tony to tell him where you and the children are?'

'If you would, as it will stop him worrying.'

'I'll ring Alan and have him go direct to Maureen's, to collect her and the children and head to number thirteen; we should all be together in this bad weather.'

'My goodness, this reminds me of the war years, and how we all looked out for each other,' Betty said, looking a little pale.

Freda placed her hand on Betty's arm. 'There's no need to be concerned. At least we don't have to worry about planes dropping bombs on our heads, or spending the night down an air-raid shelter. It's just a bit of wind; we will cope.'

Sarah felt a sense of foreboding and prayed the storm would soon blow itself out.

Freda hurried into her house and quickly gave instructions to Bessie, who had been watching the worsening weather from the front window while the children slept. Clemmie and Jessie helped her get the older two dressed warmly and collect bedding, nappies and feeds, before heading over to Ruby, who welcomed them with open arms. Freda explained where she was going, and that Tony had been notified. Ruby insisted they take rugs and a torch with them, in case they were cut off. With Ruby's promise to look after everyone and to inform Maisie where they were ringing in their ears, the three girls set off for Belvedere as the skies darkened over Erith and the wind blew more wildly still.

24

Maisie flung her arms around David's neck. 'The house is absolutely perfect, so hurry up and do the paperwork before someone else takes it. I can't believe it has taken so long for us to find a house that suits our growing family.'

David kissed her forehead and untangled himself from her arms. 'My dear wife, if you hadn't been so fussy, we could have moved a year ago. Let's face it, who wants rooms where they can set up a home-based sewing business? I'm not sure our neighbours will be impressed. Don't forget that we've moved up in the world, now we'll be living up The Avenue.'

'Oh, David, it's not as if I'll be setting up a sweatshop in the cellar and having staff working through the night by candlelight. I want a room that I can use as an office away from the factory in Slade Green, and it would be nice to have a workroom for my ladies who do the delicate hand-stitching, as I'm going upmarket, with bridal gowns and evening wear.' She snorted at her own words. 'Listen to me, acting all la-di-dah!'

'You will never be that, my love. Now, do you have time for a quick chat about the allocation of bedrooms or do you have to dash back to the factory?'

'I can spare half an hour, but I do need to be back there to see a couple of suppliers who are bringing me samples of next season's fabrics. I said I'd give them the grand tour; I'm afraid it will mean me being home late again. There's a pie in the pantry, so you will only have to peel the spuds. I do hope the girls have remembered to tidy up the work-room,' she said as her mind started to wander back to her work.

David could see the signs. It was hard to speak to Maisie when she was thinking of her work. 'I'll go and see what the children are up to, then we can have that chat.' He smiled indulgently.

'Don't let them climb the apple tree; we don't know how safe it is,' she called out as he left her alone in the large front room on the first floor of the detached Victorian house. In her mind's eye, Maisie could see her staff working on delicate beading and embroidery. The light from the large bay window would make hand-stitching so much easier on the eye. She wandered through to the other two rooms on that floor and could see where a sewing machine and cutting table would fit, leaving the room at the back for her office. The ground floor would be the family's living area, with the two top floors given over to bedrooms. Why David needed to chat about it, when she could see how the house would suit her family and her business, she didn't know. It was perfect. A thought came to her and she hurried down the wide staircase to the hall, taking a small staircase to a cellar that ran the length of the property. With a bit of work and a lick of paint, it would be ideal, she thought to herself.

'Ah, there you are,' David said as he found Maisie

scribbling in a notebook while sitting on an upturned wooden crate. 'I've gathered the children and brought them into the kitchen. It's blowing a gale outside and is much worse than when we came here. I suggest you jump into your van and get over to the factory, but don't stay long, as I feel this weather has set in for the day. I'll take the children home and stay with them.'

Maisie nodded her head. She'd been so caught up in her plans for the house that she'd not noticed the weather getting so bad. 'Before you go . . .'

'Maisie, it can wait,' he said. 'I need to collect our things and make a move. I'd like to see you on your way as well.'

She knew he was right, but even so she wanted to share her idea. 'Let me tell you as we collect everything,' she said, leading the way upstairs. 'Did you have any plans for the cellar?'

'I'd not really thought about it, but I can assure you that I won't be working from home, if that's what you are worried about?'

Maisie chuckled. 'It hadn't crossed my mind. Our new neighbours would have something to say if they spotted coffins being carried in and out of the house.'

David took her arm as they reached the top of the staircase. 'Thank you,' he said, looking serious. 'There aren't many wives who would put up with their husband's change of career to that of running a chain of funeral parlours.'

'Don't start talking daft. I'd be proud of you even if you swept the streets; not that that isn't an honest living. Besides, if you decided to give it up tomorrow, I could do with someone running the business side of things, if you didn't mind working for your wife?'

He looked horrified. 'You know how squeamish I was when I first joined Douglas Billington in the funeral business, but working for my wife – no, thank you. Now what was it you wanted to discuss about the cellar?' he asked, before calling the children to get ready to leave.

'Well, we both want our Bessie and Jenny to live with us, now we'll have a bigger house. I thought it would be nice for her to have her own place and be away from us more, now that she is a mother. The back of the cellar leads out to the garden, and we could easily have a small kitchen, a living room and a bedroom built in there and still leave enough room for whatever you wish to put there – as long as it's not a storeroom for your work,' she grinned.

'I like the idea, but let's leave it up to Bessie to decide, as she may want to live upstairs with us.' He reached for the bundle of house keys. 'I'll drop these back with the estate agent on the way home and tell him we want the house and will be paying cash for the property.'

'We are very lucky,' Maisie said as she kissed him goodbye and shouted out, 'See you later' to the children, who were still running about.

As she headed back through Erith before taking the road towards Slade Green, Maisie started to think again how lucky she was to be married to a man she loved so much. At one time her life had been so different, and she could easily have ended up in a profession that no woman in her right mind would wish to pursue.

What there was of the late-afternoon light was fading quickly, casting long shadows over the hedgerow as she drove down the narrow lane towards the marshes. Cursing herself for having purchased her small factory in such a bleak place, she momentarily forgot that she'd picked it up for a song and wouldn't have been able to afford one closer to Erith. 'Once we've got into the new house, I'm going to look into finding a better factory,' she muttered, jumping out of her skin as a branch came crashing down at the side of the lane. 'Oh, bugger this!' she shouted as she pulled into the small square of factories similar to her own and parked in front of the main door.

'Mum, you must be mad, driving in this weather,' Claudette said as she hurried from the building, holding her coat around her shoulders. 'The roof was rattling so much just now that I thought it was going to take off. The salesmen have cancelled their appointment, so I reckon we should send everyone off home early or we'll be sleeping here all night.'

'Thank goodness for that. At least the men won't be stuck here with us.'

'There are six of us still here. Daphne's husband is on his way, and she said they will take three of the women with them, as it's not safe for them to ride their bicycles. I thought we could take the rest. I don't mind climbing in the back of the van. I've made a hot drink and everyone's in the staff room, waiting for you to decide what we should do with the factory.'

'What should we do?' Maisie stammered as she hurried into the building.

'We – I mean I and the other women – thought about boarding up the windows and putting as much as we can into the stockroom, then covering it with a tarpaulin, in case the wind lifts the roof off the building overnight.'

'Good thinking. Let's have that cuppa and get cracking. I can tell you about our new house at the same time.'

'You mean Dad's going to buy it?'

'It's ours, once he's signed on the dotted line.'

'And I'll have my own bedroom?'

'That's right.' Maisie smiled at her daughter's excited face as she went on to explain about her idea for Bessie and the baby.

'You have forgotten one thing, or two really,' Claudette said as she held open the door to the staff room. 'What about Sadie and Freda?'

'Oh, bugger!' Maisie said, not for the first time that day. 'I can't let Sadie go, but I doubt she will want to walk up The Avenue every day to work for me, not while her nan's poorly; but I can't bear to lose her, after all she's done for me. As for Freda, she's started to rely on our Bessie to look after her little ones, so that she can put in a couple of days a week at Woolworths. Who'd have thought moving house could cause so many problems?'

The pair went to join the other workers, with Maisie greeting them all and commenting on the awful weather as she started to hand out instructions.

The women soon set to moving all the valuable materials and patterns into the small stockroom, covering them with tarpaulin to pre-empt any leaks that might occur during the night. 'I'm hoping the wind drops and all will be fine, but please don't take any risks coming into work. Those of you who have telephones, I will let you know whether or not to come to work. The ladies without telephones, can you make your way to a phone box and ring one of these numbers?' she asked, handing out slips of paper with several telephone numbers. 'I don't want any of you setting off without knowing that we will be open. No one will have their wages stopped if they cannot get to work due to the bad weather.'

There was a round of applause and voiced thanks, along with promises to make up their time. Claudette watched the reaction to her mother's words and vowed to herself that she would one day be as sensitive an employer as her mother.

David Carlisle gave a sigh of relief as he turned into Alexandra Road. He'd be glad when the children were inside and safe. A few times it had felt as though the strong wind was taking charge of the car and he was powerless to control it. Driving slowly up the road, he spotted Alan getting out of his car in front of Ruby's house and assisting his mum and children to the gate. He slowed and wound down a window.

'Taking refuge?' he called out.

Alan walked over to David and leant on the car. 'Sarah thought it would be a good idea to be with Ruby, as Bob and my dad are out helping Clemmie decorate her house. I've locked up early and put boards up at the window of the shop, to be on the safe side. I don't like the look of this weather.'

'I'm hoping it'll blow over by morning as we've a full schedule for tomorrow. It's always busy at this time of the year.'

'There's never a good time, when our businesses are involved. I was due at a rehearsal this evening with Claudette, but it's been decided not to go ahead.'

David chuckled. 'I never thought our Claudette would be able to talk you into joining her amateur-dramatic group, although I must say you made a great genie in the panto-mime. Our kids didn't recognize you.'

Alan guffawed. 'It was all that make-up!'

David looked over his shoulder to see what the children were up to and was glad to see they were sleeping. 'I wondered if you and Sarah were still thinking of moving house?'

'Sarah never stops talking about it. I know we are growing out of the house, but it was my dad's place, and I don't feel right selling it after all these years.'

David nodded thoughtfully. 'I may just have the answer. I'll leave this idea with you: how would you like to rent our house?'

Alan's mouth opened wide. 'Now that's a thought, as it would suit us down to the ground. I'll catch you later and we can have a chat; best not say anything to Sarah for now, as you know what she's like when she gets a bee in her bonnet,' he chuckled. 'Cheers for thinking of us, David,' he said, as David started up the engine and headed to the top of Alexandra Road and their home – for now.

'Are you sure Clemmie said she was leaving the decorating materials here? I wonder if we were supposed to collect them somewhere,' George asked as he looked around the detached bungalow in Crabtree Manorway in lower Belvedere. 'I know it's only a ten-minute drive away, but it will eat into our decorating time if we have to go back to Erith.

'That's what the message said. Ruby wrote it down and left it by the telephone. She may hate using the telephone, but she doesn't make mistakes with messages,' Bob replied.

'That's true and she enjoys a chat, now she is used to it,' George chuckled.

'Did you notice she's had me move the armchairs about, so she can sit comfortably while she has a natter?' Bob shook his head as he thought about it.

'It may take Mum a while to get used to new gadgets, but she makes full use of them once she does. Now, I'm going to check inside the shed, in case the paint has been left out there,' George said as he picked through the keys that had been left out for them. 'I may be some time,' he added as a strong gust of wind hit the back of the house.

Bob started to lay out the old sheets that had been left to cover the furniture they'd stacked against one wall. It was too early to eat the food Ruby had packed for them, so he wandered through to the small kitchen and filled the kettle. Jimmy had already installed a new electric-powered cooker, so in no time at all the kettle started to whistle. By then he'd checked the oven and had played with the various knobs.

'What are you doing there, cooking us up some dinner?' George asked as he struggled to close the back door behind him.

'I was thinking Ruby would like one of these cookers. I'll collect some brochures from the Electric Showrooms and have her choose one. It'll be a nice gift for our anniversary.'

George thought that if he was to treat Maureen to a cooker, she'd have something to say about it, but his mum liked her home comforts and would no doubt be thrilled. 'Why wait until your anniversary, as it's not until 8 May?'

Bob scratched his head. 'Fancy you remembering the

date; Ruby has to remind me every year. She starts to hint a month beforehand, in case I forget.'

'I'm not likely to forget as you married on VE Day.'

'Blow me down, I'd forgotten that,' Bob chuckled as he took a tin of cocoa from the cupboard and spooned some into two mugs. At the same time the lights started to flicker. 'Do you reckon we'll have a power cut?'

'We could well do, as it's so open out here on the marshes. I've got torches and candles in the car, but as I didn't find anything in the shed, apart from turpentine and spare brushes, we may as well head home once we've drunk this.'

Bob had just washed up their mugs when they heard a car outside and George went to see who it was. Very few cars drove down this end of Crabtree Manorway, especially in such weather.

'It looks like Freda's car,' George said as he pulled on his coat and hurried down the path to greet them.

'I forgot to give you the paint,' Clemmie apologized as she climbed out of the front passenger seat and hurried to the boot, where George helped her take out two large cans, along with a bag of decorating materials. 'Is it too late for you to get started?'

'We could put in a couple of hours,' Bob said as he joined them and gave Freda a hug. 'How was the journey?' he asked, knowing that Freda was new to driving and tended to not use the clutch properly.

'It was a bit on the bumpy side,' a young woman said, climbing out of the back seat, 'but she done better than I ever could in this weather.'

'Bob, George, this is Jessie. I'm going to take her to collect her children, who are with their relatives down

Boars Manorway. It's just along the lower road a little more; you can see the lights from the fairground caravans across the nursery's glasshouses,' she explained as Bob gave her a questioning look.

'I can stay with them, rather than bother you any more,' Jessie said, biting her bottom lip.

Freda was aware of Jessie's circumstances and why she had run away from the family fairground as a young woman, and she was not about to allow Jessie to stay at the fairground in case the troublesome uncle appeared. 'I'll take you there and bring you all back here. I've brought food, so we can all eat,' she said, looking towards Clemmie, who gave a discreet nod of agreement. 'Let's get cracking and collect your children,' she suggested as they got back into the car, waving goodbye to the others, who watched as the lights from the car slowly faded as it headed back up the Manorway to the main road.

'I'll help you,' Clemmie said to George, who was already carrying the paint into the house. 'Can you teach me how to decorate, as I'm bound to have to do a lot of this in the future.'

'We can make a start now,' George said, while Bob eyed the packages of food that Ruby had left for him.

'Perhaps we should eat first?'

George looked towards the window as another gust of wind hit the house. 'Better that we wait for Freda and Jessie to get back,' he said, hoping they weren't too long. The weather was getting worse, and God only knew how they would fare out here on the low-lying marshes of Belvedere.

25

'This is so exciting, and much better than camping outdoors,' Georgina Gilbert said as she helped her great-grandmother, Ruby, lay out cushions and blankets in the front room for the children. 'Do you think we should string a blanket between the chairs to make a tent, or perhaps some of us could sleep in the air-raid shelter in the garden?'

Ruby felt tired and was worried about Bob and George, as she'd not heard from them. 'The shelter is full of Bob's bits and pieces, and no one in their right mind would want to sleep in there,' she said, her mind going back to when Sarah gave birth to the child in the shelter during an air raid and became trapped. If it wasn't their dog, Nelson, making a commotion, they could have been there still. Her heart lurched at the thought of Nelson, as she missed him still; abandoned during the air raids, he had become her constant companion and there had never been a dog like him since.

'Nanny Ruby, I'm talking to you.' Georgie tugged on Ruby's sleeve from where she sat on the floor.

'Sorry, my love, I was away with the fairies for a minute there. Now, how many beds do we need to make up for the children? The babies have their prams and can stay in the other room with the adults. Is it warm enough in here?' she asked, looking at the embers glowing in the fire as they heard a gust of wind sweep down the road between the terraced houses. 'I'll add a few lumps of coal and fix the fireguard in place.' She was doing just that as the telephone started to ring.

'I can answer that; we learnt about it in the Brownies,' Georgie said, getting up quickly and rushing to the sideboard where the black Bakelite telephone sat on a cream crocheted table mat. 'Erith four-five-five, Nanny Ruby's house,' she answered politely. 'Hello, Granddad Bob. Nanny Ruby is right here, if you will wait a minute while I get her.'

Ruby smiled, not only because of Georgie's impeccable manners, but because of the way the children all referred to her and Bob as 'Nanny Ruby' and 'Granddad Bob', even though they were their great-grandparents.

'Thank you, darling. Would you fetch your Nanny Maureen, as she may want to speak to your Granddad George?' she asked, thinking how many grandparents the children had – even she felt confused. 'Hello, Bob. How are you getting on? Have you finished painting the room?' she asked, noticing how her heavy curtains were moving slightly as the wind worked its way through the sash windows; she'd get some newspaper and force it between the gaps to stop the draught. 'What's that, Clemmie didn't give you the paint? I thought Freda was driving her down with it. Oh, she's there now, thank goodness! The silly girl has her head in the clouds over her wedding. Are you coming home?'

'No, we've decided to put in a few hours to see if we

can get the room finished. George reckons it can be done, with the girls' help. Can you let Tony know that Freda is staying to help us? She will be back soon.'

'Back from where?' Ruby was getting confused and pulled a face at Maureen as she entered the room. 'Maureen's here, can you let George speak to her. I'll see you later,' she said, placing the receiver onto the crocheted mat and stepping aside for Maureen. 'Try to find out who is there and how long they'll be, as I'm getting confused,' she said as she left Maureen to speak to George in peace.

Back in the living room, Sarah and Mike's wife Gwyneth were clearing the table of cups and saucers, while Alan and Mike were twiddling with the knobs on the wireless. Bessie was keeping an eye on the sleeping babies.

'You need a new one of these,' Alan said, shaking his head, 'the reception is terrible.'

'It suits me fine, lad,' Ruby said as she joined them. 'What's your problem with it?' she asked as she started to help the girls.

'Nan, we thought we could make sausage and mash for the children's tea, and I've put diced shin of beef in the oven, along with carrots and onions for the adults. We can eat after the kids have been put to bed. Gwyneth brought sausages over, and Freda gave me a pound of beef before she went over to Belvedere.'

'That sounds good to me, and you'll find a treacle tart in the pantry for afters.'

'Not for me,' Mike called. 'I'm on duty shortly and it is going to be a long night, I reckon. Thanks for having Gwyneth and the children here. I like to think they are in safe hands during this bad weather.'

'Any time, there's no need to ask. I'll pack up some sandwiches and a flask of tea for you,' Ruby said to her stepson. 'What makes you think you are in for a long night? Surely a police sergeant doesn't have to go out walking the beat at night?'

'It's all hands to the pumps in this kind of weather. We are bound to be a few men down, if they can't get into the station due to the bad storm. 'I may be late home in the morning,' he said, turning to his wife, who was nursing their youngest child.

'Gwyneth will be all right here with me.'

'I don't want to be any trouble. The children and I can go home to sleep,' she insisted.

'Let's see how the evening progresses,' Ruby said. 'I'd rather have my family close by and know they are safe. I've not known wind like this,' she went on, knowing from the look on Mike's face that he was concerned. 'I'll be happier when Bob, George and the girls are back home. Sarah, can you put a telephone call through to Betty to let her know about Clemmie?'

'There's no need,' Maureen said as she joined them. 'Clemmie has just rung her, and Betty will let Jimmy know; he's with his children at his mother's house.'

'Gosh, it's like calling a school register,' Sarah grinned.

'I can go up to my mum's to stay the night, so that's one adult and a baby out of your hair,' Bessie said.

'No, you stay here with us. You'll get blown to kingdom come and most definitely won't be able to control your pram,' Sarah replied. 'Why not call Maisie and let her know?'

'I'll do that,' Bessie said, checking that Jenny was still

asleep in her pram as she walked through the hall to the front room, where Georgie, aided by Myfi Jackson, was busy repairing the tents, where Buster had pulled them down. He'd been made to sit in an armchair, out of harm's way. Bessie went to make her call and hurried back to the living room. 'The telephone isn't working.'

'The wireless has lost its signal as well,' Alan said.

Freda drove carefully down the unmade Boars Manorway towards the turn-off for the funfair winter grounds. She'd never experienced so many holes in the road, with many of them being filled with rainwater. They'd already passed glasshouses and several nurseries, and on the left allotments led to the Belvedere football ground. There wasn't a soul to be seen, and already the afternoon had turned dark and brooding. 'I can't see any lights on. Are you sure your relatives are home?'

Jessie peered through the windscreen. 'They don't have electric lights and use oil lamps in the caravans. There is a generator, but that's more for the rides and machinery.'

'Are the rides set up?' Freda asked, thinking how strange it would be to see a fairground in action during such violent weather.

'No, it only comes out to be painted and repaired ready for the spring.'

'How do people earn a living?' she asked, swerving as a small branch flew in front of them.

'They can all put their hands to other work. Some of my uncles are chimneysweeps; it's another of the family businesses. I have cousins who are casual labourers. There's a strong work ethic in the showman's world.'

'What about all the other caravans over towards the banks of the Thames, are they related to you?'

'No, they are Romany Gypsies. I know some of them and they are a decent sort. Sadly, the council is trying to move them on, and they've lived on this land for many years and are no trouble to man or beast. I went hop-picking with a family of them once; it was great fun for a kid, but again they worked hard for the little money they earnt. It was like a holiday. I'd do it again in a flash, if my kids didn't have school to go to.'

Freda was just about to ask about living conditions at the hop fields when the car's headlamps picked up an entrance between the trees.

'Here we are,' Jessie said. 'Go slowly and bear to the left once you've passed the big tree. Be careful of the guard dogs, in case they've been let loose to protect the yard.'

Freda gripped the steering wheel, wondering if she could stay in the car while Jessie collected her children. She was wary of large dogs at the best of times.

'It's all right, the dogs are still chained up in their kennels,' Jessie said as the headlamps picked up several pairs of glowing eyes, followed by the clanking of chains and loud barking. 'You can stop here. Come in and meet my nan,' she said, getting out of the car while holding onto the door as the wind tried to tug it away.

Freda followed, unsure of where she was going until a door opened, shining a light out into the dark night. 'Get yourself inside, ducks, before you're blown away,' a woman called out.

Freda quickly climbed a few wooden steps and found herself standing with Jessie inside a warm caravan, filled with light from an ornate oil lamp. On a side table a grey parrot sat inside an iron cage, quietly muttering swear words.

'Don't be minding Polly; she can cuss with the best of them, but keep your fingers away from the bars or she'll take off your finger,' the woman laughed, holding up a gnarled hand with the tip of one finger missing. 'Sit yourself down and warm your bones while I get the kiddies ready for home,' she continued, waving towards a small armchair next to a wood-burning stove, before disappearing behind a heavy brocade curtain.

Freda could hear Jessie speaking, along with the cheerful chatter of young children. Reaching out, she warmed her hands close to the stove before gazing around the caravan. This must be the living room, she thought, looking at a glass cabinet full of floral-patterned crockery; the stove was used for cooking, and she could see a small sink in one corner. There's everything here you would want, she thought to herself. The parrot was looking intently at her and, as she stared back, it swore at her, before dancing back and forth on its perch.

'Are we going to your house?' a small boy asked, appearing from behind the curtain.

'We are going to my friend's home, as soon as you have buttoned up your coat,' Freda said, helping him fasten his duffel coat securely and pulling a knitted balaclava over his head. 'Do you have gloves?' she asked.

He held up his arms for her to see a pair of matching knitted mittens hanging from each sleeve.

'So they don't get lost,' he said, showing gaps in his teeth.

'He's always losing clothes,' Jessie replied as she joined

them with her two daughters, all dressed identically in gabardine rain-macs and knitted hats. 'Thank goodness Nan's a good knitter.'

'That's what nans are for,' Freda smiled, thinking of Ruby and her plentiful supply of knitted clothes for the young-sters. 'Are we all ready?'

'Take them to high ground, as the night will become worse,' Jessie's nan said as she entered the room.

'Would you like to come with us?' Freda asked, as a sense of foreboding came over her. Was the woman a Romany who could see into the future?

'Don't mind Nan; she has a way with her,' Jessie said with a grin. 'I have family in the other caravans, so they will all be safe.'

Freda went first, hurrying to open the doors of the car and helping the children into the back while Jessie climbed into the front. The engine started after a little complaining, and they set off into the night, with the children huddled together, not speaking a word.

'We are going to a house that belongs to one of the ladies from Woolworths,' Jessie called over her shoulder. 'We will be going home later,' she added, as Freda wondered if she was up to driving far in the worsening weather.

'This looks like Freda coming back,' Clemmie said as she peered between her net curtains.

'I'll bring them inside while you finish lighting the candles,' George said as he pulled on his already-wet rain-coat. He wanted to add that just before the lights went out, the telephone had died. He'd been talking to Betty at the time, assuring her that he would look after her daughter;

he'd keep quiet about that for now, in case Clemmie panicked. Opening the door and bending his body against the gale-force wind, he reached the car and picked up the youngest of the children, while Jessie and Freda helped the others between them. They staggered inside, where Bob and Clemmie helped the children out of their coats and led them to one of the settees that had been uncovered.

'I've lit a fire in the grate and it won't take long to warm you up,' Bob smiled before joining Freda. 'What's it like to drive out there?'

'Horrendous and getting worse; my car just about got us here and then gave up out the front; we coasted the last couple of yards. Do you think we can all squeeze into George's to get back home?'

'We will have to do the best we can, even if we turn into sardines in the process,' he grinned. 'Now, shall we eat that food and give the children a hot drink before we set off?'

'It will calm our nerves for the journey back to Erith,' Freda replied, going to join Clemmie in the kitchen, where she had put the kettle on her new stove and was turning knobs back and forth.

'It's not working,' she said, getting irritated. 'It's brand-new. Jimmy won't be impressed, as it cost an arm and a leg.'

'It's electric and won't work as the power has gone down,' Freda replied, trying not to smile.

'Oh, silly me. At least we have the Thermos flasks.' She laughed at her own mistake. 'Look at us, laughing while it feels as though it's the end of the world. Everything will look much better in the morning.'

26

'It's no good, it won't start,' George said, running a hand over his face to clear the rainwater stinging his eyes. 'Water has got in from somewhere and I'm at a loss what to do. I'm afraid we are stuck here until tomorrow when, hopefully, I can telephone the garage to come out and help me.'

Bob started to cough as he held a torch out to help George see what he was doing. 'That's if the telephone is working. At least everyone knows we are safe and can muck down here for the night. Things could be worse.'

George agreed as they struggled back inside Clemmie's bungalow. 'It's going to be a bit of a tight squeeze, with only one living room with a fire. The two bedrooms don't even seem to have grates for a fire to be lit, and the boxroom is full of boxes. I reckon we've no choice but to all kip down in the living room to stay warm. But first let's get you out of that wet coat, Bob, and warming by the fire; I don't like the sound of that cough, and Mum will have my guts for garters if you are taken ill on my watch.'

'No need to worry about me; this is just the end of that cold I caught off the children over Christmas,' he replied, although he didn't argue when George led him to an armchair by the fire and covered him with one of the clean sheets that had been put aside to cover the furniture while they were decorating.

'I'm pleased we had the forethought to start moving furniture into the house, but it's a shame most of it is still in storage while we decorate, as you would have been more comfortable having a nap in a warm bed,' Clemmie said, looking worried as Bob started to cough once more. 'At least you can huddle down in the armchair; the children will have to sleep on the floor.'

'I'm fine, love. I'll soon get myself warm and dry here, and it won't be the first time I've had a snooze in an armchair and it certainly won't be the last. Once I've warmed up, the children can sit here. I could kill for a cup of tea, though.'

'I have an idea,' Freda said as she beckoned Clemmie to follow her into the small kitchen and closed the door behind them.

'Is there something wrong?' Clemmie asked.

'We need to keep Bob warm, and a hot drink would help immensely. I wonder, would you mind if we used one of your new saucepans? We could put water into it and, if we are careful, it could sit on top of the fire. I'm not sure it would do the saucepan much good, though . . .'

'That's a great idea, and don't worry about the pan as they came from Woolworths and can easily be replaced. I'd been buying bits and pieces gradually for my bottom drawer and I often browsed in the store during my lunch breaks.'

Freda chuckled. 'I've done the same myself, just like many of the female staff, no doubt.'

'Why don't we use the kettle?'

'It's a bit bulky. This pan would be better,' she said, taking a medium-sized pan from a shelf over the cooker and filling it with water. 'Thank goodness you have plenty of tea and cocoa, and is that Camp coffee I can see?'

'Yes, I've stocked up so that anyone who is here helping to get the house fit to live in won't go without a drink. I'm not sure we have enough milk to get us through the night, although there's some tins of Carnation milk in the cupboard.'

'If it comes to it, I'm used to drinking cocoa without milk; it happened often when I worked in the Fire Service during the war. Come on, let's get these drinks made and then we can all have a sleep, as it's nearly midnight.'

'You've led such an interesting life,' Clemmie sighed.

'Much of it was forced on me, due to the war and my family circumstances, and I'm no different from many other women. You will experience some hardship tonight, as there's only our coats and the floor to sleep on,' she grinned.

Ruby couldn't sleep. She'd objected when the family had insisted on her going to bed, telling them she would give it up for others, and had only agreed when Maureen said she would share with her. They'd lain awake, chatting for a while, before Maureen dozed off and she was now snoring gently.

The wind was buffeting the back of the terraced house and Ruby tried to tell herself that they'd had worse in the last war, but wasn't so sure they had. In her head she counted her family and close friends, and ticked them off one by one when she knew they were safe. That left Mike, who was on duty at Erith police station; she prayed nothing untoward would happen and that his shift was spent peacefully indoors. Then there was Bob and George; she knew they were at Clemmie's bungalow, but when the telephone failed to work, she could only imagine that, due to the weather, they would stay there until the morning rather than risk driving through the night in this awful storm. 'Night-night, old man,' she whispered.

Downstairs, Sarah and Alan had taken up residency in the front room, overseeing the children who were camping on the floor. Alan had taken an armchair while Sarah had the settee and they were talking quietly, with the glow of the open fire casting shadows over the children, who were now sleeping contentedly.

'I've got to get something off my chest,' Alan said, propping himself up on one elbow and looking at Sarah.

'Can't it wait, love? I don't want the children waking up,' she said, hearing him give a big sigh. 'All right, but keep your voice low.'

'I spoke with David when he pulled up outside earlier. It seems they've finally found a house they like and he's going ahead with the sale.'

'I'm pleased for them; they may have a three-bedroomed house now, but with such a large family it's bulging at the seams. Where is the new house?'

'Up The Avenue; it's the one close to the entrance to the park near the bowling green.'

Sarah fell silent. Of course she was pleased for her friend, but a twinge of jealousy crept into her thoughts. Why was it that she and Alan and the children were squeezed into the two-up, two-down in Crayford Road when the pair of them worked so hard and deserved something better?

'Are you awake?'

'Yes,' was all she could say, in case her voice cracked with pent-up emotion.

'The thing is, David wondered if we'd like first refusal on renting their current house?'

'Renting? Aren't they going to sell it? Not that we could afford a house in this street just yet.'

'I've been thinking it would be ideal for us; the children could have a room each and there are the two front rooms . . .'

Sarah sighed. 'I'd adore to live in the house; Maisie has decorated it so nicely and it's close to Nan. But what about our house? You mum gave it to us, and you were born there – do you really want to move?' She knew this was one of the reasons Alan had dragged his heels every time she'd mentioned moving.

'How about if we rented our house to someone, and used the rent money to put towards the rent for David and Maisie's place?'

'Oh, I don't know. It is an awful risk. What if we can't find a tenant, or they don't pay us? Then of course it's likely we won't get as much income from our house as what David will expect for his property. We can't expect him to rent it to us for lower than the going rate.'

'Good grief, no. And if he did, I'd turn him down flat.'

'Oh, Alan, it's such a wonderful opportunity; I know it's not owning our own home, but it would mean a better life than we have at the moment. Plus, if anything should ever go wrong, we would still own our family home.' She lay back, staring at the glowing embers in the fire. 'There must be something we can do . . .'

'If only the turnover was a little more at the shop, it would give us a buffer in case anything went pear-shaped,' he said aloud.

'Were you not going to expand the repair side of the business? Surely that would be a useful income?'

'I agree, but it would mean me taking on another member of staff. I'm trained enough at present to be able to under-take repairs on televisions and smaller items, but I can't be in two places at once. Besides, some repairs will be done in people's homes or the sets will be brought into the shop. I can't expect James to help, as he handles the bike side of the business. It needs someone to watch the shop and do the books.'

'What about Dad?'

'He'd help in a flash, but with all his councillor work, as well as his consultancy stuff for Vickers, I can't expect him to do more. I took the bookkeeping side back, to give him time for his own work. If we hire someone, it will defeat the object of bringing home enough money to pay rent to David. There must be a way.'

'There's only one answer: I'll do the work.'

'Love, if you give up your job at Woolworths, we'll be no better off. We will need your money more than ever. I do appreciate the thought, though.'

'No, I mean I can change my hours at Woolies, so I can work part-time behind the counter in the shop, and I can do the books in the evenings or at weekends. James is there, so he can share the counter work – didn't you say he covers for you when you go out?'

Alan got up from his armchair and crept past the sleeping children. Kneeling in front of Sarah, he took her in his arms. 'You are the most wonderful wife in the world. It'll mean a lot of hard work, but we will be so close to having your dream home.'

'With roses around the door,' she smiled, before returning his kiss.

They talked for a while, chewing over the changes they'd have to make, before Alan fell asleep with his head on the side of the settee. He woke suddenly. 'What the hell?'

Sarah sat up as the children woke.

'It sounded like an explosion over by the river.' He hurriedly put on his shoes and went into the hall, bumping into Bessie, who was walking up and down soothing Jenny.

'Whatever was that?' she asked, her face pale in the light from her torch. 'The power's not back on yet.'

Reaching for one of Ruby's umbrellas in the hall stand, Alan stepped outside and walked to the gate. Other neighbours had hurried outside and were looking up and down the road. Further up he could see David Carlisle, and the two men walked towards each other. 'What do you make of that?' Alan asked.

'It looks like an explosion over on the marshes,' David said, pointing to where smoke and sparks could be seen above the rooftops. 'I'd not be surprised if the firework factory hadn't blown up, but what would cause it?'

'The wet weather, I would think, as some of the chemicals can be volatile when wet. One of the managers was in my shop only the other week and was talking about it, after I asked why they were sited right down on the marsh.'

'It doesn't make sense unless . . .' As he spoke, a siren

started to wail, getting louder and louder. 'What the heck is that all about?'

'It's the air-raid siren, most likely being used to warn us about something.'

'Listen, can you hear someone shouting?' Alan asked, trying to distinguish what was being called out.

They both looked towards the end of the road as two policemen appeared, wobbling on their bicycles as they steered single-handed, with loudhailers at their mouths calling out warnings to go inside. The two men ran down to find out more, hoping that one of the policemen was Mike Jackson. Unfortunately Mike was not one of them.

'What's going on, mate?' Alan asked, bending over as a stitch caught his side.

'Sir, you need to go back into your home and take your family upstairs. The Thames has breached its bank at Belvedere and the area is liable to flood.'

The two men looked at each other in alarm. Alan gasped in shock, not believing what the policeman was saying. 'Bob, George and Freda are at Clemmie's house; we've not heard from them since the telephones failed yesterday evening. There's only a short stretch of marshes between Clemmie's bungalow and the Thames.' He turned to one of the policemen. 'Officer, do you honestly believe Alexandra Road could flood? We are a couple of streets from the river, and there's the dockside as well.'

'Sir, it's best to be prepared,' was all the policeman would say.

'Whatever you do, don't tell Ruby or Maureen, but have a quiet word with Tony,' David said. 'I'm going back home to get my lot upstairs. We are slightly higher than you, but with the rail line behind us, which runs to the dockside, I'm fearful the water will spill over and surge along the back of our houses. Do you have any idea where Sergeant Mike Jackson is?' he called to one of the policemen.

'He's been deployed to head a rescue team in lower Belvedere.'

Both men sucked in their breath; Alan spoke first. 'If you can get a message to him, can you let him know his father is at a bungalow in Crabtree Manorway. It's the last house at the end of the road nearest to the river.'

The policeman looked to his colleague before speaking. 'That's very close to the breach in the riverbank. If you are thinking of going there to find him, I must warn you not to do so.'

Alan hadn't thought of going to rescue them, but the policeman's words put an idea into his head. Turning away, he nodded to David. 'Is it worth driving down there to see if there's anything we can do?'

David baulked at the idea. 'From what we've been told, the rescue services are already on the job and we'd only get in the way.' He called out to the policeman who had started to cycle away, 'What was the explosion just now?'

'It was the Wells firework factory going up. A surge tide went over the riverbank and swamped the factory, causing an explosion. By all accounts, it is bad at Joyce Green Hospital, with many windows broken in and around Dartford.'

'Christ,' Alan said, running his hand through his hair. 'Can it get any worse?'

'That's not far from my wife's factory. Do you have any news of other businesses in the area?'

'There's no saying, sir, but you wouldn't want to be living on the east coast, as it's hell up there, with lives lost. The continent is even worse, by all accounts. May I ask you to get back inside your homes?'

The two men did as they were told, promising to meet up in an hour to share information.

'What's going on?' Ruby and Maureen asked as they met Alan at the front door.

Alan knew he couldn't keep anything from Ruby, as she would see right through him. 'There's some sort of surge tide, and the Thames has broken its bank down the marshes. The sound you could hear was Wells Fireworks exploding.'

Ruby frowned. 'Where exactly has the river breached its bank?'

Alan gulped. He couldn't lie to her. 'At Belvedere, over on the marshes . . .'

27

'There's water coming in,' the children shrieked, waking everyone in Clemmie's bungalow.

George came to with a start from where he'd been sitting on a dining chair, leaning on the dining table. He couldn't believe he'd slept on, as his feet were covered in water. There were a good four inches of water in the room, which was rising at speed. 'Climb onto the chairs,' he shouted to the children, as Freda tried to rouse Bob from a deep sleep. Failing miserably, she lifted his feet so that they were on a wooden crate they'd been using to stand on, while painting the walls. He checked his watch; it was two o'clock in the morning.

'Bob,' Freda shouted in his ear as she shook his shoulder. 'Bob, you need to wake up; there seems to be a flood. You will need to help George get the car working, so we can get to higher ground.'

'The car's done for. We couldn't get it working last night and didn't want to alarm you,' Bob said, as he came to, before a fit of coughing stopped him speaking any more.

'You mean we can't drive away?' Freda asked in alarm, knowing that her own car was out of action. 'Come on, everyone, we'll have to wade through the water to get up to the main road. Hopefully the rainwater will have drained away from there.'

'I'm afraid it's much worse than that,' Clemmie said from where she was looking out of the window to the front of the house. 'That is more than rainwater.'

George joined her as the children started to snivel. He sucked in his breath as he spotted the glasshouses belonging to the nurseries half under water, as were the caravans belonging to the fairground, which he could just see further over the fields. Reaching for his coat, he went to the front door. 'I need to go out and see what's happened. Can you all climb as high as you can, because when I open the door, more water is going to flood in.'

Jessie and Clemmie started to lift the children up onto the solid-oak dining table and turned to help Bob.

'Get off with you. I'll be helping George,' he said between clearing his throat, while trying to catch his breath, before another fit of coughing overcame him.

'No, Bob, I need you to stay here and look after everyone,' George said, giving Freda a grim look. 'Besides, Mum will have something to say if you go down with a cold.'

'George is right; we need you here, Bob,' Freda urged him as he tried to reach the door. 'Come along, let me help you onto the table,' she said, as Jessie took his other arm, and they manhandled him to where the children were huddled together.

'Where will you sit, Mum?' one of the children asked, on the verge of tears.

'We'll be in the kitchen, sitting on the draining board,' Clemmie said, making them giggle, even though she could have sobbed her eyes out at the state of the home that she would be sharing with Jimmy and his children, once they were married.

'It'll be all right,' Freda said, giving her arm a squeeze. 'There's nothing here we can't clean up, once the water subsides. It's best you don't upset yourself in your condition.'

Clemmie gave a weak smile. 'Perhaps it's a sign that I shouldn't be getting married?'

'Don't be daft,' Freda laughed, even though she could have cried. She couldn't help wondering if everyone back at Alexandra Road was safe; this reminded her of not knowing what was happening to her loved ones during the war. 'Now, why don't we help George out the front door, so he can see what's going on out there. I only hope he doesn't get swept away.'

'I can help with that,' Clemmie said, opening a cupboard below the kitchen sink. And she pulled out a washing line, still neatly bound in a cardboard band. 'I picked it up in Woolies the other day, along with a packet of wooden pegs. Not that it's the kind of weather to put the washing outside,' she couldn't help but giggle nervously. 'We could tie one end to George and hold onto the other, so he doesn't get lost in the floodwater.'

'It's not that deep,' Jessie said.

'Don't you be so sure,' Freda replied. 'Have you ever been to the seaside and tried to walk out of the sea? Even a few inches of water can cause you to become disorientated; there's a lot more than a few inches out there, and it seems as though it's getting deeper,' she said, looking out of the kitchen window.

To begin with, George objected to having a washing line tied around his waist, until he was shown the neat knots Freda tied, before challenging him to wriggle free. 'If I learnt anything with the Girl Guides, it was how to tie a secure knot.'

'But if the three of you hold onto the other end, you may be pulled into the water.'

'We could tie the other end to the door knocker?' Clemmie suggested.

'It's too weak,' George said as he peered through the front-room window. 'It will have to be one of the fence posts; there are some made of concrete that should hold up. Fetch your coats and we'll get started.'

'Best we don't wear our coats, then we'll have something warm to put on afterwards,' Freda said. 'We will stay warm if we keep moving.' She wasn't sure if this was true, but no one argued with her, as George opened the door, allowing a rush of water to enter the hall.

'I'm not sure if this is a good idea,' Jessie said, peering outside. 'There are three steps down to the front path, so it is going to get even deeper.'

'In for a penny,' George said, as he held onto the side fence and tentatively stepped down until he was standing on the front path. Continuing to grip the side fence, he made his way to the gate and shouted behind him, 'I need the other end of the line, so I can tie it to the post.'

'I'll go,' Freda said, taking the end of the washing line from Clemmie and trying to ignore a flashback to her wedding day, when she had almost drowned in the Thames.

'You're not going on your own,' Clemmie said, hanging onto the back of Freda's cardigan.

'And neither are you,' Jessie said, as she hung onto Clemmie's jumper and the three girls moved slowly towards George. The swirling water was around their waists, and it was hard for them to keep together, even though they were still in the small front garden. Between Freda and George, they secured the washing line and then the four of them pulled open the garden gate.

George reached inside the neck of his jumper and pulled out a torch. 'I'm not sure how long this will last, so don't panic if it goes out suddenly,' he said, sounding more determined than he felt. 'Turn your torches off, so we can conserve the battery power. We have the moonlight to see by,' he added, looking up and thanking God at the same time.

The three girls huddled together as they watched the small beam of light start to move away from them. 'Keep talking to us,' Freda shouted.

'I can't think of anything to say,' he called back.

'Then sing us a song,' Clemmie said. 'What was that one you entertained us with at Christmas?'

'*As I walk along the Bois de Boulogne with an independent air . . .*'

Freda and Clemmie joined in, '. . . *he's the man who broke the bank at Monte Carlo.*'

'You're bloody bonkers,' Jessie said as they all started to laugh, until George shouted loud and clear, 'Hey, you up there, what's happening?'

The girls stopped laughing as they tried to listen. George had seen someone in the upstairs window of a house. As the girls hung on to the fence, trying hard to listen, they became aware that the water level was rising.

'I can hardly keep my feet on the ground,' Clemmie said, with panic in her voice.

'Then both of you go back to the front door. I'll wait here for George, in case he needs to be released from the washing line,' Freda said, wishing she'd thought to bring a knife out with her, as her fingers felt so icy that she knew she'd have trouble undoing the knots.

As she watched, George started to retrace his steps and she pulled in the line, as she didn't want him getting tangled. 'What's happening?' she asked, once he was within a few feet of her.

'The lady in the house down the road said that the Thames has breached its bank. Her husband has gone to help other householders; he didn't realize anyone was currently living here, otherwise he'd have knocked on the door. They are telling people to go upstairs and try to stay warm and dry.'

Freda looked back at her drenched friend, shivering at the front door, and then at the little bungalow. 'I'm afraid we may have a problem doing both those things,' she said as her frozen fingers started to pick at the knots around George's waist, which were now under water.

'Hang on to the fence,' George gasped, as he and Freda staggered back towards the front steps, where Jessie and Clemmie grabbed hold of them, before pushing open the door as they all fell inside.

'I never thought we'd do it,' Clemmie gasped as she stood in the thigh-high water. 'Look how much it has risen.'

The door to the front room opened and Bob stood there, holding his chest as he started to cough. 'What's going on?'

'Bob, you should have stayed out of the water,' Freda

said crossly. She didn't like the pallor of his skin or the way beads of sweat had broken out across his forehead.

'There's hardly any point,' he said as they all looked at the three scared children and the water starting to lick at the tabletop where they were huddled.

George was looking at the ceiling. We need to get as high as we can; the river has breached its bank. Do you have an entrance to your loft,' he asked Clemmie, wishing the bungalow had a staircase that led into an attic.

'It's in the master bedroom through here,' she said as the pair, followed by Freda, waded through the murky water to a door at the side of the room. A short hall led to two bedrooms and a boxroom. Clemmie opened the closest of the doors. 'Oh no, look at my new bed,' she cried out, as the double bed in the middle of the room stood there underwater. 'And the beautiful wallpaper. Everyone has helped so much to get our home presentable before the wedding and now look . . .'

'Don't upset yourself; we can sort this all out later,' George said, wondering if the foundations of the old building would survive. 'For now, we need to get into the loft to escape the floodwater. Would you happen to have a ladder?' he asked, wishing he'd brought his inside earlier and it wasn't still lashed to the roof of his car.

'It's in the shed in the back garden; the ground is lower there than the front of the house, so we could have trouble getting out there, as the floodwater may well be over our heads.'

'In that case we need to improvise. Let's get the sodden mattress off the bed and prop the frame up against the wall. I can climb up it to open the hatch.'

'I'll climb up, I'm lighter than you,' Freda said, once they'd pushed and shoved until the frame was in place. 'Lean on the bed, so it doesn't slip,' she instructed as she pushed her feet into the springs and tentatively checked to see if it held her weight. She gave a big sigh of relief and started to climb, wondering if it would hold the two men, who were the heaviest of the group. As she neared the ceiling, she started to reach out with one hand until she could touch the square panel of wood that covered the loft entrance. 'I need something to push it aside,' she called down.

'I'll get the broom from the kitchen,' Clemmie said and pushed her way through the water, causing waves to form.

'Slowly,' George instructed. 'We don't want the water to shift the bedstead, or Freda will come a cropper.'

As Freda clung to the bed frame, she could feel it starting to shift away from the wall. 'Can you lean on it, please?' she called down to George as Clemmie returned, holding the broom above her head, ready to pass to Freda.

'Jimmy usually slides it to the left, if that helps?' she called up.

Freda used the bristle end of the broom to poke at the wooden loft hatch and it slid easily to one side. After passing the broom down, she slowly climbed a little higher until her head and shoulders were above the ceiling and she could see into the loft. 'This is better than I expected; we could be very comfortable up here until we are rescued. I imagined that we would need to balance between the beams, which could have been awkward for the children.'

'My Jimmy wanted to board it out, so that we had plenty of storage,' Clemmie said proudly. 'But how will we get the children up here? I doubt they can climb up the bed frame.'

'We need to bring the table in here and then, if two of us were in the loft, we could lift them easily between us,' Freda suggested.

'Even better if we could put a dining chair on top of the table,' George suggested. 'But what will we do with the children while we move the table in here?'

'Gosh, this is harder than playing chess,' Freda declared.

'We can carry them into the kitchen and sit them on top of the draining board,' Jessie said as she joined them. 'I am worried about Bob, though, as he is shivering so much, and his cough is getting worse.'

'Ah!' Clemmie said as a thought came to her. 'If you can make your way to the large wardrobe, George, I've stored spare sheets and blankets on the top shelf. There are some of Jimmy's clothes in there as well, but they may already be wet.'

George waded over to the wardrobe and, with difficulty, pulled open the two doors. A shelf that ran the width of the wardrobe held a pile of dry sheets, blankets and towels, while the shelf below it had dry jumpers and a couple of shirts. 'Everything is dry. I'll bring them over to you to put in the loft,' he called and, with Clemmie's help, they were soon passed to Freda and deposited safely.

The sound of grunting preceded Bob and Jessie, pushing and pulling the dining table into the bedroom. 'We had to bring it on its side, as it's the only way we could get the wretched thing in here,' Bob wheezed. 'What's the plan? For some reason Jessie has deposited her three kids in the sink and on the draining board.'

'You'll see,' George said as he helped Jessie right the table and place it under the loft hatch.

'I'll fetch a chair,' Clemmie said.

'I'll start fetching my kids,' Jessie grinned. 'They think it's an adventure. I'm just glad I have them with me, as God knows what's happening down my nan's yard right now. I hope they are safe.'

Freda didn't like to reply as she'd wondered the same; there must be a lot of people trying to stay alive right now.

They soon had the three children safely in the loft, with their mum encouraging them not to run about. 'Now it is your turn, Bob,' Freda said, as George and Clemmie helped him onto the table and then onto the chair balanced on top. 'We will pull you up by your arms.'

'And I'm behind shoving,' George laughed.

'I must look a right sight,' Bob guffawed, before starting to cough again. 'I'll be fine,' he said, seeing Freda's concerned face. 'I just need to warm up.'

'You are next, Clemmie,' George said, holding out his hands to help her.

'Wait a minute,' she said, wading away from them into the living room. She came back within minutes, carrying a bag above her head. 'It's the remains of the food we all brought with us, and there's a full flask – it could be soup, it could be cocoa, but it'll be filling all the same,' she said, passing the items to George, before starting to climb up to the loft.

Once they were all safe, Freda closed the hatch and they sat on the floor, looking at each other. 'Now what do we do?' Clemmie asked.

'First, we get out of our wet clothes,' George said. 'I'll

string a line between the beams up this end and hang up a sheet, so that we get changed in private,' he continued, as he started to sort out who needed what.

There was laughing and joking as Bob appeared, wearing a jumper and a blanket as a sarong, and paraded up and down in front of them. The girls followed, wrapping flannel-ette sheets around themselves. 'What about you, George?' Clemmie asked, noticing there was only a small towel left. 'That won't protect your modesty.'

'I'll use the sheet that you all changed behind, but you'll have to turn your backs while I undress.'

Once everyone was garbed in an array of dry items, Freda hung the wet clothing across the line. 'I'm not sure they will dry, as it is so blooming cold,' she said as her teeth started to chatter.

'Here, drink this,' Clemmie suggested, as she passed a tin cup containing warm cocoa. 'It's all right, I have more cups,' she said, pointing into the bag. 'I made a quick sweep of the living room and kitchen to see what we could bring up here. 'The children will have to share, though,' she added, giving them a smile. 'You've all been so good that I have a special present for each of you,' she said, reaching into the bag and pulling out a small bag of toffees. 'I had them in the kitchen for Jimmy; they are his favourites,' she went on, as she gave one each to the children and their eyes lit up. 'You can have another one later.'

'Thank you,' Jessie said as the children also mouthed their thanks. 'You've all been so kind to us.'

'I have one question,' Freda asked. 'How can we be rescued, if no one knows we are here and we can't see out?'

28

All eyes focused on George, waiting for him to tell them how they would be saved. He was at a loss to know what to say. He was cold, fed up and wanted to be at home, with Maureen fussing over him. He had a briefcase full of work to get through for Vickers, and local people would be relying on him for help with their housing and other problems. And here he was, stuck in a loft in Belvedere, dressed in a sheet while floodwater rose higher and higher.

'We need a flag,' Bob said out of the blue. 'We can wave it to draw attention to our plight.'

The eldest of Jessie's children laughed at his suggestion. 'Don't be daft; there isn't a window, so where can we wave it from?'

As Jessie chastised him for his rudeness, George got to his feet and walked to the part of the eaves that he knew looked out over the road at the front of the bungalow. 'The lady up the road knows we are here, but it is possible she will forget to inform the rescuers.' He fumbled with the slates in the roof until several became loose. 'If we had something to wave, we could poke it through a gap in the roof slates,' he said, looking around at the expectant faces staring back in the light

311

of two torches. 'We also need to conserve the batteries in the torches, as we may need them later; if we take out a few tiles, the light of the moon will help.'

Bob got to his feet with some effort and went to where the broom was propped up by the loft hatch. He disappeared behind the washing line, to emerge several minutes later with his long johns tied to the bristle end of the broom. 'This should do it. No one's going to miss a flag like this. We can take turns waving it back and forth.'

Once everyone had stopped laughing, George took the broom and, with a few adjustments and a struggle with several roof slates, managed to get the long johns waving outside.

'I'll take the first shift of waving the flag,' Clemmie said. 'Why don't you all try to get a couple of hours' sleep?'

Jessie settled against a wall, with her children lying over her legs, while George sat to one side. 'I've never thanked you for helping me that time when I had problems at home,' she said quietly.

'There's no need to thank me. I'm just pleased you have settled down, but something I would like to ask is why you allowed the children to visit your nan at the funfair, when that was the root of all your problems?' George asked.

'They're not all bad, you know, and my kids need to know their family. My problem was the one uncle, but I was sensible enough to leg it before any harm was done. I'd have done for him, if there'd been a knife handy, and that wouldn't have been good for me. Why serve time for a no-good blighter like him? What upset me more was his sisters all turning a blind eye. But my nan didn't know about it, and neither do my kids. Yes, the uncle turned up when I worked at Mitchell's, and I got the sack over being rude to him in front of the customers, but I remembered your Sarah telling me to go and see her about working at Woolworths . . .' She laughed slowly. 'And that's how I'm here now.'

'I'm glad you're now part of the big Woolworths family,' he said. 'If you ever need a shoulder to cry on, you won't have to look far.'

'That's nice to know, thank you,' she replied as her eyelids started to feel heavy and she slept, feeling safer than she had in a very long time.

'I'll take over,' Freda said as she joined Clemmie. 'You look dead on your feet.'

'I could do with a snooze. I think the water has stopped rising.'

'How do you know?'

She peered through the gap in the roof, where George had removed a few tiles. 'Look, you can see the football ground from here; the wind has dropped, and I've been watching the top of a tree. The water doesn't seem to have risen any higher in the past hour. That means there may be people coming out to rescue those who are trapped. It has made me wonder how we can get out of here, when the water level is nearly up to the ceiling downstairs. We'd have to swim underwater just to get out of the front door.'

'Crikey, I'd not given any thought as to how we would escape, and I doubt the others have either, as we were hell-bent on getting high enough to be free of the rising water. Perhaps when we start to hear people outside, and I doubt it will be before dawn, we can remove more slates so that we can be seen.'

'My poor bungalow,' Clemmie started to cry. 'It was supposed to be the new home that me and Jimmy moved into after our wedding, and where we could bring up his two children, and perhaps in time provide them with brothers and sisters. Now I have nothing.'

Freda felt Clemmie was being overdramatic, but then she was young and in love. She took her by the shoulders and gave her a gentle shake. 'Now, look here, Clemmie Billington, you still have a loving fiancé and a wonderful family. Your wedding is planned, and Reverend Mills will be declaring you and Jimmy man and wife in four weeks' time. It doesn't matter where you live afterwards, as long as you are together. You may also want to remember what you told us about . . .' she looked around her to see if anyone was listening, 'about being pregnant. You need to think of the baby right now.'

Clemmie stopped crying and looked at Freda as she thought about her words. 'You are right, I'm acting like a spoilt brat.'

'I didn't say that.'

'I know I am, and I need to grow up. How would you cope, if you were me?'

'I'd ask myself what Clive Danvers would do.'

'The character that movie star Johnny Johnson plays in the B films?'

'That's the one,' Freda chuckled. 'Come on, let's try to get some sleep, as the flag can wave itself for a while. It's not as if anyone is going to miss Bob's long johns flapping over the rooftop, is it?'

*

Ruby couldn't sleep and decided to give up trying and go downstairs to make herself a drink, then she heard murmured voices and realized Sarah and Alan had beat her to it. 'Great minds think alike,' she said as she joined them. 'I can't help wondering what's going on down Belvedere,' she went on, accepting a steaming mug from Sarah. 'I only hope Bob is keeping himself dry and not doing anything silly; any chill seems to go to his chest these days.'

'Oh, Nan, he is sure to be sensible, and it is not as if Dad and Freda aren't there to keep an eye on him.'

'I suppose you are right, but I can't help worrying all the same.'

'Actually, Nan, we'd like your advice,' Sarah said, glancing towards Alan to continue.

'I've been offered the opportunity to rent a larger house; it would be ideal because, as you know, the two kids have to share a bedroom, which isn't going to be convenient as they get older.'

'Please don't say you're moving away,' Ruby said, looking miserable. 'It may be selfish of me, but I like having you around. Besides, it would be madness to move away from the town and your business; think of the time you would spend travelling.'

Alan spoke quickly, before Ruby became too upset. 'It's not like that at all; in fact we would be living closer to you.'

Ruby pulled a face. 'Now I'm confused. Why, your house almost backs onto mine, with only the railway sidings in between. How can you live closer?'

Sarah chuckled at her nan's expression. 'David had a

word with Alan and gave us first refusal to rent their house up the road.'

'Where are they moving to?'

'You know they've been crowded in the house for some time, and that's why Bessie and Jenny are lodging with Freda, even though that is now a tight squeeze. David and Maisie viewed a large house up The Avenue yesterday and have decided to purchase it,' Sarah tried to explain.

Alan butted in. 'David thinks it would make economic sense not to sell their house in Alexandra Road, but to rent it out instead; that's how he thought of us.'

'That makes very good sense and would be ideal for you and the children. Will you sell your own house?' Ruby asked, thinking how it would be lovely to have her family living in the same road; perhaps she was being selfish, but she could not see any obstacles to them moving. However, by the glum looks on their faces, there was indeed one. 'So, tell me what the problem is?'

'We are very attached to our house in Crayford Road and, as Maureen gave the house to Alan, it doesn't seem right that we should sell it. We thought of renting out the property, just as Maisie and David are doing, but it can be so risky: what if we couldn't find a tenant?'

'Or, worse still, they didn't pay their rent and damaged the house,' Alan chipped in. 'We'd both feel as though we'd be letting Mum down, as the house, to all intents and purposes, belongs to her.'

Ruby sipped her tea thoughtfully. 'Tell me to mind my own business if you think I'm asking too many questions, but when Maureen gave you the house, was it all done and dusted legally?'

'Our names are on the deeds, if that's what you mean?' Sarah replied.

'Yes, we used a solicitor, as Mum was insistent that we did everything professionally; she was worried that we'd lose out after she passed away. She'd heard all sorts of stories and wanted to do the best for us, without causing any distress at what would be a sad time for the family,' Alan added.

'She's a sensible woman, and no doubt George advised her as well,' Ruby added proudly. 'For my two penn'orth, I would add that whoever rents your house should provide references and pay a reasonable deposit. Check them out thoroughly and do not, under any circumstances, rush into any hasty decisions.'

Alan agreed with Ruby's advice. 'I get the feeling David wants a quick decision from us, so that if we decline his generous offer, he can place an advertisement for a tenant in the *Erith Observer*.'

'You need to sit down with David and talk over everything, rather than try to guess what he wants from you as a tenant. I bet you don't even know how much the rental will be?'

Alan's face turned red. 'No, we haven't given it a thought. It could be that we can't afford what he is asking. I feel such a chump for telling you this, Sarah, before I had more information'.

'Don't blame yourself, love, as I would have guessed there was something on your mind. Nan is right: we need to ask more questions. I do hope we can afford the house, as I'd adore to live in Alexandra Road.'

Ruby went to the sideboard and rummaged in one of

the drawers, pulling out a notepad and pen. 'There's no time like the present; why not jot down your thoughts now, while the house is quiet. Once Bob is back, peace will go out of the window,' she said, looking towards where the curtains were pulled across the living-room window and wondering what the dawn would bring.

'I can hear something,' Freda said, nudging Clemmie.

'Quick, let's start waving the flag so it can be seen,' Clemmie said, getting to her feet and reaching for the end of the broomstick. 'Can you wake George? It's time we started to make a larger hole in the roof; it is the only way we will be able to escape, as I don't wish to sit here until the floodwaters subside.'

George joined them and started to carefully remove slates until he could stick his shoulders through a hole and call out into the darkness, 'Is there anybody there?'

Freda crossed her fingers, hoping someone would call back. 'Try again, George, and then we can all shout for help.'

George dislodged a couple more slates until he could lean out as far as his waist. He reached for their home-made flag and waved it frantically, while bellowing, 'Help, there are people trapped in this bungalow . . . we are in the roof space.'

'Any luck?' Freda asked as he came back into the loft.

'There are people out there, but they seem to be further back towards the main road,' George replied as he rubbed his chin thoughtfully. 'Perhaps if we shone the torches in their direction, they might spot them?'

'Then you need to make a larger hole in the roof. Besides,

if we plan to get out that way, we will need a much larger gap,' Clemmie said as she poked her head through the hole. 'Crikey, the flood must be touching the ceiling downstairs.'

Freda went to the loft hatch and pulled back the cover before crying out, 'It's within six inches of the ceiling.'

The children started to cry and clung to their mum.

'We need to prepare to get out of here,' George said.

'What do you mean?' Bob asked from where he still sat.

'We are going to have to climb out of the hole and get up onto the ridge of the roof,' Freda explained, as she looked through the hole and shone her torch left and right. 'If we are careful, we will be able to crawl out and follow the edge of the roof until we reach the chimney stack, where we can scramble a little higher; we can use the washing line to tie the children to the adults, so they don't fall . . .'

'I'm not sure I'm up to climbing on a roof,' Bob apologized while coughing, as the children started to panic and scream with fear.

'Quiet!' George bellowed as everyone fell silent. 'As good as the idea is, I don't think that's possible.'

'Then I'll go alone and make them aware we are here,' Freda said, going to the washing line to remove her clothing. 'These are wet, but I need to be respectable to climb along the roof slates. Clemmie, can you take down the rest of the wet clothes and roll up the washing line. I'm going to need it on the roof.'

'You can't do this on your own. I'll come with you,' Clemmie insisted.

Freda shook her head. 'Clemmie dearest, in four weeks you will be walking down the aisle to be married and you can't do that if you have broken bones.' Or worse, she thought to herself. 'Perhaps you could help George make the hole in the roof much larger for when the rescuers get here?'

'I can do that,' Clemmie said, looking relieved.

When Freda was ready, she rolled up the washing line and slung it over her shoulder. George and Clemmie had started to stack the roof slates out of the way on the other side of the loft.

'You will be able to reuse them,' he said.

'Only if I have a home with a roof left, after all this,' she said, giving him a small smile. 'I'd rather everyone was safe away from here. I'm not even sure I want to live here after this.'

'You will feel different once the flood has subsided and your home has been cleaned and decorated,' he said, feeling sorry for the young girl about to start her married life. 'At least Jimmy's children weren't here.'

'I must be grateful for small mercies.'

'Stop chatting, you two, and help me, will you?' Freda said as she tied one end of the rope around her waist. 'Can you hand me the torch. I'll carry it down my jumper.'

'Are you sure you want to do this?' George asked as Freda carefully stepped through the hole in the roof and turned to hold onto the rough edges of the tiles.

'Let's be honest, George. I'm younger and fitter than you, so it is best I do this. I'd rather not be here at all, but if I can attract someone's attention, we could be home and in our beds within the hour,' she replied, sounding more optimistic than she felt.

'But you've not long had two babies . . .'

'That doesn't make me an invalid,' she laughed. 'Here, take the end of the washing line and, whatever you do, don't let go.'

George fed out the line as Clemmie kept the beam of the second torch focused on Freda's retreating back as she carefully took one step at a time, clinging to any protruding tile that gave her purchase as she crept closer to the chimney stack. Once there, she sat down on the sloping roof and undid the line tied around her waist. After looping it around the stack several times, she again secured it around herself. Reaching for her torch, she flashed it towards where she thought there would be rescuers and used the SOS code, thankful once again that she had learnt so much whilst helping to run the Brownies and Girl Guide groups. Waiting two minutes, she sent the SOS message again.

It felt like hours that she sat leaning against the chimney stack, praying someone would see her appeals for help. The wind had dropped and there was an eerie silence, broken only by the sound of the waves as the floodwater continued its relentless onslaught across the marshes. Looking down, Freda could see that the water must have risen another six inches since she had climbed onto the roof. 'It's time to start evacuating the loft,' she called to George and Clemmie, who were watching her. 'Tear up the spare sheet into strips and secure them to the children. Each of you take one and get them up to the top of the roof. Hurry!'

She kept flashing the SOS signal towards the main road, thinking that was where the rescuers would come from, as George and Clemmie helped Bob out of the hole in the roof and led him slowly towards her. She settled him against the chimney stack and secured him safely with a length of the sheeting. 'It may not be very comfortable, but it won't be for long. Do you think you could flash the SOS signal while I help the others?' she asked, worrying how weak he seemed.

'I'm fine. You go and help those little kiddies,' he said, giving her a wink. 'I will need your help once we are home, though . . .'

'Anything,' Freda promised, wondering what he wanted her to do.

'I'll need you to explain to Ruby why I've lost my long johns,' he laughed.

'Oh, Bob, you had me going there,' Freda laughed, before turning to help the children onto the roof, until they were sitting between Jessie and Clemmie on the top of the ridge.

'Why don't we sing?' Jessie suggested. 'The sound will carry across the water.'

'As long as it's not "Old Father Thames",' Bob grumbled.

'I know, let's sing one of Vera Lynn's songs; they cheered everyone up during the war,' Clemmie said and broke into 'There'll Always Be an England'.

Even George joined in, although he had to keep stopping to cough.

They'd sung their way through 'The White Cliffs of Dover', 'The Lambeth Walk', 'We'll Meet Again' and 'Land of Hope and Glory', during which both torches were waved on high, when Freda shouted for them to be quiet.

'I can hear something.'

Up ahead there was the steady movement of oars. 'Ahoy there!' a familiar voice called out.

'Thank God,' Freda cried out. 'It's Mike Jackson.'

29

~

'I'll get it,' Alan said as there was a knock on the door. It was five o'clock in the morning; no one brought good news at that time.

Sarah clung onto Ruby and Maureen as Alan pulled back the bolts and opened the front door. The four of them had given up on sleep and had sat around the dining table, hardly speaking as the clock ticked away on the mantelpiece.

There were muffled voices at the door before Alan led a policeman into the room.

'Oh no!' Maureen cried out, which disturbed the children sleeping in the front room. 'Please don't say anything has happened to them . . .'

Tony came bounding downstairs, taking two steps at a time, followed by Gwyneth. 'What's happened – are they safe?'

The policeman cleared his throat. 'We've rescued Mr Bob Jackson, Mr George Caselton, Mrs Freda Forsythe and a Miss Clemmie Billington from the roof of a property in Crabtree Manorway. They've all been taken to the cottage hospital.'

'What about Jessie and her children – Freda had taken her to visit her family at the showmen's yard in Belvedere?' Sarah asked, praying they were safe.

The policeman checked his notebook. 'Ah yes, they too are at the hospital.'

'We need to go there, now,' Ruby said. 'I need to see they are all right.'

'Nan, it's the middle of the night; I doubt we'll be allowed to see them,' Sarah replied, although she too wouldn't rest until she knew her loved ones were fine.

'Under the circumstances, it may be allowed, if only for a few minutes,' the officer said.

'But what about the children?' Tony asked.

'I'll stay with them,' a yawning Bessie said, appearing at the top of the stairs. 'You all go.'

'I'll stay as well,' Gwyneth added.

'I'm not sure I can fit everyone in my car,' Alan said.

'I can take someone in my car,' the police officer suggested.

'That's very good of you,' Ruby replied. 'Hurry and get your coats, everyone.'

The drive to the cottage hospital only took ten minutes, but as Alan concentrated on the road ahead, he thought it felt more like an hour; no one spoke as everyone in his car remained silent, wondering what they would find at the hospital. Once he had parked, they joined Tony, who had travelled with the policeman. They were led through the main entrance and were met by a nursing sister, who placed a finger to her lips, indicating they should remain quiet. 'You will find your family in here,' she said, opening a door into what seemed to be a doctor's office.

Freda and Maureen flew into their husbands' arms, while Clemmie already sat in a corner with Betty and Douglas; by the look on the girl's face, she had been weeping, but now seemed resigned to what had happened.

Sarah hugged her dad, who assured her that he would be as fit as a fiddle, then she went to where Jessie was sitting with her three children. 'What an adventure,' she said to the youngsters, then mouthed to Jessie, 'Are you all right?'

'Just very tired, but at least now we are warm and dry,' she said, indicating the mismatched garments that all four were wearing. 'The hospital provided us with clothing until ours are clean and dry. The policeman said he would drive us home, but I wanted to wait until I knew how Bob was.'

It was then that Sarah realized Bob was missing. Ruby stood alone in the centre of the room, looking around her in confusion. George was whispering to Maureen and they both went to Ruby, as Sarah did the same.

'Where is Bob?' Ruby asked, looking bewildered.

Never had Sarah seen her nan look so old as at that moment, and it dawned on her how much she must love Bob; she would be lost without him. 'Dad, what has happened?'

'Mum, you mustn't get upset, but Bob is rather ill. The cough he's had for a while got much worse while we were waiting to be rescued. Being cold and wet did nothing to help matters. He held on until the rescue boat appeared with Mike at the helm, then he weakened rapidly and was out of it completely by the time we reached the edge of the flooded area. There was an ambulance waiting, and Mike accompanied him here. I've been in to see him, and Mike has stayed at his side all the time. I've been told to take you in to see him, once you arrived,' he said, putting his arm around his mother and leading her from the room.

'Oh no, not Bob.' Sarah started to shake uncontrollably.

Freda led her to a chair and encouraged her to sit down. Turning to Alan, she said, 'A nurse is supposed to be bringing hot drinks. Would you help her, please?'

Kneeling in front of her friend, she handed Sarah a handkerchief and waited until the tears had stopped. 'Bob is very poorly, Sarah. I had a quick word with a doctor, but all he would say was that it is touch and go. Your dad may be able to tell you more later. At the moment your nan is your priority; she's going to need as much help as possible to face the days ahead, come what may.'

Sarah blew her nose and pulled herself together. 'You are right. It was just seeing Nan standing there alone, and then the news that Bob was poorly. He is such a lovely man and is devoted to Nan. Thank goodness it was Mike who rescued you and could be with Bob. But what about Gwyneth, does she know?'

'No, not yet. Mike asked if one of us could tell her. He doesn't want one of his colleagues knocking on the door, as she may think the worst. If you are agreeable, I thought Tony and I could go back home and at the same time break the news to Gwyneth, as she's only a few doors down from where we live. By the way, where are my babies?'

Sarah couldn't help but give a small chuckle at the look on Freda's face.

'I'm only smiling as it's taken you this long to wonder about your little ones. They are fine and are still at Nan's house; Bessie and Gwyneth are caring for them. If you wish to wait a little, while why I look in on Bob, you can both travel back with us, as Alan drove up here in his own car.'

'Thank you,' Freda said as she looked at Tony, who had joined them. 'I have a confession to make: our car is still under the floodwater in front of Clemmie's bungalow.'

'Don't worry about the car, I'm just pleased to have you home and safe,' Tony replied.

'If it's any consolation, it broke down before the flood started; perhaps it is time we thought about getting another one?'

Betty joined them, putting her arms round the two girls. 'I know I shouldn't be thinking about the store at this time, but I don't want either of you coming into work on Monday, as having today to recuperate will not be enough. In fact let's play it by ear, as Ruby may be needing you more than Woolworths does for the foreseeable future, Sarah.'

Thank goodness we have you in charge, Betty. I tried to think what it would have been like if Mr Harrison was still the manager, as he'd have been banging on my door demanding I come into work . . .' She suddenly realized what she'd said and stopped speaking until Tony laughed.

'Don't walk on eggshells around me,' he begged. 'Being given the Dartford store to manage is a big feather in my cap. As much as I would have loved to have worked in Erith, I have to think of the future; Dartford is a much bigger store and I have more staff – it is most definitely a step up in my career.'

'Whereas I'm quite happy to work at the Erith branch, with everybody I know and love,' Betty said. 'Now we are going to take Clemmie home to her bed; she wants to speak to Jimmy. The poor lad has been beside himself with worry, and only a long chat on the telephone will convince him that Clemmie is well, even though she seems to be in shock. Goodness knows where she and Jimmy will live after the wedding. I have already suggested they move in with us, but Clemmie has refused; she wishes to run her own household and wouldn't be able to do that, living with us. That is something we will have to work out, but it can wait until another day,' she said, before kissing them all goodbye.

'She's a decent sort, isn't she?' Tony said. 'When I first worked with her, she frightened me to death, along with all the other trainees.'

Sarah and Freda looked at each other and smiled. Both were thinking of their first encounter with Betty at their interview back in 1938. Neither knew then that Betty was as nervous as they were, with it being her first day as a staff manager.

Sarah stepped into the side ward where Bob was being cared for. He looked so pale against the white pillows, with none of his normal ruddy complexion. Usually a sturdy man, he seemed to have shrunk immeasurably. Was that possible? Sarah wondered. Mike sat on one side of the bed, resting his hand close to his father's arm, while Ruby sat on the other side, holding his hand and talking quietly to him. George sat at the bottom of the bed, deep in thought; he stood up to give Sarah his seat when she entered the room.

'How is Bob?' she asked.

'It's early days and he's been through a lot,' Mike said.

'I told him to go and see the doctor weeks ago about this cough, but would he listen to me? No, the obstinate old fool wouldn't listen, and now look at him,' Ruby said in an angry voice. 'He still thinks he's a young lad who can do anything, and now it'll be the death of him . . .' She broke down, resting her head on the bed. 'If you leave me, I'll never forgive you, you old goat.'

Mike looked away as he wiped a tear from his eye, while George wept openly. Even in sickness, Ruby spoke to her beloved Bob in the same way she always spoke; it was a sign of true love, he thought, as he put his arm round his daughter to comfort her.

'I'm going to have a word with the doctor when he comes back on duty in the morning,' Mike explained. 'Hopefully by then we will have a clearer picture of Dad's condition and what they plan to do to help him. I'm going to stay here until then. Why don't you go home and put your head down for a couple of hours, Ruby? If there is any change we will get hold of you immediately.'

Ruby lifted her head. 'Our telephone isn't working, so I'd best stay. I wouldn't want to miss . . . I wouldn't want to miss his waking up.'

'Nan, you really need to rest. Bob will need you when he wakes up.'

'And if the telephone isn't working, I'll have someone from the station on your doorstep in seconds,' Mike promised.

'Maureen and I will stay at home with you tonight, then I can drive you up here when—' George started to say, before he stopped. 'Blast, my car is under eight feet of water in Belvedere.'

'You can use ours,' Sarah was quick to say. 'We will leave it in front of number thirteen and walk round to our place. We have the shop's van if we need to go anywhere.'

Ruby reached out and touched her loved ones. 'We do appreciate your help. I speak for Bob as well when I say that.'

'It's what families do, Mum,' George said as he gave her a hug. 'I'll be outside while you say your goodbyes.'

Sarah kissed Bob goodbye before joining her dad outside the room.

'Hang on a minute, George, I want a word,' Mike said as he joined them, closing the door behind him.

Sarah could see that Mike wanted to speak to her dad on his own. 'I'll go and find Alan,' she said, hurrying away.

'I didn't want to say this in front of Ruby or Sarah. The doctor doesn't seem to think Dad will make it . . .'

George was at a loss for words as he saw the agony in Mike's eyes.

'What is it?'

'Ruby doesn't know, and Dad swore me to secrecy; he will kill me if he knows I've told you. He has been to see the doctor about his cough, which has been hanging around ever since that bad smog last December. The doctor did some tests, and it seems Dad has a weak heart. Ordinarily he could live for years if he doesn't over-exert himself, but with what happened today, things don't look so good.'

'My God, I had no idea.'

'My one thought at the moment is: should we tell Ruby?' Mike asked with a bleak look in his eyes.

'She deserves to know,' George said. 'Leave it with me to tell her. I'll do it when we get back to her house.'

The door opened and Ruby joined them. 'Are you going back in with your dad, Mike?' she asked, looking between the two men.

'I'll go right now,' he said, kissing her cheek. 'See you both later.'

'What was that all about?' Ruby asked.

'Nothing important; just something Mike wanted me to tell Gwyneth.'

Ruby frowned. She knew when George was telling lies.

30

~

Sunday 1 February 1953

'Let's go into the front room; the fire still has a few glowing embers and we can drink our cocoa in comfort,' Maureen said the moment Ruby and George arrived home.

George led his mum to her armchair by the fire and placed a cup in her hands. 'Drink it up, Mum, it'll do you good,' he said, before helping Maureen to fold up the rugs and blankets that the children had used for their camping adventure.

'I'll go up to bed,' Maureen whispered to George. 'See if your mum will talk. It will help her troubled mind,' she said, kissing his cheek gently.

George could only nod his head as he watched his mum. Her body might be sitting in the armchair, but her mind was visiting past memories, thinking of the man she loved, lying in bed half a mile away at the cottage hospital. He picked up a stool and moved it next to Ruby, leaning on the arm of her chair as he had done as a young boy while she spoke of her family and people he never knew or had long forgotten.

'We've not sat together like this for a while,' he said. 'Drink up before it gets cold.'

Without uttering a word, Ruby sipped the drink until it was gone.

'That's better,' he spoke to her as if she was the child and he the parent. 'Do you remember when we first moved here, and Stella lived over the road where Freda and Tony live now?'

A fleeting smile crossed Ruby's face. 'She was like a mother to me; I miss her.'

'And Dad, when he would disappear for God knows how many years at a time.'

This time Ruby gave a faint laugh. 'I fought to hang on to that man and he always came back, because we were meant to be together.'

'And then Bob came along to take care of you,' he said, trying to draw her out.

'I loved him too, and now he's going to leave me . . .' she said as a sob shuddered through her body.

George's heart was broken as he took his mum into his arms, rocking her back and forth until the tears subsided. 'He's still here with us, Mum.'

'No, when people creep away to speak in hushed tones, it means the patient is at the end of their life. I've seen it before. Bob's going to leave me,' she said, turning to look him in the eye. 'Tell me it's not true.'

George had expected to break the news to his mum; he had not expected her to ask him if Bob was going to die. He sighed before taking her hand. 'Mike told me this evening that Bob is very ill; but we could all see that. What we didn't know was that he has been ill for a while now.'

'That cough? I bought him all kinds of remedies from the chemist; he refused to take them or go to see the doctor.'

'Well, he did go to see his doctor, but he didn't want to worry you.'

'I assume that whatever medicine he was given, Bob refused to take it. He can be a curmudgeonly old bugger at times.'

'No, Mum, there isn't any medicine. After tests, Bob was told he has a weak heart and should avoid over-strenuous work.'

'Why didn't you tell me?' she demanded, her voice getting louder.

'I only knew this evening; I'm as shocked as you. Bob made Mike promise not to say anything. The poor man was relieved to be able to tell me.'

Ruby pushed Bob away from her and sat up straight in the armchair, the empty cup falling to the floor and breaking into a dozen pieces.

'The silly old fool,' she muttered angrily. 'What's the time?'

George had lost all sense of time, so he looked up at the black marble clock on the ornate wooden mantelpiece. 'It's just gone seven o'clock in the morning.'

'Too early to go back to the hospital. They won't like us trampling about the place while patients are trying to sleep. What time can we go back there?'

George was flummoxed, as he had no idea. With Bob being so poorly, he assumed it was what they called 'open orders' and that family could visit at any time. 'I would think we can go there late morning, after the doctors have done their rounds.'

'Then that's what we'll do. If Bob thinks he's going to die without me speaking to him first, then he has another thing coming. Now get yourself to bed. I'll be up as soon as I've locked up and put the dog out . . . By the way, where is that dratted dog?'

George laughed; his mother had never got on with Bob's greyhound. 'David Carlisle collected him. He's being spoilt by their children until he can come home.'

Ruby shook her head and gave a sad sigh. 'With the dog gone, it's like Bob has gone as well – those two are joined at the hip.'

'Four hours' sleep is not good for anyone,' George groaned as he joined Maureen in his mum's living room. 'I hope everyone else feels better than I do. I'm too old to be climbing on a roof in the dark. I tell you, when that boat came alongside us I was so glad to see them I could have hugged Mike Jackson, until I realized that I had to get from the roof to the boat without falling. And then it came to me that if I wasn't able to do it, how would Bob manage?'

Maureen put a plate of eggs on toast in front of him, along with a cup of coffee. She sat down opposite, wiping her hands on her apron. 'However did you manage to do it? With all that was going on earlier this morning, I didn't hear the details.'

'I held back and helped the two firemen who were in the boat with Mike to bring Bob down gently, while Mike used a hook to hold the boat steady to the side of the bungalow. The water was that high, it was just a case of passing Bob to the other policeman, who settled him in

335

the boat. To be honest, I thought Bob was a gonna; it must have been a shock for Mike to see his dad like that.'

'It doesn't bear thinking about. I've been listening to the wireless; yes, it's working again, as is the telephone. The flood's a major disaster, by all accounts. The Sunday newspapers are full of it. I've left them in the front room in case Ruby doesn't want to read about it.'

'Read about what?' Ruby asked as she joined them, wearing curlers in her hair and a candlewick dressing gown over her Winceyette nightdress.

'You should have stayed in bed for a while longer. I was about to bring you a cup of tea.'

'Maureen's right, you need to rest.'

'What I need is to get myself ready to visit my husband; that's if he hasn't passed away in the night. Have there been any messages, or are you keeping that from me as well?'

George flinched under the steely stare of his mum. 'We were talking about the newspapers reporting on the flood. They're in the front room if you want to see them?'

'I've no time. I want to get to the hospital to see how Bob is and talk to the doctors. I take it they work on Sundays?'

'They are at the hospital every day, Mum,' George said, pushing his plate away.

'Would you like me to sort out your hair?' Maureen asked, looking at the haphazard way Ruby had pinned the metal curlers into her grey hair.

Ruby's stern face visibly melted into a warm smile. 'I'd be grateful, love. It came to me in the night that I'd better look my best. Bob doesn't want to be feeling poorly, then see me looking a mess. It's my duty to do the best I can

336

with my appearance, so that he is proud of me; I'll wear my best coat and hat as well.'

'Then once I've sorted out your hair, I'll give your coat a brush, in case that blooming dog's hairs are on it. They seem to get everywhere.'

'I find a damp cloth does the job,' Ruby said, before looking at George. 'Aren't you going to eat that? It's a shame to waste good food,' she added, leaning over to take one of his slices of toast. 'Perhaps I will have some breakfast; we've got to keep our strength up.'

Just then the telephone rang in the front room. They all looked at each other.

Maureen urged George to hurry. 'Best get that, in case it's the hospital,'

'I can't listen,' Ruby said as she pushed the door to. 'Let's have that cup of tea.'

Maureen thought Ruby was putting on a brave face until she saw how much the older woman's hands were shaking and put her arms around her to hold her close.

'If I was a religious woman, I'd be on my knees right now,' Ruby whispered, allowing Maureen to help her to one of the chairs set around the dining table.

Maureen closed her eyes and whispered a silent prayer.

George entered the room with perspiration on his brow. 'That gave me quite a scare.'

'Was it the hospital? What did they say?' Ruby asked.

'It was David Carlisle. He said he'd bring his car down in the next half-hour and that I've got full use of it to take you to the hospital.'

'That's good of him,' Maureen said. 'We have some thoughtful friends.'

'Where's your car?' Ruby asked.

'The last time I saw it, it was under seven or eight feet of water outside Clemmie's bungalow, alongside Freda's.'

'Sorry, lad, I should have asked how things were when I saw you last night, but there was so much going on. I didn't even ask if you or the others were hurt. Were the little kiddies all right?'

'How about I tell you while we drive to the hospital. It's best we get ourselves ready. Are you coming with us, Maureen?'

'I thought I'd stay here and man the telephone, as there are bound to be a lot of people enquiring after Bob and someone needs to let your sister Pat know.'

'That's a good idea. And Maisie sent a message to say she was cooking a roast dinner, but would plate it up and bring it down later, so we can eat when we are hungry.'

Ruby started to pull the curlers from her hair. 'What a lovely girl she is, to think of us when she is so busy. Now let's get cracking, as Bob will be watching the clock and wondering where we are.'

Maureen looked at George and raised her eyebrows. If only Bob was awake and talking . . .

'Ruby, Ruby. Wait a minute!'

Ruby groaned as she looked up the road. 'Maureen, can you do something, love? I can't face talking to Vera.'

'Don't you worry. Get into the car right now and I'll cut her off at the pass.'

George gave Maureen a quick kiss on the cheek before jumping into the car.

'Hello, Vera, I didn't see you there. Can I help you?' Maureen smiled sweetly as Vera reached the gate of number thirteen just as George drove off.

'I wanted a word with Ruby about . . . well, about some private business. When will she be back? Isn't that David Carlisle's car? Can I wait?'

'I'm sorry, Vera, that's the telephone ringing; I must go,' Maureen said, rushing into the house and closing the door behind her before Vera could follow. Thank goodness for that, she thought to herself as she grabbed the receiver, before fear clutched at her heart. Was it the hospital? 'Erith four-five-five. Oh, hello, Alan love, thank goodness it's you. No, nothing is wrong. I was worried you were the hospital. I'm here on my own, as George has taken Ruby . . . They left just now. I will let you know as soon as I hear anything. Bye-bye, love.'

Maureen replaced the receiver and the telephone rang again. This was how her Sunday continued.

If Ruby had expected to see Bob sitting up in bed, she was to be disappointed. When they entered the side room, the curtains were drawn and Bob lay still, with his eyes closed.

'I thought there'd have been a bit more colour in his face today. He's still as white as a ghost and looks half dead,' she said, stepping closer to the bed.

His eyes fluttered for a moment before opening. 'It'll take more than a flood to carry me off,' he said, attempting to laugh, until a fit of coughing had him gasping for breath.

'You silly bugger, you had me thinking you were at death's door,' she scolded him.

'Mum, the doctor's here,' George said, looking embarrassed as a portly gentleman in a tweed three-piece suit walked in, followed by a clutch of younger doctors wearing white coats and looking flustered.

'This is Mr Robert Jackson, sir. He was brought in during the night, a victim of the floods,' one of the men in white coats explained. 'He has a rather nasty cough and his medical records show there is a problem with his heart.'

Ruby frowned and glared at Bob. As ill as he was, she would be having this out with him. How dare he keep a secret like that! 'I would like an explanation, please. I can't rely on my husband telling me.'

'Perhaps if you come to my office we can talk quietly. I don't wish to upset the patient. Let us say in one hour? The sister will show you the way,' the doctor said, before continuing his ward round.

Ruby sank into a chair close to his bed.

'I didn't want to bother you, love,' Bob told her. 'Those medicines you kept getting me weren't clearing this cough; it got to the point where I was trying not to cough in front of you as you'd worry, so I went to see the doctor.'

'Which doctor?'

'Old Dr Baxter.'

'And he told you your heart is failing you?'

'Yes. I only told Mike as I wanted to get my affairs in order and not worry you until closer to the end.'

'Oh, Bob,' Ruby said, bursting into tears.

George slipped out of the room and hurried to a public telephone box in the hallway. Dialling a local number, he waited for it to be answered. 'Mike? It's George, are you able to get up to the hospital? No, he's not worse, but

340

something is worrying me about Bob's diagnosis. Thanks, I'll wait at the front of the hospital. I don't want to worry Mum for now.'

George paced up and down, deep in thought. The hospital was emptier than the night before, when many people affected by the floods were waiting to be attended to. The cottage hospital might be small, but it served the inhabitants of Erith well. When he spotted Mike's car, he hurried over to greet him.

'Let's get inside, out of the cold,' George said as they walked briskly to an empty waiting room, closing the door behind them. 'What has Bob told you about his heart problem?'

'Very little. He swore me to secrecy, then wouldn't discuss it. I made a point of trying to take on his work up at the allotment and drove him around as much as possible, so that he wasn't walking and exerting himself. To be honest, he seemed a lot better in recent weeks. I suppose getting cold and wet set it off again. I've been at my wits' end worrying about his health. When I heard he was trapped by the rising floodwater, I thought it was the end and I'd not see him alive again.'

'Do you happen to know who diagnosed his condition?'

Mike shrugged. 'I assumed he saw young Dr Baxter.'

'He's just said it was his father: the old Dr Baxter who has retired.'

Mike frowned. 'Does it make any difference? After all, a doctor is a doctor.'

'I want to tell you something in the strictest of confidence. I'm talking now to Mike Jackson, son of Bob Jackson. I'm not talking to Sergeant Mike Jackson, do you understand?'

341

Mike thought for a moment. 'I only have one father and I must remain loyal to him, unless he has broken the law, that is. Whatever you tell me, it will remain between the two of us.'

'And young Dr Baxter?'

'What do you mean?'

'I have evidence that Dr Baxter senior has misdiagnosed quite a few patients, hence his early retirement. For some reason, Bob saw Dr Baxter senior that day.'

Mike frowned. 'I'm not quite sure what you are saying . . .'

George got to his feet and walked up to the window and stared out for a minute or two. 'In my position as a town councillor, I've seen a few people with similar problems. I took their cases to the son, and he examined them carefully. Sadly, it was found that his father had misdiagnosed ten of their patients. It was then agreed that Dr Baxter senior would retire immediately. I'm ashamed to say that I agreed it would go no further, and now Bob is a victim of the man's incompetence,' George said, sitting down and putting his head in his hands.

Mike patted his back. 'It's not your fault, but what a mess. To think Dad's been carrying this burden all these months. What can we do?'

'One of us needs to see Dr Baxter junior as soon as possible, and one of us must accompany Ruby to see the doctor here.'

Mike agreed. 'You should go and see Dr Baxter junior right now. He knows you as a councillor, and associates you with the problems of other townspeople. It would be ideal if he would look at Dad's records and tell us if he was misdiagnosed. I can stay with Ruby and, if you aren't back by the time of the appointment here, I'll go in with her.'

'I'll head off this minute. Can you tell Mum I've been called to an important meeting to do with the flood situation? It's not far from the truth.'

'Will do. Good luck, and let's hope you get to the bottom of this soon.'

31

~

'Why, Betty, what a lovely surprise,' Sarah said, seeing her friend standing on her doorstep holding a bunch of flowers.

'I hope you don't think this is an imposition, visiting on a Sunday. I wanted to find out how Bob is today and to leave some flowers, then I thought it would be better to ask you in person; using the telephone doesn't seem right, under the circumstances.'

Sarah ushered her inside, thinking how she had been about to ring Betty to check on Clemmie after the events of yesterday. 'Excuse the mess,' she said, removing toys and newspapers from the settee. 'I'm behind with everything today. Alan's taken the children for a walk, so I can catch up on myself.'

'Then I won't delay you too long,' she said, placing the flowers on a cluttered table and removing her coat.

'I always have time for you,' Sarah insisted. 'I'll put the kettle on.'

'That would be delightful,' Betty said as she sat down and then winced, removing a tin soldier from the seat beneath her. She looked around her and thought how it was such a cosy and welcoming house. 'I wondered if there was news of Bob?'

'I'm waiting to hear more,' Sarah said, glancing towards her telephone. 'Imagine what it would have been like if this happened when we didn't have telephones in the house?'

'We are fortunate to have them, because of our husbands' businesses, as so many people don't.'

'That is true. I've been wondering about Jessie and her children. Alan promised to drive me to Slade Green after dinner, so I can check on her. He said he would pop in on Aunty Pat at her farm and check on things. Nan will be fussing if she doesn't have up-to-date news on all her family. Speaking of which, how is Clemmie today after her ordeal? Is she staying with you?' Sarah asked.

'Oh yes, she won't be living with Jimmy until after the wedding. Douglas and I insisted on that when we agreed to the engagement. However, the plans are now in disarray, with their proposed home under water. Douglas is of the opinion that the bungalow may never be fit for purpose and may have to be pulled down, and that is before he's even been to Belvedere to see it.'

'Crikey, that's rather drastic. Surely it will be fine once it has dried out; that's if the floodwater ever subsides. We were reading about the floods this morning in the newspapers. Alan popped out and bought every one of them, as we are trying to explain to the children how the awful weather started in The Netherlands and affected so many people. Georgie soon understood, once we showed her the maps in her junior encyclopaedia, although Buster was more interested in the photograph of dead cattle in the fields and wanted to know how his great-grandfather climbed into Clemmie's loft.'

Betty smiled. She couldn't understand why Sarah's son had such an awful nickname; it still made her shudder. 'I hope, in years to come, children will be taught about this in their schools, along with how it has affected people's lives. I don't mean Clemmie and Jimmy's home being flooded, although I have no idea where they will live after the wedding, but the overall effect on industry and farming, and in more than one country.'

Sarah agreed. 'I have something to discuss with you, but first let me fetch our teas, as I can hear the kettle whistling.'

Please don't say she is handing in her notice, Betty prayed. The store was ticking over nicely now, and she had such a hard-working team under her. 'I've decided to give Clemmie, Jessie and Freda the day off tomorrow; it is Freda's day to come into work. I feel they need time to get over the shock. Would you inform Jessie when you see her later and reassure her that she will be paid.'

'Of course, that is most generous,' Sarah said as she placed the tea tray containing her best china on the table. 'We were due to have our meeting about the Queen's coronation celebrations and how it will affect the store. Should we cancel it for now, until we have those who are involved back at work?'

'Yes, that would be a good idea, as was your suggestion that we involve the general staff in putting forward ideas. I'm looking forward to hearing the staff's suggestions. It will be such a glorious day, and the second of June will be perfect; hopefully the sun will shine. Now tell me, what is it you wish to discuss with me,' she asked as Sarah passed her tea.

'It is early days and it may all fall through, but Maisie

and David have found the ideal house for their family. When they move, they plan to rent out their house in Alexandra Road and have given us first refusal. It will be wonderful for the children to have their own bedrooms, as well as a proper garden.'

Betty, although pleased for her friend, had one concern. 'That will mean you are no longer property owners.'

'Oh, but we will be, as Alan wants us to hold on to the house and rent it out instead, rather like Maisie and David intend to do.'

'That is certainly a big step, but I can see the allure of living in Maisie's house, as she has made it such a beautiful place to live. Of course, being selfish, I'm so pleased you are still living close to the town and Woolworths.'

'And therein lies my problem.'

'Please don't say you are resigning!'

'No, not at all. I know what I'm about to tell you won't go any further.'

'I promise not to say a word to anyone,' Betty said, looking worried.

'As you know, Alan has invested heavily in the new business and has such wonderful plans to expand. There is a big difference between what Maisie and David will expect in rent and what we will get for this place, so we have had to think carefully about our income. Alan believes he can continue to expand the shop without taking on another staff member, as he had originally planned, so that will make a big saving. However, it means I am going to have to work at the shop, as well as help with the accounts. We can't ask my dad to help as he has so much on his plate as it is, let alone supporting Nan now.'

Betty nodded as Sarah continued to explain their plans.

'I so want to grab the opportunity to move, and doing it this way means we still own Alan's family home.' She stopped talking and drew a deep breath. 'I wondered if I could change my hours at the store in order to be able to work at the shop as well; that's if you are agreeable. I've written down how it could be achieved,' Sarah went on, taking a sheet of paper from the table and handing it to Betty.

Betty was silent and gave no indication of her feelings as she read Sarah's notes. Once read, she finished her tea without speaking.

'I'll understand if you don't agree to it.'

'Oh, but I do agree; in fact I'm one step ahead of you. We've been thinking of taking Clemmie on full-time, now she sees her future with F. W. Woolworth. It would be good training for her to take on some of your duties.'

Sarah's heart plummeted to her boots. Was she being replaced by Betty's stepdaughter?

'There's no need to look so glum. I'm not asking you to resign,' she chuckled. 'In fact we can work around Clemmie's cashier work, and she can take on some of your minor tasks. I'll leave that up to you. In time, Clemmie will be leaving to have her family, but until then she can be of use to you while you help Alan. This could work very well, unless of course Clemmie and Jimmy decide to live further away until their bungalow is either repaired or rebuilt. Douglas is looking at a rebuild and says it will be a year at least before it is liveable.'

'But Clemmie told us only a few days ago she thought she was expecting . . .'

Betty wrung her hands together, trying to find the right words. 'Let us just say that, with the excitement of last night, she's had a visitor.'

Sarah frowned until the penny dropped. 'Oh, I see, but what about her putting on weight?'

'Too many biscuits and sweets while she'd been at the bungalow decorating,' Betty smiled. 'I shouldn't be pleased, as the poor girl is upset, but I feel it is for the best. They have plenty of time in the future to add to their little family. Any notion Clemmie had of starting her own family early on has been forgotten.'

'So she just has to sort out where to live after the wedding,' Sarah said.

Both women looked at each other and smiled as a thought came to them.

'Would you give us first refusal on this house, if you decide to rent it out? Douglas and I will be responsible for the deposit and the rent; we could say one year to begin with.'

'Gosh, it would be a dream come true. My one worry was that we'd be messed about by people changing their minds and not renting – or not paying the rent. I know we can rely on you.'

'It would be a big weight off our minds. Clemmie is so miserable about losing her bungalow. It is four weeks till the wedding; I have no wish to push you, but . . .'

'But could we be out by then? We would have to speak to Maisie and David, as it depends when they can move into their house in Avenue Road. Alan said it is empty, so there might be a chance we could all have moved by the end of February. But let's not jump the gun for now. The men can sort all that out,' Sarah said, not noticing Betty's disapproving look.

'There is something I'd like to ask. You don't think you'll be burning your candles at both ends? Two jobs, as well as keeping on top of the books at home, is going to be a struggle.'

'It's not forever, I'll cope,' Sarah replied, feeling excited about her future.

George hurried as fast as he could from where he'd parked David's car through the hospital to where the consultant's office was situated, earning a reprimand from a nurse along the way for running. Reaching the closed door of the office, he stopped to listen for a moment, in case it was the wrong room. Upon hearing his mum's raised voice, he knocked and entered without waiting for an invitation to do so.

'I'm sorry to arrive late. I'm Councillor Caselton, Mr Jackson's stepson,' he said, leaning over the desk to shake Mr Broadbent's hand. 'Have I missed much?' he asked, before sitting down next to Mike, giving him a nod as he did so.

Mr Broadbent cleared his throat. 'I was explaining to Mrs Jackson that her husband was a very poorly man, even before his . . . er, adventure yesterday. I've had time to read the notes from his GP, where it shows the diagnosis.' He put down the papers he was holding and placed his elbows on the desk. 'Mrs Jackson, I don't know how to put this, considering that you were unaware of how ill your husband is, but I cannot give a reasonable prognosis. We will keep him as comfortable as possible and must put his chances in the hands of God. Now, if you will excuse me, I have an appointment.'

There was an uproar in the room, with Ruby jumping to her feet and shouting, 'What?' to Mike's more reasonable, 'Now look here!'

It was George who raised his hand for his relatives' silence. 'If you would allow me to speak, please?'

Mr Broadbent looked at the gold watch on his wrist. 'I can spare you five minutes.'

'Thank you. I can see that you have information about Mr Robert Jackson's visit to his GP, along with his diagnosis.'

'Yes, I've based my conclusions on these notes.'

'They are wrong,' George said, throwing a folder that he held in his hand onto the desk with a flourish. 'My stepfather's appointment was with Dr Baxter senior, who was no longer practising due to . . . Well, let's just say that due to a few ill-thought-out diagnoses in the recent past, he had been advised by his son, Dr Baxter junior, to retire. It was Mr Jackson's unfortunate luck to attend the surgery while the younger doctor was absent.'

'That is all well and good . . .'

'Please, may I finish? I have here Mr Jackson's file, which his GP generously allowed me to show you. And this is a letter from him, with today's date. I was able to see the younger Dr Baxter and, due to his concerns, he wrote this letter. You can see—'

Mr Broadbent raised a hand to silence George, while he read the letter and went to look at Bob's file.

Ruby didn't know what to think and opened her mouth to ask George what was going on, but was silenced by George shaking his head at her and by Mike putting a finger to his lips. The three sat and watched the consultant.

'Very well, I can see there are anomalies in the diagnosis. I will arrange for Mr Jackson to undergo more tests and then re-evaluate the situation. This may take a few days, and in the meantime I will put the gentleman on a course of antibiotics for his cough. And no, he cannot go home just yet,' he said as he spotted Ruby raising her hand to speak.

Ruby hadn't finished. 'I have a question. Can you tell me if you dismissed my husband because of his age and would have let him die, if my son hadn't intervened?'

'Mum, really!' George was shocked, while Mike's chin almost hit the floor.

Mr Broadbent had the good grace to smile at Ruby. 'We will never know, Mrs Jackson, as I will be giving your husband the full belt-and-braces treatment. Now, if you will excuse me,' he said, standing up.

As George went to follow Ruby and Mike from the room, Mr Broadbent called him back. 'I take it you were instrumental in aiding Dr Baxter senior's retirement?'

'You could say that,' George replied, not sure where the conversation was going.

'Good work,' Broadbent said, holding out his hand and shaking George's hand warmly. 'We need more good men like you in Erith.'

32

~

12 February 1953

Betty looked around at the eager faces in her office. 'Thank
you all for giving up your lunch break for us to start planning the Woolworths celebrations for our Queen's
coronation. Before we start, Sarah, is there any news yet
about Bob?'

'Thank you for asking. He's getting stronger every day,
and is still complaining about the hospital food and asking
when he can go home. Nan and Mike went to see the
consultant yesterday afternoon, and the good news is that
he does not have the heart problems that were first diagnosed. He will never be one hundred per cent healthy, as
he will always have a weak chest, but if he takes care of
himself, then there is no cause for concern.'

'Why, that is wonderful news,' Betty declared as the staff
members in the room all cheered.

'Will he be out of hospital for my wedding?' Clemmie
asked. 'Jimmy and I would very much like him to be there.'

'I doubt it. He may still be in hospital, but if he is home,
the exertion would be too much. From what Nan has told

353

us, Bob will have to be careful of the cold weather and smoky places, as cigarette smoke could play havoc with his chest.'

'Then I will send him a slice of our wedding cake,' she replied.

'He will enjoy that, thank you. There is talk of him going to a convalescent home for a while to recuperate. I'm not sure that Nan wants him out of her sight, though.'

Maureen came into the office, carrying a large plate of sandwiches. 'Here you are, ladies, you can't have a meeting on empty stomachs, so tuck in. Keep me posted on what is planned, as I can help with the catering. I think it's a jolly good idea to have a party for the children of the staff; we've had some fun parties since I've been here, but never one for the children alone,' she said, before going back to the staff canteen.

'Now, what about the decorations for the store windows?' Betty asked, pen poised over her notepad.

'All in hand, and I have Dorothy and Jessie in my team. We will be working on the windows after the store closes, so as not to disturb our customers,' Freda replied.

'May I ask if Woolworths will be selling coronation souvenirs?' Clemmie enquired.

'I'm glad you asked,' Betty said. 'Most certainly there will be memorabilia, and I propose that the staff on that counter wear a special uniform; perhaps some gold or silver braid on their lapels.'

'And they have to wear tiaras,' Claudette suggested. 'I can ask Mum about the trimmings.'

'That is super, although I'm not sure about the staff wearing tiaras,' Betty chuckled.

Freda raised her hand to get Betty's attention. 'I was

wondering if staff were going up to London to watch the coronation and, if so, will the store be open that day?'

'To be perfectly honest, I have no idea. This is just a preliminary meeting, so we have plenty of time to plan. The coronation is on a Tuesday, and I would think the store will be closed for the day. Were you thinking of going to London, Freda?'

'Gosh, no. We went for the royal wedding, and it was such a long day. Besides, I have the children to consider these days. We are going to have a street party in Alexandra Road during the afternoon and will also include the surrounding streets. We will watch the event beforehand on television; it will be a wonderful day,' she beamed.

'Does that mean I can attend, as I'll be a resident of Crayford Road by then?' Clemmie asked.

'Attend? No doubt Ruby will have you give a helping hand. She's already making plans to decorate everyone's windows and make red, white and blue bunting to hang from house to house.'

'Oh, what fun!'

Betty looked at the clock, aware that her girls were giving up their lunch break. 'What I propose is to give you all a copy of my notes, and I would appreciate feedback and suggestions that we can build upon. Now, eat up, and thank you for attending. Sarah and Clemmie, can I have a word before you go? Sorry, Sarah, I know you have to shoot off to get to your Alan's shop, but I wondered if there was any more news about your moving date?'

'Oh, Mother, it's all in hand,' Clemmie smiled. 'Sarah and Alan are moving into Maisie's house on the twenty-second, and we will have the keys the day after. That gives us plenty of time to move our furniture in before the wedding.'

'Oh my, that's less than a week. Are you sure you will have time?'

'Plenty of time, so you needn't worry. Just concentrate on being mother of the bride and looking glamorous for our guests,' she replied, kissing Betty's cheek before hurrying back to her office.

'I must go,' Sarah said. 'As Clemmie told you, there is no need to worry. We will leave the house spick and span, so they won't have to worry about cleaning the place. I'm so excited finally to be having a home of my own; with our house originally being my in-laws' home, it never quite felt like my own.'

Betty gave her a quick hug. 'I'm so pleased for you and a bit jealous, with all my friends moving house. It is quite a celebration. If I can be of any help, please do ask. But try not to overdo things, Sarah love.'

'I promise not to,' Sarah said as she hurried off to fetch her coat. Walking down Pier Road and into the High Street, where Alan's shop was situated, she did indeed wonder if she was doing right in helping Alan, as she was finding it hard to have her husband as her boss. On top of that, she wasn't familiar with what was sold in the shop and would have made some embarrassing and costly mistakes, if James hadn't come to her aid. He reassured her that she would soon learn and wasn't to worry. Sarah felt the real reason she wasn't learning quickly was because she really didn't have much interest in advising customers on televisions and wireless sets. There was also a small counter where they still sold parts for bicycles and other accessories; this was

James's domain, but if he was busy elsewhere she'd be called upon to serve customers. It wasn't that she didn't wish to support her husband, but more that everything was so confusing. She checked her watch and walked faster, knowing that Alan was waiting for her before he headed out to visit several customers and deliver their television sets.

'I'm sorry I'm a few minutes late,' she said, pulling her coat off as she hurried into the shop. 'Betty had a meeting about the coronation-day celebrations, and it ran over slightly.'

'Not to worry,' he replied, giving her a grin, which reminded her so much of the young man she first knew when she went to work for Woolworths. Where had those years gone? 'I've had a new item of stock arrive and I wanted to go over it with you, in case someone comes in to purchase one while I'm out.'

Sarah groaned; not something else for her to learn. Whatever had he added to the stock now? 'Oh, Alan, my head is already in a spin trying to learn about televisions. I had a lady the other day asking me why we didn't sell lace doylies that she could put on top of the set, so as to stand a vase of flowers on the television.'

Alan roared with laughter. 'Whatever did you tell her?'

'I sent her to Woolworths and suggested that she purchased a pattern and made her own.'

'Well done,' he said as he put his arms around her.

'I'm not sure this is the right place to be affectionate,' she said primly, looking towards the glass window in case somebody was watching.

Alan ignored her comment and instead turned her to face the other way. 'Look at this,' he said.

Sarah could hardly contain her joy. 'Oh my, it's an

electric washing machine, and there's a mangle attached,' she noticed, as she ran a hand over the white shiny metal. 'I thought we'd decided not to sell them for a while, and to concentrate on television sales. Mind you, that one you had in the shop when you first opened was very popular. I know I'd have loved one, if there'd been room in my kitchen . . .'

'Circumstances changed my mind.'

'Whatever do you mean?' she asked as she lifted the lid to look inside at the agitator.

'Well, there's a working woman who really needs one of these to help with her housework.'

'Oh, you've sold it already.' She was disappointed, as she'd love to have shown it off to the customers.

'I ordered two: one for the shop and one that has to be delivered next week when the lady moves to Alexandra Road.'

Sarah frowned for a moment, before throwing herself into his arms.

'Careful, Sarah, someone might see us,' he grinned.

'You do mean it is going to our new house, don't you?' she asked, suddenly unsure whether it was hers.

'I'm not delivering it to Vera Munro, if that's what you're asking. Besides, if you know how to use it, you can advise our customers. The men will come in to look at television sets and this will give the wives something to admire.'

Sarah would normally have put her husband straight about duties around the house being shared by husband and wife jointly, but on this occasion she was too excited and let it pass. Suddenly she could see that she would enjoy working in the shop.

*

George and Maureen were just leaving the cottage hospital that evening as Mike and Gwyneth arrived.

'How is he?' Mike asked.

'Bright and chirpy, and he has some colour in his cheeks at last. Mum's over the moon and was talking about bringing Bob home; she's jumping the gun, but she won't be happy until he is back home and being mollycoddled.'

'Is there any more news on whether he will be sent to a convalescent home?' Gwyneth asked. 'I've heard they can be very nice places.'

'I've heard the same,' Maureen agreed, 'and, to be honest, Ruby could do with a rest; going up and down to the hospital twice a day is taking it out of her. We've told her she doesn't have to be there for every visiting time, but she won't listen. Even with the family driving her, she is starting to look tired.'

'I'll try and have a word with her, but I doubt she will listen. The pair of them are as stubborn as mules,' Mike grimaced. 'By the way, some news came through today about Vera's son. There's been a whisper that he's planning to come back into the country. When he does, we'll be waiting, as there's a fair list of things we want to talk to him about.'

'That's interesting, but perhaps don't say anything to Vera, as she'd not take kindly to being told he's a ne'er-do-well. Best to let her live with her fantasies.'

'I agree with that,' Mike said, as he wished them good-night and entered the hospital to visit his father.

33

~

28 February 1953

'That was such a lovely wedding,' Freda sighed as she kicked her shoes off and collapsed onto the settee in her front room.

Sarah joined her while Alan and Tony took the armchairs. 'Maisie pulled out all the stops with the beautiful bridal gown; Clemmie looked as pretty as a picture. And what about Betty? I've never seen her look so glamorous.'

'Fancy a beer?' Tony asked Alan. 'It looks like the girls will be talking about the wedding for hours.'

Freda threw a cushion at her husband. 'We'll have a drink as well, there's some port in the cupboard. I thought your song at the reception was wonderful, Alan. You sounded just like Mario Lanza when you sang 'Be My Love' and all the old dears were swooning,' she laughed.

'I was singing to my lovely wife. Do you know she sold three washing machines in the last week? At this rate I'll be able to retire in another year or at least buy Maisie and David's house, rather than rent it.'

'Would you do that?' Tony asked as he handed Alan a beer.

'There's always that option. Sarah loves the house; it's what she's always dreamt of. Did you see that I had a couple of rose bushes planted on each side of the front door? Granted, it's still winter, so they aren't flowering yet, but it'll look lovely in the summer.'

'Look at you, getting all romantic,' Freda giggled. 'You'll have to have a new dream, now that Alan's fulfilled these ones, Sarah. Sarah? Oh, bless her, she's fallen asleep.'

Alan shook his head. 'She does that a lot these days. I've found her dropped off over the accounts some evenings.'

Freda frowned, as that wasn't like her friend at all. 'You'd best get her home. At least you don't have far to walk and, with Georgie and Buster going home early from the reception with George and Maureen, you can have some time to yourselves, so let her have a lie-in tomorrow; she deserves it.'

Alan laughed as he pulled a complaining Sarah to her feet. 'Fat chance of that, as we are stocktaking in the morning.'

Ruby spotted Sarah in Woolworths as she sneezed into her handkerchief. 'Don't you go into the hospital with that cold or you'll give it to Bob, and they'll cancel him going to that convalescent home next week. He's looking forward to his visit to Margate,' Ruby scolded her. 'You shouldn't even be at work in that state.'

'I've got no choice, Nan, and when I finish here, I've got to put in a couple of hours at our shop,' Sarah sniffed into her handkerchief. 'It's only a head cold. I'll soon shake it off, I'm young and healthy.' She tried to grin.

Ruby gave her a stern look. 'You've lost weight and are

as pale as a ghost. Get yourself sorted out or I'll be having a word with Alan. He's working you far too hard.'

'I'm fine, Nan, please don't worry about me; you concentrate on Bob. Now what are you here for?'

'I'm picking up some navy-blue darning wool; your Buster has gone through the elbows on the last one I knitted.'

Sarah was downcast. 'I'm sorry, I'd not noticed.'

'That's what comes of working too many hours. A mother should be putting her children first, not spending all her time at work,' Ruby scolded.

Sarah stood listening to Ruby until she'd run out of things to tell her off about, then waved goodbye to her before going back upstairs to her office. She checked the time; she had two hours before she needed to be at Alan's shop. Time to check the work rotas and sort out applications for holiday leave, then have some lunch . . . She gave herself a shake and reached for the telephone, which seemed to have been ringing incessantly. 'Sarah Gilbert,' she said, still trying to clear her fuzzy head.

'Sarah, it's Alan. You should have been here an hour ago – what's going on?'

Looking up at the clock, she was shocked to see that she'd slept at her desk for over two hours. Whatever was wrong with her? 'Sorry, Alan, I'll be with you in ten minutes,' she apologized.

'I just need a tonic,' Sarah explained to old Dr Baxter later that day when she popped into the surgery. 'I can't seem to shake this cold off and I feel so tired all the time. It's probably because I'm putting in extra hours at work and we recently moved house,' she said, almost apologizing for wasting his time. 'On top of that, I'm on the committee for our street party in June.'

'Be quiet,' he said as he listened to her chest with his stethoscope. 'There's no congestion, your chest is clear,' he went on, as he put a thermometer under her tongue while feeling her pulse. 'I can't find anything wrong with you, but I will give you a tonic, as you requested. My suggestion is that you don't work such long hours and stay at home with your children.'

Silly old fool, Sarah thought as she queued up in the chemist to hand in the prescription. He sounded just like her nan. Wasn't something said about the old doctor when Bob first went into hospital after the floods? She couldn't remember what, as her brain felt so foggy. She'd take the tonic and would be well in no time.

34

~

2 June 1953

'You girls have pulled a blinder decorating the road,' George said as he stood at the gate of number thirteen and looked up to the top of the road where Sarah lived. Why, you must have decorated every window of every house. It looks splendid.'

Sarah beamed with pride. Even though she was still feeling awful, she had done her utmost to play her part in preparing for the big day and had been climbing ladders attaching bunting to the gutters, as well as helping older residents decorate their bay windows in red, white and blue. 'I've just got this one length to pin up, then we are done. Would you hold the bottom of the ladder, Dad?'

'Be careful,' he said as he held the wooden ladder steady. 'Perhaps I should do that?'

'Oh, Dad, I've been up and down this ladder dozens of times. There's no need to worry about me. There, it's done,' she said as she climbed down, stepping back to check that the bunting was in line with the rest, before collapsing to the ground in a dead faint.

'Sarah, Sarah, here, sip this,' Ruby said, holding a glass of water to her lips. 'You've given us a real fright, girl.'

Sarah blinked her eyes and looked around. She was in her nan's front room, stretched out on the settee. 'What happened?'

'You fainted and gave me the fright of my life,' George said as he stroked her head.

She struggled to get up, still feeling wobbly. 'I went up the ladder one too many times.'

'No, it's more than that. You've been poorly on and off for ages and it's time to get to the bottom of this.'

'What do you mean?' Sarah asked, not liking the determined look in Ruby's eyes.

'I'm taking you up the surgery to see Dr Baxter.'

'That's a good idea, Mum,' George said, looking relieved. 'I'll drive you up there.'

'There's no need. I saw old Dr Baxter a while back and he gave me a tonic.'

George frowned. 'Old Dr Baxter? I thought he'd retired,' he said, not wishing to alarm Sarah or his mum.'

'Yes, but his son was laid up with a broken ankle, from what the receptionist told me.'

George shook his head. 'I'll take Sarah to the surgery. You stay here and oversee the preparations,' he told Ruby, then bundled Sarah out of the house before she could argue.

'Dad, is there something you're not telling me?' Sarah asked as they drove to the surgery. Even though she felt so dizzy, she couldn't help but notice how most houses and shops in Erith had pulled out all the stops to celebrate the young Queen's coronation.

'Old Dr Baxter is supposed to have retired; it was either that or be reported and struck off,' he said, explaining what had happened at the time Bob was taken ill.

'Oh my God, he could have misdiagnosed me too,' Sarah said, feeling weepy. 'What if I have something seriously wrong with me? Please, can you stop the car. I'm feeling sick,' she cried, holding a hand to her mouth.

George pulled over to the pavement and rushed to the other side of the car to help Sarah out, whereupon she went over to hold onto a wire fence that bordered the railway line some twenty feet below. He rubbed her back as she leant over and was violently sick.

'Has this happened before?' George asked as he handed over his large handkerchief for her to wipe her sweaty face.

'A couple of times, but I've hardly eaten, so I have no idea what the problem could be. I must have something seriously wrong with me.' She started to sob as George helped her back into the car. He tried to pacify her, but felt as fearful as she did.

'We are very close to the surgery and, even if it is shut, I'll bang on the door until young Dr Baxter opens up. Whatever is wrong, I promise I'll make it better. Why, I'd not be your dad if I couldn't put things right,' he said, pulling out into the traffic and trying not to worry. But what if he couldn't help his daughter? 'Here we are,' he said as they pulled up outside the old house in South Road where the Baxter family had their surgery. 'I'm going in to see the younger Dr Baxter before you see him.'

'All right, whatever you say, but it may be too late for me . . .'

'Are you sure you are going to be able to fit everyone in?' Tony asked as he looked around his front room.

'People won't mind squeezing up; it's a special occasion. Besides, after the ceremony they will be out in the street, having a party, and they can stretch out all they want,' Freda said. 'I wish I knew where Sarah had vanished to, as she said she was going to bring down a couple of stools. Could you?'

'Find Sarah or collect the stools?'

'Tony, I'm in no state of mind to joke; there's too much to do. I've given Ruby pride of place in the armchair. It's such a shame Bob couldn't be home for today, as he's so much better. I said as much to Mike, but he didn't seem interested.'

'He's probably got a lot on at the police station. These big events seem to attract more crime.'

'Yes, do you remember the pickpocket, when we went to London for the royal wedding? Maisie gave chase after him. She was so brave,' she chuckled. 'I'll walk over and collect Ruby now, so that she doesn't have to rush. Maisie and David will be here soon with the children, and Betty and the family should be arriving around the same time. I hope we have enough beer. I wonder, could you check?'

Tony hurried away before Freda gave him any more jobs. Walking up Alexandra Road, he smiled at the happy faces and the children running about in fancy dress, while the women in charge of the catering were laying out trestle tables down the middle of the road. He marvelled at the community spirit in this one road in Erith, regardless of the weather, and thought how it would be the same up and down the country. We have a new monarch, and long may she reign, he smiled, while he choked with emotion, realizing that at long last he and Freda had their own family and friends, something he'd longed for when he first arrived in the town. Reaching Alan's house, he was surprised to see Mike at the gate; perhaps he wasn't on duty after all. That meant the whole gang would be together for the day.

Mike waved to Tony. 'Just the man I wanted to see. Can you give me and Alan a hand?'

Freda stood at the door to her front room and gazed over her friends and neighbours, all waiting for the coronation procession to start. She felt a deep contentment to be part of such a special occasion.

'Sorry we're late,' Sarah said as she squeezed past her friend. 'Dad and I had something urgent to deal with,' she continued, as she looked around for Alan. 'Where's my husband?'

'No doubt with my husband. I sent Tony to collect the stools an hour ago.'

'I'll pop up the road and hurry them up, or it will all be over before they get here,' she said as she went outside. She didn't have to go far, as Alan and Mike, along with her dad, were assisting Bob out of a taxi.

'I couldn't miss a street party with my family and friends,' he said as Sarah flew into his arms.

'Let's get you inside before Nan spots you through the

window,' she said as Mike took his father's arm and assisted him into the house.

'Is there room for a small one?' he asked, stepping into the room.

Amongst shrieks of joy, he took Ruby in his arms. 'I've missed you,' Bob said as people made room for him to sit next to her.

'How did you escape from Margate?' she asked, before kissing him soundly on the lips, to cheers from everyone in the room. 'Now take my armchair,' she urged him. 'It'll be more comfy than the dining chair,' she continued, nodding her thanks to Freda, who shunted people about in order to fit in a seat next to Bob. 'It's starting,' Ruby said. 'No more talking,' she hissed at Vera.

'I was just about to say that my son is likely to be in London today, as no doubt he has an important position in the goings-on,' Vera said.

Ruby rolled her eyes, but kept quiet. Vera would never change.

Sitting at the back of the room, Mike turned to George. 'Vera's long-lost son was picked up today. We have him in custody on a list of charges.'

'Will you inform her?'

'No, there's no point. Let her live with her dreams, as it won't harm anyone.'

George looked towards where Sarah stood by the door with Alan and gave her a wink.

'Your dad seems happy,' Alan said as he slung an arm around her shoulders, unaware that she'd fainted earlier.

'He was with me when I received some news from young Dr Baxter. It answers all my questions as to why

I've been so poorly lately. It's early days, and we must wait for the test to come back, but he's more than confident we will be expecting a special little present in time for Christmas.'

'You mean . . .'

'Yes, I'm pregnant.'

Alan kissed her and hugged her close.

'Just like this country, our family and friends have so much to celebrate and look forward to. We are the luckiest people in the world.'

Acknowledgements

~

Gosh, where to start as there are so many people to thank. Top of my list are my readers who do so much to let the world know about my books, with your 'shelfies' and posts on Facebook and Twitter. I can't begin to express how honoured I am that you love my stories so much; at times I have been reduced to tears at your kindness. Bless you all.

My editor, the wonderful Wayne Brookes, who seems to keep everything running and always answers my endless questions – you are a star! Susan Opie, for her eye for detail at the structural edit stage and, not forgetting, press officer Chloe Davies for getting word of my book out to readers, which was such a success. I also need to thank the many other people at Pan Macmillan who got my book from the page to the shelves on time. Thank you all!

I love writing short stories, it was part of my freelance writing job long before I wrote my first novel. To the commissioning editors at the fabulous weekly magazines, I thank you for featuring my work. I mustn't forget the radio presenters, bloggers, librarians and journalists who take time to promote my writing in so many ways.

Finally, my literary agent, Caroline Sheldon, and her lovely team. Thank you, thank you, thank you, for all you've done for me.

Oops, I almost forgot the home team, my husband Michael and Henry the dog. It goes without saying how much I appreciate you both.

Thank you one and all!
Elaine x

A Letter From Elaine

~

Dear Readers,

Celebrations for the Woolworths Girls was written in tribute to our late Queen Elizabeth II, with many events leading up to the Coronation on 2 June 1953 being true both nationally and locally. I included the terrible floods at the end of January 1953 with some of our well-loved characters experiencing what my own mother went through on that awful night at the end of January; in fact, one of the girls shares my parents' wedding day of 28 February 1953 and the same venue. Memories are important in my books, as that is all we have left of the past and our loved ones.

Little did I know when working on this book that we were to lose our wonderful monarch and, by the time of publication, that we would have welcomed King Charles III. Long may you reign, sir.

It was lovely to hear from so many of you after you'd read *A Woolworths Girl's Promise*. Thank you for your kind comments and Amazon reviews, they mean so much to me.

Please do let me know what you think about *Celebrations*

for the Woolworths Girls, I love to chat about memories of Woolworths and 'the good old days'.

If you would like to get in touch or chat with fellow readers, please join in with the links on the Keep in Touch page.

Until next time,
Elaine xx

Keep in Touch

I love to hear from readers, and there are many ways you can not only follow me but contact me to chat, as well as enter competitions.

Twitter:
Find me as @ElaineEverest
I will often tweet book news, so if you follow Twitter, look out for me.

Facebook author page:
Come and chat and hear my news on Facebook.
www.facebook.com/ElaineEverestAuthor

Instagram:
I have an account on Instagram, so why not find me and say hello?
www.instagram.com/elaine.everest/

Website:
This is where you can not only read about me and all my books, but also read my blog posts where I chat about my life and everything to do with my books.
Go to www.elaineeverest.com

My newsletter:
Sign up to receive a copy of my monthly newsletter, where I not only give you the latest news about my books but also run some fab competitions. In the past there have been competitions to win a sewing machine, leather handbag, hampers, jewellery and signed copies of my books. You will find the link to sign up on my website: www.elaineeverest.com

Discover the first book in the Woolworths series

The Woolworths Girls

Can romance blossom in times of trouble?

It's 1938 and as the threat of war hangs over the country, Sarah Caselton is preparing for her new job at Woolworths. Before long, she forms a tight bond with two of her colleagues: the glamorous Maisie and shy Freda. The trio couldn't be more different, but they immediately form a close-knit friendship, sharing their hopes and dreams for the future.

Sarah soon falls into the rhythm of her new position, enjoying the social events hosted by Woolies and her blossoming romance with young assistant manager, Alan. But with the threat of war clouding the horizon, the young men and women of Woolworths realize that there are bigger battles ahead. It's a dangerous time for the nation, and an even more perilous time to fall in love . . .

Available now